The Servant's Voice

The 3rd Tale from Ragaris

by

Penelope Wallace

A Mightier Than the Sword UK
Publication

©2019

The Servant's Voice

The Tales from Ragaris

By Penelope Wallace

A Mightier Than the Sword UK Publication

Paperback Edition

Copyright © Penelope Wallace 2019

Map of Ragaris by Stephen Hall

Cover Illustration by Ian Storer

Cover Design by C.S. Woolley

Paperback ISBN 978-0-9951475-0-8
Hardback ISBN 978-0-9951475-1-5
ePub ISBN 978-0-9951475-2-2
Kindle ISBN 978-0-9951475-3-9
iBooks ISBN 978-0-9951475-4-6

"Nothing is covered up that will not be revealed, or hidden that will not be known. Therefore whatever you have said in the dark shall be heard in the light, and what you have whispered in private rooms shall be proclaimed upon the housetops."

(Luke 12: 2-3)

Contents

Cast of Characters

<u>Residing in City Qayn</u>

Aigith, King for the Evening

Zinial, Queen for the Morning

Gridor, a delivery-man, sometimes called Flower-in-Hood

Miya, his wife; their children Gita and Vren

Brinnon, his nephew; Brinnon's wife Lulet; their children Minna and Jof

Hridnaya, his niece, serving the b'Nida Family

<u>B'Nida Family</u>

Riodran, Lord b'Nida

Irramatti, Lady b'Nida, Chancellor of the Great College

Jeruma, their eldest daughter

Lindet, their youngest daughter

Narrim, their Housemother in City Qayn

Hridnaya, Jantorad, Attar and Gabo, servants in the household

Other Family members and servants

<u>B'Shen Family</u>

Jeriet, Lady b'Shen

Yettrid, her son, acting head of the Family
Rommi, Yettrid's niece (later Queen for the Morning)
Mejorad, Rommi's son
Eyanda, Rommi's sister
Tor and Yikkeri, servants in the household

Nadya b'Astith, Eyanda's lover
Adjefi b'Trai, a judge in the Evening King's courts
Krothon b'Trai, Chamberlain to the Morning Queen
Brechad b'Iri, Chamberlain to the Evening King
Narod, a friend of Mejorad b'Shen
Simoren b'Asa, another judge
Sister Felicity, a priest

Balki, an imaginary friend

<u>Residing in Sapientia</u>
Bekonin, First Doctor of Theology
Akraib, Second Doctor of Theology
Dirria, Second Doctor of Law
Madrasun, her predecessor (deceased)
Rorash b'Shen, a student, cousin of Mejorad
Bada, keeper of The Morning Dream tavern
Shina, a customer
Mobira, the Evening King's agent
Ittrad, a student-servitor

<u>Foreigners</u>

Kelji of Makkera, a distant kinswoman of Nadya
b'Astith and envoy from Queen Nerranya

Fejederic ("Jedder") her husband

Vaddras and Imadal, their servants

Historical Note

This story takes place in the land of Ricossa, in the east of Ragaris.

The land of Jaryar is to the west. In the year 619 AL, the nobility of Jaryar gathered at the Great Council of Vach-roysh to choose who should rule them after their childless king died. The choice fell on Nerranya, then Queen of the northern land of Marod.

Accordingly, a year later Nerranya became Queen of the two countries, Jaryar and Marod, and moved south with her husband to the city of Makkera.

At the time this story starts, she has been ruling for twenty-one years.

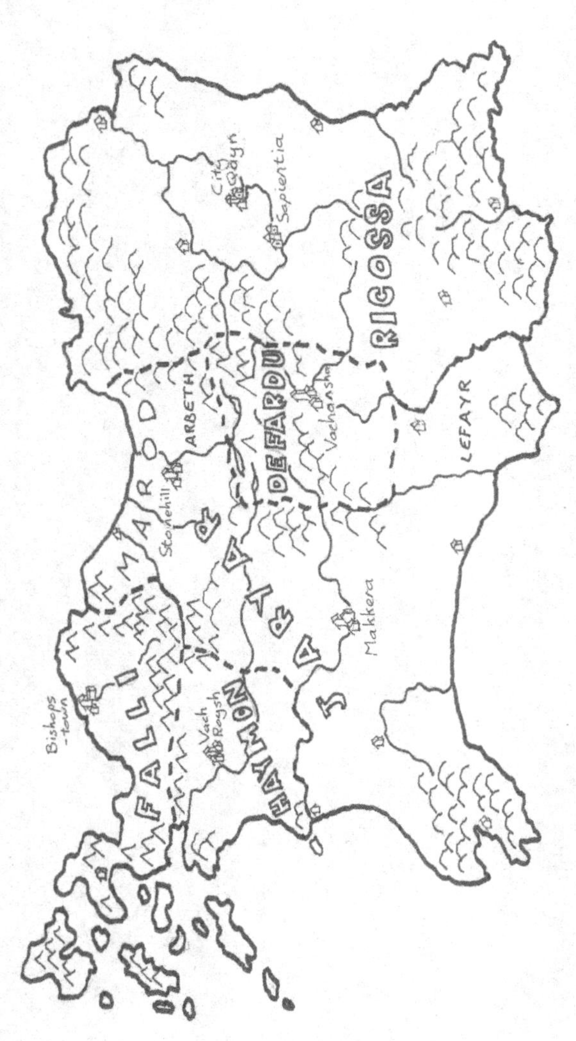
RIGOSSA
City of Qayn
Sapientia
DE FARDUN
ARBETH
MARODA
Vachaasha
LEFAYR
Stonehill
HAYMON TAPRA
Makkera
FALLIM
Bishops-town
Vach Roysh

Part One

Legal Proceedings Following Two Deaths

I

19th June 641 After Landing

Gridor conceded that he was lost, a new experience.

He'd lived forty-two of his forty-eight years in City Qayn, mostly employed delivering rich people's purchases, so he knew that city well, almost every alley. But two hours ago he'd arrived in the town of Sapientia, where he'd never been before. The Lake was *that* side, downhill, and he supposed the Great College would be a big building – or more than one building? – but this knowledge wasn't enough.

The streets themselves were confusingly similar to those at home. Tenement blocks three stories high; churches on patches of green; one big square with gallows, pillory and whipping-post; occasionally wider streets with larger houses set apart. A few of these houses had brightly coloured doors, proclaiming that they belonged to one of the Ten Great Families of Ricossa. All around, the greyness of stone; above him a narrow passage of paler grey sky. People passed by, normal people. Rich and servanted; poor alone or with friends; clergy.

"The north side of the Third Quadrangle," he'd been told, weeks before, and his old brain had been so excited at the invitation that it hadn't occurred to him to ask what a Quadrangle was.

So now after a longish time of wandering, he tried to ask for directions – politely, smilingly – but the inhabitants of Sapientia were not helpful. They stared, shook heads, or shied off – one man did say, "That way," and waved a vague arm. Was it his destination they didn't like, or his accent? His appearance, or his reputation?

Both appearance and reputation, Gridor would've admitted, were odd.

He was a brown-faced thin getting-old man, whose wiry black hair and beard were greying. There was nothing strange about any of that, though it was a small shame to be so obviously thinning on top. Over his Sunday-best blue jacket and hose, he wore a grey cloak. Its hood was thrown back on his shoulders, which in itself was also ordinary, for only in the worst weather does a Ricossan cover their hair, and this was June.

But the hood was not ordinary. Inside it he'd asked his nephew to sew a small woven basket, and a flowering plant – a geranium, he understood it was – grew there in its own soil. Its dark-edged green leaves and pink blossoms waved above his head, and sometimes falling petals pattered onto his scalp, or lost themselves irritatingly down his neck. And this was very odd indeed – had been odd for over fifteen years. It also ached his shoulders sometimes. But he'd made a vow.

The vow had brought him to Sapientia, and hope had burned strong in him that this was God's leading, this was the year, he was stepping forward at last. There was fear also, for he might be annoying powerful people, but the hope was stronger, when he set out. But a bumpy day-and-a-half in a goods wagon (beautiful countryside views though, reminding him of his childhood in the northern b'Iri lands) followed by two hours of wandering, had discouraged him. He looked at the high roofs on either side, and they seemed to curve down threateningly, and even waver like tall grass. His head was swimming.

It was starting to rain, and people were leaving the streets.

There was a patter, a murmur, behind him. Or was it a giggle? He looked round, and thought bright cloth flickered behind the last corner, and the patter stopped. It was absurd to be nervous, but his back stiffened, remembering old scars. He walked faster, turned again, and saw what was obviously a tavern ahead. Light shone from unshuttered windows, and a buzz of talk trickled – on a summer evening that might be any house. But this door had a jug hanging beside it, and above the lintel swung a board with a brightly painted picture of sunrise over the Lake. He hadn't much money, but he'd enough for a cup and a slice of pie, and as a paying customer he'd surely deserve directions.

And the provisions he'd brought for the journey were finished, so he was hungry.

Gridor pushed at the door – too hard, it thumped against the wall – and stumbled in with a blast of cool air. Those inside looked up. Not many of them. A thin woman in an apron stood behind the counter. At one table an old couple sat stroking each other's hands (*ah, Miya, when did we last sit like that?* he thought a little guiltily) and at another three smarter folk, perhaps merchants or craftspeople, were gossiping in low voices. "I hear the messengers are all saddled to ride out, as soon as she goes," one of them said. So they believed here as well that Queen Zinial was dying. *Might that make a difference?*

The tavern had two fires in braziers, and lamps in cressets round the sides. One wall was actually painted all over with a huge version of the sunrise picture he'd seen outside, complete with a town in the foreground, boats on the water, and a large crown at the edge. It was pretty. As he made a slow path over to the hostess, the place felt snug and welcoming.

"A pleasant afternoon to you. Welcome to The Morning Dream. What's your desire, sir? Are you alone?", for he'd been peering back at the door.

"Thank you. A cup of ale, if you please, madam. I'm alone, unless – was there someone behind me?" Why had he said

that? He glanced behind, blinking in the brightness, head whirling;
and the braziers' flames looked taller and more dazzlingly
coloured than they surely were. "And if you would -"

She looked up from him as the door opened again. Two
young dark-skinned men came in, drawing all eyes in the place.

They were people of importance, people of Family. Their
easy, entitled-to-be-here manner would have proclaimed this,
even without their clothes. They wore bright knee-length gowns
with sleeves in contrasting colours, brown for the red gown, and
green for the blue. The red-and-brown man wore his hair combed
back in loose ringlets that curled on the shoulders, and his beard
was neatly pointed. His companion in blue was less tidy, and had
only a boy's beard, but he was the one wearing a sword.

The hostess smiled politely at them, curtseying. The eyes
of the smarter one were on Gridor. He murmured something to
his companion before waving the woman permission to carry on,
while looking around for a place to sit.

Gridor cleared his throat, resumed, "Thank you," and
took his cup. He swallowed. "That is good, my head's sore and
my throat. Can you tell me, madam, where I can find the Great
College?"

"The Great College? What part of it?" she asked - and then
everyone was looking at them.

One of the drinking merchants laughed. "You look like a
decent Christian. Why'd you want to go there?"

"I - I am to meet someone."

"Well, beware," she said, leaning back against the wall.
Her eyes narrowed in her pale face, and she looked beyond him
at the newcomers, the finely-dressed lads. "The College is where
they teach the rich how to mix poisons. They cut up beggar
children for entertainment, just to see how they're made."

"Shina," said one of the men with her warningly.

The young man with ringlets said loudly, "That is nonsense."

"Is it?"

"I – I only need instructions -" Gridor heard himself bleat.

The young man pushed himself up, and said past him, "I must ashk, madam, that you show more reshpect. Respect."

"I'm a merchant in this town, and a child of God. Who's calling for respect? Who are you, *student?*" The woman Shina stood also.

"Yes, I study at the Great College, and we do nothing vile."

"And you are?"

"My name is Rorash Adam b'Shen," he answered with a defiant note. *Poor lad,* thought Gridor, whose wife was a daughter of Eve, but the woman laughed again.

"Rorash *Adam?* At least my parents were married, you arrogant drunk bastard."

The rich boy plunged forward with a shout. His friend was also moving. The woman's companion grabbed her arm. *These young idiots.* Gridor had stopped many stupid fights in his time. He lifted his hands, said mildly, "There's no need -" and stepped between.

The young man flung him aside, a forceful shove to the chest, *pain*, and he tipped over backwards.

His head banged hard on the wall. More pain. He was flailing, and falling. He was on his back on the floor, in agony.

People were punching each other above, and someone tripped and fell onto him. The other rich lad. A dark face stared into his own. He heard himself make a noise.

But the pain was too great, and he could no longer see.

And suddenly Gridor wondered in terror if he could possibly be dying – *Lord have mercy on me, a sinner!* – and knew if that were so, he had utterly failed.

*

That same evening, thirty miles to the north-east, Riodran, Lord b'Nida, left his home in obedience to an invitation from the Palace. He took two servants with him, Attar in case of attack, and Hridnaya in case he needed a witness to an otherwise secret conversation. The three walked silently along wide well-lit damp streets, across the Square of Silent Remembrance and the Great Square, through the Royal Gate and into the Palace courtyard. Up to this point, all seemed normal, but once they were inside the magnificent doors, the clumps of people in the Mosaic Corridor were smaller, more closely huddled, with twitchier looks around them. So probably the rumours were true.

He should be grieved, but sorrow was elbowed out by anxiety. What next, and who next, after she died? He'd been very fond of Zinial, long ago; and when she'd become Queen, he'd been hopeful for good. But over the last seven years she'd disappointed him steadily.

And deathbeds are places of pain and mess, such as he usually tried to avoid.

There were a few calculating stares and whispers from Palace people as they passed.

Riodran's servants peered eagerly at the pictures made of tiny stones on the Corridor floor, and the portraits on the huge staircase. He would have liked to give them a little time to look around and savour the building, but courtesy forbade. They weren't here to gawp.

They walked through a white door to the Morning Queen's private apartments, and here Attar was told to wait.

"Lord b'Nida. Thank you for coming." A tidy plump man in his fifties waddled up with a grave smile, and bowed. Krothon wore the long plain gown of a secretary – for that after all is what

22

a Chamberlain is. Unlike many of his rank, Riodran respected secretaries, but he had no reason to respect Krothon. People said he spent as much time in Queen Zinial's bed as at his desk. Moreover, *as* her Chamberlain, he was in part responsible for her neglect of her duties, in particular neglect of the College. Riodran almost preferred the other Chamberlain, the King's, who never bothered to hide his enmity.

However, only a fool dwells on people he doesn't like, and only a very great fool shows the dislike, so he bowed in return replying, "I am honoured by the call. How does the Queen?"

Krothon indicated another door with a ringed hand. "She's in her bed, this way. I fear you'll find her much altered." They went through two more doors, the last one guarded, and into a stiflingly hot room with many candles.

Hot and full. As he'd said, the Morning Queen lay in bed, the curtains drawn back. A physician stood chewing her lip on one side; a priest sat praying in a whisper at the other. There were two maids standing with their backs against a shadowy wall, and a Guard to shut the door on the draught. Krothon, Riodran, and his one servant filled most of what space was left.

Queen Zinial was not many years older than her visitor. He remembered her dancing, glowing; cackling at some stupid joke – long ago, before she was a Queen. He stepped onto the blue-and-gold carpet that he'd need to be able to describe to his youngest daughter when he got home, and nobody stopped him taking more and more steps until he was standing next to the bed, looking down and yes, feeling pity.

Her brown face was taut, but her cheeks had sunk in. Both hands were on the blanket, one clutching a crucifix. Her black hair had been combed fanlike over the pillow, but she jerked her head wearily about, disrupting the pattern. "Your

Grace," said Krothon behind him, "Lord b'Nida is come, as you asked."

"Riodran," she said in a tired voice, looking up.

She is finally dying, after all these months. It's true.

"Your Grace, I am here."

"Yes," she said slowly, a sigh. Then, in a more energetic tone, almost a squawk, "*Yes.*" She lifted and waved her free hand in a weary but unmistakable gesture. The physician and the priest stood up and moved away. Riodran jerked his head at the woman he'd brought, and she retreated also. The Queen kept waving until everyone was on the opposite side of the room - except Krothon, who stood, a chunky pillar, in the middle.

Riodran sat down on the vacated chair, and bent forward, smelling medicine on her breath. "How can I serve you?" he asked formally.

Her lips twitched, smile or grimace. "Do you remember, Riodran?" she asked clearly. "Long ago, at Christmas, you and I?"

Oh, that Christmas. Pity mingled with annoyance. *After seven years aloof, have you brought me to your deathbed to reminisce about old times? Yes, I kissed you twenty or thirty years ago – did a lot more than kiss you, before we both married other people, but –*

"I remember," he said, and made himself smile.

"My friend." Her chin jerked and her hand clenched, he guessed with pain. Then, more softly, "My friend." She beckoned him to bend down. "Do you remember Madrasun?"

Madrasun? A much more recent, much sadder, memory. "Of course."

Her free hand was on his, and her mouth was almost touching his ear.

"Speak soft. Secret. Before I die – I'm dying – must warn you. Should've done before. Madrasun. How did he die?"

"I don't – he had a fall. Down the stairs from his room." But there was cold between his shoulder-blades.

"He came to me – worried." He watched her gasp, and realised the effort in every word. "Soon – foreign woman's coming. To your College. Yes?"

"Yes." The envoy from Makkera, bringing Queen Nerranya's gift. A project *their* Queen could and should have taken more interest in. What of it?

"Madrasun thought – trouble was planned. Bad trouble. Mobira – you know her?"

"Of course. What trouble? What are you telling me?" He frowned, trying to remain patient.

"I told him – 'be calm, don't fret.' But then he died. I did nothing. Be careful, Riodran." She lifted her eyes to the bed canopy above them, patterned with huge flowers. "I told them to fetch you. A fond farewell. So I could warn you. Do my duty. God forgive me." Then, louder, "Tell me you remember dancing that night in the gardens, in the snow? The best Christmas. Riodran!" Suddenly she was exclaiming in pain, and clutching at him. The physician bustled back.

"Your Grace – I think you need another dose."

"Yes, yes, hurry!" Her eyes rolled.

Lord b'Nida took her fingers from his wrist. He kissed her knuckle before laying them down. This seemed a bad time for play-acting, but "I will never forget," he said. "God bless you, Your Grace. Zini. Always."

Wondering, he stood up and stepped back again. The priest and the maids brushed past him until the bed was surrounded. He was standing next to Krothon now. The other man was very still, but then his right hand moved to cross himself. "May God indeed bless her," and then he looked up. "Thank you, my lord. I don't think she has long." His eyes were glistening.

Perhaps there was affection there, after all, not merely pocket-lining.

So this meeting is over. What was she saying – and what was so important, to tell me now? Madrasun, Mobira, the Jaryari visit, the College – what was she warning me of, or asking me to do? Has she only just noticed that Mobira means trouble?

And why so secret? She's the Queen! Does she think her Chamberlain or her maids are reporting to Aigith? Are things as bad as that?

What is the Evening King doing?

He beckoned for the maid Hridnaya to follow him, and walked out of the room without looking back.

*

"They're calling Rorash a murderer!"

Mejorad b'Shen's face bounced in surprise at his aunt's cry.

He'd been spending the evening sitting unobtrusively in the corner of the music-room. If challenged, he was reading a book called "An Assessment of Military Strategies in the War of the Throne." In reality he was cutting out the dullest-looking pages, folding them into triangles of varying sizes, and feeding them one by one to his candle to darken, curl and be consumed.

Trying not to remember the huge black terrified eyes of the pauper dying under his hands the day before. How he longed to run away to a tavern! But today of all days his family would not have approved.

Now he looked up as mother and aunt swished towards him. One was ferocious, the other business-like. "Mejorad! Did you hear me?"

"Aunt Eyanda, I – I don't understand."

"That man's family are claiming it was a deliberate assault – murder! They're demanding a *trial!*"

Eyanda b'Shen's energy and fountain of black hair always made her look taller than she was. Her face, nose and ears were long and thin. So were her fingers, one of which was pointing accusingly at Mejorad. Her sister Rommi, his mother, was shorter, plainer, quieter. By chance today they were both wearing blue gowns, which looked better on Eyanda, as everything did. Mej scrambled up, brushing burnt scraps off the desk to flutter downwards, and stared from one to the other.

"The man yesterday? How could it have been deliberate? I told you – Rorash told you -"

Rorash had been sitting all day alone in his chamber upstairs.

"I know what you told us. What is the *truth?*"

He looked away from her furious eyes – then made himself look back. "It was an accident, I swear to you! We had no intention of causing trouble, of doing any damage – Rorash would never hurt anybody! You know that! I swear!"

"How drunk were you?" asked his mother, her voice quiet.

"Not very – somewhat, me more than him. We'd never spoken to old Flower-in-Hood – seen him around the city, is all! He was just there in the tavern, and it happened. Rorash didn't even strike him hard."

"And yet he died. It seems his kin have a tale that he was being watched and spied on, and that this wasn't chance."

Mejorad went a little cold.

"How dare they? How *dare* they?" cried Eyanda. "Slandering my son – one of the Families! I want them punished! This is treason!"

"No, it's not." Rommi's voice was timid but clear.

Eyanda threw up her hands wildly, and turned away. "Why did I let him go to that bloody College? What use are those doctors and books to someone like him? And now – he's to be tried for murder! He could be -" and there she stopped. Convicted murderers are hanged. If they're lucky.

Mejorad felt his mother's gentle unchanging eyes on him. "We meant no harm," he said again. Still she stared.

"What can we do?" Eyanda wailed.

Rommi laid a hand hesitatingly on her arm. "Accusation isn't yet trial, and trial isn't conviction. There would have to be very strong evidence to convince a judge that Rorash, for no reason -"

"We must find out which judge! Persuade them – talk to them! How much money do they need?"

"Sister, don't. An honest judge would be insulted, and most of them -"

"Very well for you to say! It's not your son accused! There must be something I can do! And don't just tell me to pray!" She whirled around, fixing Mejorad with an unfriendly look, and then put her hands over her face.

There were times when Mejorad envied his cousin; wished that he too was Eyanda's child. This was not one of those times.

Suddenly the door banged open, and his great-uncle pushed his face in. *"There* you are! Have you heard the news?"

"About Rorash?"

"Rorash? No. Queen Zinial is dead."

II

Two weeks after her master had taken her to the Palace to visit a dying Queen, Hridnaya was out on the streets again, but this time she didn't leave by the front door.

"Where are you going?" the doorguard demanded; but

then he recognised her, and changed the question. "D'you have leave from Narrim?" Hridnaya nodded, and he threw up the latch, and allowed her out into the alley.

Left, and down, and out into Scholars' Street. "If someone would kindly burn down the Great Passage, this would be the best address in City Qayn," as Lord b'Nida had once joked. Scholars' Street was broad and tidy, their huge but shallow mansion taking up most of one side. The great b'Nida banner hung above the front door, which was raised a few steps, and painted purple. The doorguard's jacket matched it. Carved on the lintel above were the letters R 403 M. They were the only letters Hridnaya knew.

At the end of the street, she turned right, and past the Saints' Bakery, right again. She was out in the city, by herself, and it wasn't even Sunday. She grinned.

She was a little nervous of the great tall bustling people flowing past her; and a little puzzled about her strange errand; and she felt a little grief at its cause, a little worry about her family, and a little - yes, a little simple pleasure at being out in the sun. Seeing pretty-shaped clouds in the gaps between high buildings, feeling the breeze, on her own errand, her own

But most of all, curiosity.

Wednesday was the day many people were allowed half-holiday, a day for laundry and marketing. In lower parts of the city Hridnaya might already have seen clothes hanging across streets to dry, but not in the First Quarter, of course. Shops and taverns were open, market stalls sent out a gorgeous mixture of smells, and everyone was walking weekday-fast. All on important business.

No, she thought. *Some walk fast because they have business. Some walk fast to pretend to have. Some walk slowly, because they're happy and at ease; and others to show they're too*

rich to work.

Hridnaya had business: family business, not Family. She was going to watch Rorash b'Shen tried for murder.

She'd had to plead for the morning out with gestures. Housemother Narrim hadn't wanted to be worried, busy with preparation for the Conclave visitors. "You went to the funeral. Now this as well. Did you love your Uncle Gridor so much?" Her parting words had been, "Be back by sundown. And don't expect any more favours from me till Christmas at least."

Now, "*Did* you love him so much?" asked Balki, the friend-in-her-head.

No.

Fond, perhaps – but they hadn't met often in the last eighteen years, and the meetings there'd been were awkward. He'd always been odd, kindly but strange, and got odder over time. *Flower-in-Hood,* people called him, and laughed. She wasn't really doing this for him. She was doing it for her brother Brinnon, who had loved him - and for Aunt Miya, Gridor's widow, bereft with two children. And she was also curious – why murder? Surely the death hadn't been meant? "One of the Ten pushed him over in a tavern," her cousin Gita had told her, eyes peeping round in awe at the b'Nida hall.

If Uncle had been rich, and the man who pushed him poor, I could understand it. Then there'd be accusations of riot and all manner of things -

"So does this mean the courts give a lowly delivery-man the same justice as one of the Families?" asked Balki. "Is that a Question for the Box?"

I suppose so. Question 34.

She'd reached the Square of Silent Remembrance. All round the edges the buildings rose even higher than on Scholars' Street. They weren't houses or shops, they were Offices - places where business was done by the Morning Queen (Queen Zinial, *God rest her soul,* and soon her successor) and the Evening King, and their consorts and Councils, and the Church.

Long ago, she'd heard, the Square had housed a market, but its centre was now empty except for the ten huge pillars, a door's length each side, and a two-storey house tall. On them were carved the names of dead people, from the War.

It was unlucky to walk between them, so she edged round the outside, crossing herself dutifully as she passed the b'Nida pillar. She turned off left out of the Square. Because this wasn't familiar ground she needed to concentrate, and remember Brinnon's instructions. There were people about, a few, well-dressed; but of course she couldn't ask them. Along past the city's grandest childpen, from where she heard sounds of gleeful battle, and the scaffolding where a great house was having its roof repaired. She stepped aside for two gossiping young women on horses, and entered the Great Square.

There were no pillars here. Here stood the gallows that could hang ten people at a time on its long platform; the pillory and whipping-post; and, in the centre, the stake for burnings. There hadn't been a burning for over a year. Hridnaya had never watched one, and didn't want to. She marched through, heart beginning to thud, to the foot of the steps.

She had arrived at the Hall of Justice, wide enough to fill one side of the Square. The steps were as broad as the building. There was nobody on them, but at the top there were Guards with maces.

"You could just leave," said Balki. "You could walk away and have a free morning; buy something tasty, eat in a tavern maybe, play with the children –" But instead she took a deep breath, and put one foot on the lowest step. There weren't many people in the Square, but she wondered if all of them watched as she climbed. The Guards certainly did. Their eyes dragged her upwards, and she stood before the doors.

They made her take off her cloak and lift her arms to show she wasn't carrying a weapon, but let her in without other trouble. She went through an anteroom whose walls were covered with portraits, a room large enough itself for a b'Nida dinner. One or two people were standing about - more Guards - and finally into the Court.

This was a bigger room, almost too big to understand. Across its far end a wooden wall reached half-way to the roof, and behind this there were two more doors, higher up. Hridnaya had heard enough anecdotes in the b'Nida house to recognise this as the "bench". The Judge and the prisoner would sit or stand behind it, along with the witnesses, all elevated for everyone to see them.

She began to edge forward, through a few folk chattering. *People have heard of Flower-in-Hood,* she told Balki. Before the bench on the left side was a more solemn group, six or seven people, most of them dark-skinned, as the b'Shen tended to be. Men in gowns rather than jackets, and women with lace-edged bodices and wide skirts; lovely sleeves in different colours. Their belts looked as if they normally wore swords.

Hridnaya's family was respectable. Brin had a good place, and she herself was a trusted maidservant to one of the Ten Families. But these people were different. They stood as if they had a right to be there. Or anywhere.

"Hridna, greetings!" Her sister-in-law Lulet flung arms around her. "Thank you for coming."

"Yes, thank you." Over Lulet's shoulder stood Aunt Miya, Gridor's widow, tall and red-eyed, and beside her her son, newly-apprenticed Vren.

But where was the person she'd come for? She pulled

back, and looked questioningly at Lulet's chubby deceptively child-like face. "Bih?" she said awkwardly.

"He was here. The Guards said they had questions." She now saw that Lulet was trembling.

"He's coming!" cried Vren in a voice of relief, and pointed. Two black-and-grey-clad Guards, a man and a woman, not looking particularly vicious, were walking over with Brin between them. In a moment, he was there, and squeezing her tightly.

"I couldn't make the funeral. I couldn't ask for two days off, and this was more important. It's good to see you, even -" He swivelled his head around to indicate the sad circumstances.

Her twin's shoulders were slightly hunched from his work as a tailor's assistant. Like Hridnaya, he was small and slight, and pale-brown in face. Both had black hair, currently cut short for mourning - hers rapidly but imperfectly trimmed by Housemother Narrim, who was pretty kind to the maids on the whole; his with careful neatness by his loving wife. He was wearing his smartest green Sunday jacket. Beneath the cloak that was too warm for the day, Hridnaya wore a colourless kirtle with the b'Nida Family's sleeveless purple tabard.

"What did they want?" Lulet asked him.

"I had to look at some people, say if I recognised any of them -" But then there was a sudden trumpet-blast, all conversation stopped – and Hridnaya's heart banged in her chest.

Through the middle door above them an oldish woman appeared. She was broadly-built, with a stern look and a beaked nose. What could be seen of her gown was white, but on her smooth greying hair rested a black circlet, showing that she had the authority to order death. Everyone bowed, and she sat down. The Judge. Two Guards followed, and took places behind her.

Through the second door walked another man, also guarded. There were no bows, but there was silence. Vren clutched his mother's hand, and Brin was very still.

He looked rich, but otherwise ordinary, Hridnaya thought. Youngish, almost but not quite black-skinned, a round bearded face; dressed in a fine gown of red and silver. The noble's look of calm disdain. As he looked round and down at the little group that was presumably his family, he smiled at a woman in blue with red sleeves. She was too old for wife or sweetheart – "I guess his mother," said Balki.

A secretary stood up. "This court of justice is now in session, under Judge Adjefi Dir Ray b'Trai. May God guide its deliberations. May God punish all liars."

"Amen," came a general murmur.

What do I know about the b'Trai? Not much. Their lands are in the south: they're in feud with the b'Met, or some of them are -

"Listen," said Balki reprovingly.

Judge Adjefi b'Trai turned to the young man. The prisoner. The killer. "Are you Rorash Adam b'Shen?"

"Yes, my lady."

The Judge snapped her fingers, and a Guard handed her a clinking bag. "You, I think, my lady," she said to the woman in blue, "are Eyanda b'Shen? And what is *this,* that was delivered to my house last night?"

The woman stared.

"I will tell you what it is. It is a bribe." She opened the bag, and dribbled a few gold coins through her fingers. "A bribe to the Evening King's courts, to steal a favourable judgment for your son." She fastened the bag again, and tossed it down to her. "Nine gold pieces. Count them. Are they all there?"

There was no sound in the court as the woman counted. Then there was more no-sound. The Judge turned back. "Take him out and thrash him. Nine strokes."

The young man gasped, just a little. And before anyone fully understood, he'd been half-pulled back out of the room, and his place was empty.

"No – please!" cried the woman Eyanda. "My lady, please – it wasn't his fault, it was me – have mercy!"

"You seek *mercy* here?"

She began to cry.

"Perhaps this Judge will give us justice," young Vren whispered.

"Nine strokes – yes, and that's all they'll do to him! For killing a man! Not even a real flogging! It's nothing!"

It's not nothing, Hridnaya thought. People weren't often beaten in the b'Nida household, but it did happen. *It depends. But -*

"But maybe it's just for show," said Balki in her head.

Yes. Question 34.

Everyone waited. Above them was still warm air; and above that a ceiling divided into squares. There was painted lettering in each square.

Her brother touched her shoulder, and pointed to the bench. He whispered, "Do you think – up there – is that where the witnesses stand?"

She nodded, and then looked questioningly at Aunt Miya.

"Yes, she's to give evidence, and so am I. I have to tell them -" He pressed his mouth together, and blinked. He was very scared. Lulet lifted a finger and gently touched her husband's forehead, then nose and mouth. It was a thing they did.

At last the Guard brought the prisoner back. He was moving with some pain, Hridnaya thought, but his face was almost as calm as it had been.

The Judge looked slowly from him to Eyanda. "Please remember," she said, "that this is a court of justice. Mercy is for

God, and vengeance for barbarians. Now," as she turned back, "you are accused of murdering the man Gridor, son of Arro, sometimes called Flower-in-Hood, a delivery-man of this city, on 19th June in the town of Sapientia, by thrusting his head violently against a wall. Are you guilty or not guilty?"

Rorash swallowed. "Not guilty of murder, my lady."

"Then let us begin."

*

Two hours had passed. The Judge leaned back to the Guard, and requested a cup of wine, which was poured. She drank it. The prisoner lowered his eyes. His mother stared at him. The space on the Judge's left, where the witnesses had stood, one after another, was empty.

Aunt Miya held young Vren in a long embrace which Hridnaya thought he found uncomfortable. One of the rich witnesses, the young man with hardly any beard and untidy hair - Mejorad b'Shen was his name - fidgeted.

Hridnaya shut her eyes, reciting.

The Judge cleared her throat, and the hall jumped.

Her voice was calm and cold. "I have heard and considered the evidence. I have heard from the physician Vreddo on the cause of death. I've heard from the widow Miya, and from Gridor's nephew Brinnon, who claims that the dead man feared attack, and says that people were watching him, but could not identify any. I've heard from the prisoner, and from two other people who were present - Bada, the keeper of The Morning Dream tavern, and the prisoner's cousin Mejorad.

"I find that Rorash b'Shen killed Gridor, son of Arro, in an act of unplanned drunken rage. If Gridor indeed feared an attack, there is no evidence that his fear was correct, nor any link to the b'Shen family or the prisoner. Or that any attack would have meant worse than a sound cudgelling, to teach respect. There's

36

no reason to think that the meeting in The Morning Dream was other than accidental. I therefore find him guilty of manslaughter, but not of murder."

A sigh went up from one side of the hall. Hridnaya felt empty, neither pleased nor disappointed.

"So, as to the consequences. A man is dead. Rorash b'Shen or his kin will pay the sum of three gold pieces to the widow Miya. And he himself -" one of the Guards nudged the prisoner to make him look up - "As a killer without evil intent, you are sentenced to the Prelate's Penance. You will be taken from here to the city of Vachansha in Defardu, the City of Refuge. You will kneel before Prelate Susanna, and she will give you your orders. You will not return to Ricossa until two years from this day. Do you understand?"

"Yes, my lady," the young man whispered.

"This matter is ended." The Judge stood up. "In the Name of the Father -"

As soon as the prayer was over, she vanished.

"What does that mean?" Vren was hissing. The woman Eyanda had run forward to clasp her son's hands. A pink-cheeked elderly servant wearing the holly-green tabard of b'Shen crossed the room, carrying a bag, a pen and a parchment.

"Miya, daughter of Eve? Three gold pieces. Please make your mark to acknowledge receipt."

*

The five of them wandered out into the Great Square. Other people, who knew nothing about it, passed by on their ordinary lives.

Lulet explained, "I think it's - he'll do whatever the Prelate orders – hard labour or prayers or some such – in Defardu for two years. When he comes back it's all supposed to be forgiven." She raised enquiring eyebrows towards her sister-in-law, but in this case Hridnaya knew no more than she.

"I'll never forgive my father's murderer," said Vren. He stared across the Square, blinking.

"The Judge said it wasn't murder; he didn't mean to kill him."

It was over, funeral and trial. This evening Hridnaya would have to go back to work. But for now she stood quietly, part of her soul enjoying being with her family, and another part running through the evidence, all that had been said. At the back of her mind somewhere, Uncle Gridor waited to say a last goodbye.

"Your pardon?" They all seemed to jump. It was a woman, not young; a priest with black robes, and short hair the colour of flame, but with ashy streaks. "You are Gridor's widow, I think? And his kin?"

Aunt Miya, who was staring at her hands, shrugged.

"He was our uncle," said Brin gruffly. The priest looked at them all, but for some reason her eyes stopped with Hridnaya.

"My name is Sister Felicity. I was acquainted with Gridor, son of Arro. I wished to… give you my small share of your sorrow."

Hridnaya had heard this phrase, read out of formal letters of condolence. No one had ever said it to her before.

The priest went on. "He was a good man. I think the best I have ever known."

They all stared.

"If I've ever met a saint in my life, your husband, father, uncle, was that man." She seemed to feel their astonishment, and her distinctive pale face grew pinker. "And, if I may ask, are you Hridnaya, daughter of Haidi?"

Hridnaya nodded. The priest looked at her solemnly for a moment (she seemed a very solemn woman) and then beckoned her a few steps apart.

What's this? What have you to do with me?

"Your uncle spoke to me of you." Hridnaya felt her face grow hot. "I'm sure you know how distressed he was by what happened many years ago. Fifteen years?"

Eighteen.

"It changed his life." The priest paused. Plainly there was nothing more to say. But, "God bless you, Hridnaya. If you – or any of his family - need help, *any* help, come to me. Sister Felicity, the Church of Holy Mourning, on Redman's Street." She hesitated; then made the sign of the cross in the space between them, and turned away.

"What did she mean?" Balki asked, and Hridnaya had no answer.

"What did she say?" Brin was wondering pointlessly, when Aunt Miya cried out, "I don't want their money!" She unhooked the little bag from her belt, and looked around as if for somewhere to throw it.

"Don't do that, aunt! You need the money, now there's only you and Vren to earn."

"I don't want it!"

"*Mother -*"

Uncle Gridor and his wages were gone. Uncle Gridor, that saint *(saint?)* that amiable talkative fool who kept offending employers and having to search for new ones. And they were all feeling sad and a little empty, but that would pass away, as sadness and pain did.

It was starting to rain. Lulet said, "Let's go home."

*

Rorash was gone. They'd been allowed a half hour to say farewell. This was just enough time for Mejorad's mother Rommi to send one of the servants back to the mansion for a satchel of clean clothes and a prayerbook. And, because this was Rorash, a book of poetry.

Half an hour in an evil bare room, with a Guard standing in the corner.

Eyanda flung her arms around her son, and he cried out. His pain was her fault, and she jumped away and burst into tears.

"I will be well, mother," he said.

Rommi said shyly, "It's only two years."

"Only!" Eyanda exclaimed. "We could all be dead in that time!"

Great-Uncle Yettrid, who'd been scowling throughout the trial, said, "That's not probable. We warned you not to annoy the Judge, Eyanda. Almost none of them are corrupt. Rorash," more solemnly, "God go with you. Live to the honour of the b'Shen, wherever you are." He laid a hand on Rorash's bowed head. Then he turned and walked out. He was a busy man, acting head of the Family.

"Please look after my daughter," Rorash said, a little hoarsely, and the women nodded.

Mejorad clasped his cousin's hand, and met his eyes. They shared a shrug. There was nothing to say. Stepping back, he felt again his mother's eyes on him.

Rorash had stood straight and tall in court, and said,

"What the tavern-keeper - and my cousin - said is what happened."

And that was true. Almost.

The satchel arrived, and no one could think of anything more to say.

They were now outside in the Great Square. Mejorad, his mother, his aunt, and a few servants.

"We must be able to do something! It's intolerable! We must!" Aunt Eyanda was angrily slashing tears off her face with her hands. Her maid passed her a handkerchief.

"There's nothing to do. We keep an eye on your beautiful granddaughter, and we pray. Defardu isn't a prison. It may even be a blessing for him."

Mejorad watched his aunt not screaming. She managed to say, "Thank you, sister. I will see you at supper," and then she whirled away, snapping her fingers for her maid to follow. She was probably going to seek consolation at her lover's fireside, or in their bed. Mejorad bowed to his mother, told his own man, "I will be alone," and turned rapidly away. *What, oh what, to do now?*

He could beat on all the doors in the First Quarter until he found a friend to talk to. He could seek out a whorehouse. He could walk into a tavern and get drunk.

He was cold, actually cold. It was raining, in July. He wandered over to the edge of the Square, where a few stalls with canopies provided a little shelter. Baskets were piled high on this one – large and small, willow and reed and rush –

Mejorad grabbed the table and pushed it violently up and over backwards. People leapt away, baskets bounced through wet air. "Sir!"

He ran, ran to the nearest street, and down it. As he went, he looked upwards for a ledge or porch to climb on and escape, but the rain still pattered, and even he wasn't mad enough for slippery roofs in this weather. In any case, no one came after him. He was one of the b'Shen. So he just went on running.

He ran through puddles, splashing dull middling and poor folk. Around corners, down to the docks, along them and away again. Running, running. It seemed he ran all over the thumb-stuck-out-into-the-Lake that was City Qayn. At last he stopped, panting, in a non-descript street he didn't recognise.

Though not heavy, the rain was constant, and few people

were about. Some who were had pulled hoods up, which was rather unRicossan of them. *It's the flimsy Westerners who worry about a little damp on their hair.*

Tonight Rorash would be sleeping on the muddy ground, on his way to Defardu under guard. Tidy cleanly Rorash.

But Mej was too tired to run any more. Around a corner was a tavern. He walked in and ordered a cup of foreign wine. "At once, sir." It was a dim and almost empty room. He pulled off his wet cloak and slung it onto a chair, or tried to. The bloody thing slid off and landed on the floor.

No one had seen, but for a moment he wanted to die.

*

The family went back to the square pleasant room on Jaydrich's Street where Hridnaya and her twin had been born and brought up, where he and his family lived now. Hridnaya breathed deep the wonderful smell of freshly-cooked bannocks.

"Manslaughter. He's to go to Defardu for two years, and they paid a blood-price," Lulet told Vren's older sister, who'd been taking care of the children.

Brin offered his bereaved aunt the only chair and sat slumped against the wall, while Lulet, Vren and Hridnaya poured ale and passed round plates. Lulet also opened a sealed pot of mizzum, the mashed-up food mix sold in the markets for people who for any reason couldn't eat properly. It was their kindness always to keep some on hand for her sister-in-law's visits, and Hridnaya dipped a finger in a bowl, and tried to push the stuff down tidily, between sips.

So many years had passed since her baby memories of this room. The time had brought changes, thanks to Brin's sewing skills and Lulet's imagination. The box beds on the left wall were hidden by curtains - one embroidered with a night sky, and one with a sunny mountain. Brin had greater skill than his master acknowledged. There was more space, now that their father's loom had gone.

The people had changed too. Her father and her little sister, both dead. Her older brother and their mother, now living three days' journey to the south-east. They wouldn't know what had happened yet, as there was no way to tell them until Gardyish chose to visit the city and his kin, which he'd surely do before winter, anyway.

The last time she'd seen Uncle Gridor alive had been in this room, on the fourth day of last Christmas. They'd managed to fit a family feast in between the needs of their various employers. She remembered him lying on the floor, letting baby Jof crawl over him, telling the tale of Three Cats on the Moon, and not telling it as well as usual, because he was Christmas-drunk. Brin and Lulet had been sitting in a well-fed doze in each other's arms. Aunt Miya, never idle, had been sewing her new blue false-sleeves on top of her green gown, so that she could put her nose up and pretend to be a well-born person at the Twelfth Night mass.

That was six months ago.

Now Brin was silent, sitting against the wall. But Lulet said, "Will you – will you be able to manage, Aunt?"

"By God's grace." Aunt Miya sighed sourly. "I suppose their money will provide Gita's entrance-gift to the monastery – she's going next Wednesday. And it'll help with the rent, and pay for the funeral. I'm earning, and Vren's settled."

Vren, who was thirteen, had recently started fish-cleaning down at the docks. He slept in one shed with the other apprentices, spending most of the day scaling, gutting, chopping and packing in another. Already he smelt of fish all the time, as he probably would for the rest of his life, but it was steady work.

If Gridor had earned more, or more reliably (Aunt Miya

had complained at Christmas) they might have hoped to place him better and wouldn't have had to rely on their Voiceless niece's money to help. Miya herself washed dishes at a tavern near the Cathedral, and earned extra by singjng to attract and entertain customers. It was her voice that Gridor had fallen in love with, he'd always said, long ago.

She sighed again, her face twitching. "Gita, we should be going home. How long are you permitted, Vren?"

"Till sundown, and I'm losing a whole day's pay, so I'll take it all. If my aunt and uncle permit?" he added hastily.

"Of course."

He stood up, and allowed his mother to embrace him. Hridnaya saw a tear on her face.

"Fare well, Aunt," said Lulet, casting a look at her silent husband. (*The Glowering Twin*, Hridnaya remembered.)

Aunt Miya scrabbled in her satchel. She surprised them all with, "I have some things here, if you'd wish them to remember him by. This is for you," to Vren. It was a plain brown earthenware plate, nothing beautiful, but it must have been his father's. Vren took it, nodded, snorted up tears, and wiped his face again.

"Niece, you collect these, don't you? From that cloak of his, with the absurd hood." A large green button, which Hridnaya took with a grateful pang. This made fourteen buttons in her box. "Fa – oo," she managed to say.

"And for you two – this was also his. I found it in his satchel, when the Guards returned it." A small white square of cloth, a handkerchief. There was stitching on it, some kind of pattern.

"Thank you. That is very kind," Brin said, his voice sounding rusty.

"So fare well."

"Wait," Lulet said suddenly. "A last drink." So they all made a circle, the children sitting on the floor at their mother's feet, and lifted their cups. "Gridor, son of Arro. God rest his soul. And may God bless all of us till we meet again. Father of all, we pray you bless Vren at the fish-house, and Gita at St Tabitha's – and Hridnaya at her place – and – all of us. Amen."

"Amen."

Trying to be cheerful, "The Conclave will be soon, will it not? Your Lord and Lady must be wondering who'll be chosen. *Do* you know how they do it?"

Hridnaya wanted to help, and smiled as she shook her head, untruthfully.

Vren said without much interest, "By the docks they're all betting we'll have a Morning King this time. We've had two Queens in a row."

There seemed nothing else to say about the Conclave. They drank. Aunt Miya and Gita left. Vren knelt down, staring into the fire.

Brin began to gather the plates, his silence oppressing them all. Hridnaya moved over to him, and tapped his shoulder.

He looked up at her, and then he leaned close, private from the others.

"D'you know what I heard once from the Bible, the *Bible,* in church? 'Woe to the rich.'"

What?

"They murdered him," he said. "Woe to the rich." After a moment, "I'm sorry," and he turned away.

Balki said in her head, "But if it was an accident indeed, then justice has been done."

If it wasn't an accident, it hasn't. But murder – that does seem unlikely. What have the b'Shen to do with us?

"He was very distressed," the priest had said. *Yes, I know.*

I remember him shouting.

    "If I've ever met a saint in my life -"

    What did she mean?

*

Some years ago, Hridnaya had heard Lady b'Nida tell her children that the world is not flat, as you might think, but round like a bubble.

So at night, if she had nothing else on her mind, she would imagine the round world hanging in the sky, held in the hands of God – He might even bounce it gently on His palms. She would draw her thought down from the heavens, and float it around the countries and seas, until she fixed it on the continent of Ragaris, counting the nations. She'd move to the east, to Ricossa; and then to the middle of the north, the Great Lake, and the city that stuck out from its eastern shore, City Qayn. On and on, smaller and smaller, through streets and squares, to the First Quarter, to Scholar's Street, to the b'Nida house, and this little room - and finally her own bed. If she wasn't asleep by then, she would lie and think what a privilege it was to be a tiny part of all that creation.

But that was if she had nothing else to do.

The night of the trial, she lay very still and carefully recited evidence, as near to the exact words as she could.

My name is Brinnon, son of Tren. He was trembling, but his voice was clear. *I live on Jaydrich's Street, and I work for Hanno the tailor on Firstbattle Street. The dead man was my uncle, my mother's brother.*

I wasn't there when he died, but I know he'd been expecting,

fearing, that he'd be attacked. There were people watching him, he told me so, and he told his wife, and I saw one of them.

The Judge said: *What people?*

I met him after work I think a month or two before he died, and we walked back to his house. It was maybe about Easter. He

pulled me aside and said there was a man following us, who'd been standing outside the shop, looking at him. I saw this man too, but not clearly. He walked with a limp, he had a stick, but I think he was quite young, not thin. I asked my uncle why anyone would want to spy on him, and he said, "They did before, and they may again. You know I talk too much." And he said he'd seen another different man, taller, near his house, and also a woman. His wife had seen them, or one of them, I think. Both of them had been there more than once, and not long

past. And a little later, the next week, he said he was still seeing them, or sombody.

The Judge: *Did he say any of these people had spoken to him, or threatened him?*

No, my lady.

The Judge: *What did he mean about talking too much, and 'before'?*

He – he used to offend people sometimes. He says, used to say, begging your kindness, the Ten Families didn't need to - to burn houses and beat folks and such like things. Once three people came to where he was working, ordered his mistress to dismiss him, and then thrashed and kicked him in the street.

The Judge: *How long ago was this?*

About seven years ago, just before I was married in 634. He told me about it, saying he was sorry if he was causing me trouble, if my wife's family would think it a disgrace to know him. He lost his place, and had to find another one, and then he lost that one, and went to work for Garida, daughter of Lim.

The Judge: *Do you know who these people were who beat him?*

No.

The Judge: *Were they connected to the b'Shen?*

I don't know.

The Judge: *Did he mention the prisoner Rorash, or that he was afraid of the b'Shen in general?*

No, my lady.

The Judge: *Did he speak against the b'Shen Family?*

Not that I remember.

The Judge, sighing: *Hmm. Do you know why he went to Sapientia that day?*

He told me the Sunday before he died that he was going to arrange to go there. He was managing time away from work with his mistress. He was very pleased about it, he said he was going to see someone, he didn't give a name, but it was important. "It's what I've been hoping for," he said.

The Judge: *Did he explain any more than that?*

No.

The Judge: *You have described an insolent commoner. One might say he deserved whipping, but why would anyone go to such trouble as you imply, watching him, plotting his death?*

I don't know, my lady. But he said they were. He was afraid.

The Judge: *Drink makes some men cowardly. I asked Lady b'Shen to send all their servants, male and female, here today, so that you could view them before the trial began. The Family gave their full co-operation. Did you see anyone you recognised?*

No. I didn't see the man clearly.

The Judge: *Have you ever seen the prisoner before, or any of his family who are here?*

I may have done, but I don't remember.

*

48

Zinial, the Queen for the Morning, was dead.

Messengers had duly ridden out to all parts of Ricossa, summoning the chosen from each of the Ten Families. They came for the Conclave of One Hundred and Two, gathering to choose - or discover - or be God-given - a new queen or king. (One ruler for the Morning, for commerce and art and beauty and the Faith; one for the Evening, for war and justice and the defence of Ricossa. So it had been since the War. King Aigith had been the Evening King for many years, since Hridnaya had been a tiny baby.)

The Conclave would mean guests and hubbub in the b'Nida household, as in all the great households, and of course extra work in preparation. Even the Family grandchildren were occupied learning genealogies by heart, so that they could correctly and courteously welcome all their relatives. Narrim the Housemother had piles of linen, stacks of dishes, lists of tasks, and a permanent frown on her face. Hridnaya, like most of the servants, scurried as directed between darning old sheets, removing cobwebs from guestrooms, and washing or polishing everything washable or polishable.

Unlike most, she also waited at table for the more private discussions that Lord and Lady b'Nida were starting to have over breakfast or supper. For some of these, even Narrim wasn't present. They were pondering the needs of the realm, and of the Family – which were almost the same thing, but not, Lord b'Nida conceded with a smile, identical.

The realm needed someone whose interests extended beyond border troubles, money and rooting out heresy. Someone who could persuade King Aigith to talk to people outsidehis own Council (growing smaller every year), his b'Iri Chamberlain and others of that Family. Someone who could occasionally refer to Jaryar over the mountains without calling it a "den of filth and sin", and to its Queen and King without obscenity. Someone who understood the principles of the New Governance, and valued peace and learning. So, again, not one of the b'Iri.

Such a person would also be good for the b'Nida, for valuing learning surely meant allocating money and honours to the Great College and its doctors. The b'Nida had invested much in the College, and Lady b'Nida managed it as its Chancellor, but few other Families shared their enthusiasm.

They also discussed their own guest-list, and for a few moments of foolish terror, Hridnaya waited for them to perhaps name Sinavid b'Olim. Sinavid, who'd raped her, and possibly other servants too, when staying for Christmas four years ago. Of course, as she told Balki firmly, there was no reason for him to stay anywhere other than with his own Family, if he came at all. Nonetheless she listened tensely to the names, and his was not one, and her skin could relax.

There was much going on. But Uncle Gridor and Sister Felicity would not leave her head.

"If I've ever known a saint in my life, your uncle was that man. Come to the Church of Holy Mourning, on Redman's Street."

What could that mean?

It was a question, and questions were the fascination of Hridnaya's life.

*

The physican who'd examined her uncle's body was called Vreddo, son of Bandar. He was a comfortable-looking man in grey and red, hair cut short on the scalp, beard growing pale in the centre.

I was called to the Sapientia Hall of Justice at the eighth hour of the evening on 20th June to examine the dead body of an elderly man. Miya, daughter of Eve, identified the deceased as her husband Gridor, son of Arro, and said he worked for the saddle-

maker Garida on Gallows Walk Street.

Death was caused by striking the back of the head against the wall. There was a single wound, which had bled somewhat, and there were grains of stone dust and paint in the blood. Also some soil, because he carried a flower in his hood, I believe. There were no other injuries.

The Judge: *It must have been a forceful blow?*

Yes, yes, indeed. Not just a shove, as one might give a beggar in the street, but there would have been strength and determination, or anger, to push so hard.

*

Hridnaya rarely left the mansion, save for attending Sunday Mass along with everyone else. The b'Nida went to the Church of the Fear of the Lord. As far as she knew, Holy Mourning wasn't Gridor's and Miya's church, nor Brinnon's. She'd never heard of it, nor of Redman's Street, and she couldn't ask anyone.

But at supper in the Large Kitchen, on Saturday night, everyone silent with exhaustion, Narrim rapped the table and said, "We have made good progress so far. The Lord and Lady will permit everyone a free day tomorrow, once Mass is over," and there were tired cheers.

A free afternoon! She must do something.

Could she wander round the city, staring at every church until she found the pale red-haired old priest? *No.*

But there was something she could do, if she dared.

Balki didn't approve.

One morning in the first weeks, when she was wondering if the pain would ever go away, and aching for her twin and her parents, she'd turned to stare at a stone in the wall by her pillow, and thought that the cracks and bumps in it almost made eyes and a nose – and so Balki was born. Balki had a white squarish hairless face, a white squarish body, with tiny paws at the corners like a rat's, and a huge blue and green fan tail with eyes, like that bird in the tapestry downstairs. Balki could scuttle up a wall like a spider, and caper upside-down on the ceiling. More importantly, she smiled when Hridnaya needed a friend, and was nervous when she needed someone to reassure - and asked questions when she needed to think things through.

Talking to Balki was a childish thing, but she had no one else to talk to except God, and she couldn't force God to talk back.

*

Miya, daughter of Eve, had clutched the bench in front of her, and stared straight at the Judge.

We were married twenty-two years, my lord, and never a cross word. He got drunk sometimes, spoke out of turn to people, but such a good man! And two children to provide for, one apprenticed, but his sister has a holy vocation and that costs money -

The Judge watched as she wiped away tears, and took a deep breath.

He wouldn't tell me why he was going to Sapientia. He had some odd notions. He'd never gone there before.

He never mentioned the b'Shen.

The Judge: *Did he tell you he was being followed?*

Yes, he did say, but I don't think he was sure. He did mention a man with a limp, as my nephew said, and also a woman who seemed to be looking at him, but he might've imagined it. Sometimes, when he'd been drinking, he used to be fanciful. But he described her – I mean this woman - to me in case I ever saw her: middle years, and very pale, and fair-haired, not grey but like straw.

The Judge: *Did you ever see this woman yourself?*

Yes, I think so. One night he lifted the shutter and called me over, just before we went to bed. There was someone standing on the other side of the street. A woman, just standing there.

The Judge: *Did she look as he'd described?*

I couldn't see her clearly enough, but yes, she was pale-skinned. I could only tell it was a woman by the kirtle and the – the shape of the head, with plaits. Even he wasn't absolutely sure it was the same one.

The Judge: *Did he go to talk to this woman?*

He would have done, that night, but I told him not to. I was afraid. I thought he might get into trouble, if she was working for someone important. We barred the door, and she was gone in the morning.

*

Hridnaya had put a shoe on her pillow, and as she'd hoped, she rolled over, scratched her cheek, and woke up. The tiny room was dark and silent. Only her heart thudded, as she dragged herself out of bed and opened the door.

Balki hovering at her shoulder, she found the stairs. So far, she was doing nothing wrong, but still she placed her feet carefully to the side to avoid creaks.   There was a faint light from below. "What's that?" asked Balki.

Attar guarding the front door. But the stairs run along the back. We can avoid him.

Down one flight, breathing through her mouth to make less noise, past the Family's sleeping chambers. The strangeness of being awake, while everyone else lay far away in slumber, held her for a moment. Then down again, and left. The door to the private study, which she had been in perhaps a dozen times.

She'd done nothing wrong. That was about to change. She lifted the latch, and entered.

It was darker than the landing, and she had to pause to

remember the layout. The desk; the window; the fireplace; the
cabinet. The map.

Careful not to bash into anything. Open the shutters.

Greyness slid over the room.

The candle and flints are on that shelf. A scrape and hiss,
and sudden light. She held the candle up to the cabinet, trying to
remember which rolls and books and documents went where.
This one.

Hridnaya rolled the parchment out on the desk, weighing
down the corners. She was stealing her employers' candle-wax.
She was standing in their study without permission, peeking at
their documents. There was no excuse. If anyone caught her, she
would be whipped, and her body and bowels cringed.

"Is this a map?" Balki asked helpfully.

*Yes. It shows the streets and buildings of the city. I need
to find the Church of Holy Mourning.*

It was a square parchment, which she'd seen once or
twice before, and there was a large blue shape, un-neat like spilt
water, painted on it, and around the blue were black lines and
little drawn boxes, which must be meant for buildings. And words.
Lots of words.

The blue shape was the Great Lake.

She stared at it, and frustration rose, clawing at her throat.
She'd expected the map to have actual pictures, recognisable
buildings – a church is not like a house, after all! But it was just
lines, and *writing.* She'd seen letters often on inscriptions and
documents, and could remember most of their shapes, but she
didn't know how they sounded, or what words they made.

She'd crept down for nothing; wasted all the courage she
had.

The blue shape is the Lake. Along the edge of it were the
cities: City Qayn to the right, sticking out into the water; Sapientia,

where the College was, to the left, much smaller. At least she had it the right way up. And at least she knew which pattern of lines she was standing in. She bent the candle forward, watching with one corner-eye for drips of wax. Not all the boxes were the same! That one had a pointed top and a cross - that must be a church! But was it the right one? "There's another," said Balki. "And there…" *How can one city have so many churches? And which one's Holy Mourning?*

In one or two places, the lines spread open to form four-sided shapes. There were two quite close together, blank except for teasing words – words that started with the same wriggly letter.

It came to her in a gasp. *Square!* The Great Square and the Square of Silent Remembrance! Her hand shook, and a melting drip trembled on the edge of the candle. She just managed to catch it on her knuckle. *Ow.*

But *S is ess, and it means Square. And -*

"What are you thinking about?" asked Balki.

I can do this! All the little churches (*that's what they must be*) had words beginning with the shape C. C must be for Church. That didn't help much, but - *The Church of Holy Mourning. I know the letter M,* she told Balki. *It's above the front door. R 403 M, for the marriage two hundred years ago. Just as I know b'Nida….* She forced herself to search the map systematically, eyes buzzing with strain in the dimness, for a church with words beginning C, and then something else, and then a longish word beginning with M.

And she found it.

She marked it with a tiny piece of dirt from the floor, and let her eyes rest. And then she thought: *The Family houses must be marked. I know S. Can I find b'Shen?*

She took a deep breath before plunging back to work. "Be careful," said Balki. The floor creaked under her foot, and terror stabbed her.

Oh God help me. Jesus, Word of Truth - If anyone came in -

Go back to bed <u>now</u>. Moments passed. *Lord save me, Lord save me, Lord save me,* as women rich and poor screamed in labour.

She bent back over the map. *If that's the Square of Silent Remembrance, then Scholars' Street is here. More S's! Yes, that is b'Nida, shaded purple - all the Families have mansions round here - there is b'Iri - there is b'Shen!* A long narrow box-shape, coloured green, which was right.

So. Triumph all through her, tingling on scalp and in toes. She grinned up at the shelves opposite, imagining a delighted expression on Balki's square non-existent face. But she wasn't finished. Now she had to learn how to get there. She bent again, staring, staring, then shutting her eyes and silently chanting, making a list of instructions, Scholars' Street to the Church, Scholars' Street to the b'Shen. It was difficult to hold in her head.

"And then we'll go back to bed, and to sleep, and by morning we'll have forgotten it all."

Balki was right. She almost cursed.

There has to be a way. She'd lived long enough to know that this isn't always true. *Nevertheless.*

Steal a piece of parchment, and make her own map? No, Narrim surely kept count, and theft is theft.

After thought, she moved over to close the shutters. She picked up the flints and candle, and a piece of coal from the grate, and blew out the light. Out of the door, up the stairs without creaking. *Please let no one be getting up yet.*

She was a privileged servant, or an isolated one, and had her own tiny room. There she lit the candle and knelt on the floor to draw the map with the coal. Even if anyone else saw it, it was just a design underfoot, and why should she not want to remember the way somewhere? Then downstairs again to return candle and map to their places.

In bed at last, her whole body began to shudder. It didn't stop for some time. But at last she slept, and the next thing she knew was Narrim banging angrily on her door.

*

It was a smaller church than the one the b'Nida Family attended. There was a tree heavy with ripening apples growing just outside, and tear-drop shapes carved on the door. The Church of Holy Mourning.

Hridnaya had hurried, and she paused to catch breath and calm spirit. Inside her head, Balki said, "I don't like red-haired people," which gave her an excuse to tell them both firmly, *They're no worse or stranger than anyone else. Sister Felicity is not Sinavid. And this is a church.* She put a hand on the door, and pushed, and went in.

She found pale light through glass windows, lighting statues of weeping saints, but no living people.

She hadn't dared to miss Mass with the Family before slipping away here - so it was all over. Everyone was gone, including the priest.

Bloody bloody hell, as Lindet b'Nida would say. "Wash your mouth," said Balki, but Hridnaya scowled.

Then there were creaks behind her. A man and a woman came in, and the woman was Sister Felicity. "I'll have left it in the vestry."

"Hurry up, then," said the man.

They saw her.

"Oh! Be welcome in the Lord's name." The priest put on, perhaps reluctantly, her serving-the-parishioners face. "Can I help you?"

57

Hridnaya stepped towards the light, lifted a finger and touched her shut mouth. A gesture understood, she hoped, throughout the city.

"I don't understand - oh. Hridnaya, Gridor's niece. Oh."

"Don't," said the man. He marched past and through a door, presumably to find the "it" they'd come back for.

Hridnaya kept her eyes on Sister Felicity's, and placed her palms together before her. Narrim would've understood at once that she had a request to make, but Narrim wasn't here.

"You've come to pray?"

She shook her head, and made a pleading gesture, pointing. "Oo." She mimed talking.

"To talk to me. I see. I shouldn't have said -" The woman looked away, biting her lip.

Her probably-husband walked back, carrying a cloak, and glaring. "Have you forgotten?" he asked the woman. She met his eyes; then they both looked at Hridnaya, not welcomingly.

You're scared. Someone has frightened you, since you spoke to me in the Square.

"Just a little, and then I'll come."

"Be careful." His feet slapped towards the door.

"Sit down, please." Hridnaya was gestured to move rapidly to a bench by the wall. They sat together. Brusquely, "What d'you want me to say, to tell you?"

She moved her hands behind her head, trying to demonstrate flowers. Then she pointed at a statue, and made a halo circle.

After a pause, Sister Felicity said, "I called your uncle a saint."

Yes.

The priest swallowed, and then stared down at pale hands, swollen-veined, in her black lap.

Hurry up.

"Do you not know - what your uncle did?"

What manner of question is that? He delivered horse-wear to

people's houses and stables. Hridnaya mimed carrying something, handing it over, and receiving money.

"Yes, he worked for Garida the saddle-maker, and before that for Pijic the armourer, and before that he was a guard for the whorehouse on Unholy Lane." (The family had been embarrassed by that one.) "Has nobody told you why he had to keep finding new places, why he kept losing them? What else he did?"

No. Aunt Miya said once he couldn't keep his jabbering mouth shut.

"He lost places because he made trouble." The priest looked down again, and then up, her mouth a thin line. She spoke quietly. "I suppose you have the right to know. It was because of you. After it happened – twenty years ago? – that was when I met him first. This wasn't his own church, but he wandered in to confession, he was distressed, and then he came again, and we talked. I don't know why he chose me." She sighed crossly, lifting and dropping her hands in exasperation, reminding Hridnaya of Aunt Miya. Except that Aunt Miya's hands would always have sewing in them.

She went on, "He said - he said such things shouldn't be done. I told him of course they don't happen often, only sometimes, the Families need people like your niece, they're paid well, it's the way things are. He said, 'That will change.' I remember him saying that.

"Well! He threw away twenty years on that idea. I let him talk; he said nobody else would listen. I should have been firmer, and told him to forget it. What could a man like him do to change anything? He had no power, he knew nobody in authority, and he wasn't mad enough for violence.

"First he went round all the Family houses asking them, or trying to, why they needed Voiceless servants. All of them except yours, I think. He didn't want to cause trouble for you. Someone complained to his employer, and that was how he lost the first place, years ago. Then he talked to people in the street or at church, especially anyone he thought was from the Families, or had money, he put that flower behind his head, to attract notice - he said that came to him in a dream. People complained again, and he lost another place. He quarrelled with his wife when she told him to stop. He said it was a vow, and I couldn't tell him to break a vow. Perhaps I should have done. I had charity enough to listen to him when no one else would -" She swallowed and blinked.

Very scared, and so you're scaring me. But why?

"Last year he was growing desperate, and he persuaded me to write a letter for him to the Bishop. That was foolish. Nothing came of it. It was all foolish.

"Do you understand? Twenty years talking, and annoying people, and neglecting his family, and he achieved nothing. Of course nothing. Except trouble. But he went on." Hridnaya saw her hands trembling. "Does that make him a saint - or just a fool? I chose the gentler word at the funeral, but perhaps I was wrong."

Hridnaya's head was whirling, but she remembered the trial, and Brin's evidence. "Sa – Sa," she said, and made her fingers walk along her thigh. *You must understand, please!*

"What was he doing in Sapientia? Does your family not know?" Sister Felicity bit her lip, and looked quickly up and around. "Very well, but don't ask any more! He told me a man came to see him; said one of the College doctors would talk to him if he could find a way there." Very low, "A Doctor Dirria. How she'd heard of him, I don't know. I don't think he knew. But he made plans to go. He hoped -" She looked away again suddenly, and then back, leaning forward. "I'm sorry, but you can't come back here. Don't ask more questions. People are – Have you heard of the King's Cousins? They're watching, and they don't want - Leave him to God."

The King's Cousins? Why? Hridnaya stood up. Carefully she made the grateful sounds "Fa – oo," and curtsied.

The priest stood too. Slowly she reached a hand out, and patted Hridnaya's shoulder. Slightly friendlier now the nuisance was on her way out, she asked, "Do you – are you well, daughter? D'you need money, or anything?"

The one thing the Voiceless have enough of is money. Hridnaya shook her head, curtsied again, and left.

All the way home she kept Balki silent, as she repeated what Sister Felicity had said, learning it by heart. She climbed upstairs to her little room.

He said, "That will change."

She lay on her bed, and cried and cried.

But she had the whole day free, Sunday, and she might as well use it. She got up, and went to visit her brother.

*

Eighteen years earlier, the twins had been twelve years old. This was a suitable age to start work, and for them it was more urgent than most, their little sister being sickly, and taking up so much of their parents' time and money. An apprenticeship was found for Brinnon with the tailor Hanno - and then a neighbour told them that the b'Nida were looking for a servant – presentable and silent and alert. "That sounds like you," said her mother. "D'you think so?" Hridnaya asked in shy awe. The b'Nida had a good name.

A good name, but still somebody should accompany her to their house, and her parents were busy, so it was Uncle Gridor who walked with her to Scholars' Street. Hridnaya wouldn't have chosen him. He was cheery, and told good stories, but he was also the embarrassing uncle, the one who ruffled your hair, and laughed too loudly, and sometimes got drunk, to his wife's loud annoyance. But that was the way it was.

They went to the side entrance and were allowed inside (how could a house be so big?), and escorted upstairs (stairs *inside*, with pictures on the walls!) and into a room with ceiling-to-floor tapestries that she longed to study. Uncle Gridor stood behind her, as she was beckoned to a seat on one side of a table, and she sat down opposite Lord b'Nida himself, and the Housefather, Bakker. Narrim was only a deputy then. The Lord was dignified, with hair beginning to thin, and a very tidy beard; Bakker was a solid old man with a gravelly voice.

She trembled, a shy girl who'd never been addressed by such high people before.

Bakker asked questions, and she answered as well as she could. Then he told her a list of names and made her recite it back, to test her memory. He sent her scurrying around the room with plates, to see if she dropped things. He watched her sew a seam, and make up a fire in the hearth. And he asked for her priest's letter as evidence that she was of good character and attended church regularly - and then she recited the Apostles' Creed, to prove she listened when she was there.

"You'll have your own sleeping chamber, and three meals a day. You may take Sunday afternoons for yourself if you're not wanted for anything particular. And the Lord and Lady will pay you one silver piece every month, in exchange for your loyalty," he said.

Hridnaya gasped.

"How many is that in two years?"

"Er - twenty-four, sir," she answered, passing a test in arithmetic. But the world was shaking around her. A silver piece every month! How could anyone be paid so much?

"If you are willing to be employed, please write your name here." There was a piece of parchment with writing on it. Hridnaya went cold. Now she was going to fail.

"I am sorry, my lord, honoured sir. I cannot write."

"Make your mark, then," Bakker said a little irritably. "Underneath where it says 'on this day.'"

She stared miserably at the parchment. "I can't read those words."

"Ah."

Long afterwards she realised that this was the final test, the test of illiteracy, and she'd just passed it.

Bakker looked at his master. "Satisfactory?"

The Lord nodded.

Hridnaya's stomach fizzed with triumph. They'd never want for money again! Little Siri might even get well!

But Lord b'Nida looked thoughtful. He hadn't spoken before, but now he leaned across the table, and said, "Hridnaya, daughter of Haidi. You're very young. Do you understand that this is a Voiceless position? Do you know what that means?"

"To be silent, to be secret, yes, of course, my lord," she gabbled.

He opened his mouth, but then from behind her Uncle Gridor spoke. "*Voiceless?* Is that-? No, she didn't know, and she doesn't want the place. Come, niece."

She hated being called "niece." She had a name. "I do want it!"

"No, Hridnaya! No, you don't!" He put a hand on her arm, to pull her up and away. Hridnaya burned with shame. He was disgracing her in front of her employers; they might withdraw the offer; they might never forgive her.

She stood up, but wrenched her arm free, and turned to

the two men. "I will do it, if I may - I will – Please -"

"You don't know what it means!"

"It's her choice," said Lord b'Nida, and he and the Housefather stood also, and beckoned her to the back entrance of the room.

And she walked round the table, and went with them.

"Voiceless is for life! You mustn't do this! Hridna, listen to me!" she heard desperately from behind her.

Later, she heard that he went on shouting until they had him thrown out into the street. She heard that her parents didn't speak to him for a month, and he spent much of that month drunk.

But that was later. On that day eighteen years before she walked into the hall of her new home, and learned what being Voiceless meant.

*

When Brin and Hridnaya were small, irritating smiling adults sometimes asked their parents, "Which of them is the Good Twin?" As people do. Their mother's usual response – at least when the children could hear – was "They're both good four or five days out of seven," swiping the nearest child gently on the back of the head, to remind them to improve the ratio. But as years passed, she began to say she didn't have a Good Twin and a Bad one; what she had was a Glowering and a Merry.

Brin welcomed her with a smile and an embrace, but something about him was still glowering.

Sitting at her brother's table, Hridnaya clutched a piece of coal and drew as well as she could, which wasn't very well. She scrawled a person, with flowers at his back. Brin looked at her. "Uncle Gridor. What of him?"

Slightly embarrassedly, she opened her own mouth, and pointed inside. Then to her picture. "Mm?"

"Oh. How did you guess?"

She gestured a halo around her head, and pointed at the picture again.

"That priest," he said, and she nodded.

Lulet had taken the children out for a healthy walk-around-in-God's-good-air. Brin had been breaking the Sabbath by adding final trimmings to some lord's riding jacket when she called. Now he looked at her, and away at the fireplace, drinking more ale. Glowering.

She nudged him, a cross sisterly nudge.

He sighed. "I don't know why she said a saint. Saints convert the heathen, and stop battles, don't they? He only went round talking to anyone who'd listen. About the Voiceless, why they – you're - needed. Aunt Miya hated it. She said it'd cause trouble, and I suppose it *has*." Reading her question, "He wouldn't let us tell you, in case you blamed yourself. All those years. And no one ever did listen. At least -" He leaned forward. "That must have been why he went to Sapientia – he told me, and he told Aunt Miya he had someone to see. Aunt Miya made a screech, accused him of having a lover somewhere, and he laughed, and said none of those great folk would want to bed him, and the students were all too young for him anyway. She didn't like that either!" He gave a sighing laugh. "Poor Uncle. But after eighteen years – he said someone was interested. A woman in Sapientia wanted to meet him but he didn't say who."

Dirria. Doctor Dirria.

"I was at hand when the Justice people questioned Aunt – she was taken to Sapientia to identify his body, and when she came back she ran here to cry over Lulet. They came, and I told them about people watching him. I said it wasn't chance that killed him. Lulet thinks – they had that fine trial, and it's all ended. Maybe you think that too. But it isn't."

The room was quiet. He met her eyes, and they looked down together at the image scrawled on the table. "The b'Shen killed him. I don't know how they managed it – made it look innocent – but someone planned it. That limping man I saw one night – I keep wondering if I see him again, in corners. They spied on him, they killed him, and we can't get them punished, because we're nothing. We have to leave it, and pray they suffer in hell." There were tears in his eyes.

Hridnaya made a face, which he interpreted correctly. "I don't know why! Who knows how the rich think?" Suddenly he sprang up and crossed to the wooden chest beside the fireplace. Rummaging inside, he came back with a cloth. "D'you remember this? Aunt found it in his satchel after he died."

It was a white cloth, good stuff, perhaps a napkin. Hridnaya had seen so many b'Nida and their guests wipe greasy lips and fingers, or smother sneezes, in such things. But this one had large stitches sewn on it. Not a pattern, surely? No, these were letters. *Writing*.

"You're not telling me that's for decoration," said her brother, the tailor. "It's a mess, done by someone who can barely lift a needle, who was in a hurry. It's a message."

They looked together at the letters, six in all, two of them the same. None of them was an S, a C or an M. One, she thought, might be a clumsy R. They might say DIRRIA; they might not.

"You can keep it if you like," Brin said. "Lulet thinks brooding on it will drive me mad."

Hridnaya silently folded the cloth, and squashed it into her pouch. Then she had to take it out again, so she could lay her money on the table. One, two, three silver coins.

"What's this? I don't need anything."

How Brin hated not understanding her, when once they'd shared every thought, mischievous twins teasing their elder brother. But she had to mime – *you sew, customer gives you money, you sell.*

Until at last he said, "Oh. Very good. What d'you want to buy?"

*

My name is Bada, daughter of Ebbi. I'm the keeper of The Morning Dream. The woman was thin and unsmiling, and her voice slow.

I'd never seen the man who died before, Gridor, but I'd heard of him, him and his flower. He came up to the counter. I thought he looked drunk; he staggered a bit, but he was polite. He ordered some ale, said his head ached; then he asked for directions somewhere, I forget where. He looked around and said something about a person behind him. I can't remember exactly. I think I was still talking to him when the prisoner and his friend came in.

The prisoner had been in the Dream a few times before – with
friends, never alone - drinking and talking. Only once or twice, quite recently. He never caused any trouble. That night he had a friend with him, but I didn't know this one.

They went to sit down, and then the prisoner took offence at something one of the other customers said, a woman called Shina. I've known her for years; she means no harm, but she likes a row sometimes. They had words – she mocked him, the prisoner, and he ran over. What she said – I wasn't surprised he was angry; she called him a bastard. His friend jumped up too.

The old man stepped between them, and the prisoner pushed him aside. It was a hard shove, no wonder he fell. He fell, you might say sideways, and soil flew out everywhere from his flower-thing. He hit his head on the wall, I think, and then went down on the floor. But then he didn't get up. The other young

67

man tripped over, and landed almost on top of him. And then the man was - he just gasped, and died. The

prisoner hadn't done anything else to him, only that one blow.

The Judge: *You're certain that no one else came near him? Could anything have been thrown?*

No, I'm sure not. There was no one behind him.

The Judge: *Had he had anything to eat or drink?*

I'd just handed him a cup of ale. He may have taken one or two swallows, no more than that.

The Judge: *Was there any sign of recognition between him and the prisoner Rorash b'Shen, or the prisoner's friend?*

No, no. Except I think the prisoner may have said something about a flower when he came in. And afterwards I heard that the man was called Flower-in-Hood.

*

The last time the Conclave had happened, seven years ago, it had been almost unbearably exciting. Over and over again she'd explained to Balki: *Each of the Ten Families chooses ten people – that's one hundred; and they meet in the Palace with King Aigith – and we all pray that God will be with them also, making One Hundred and Two – and then it happens. No one's told how – it's the Ricossan Secret.*

Waiting at suppers and watching at meetings before and afterwards had told her the Secret, but this she didn't say, not even to Balki, who wasn't real and could betray nothing. She was allowed to know, because she could betray nothing either. She hugged this wonderful fact to herself in bed.

That was seven years ago. But this time she had other matters on her mind. (And in any case, what difference does one king or queen make over another? That was one of the Questions in Hridnaaya's Box.)

The visitors had arrived in Scholars' Street, and settled in.

68

On a windy morning in mid-July, the b'Nida Ten walked out solemnly to the Palace, taking a single messenger, young Gabo, to wait outside. Riodran, Lord b'Nida, led them, gait measured and face unsmiling but benign, nodding slowly to the people lining the streets. He wore his deep blue gown, with silver feather patterns embroidered on it, silver sleeves and hose. Fifty-four years old, and his brown head was now almost bald, which a lesser man would have found embarrassing. His grey beard was long, and trimmed to a sword-point. His wife Irramatti, Chancellor of the Great College, the Lady of the Unchanging Expression (Balki's joke) had arrived back from Sapientia last night.d her hand on his arm, and matched her step very deliberately to his. Like her husband, she was tall; unlike him well-rounded and comfortable-looking in figure and plump face. This was deceptive – anyone who wanted sympathy in the household went to Lord b'Nida or, more probably, Narrim. Her gown was purple with white sleeves, and her river of grey hair still long and thick.

The Lord and Lady, especially the Lord, were great assets, Hridnaya knew. Without their dignity and wisdom, the b'Nida would have been one of the less regarded of the Ten.

Behind them in the house, other Family members and servants speculated for the twentieth time whether glory would at last fall on b'Nida, and if so, on whom. "'King Riodran' would sound so well, and he'd look the part, and be wise," was the general thought, but Narrim pointed out that if their Lord became King, they'd lose him, completely and forever, and then the household, the Family's far-away lands to the south-east, *everything*, would be run by his daughter Jeruma, "whose temper is, um, delicate", the Housemother said tactfully, and whose husband was widely disliked. It might be better if the great choice fell on one of their children, or on Riodran's brother Feodor, who'd arrived last Monday after nine days' travel. "What do kings and queens do, when all's said?" asked Lady b'Nida's maid. "Walk up and down and have people bow to them. The Evening King declares war, but the Morning Queen just makes gifts to singers, and complains about prices in the city." A few people giggled nervously.

The morning passed, and it was shortly after midday when Gabo came racing back, desperate to be first with the news already being shouted around the city. "Rommi b'Shen!" he gasped between heaving gulps. "Another Queen for the Morning!"

"Rommi b'Shen?" asked everyone. "Who's she?"

Rommi b'Shen.

B'Shen.

*

Hridnaya remembered Mejorad b'Shen. A young man in a fine gown a little too big for him, who looked as if he'd just combed his hair, and smiled shyly and pleasantly at the Judge.

I was visiting my cousin Rorash in Sapientia. He's been studying there since last autumn. We walked round a little, and then we went to a tavern, The Young Queen was the name, and Rorash had a

few cups of wine, I think three. He doesn't normally drink much, and I could see it went to his head. I told him he'd had enough, and it wasn't a very good place anyway. So then we walked out again, but it was cold

for June, raining a little. We passed this place, The Morning Dream, and I said I liked the name, and "Let's try this one."

The Judge: *He was a little drunk, you say? And you?*

No, I only had one cup, and that watered. I'm to be a priest some day, and I try not to act unseemly.

We went in, and then we saw the man, this Gridor, at the counter. Rorash commented that it was Flower-in-Hood. We've both seen him around City Qayn. I've had no speech with him,

70

and I've no reason to think Rorash had.

He didn't talk to him, not a word. It was the woman. I didn't know her, but she was very insolent, calling Rorash an arrogant bastard. He was angry – so I would've been, anyone would, my lady. But he hadn't a weapon, and Flower-in-Hood just got in the way. Rorash pushed him.

Somebody tripped me up, and I fell on top of the man, but I rolled off at once. Then I saw that his face looked strange. It was - twisted, as if he was hurt and trying to talk, but he couldn't. His eyes were all black; he looked scared. And then he died. I remember someone shouting to call the Watch.

My cousin's a gentle man, I swear, my lady, not violent.

The Judge: *But he is trained to fight?*

Only as we all are. He'd done his military service, yes. He'd no reason to want to hurt the man. It was just a push – caught him off balance, that's all.

*

The b'Nida Ten returned from the Conclave, and were reunited with their spouses, siblings and adult children for a great dinner in the Gallery. This was a long room, usually furniture-less but with portraits of distinguished and dead Family members painted up and down the walls.

There were empty places still, and younger b'Nidas had been known to bargain with each other for their future space. Anyone caught doing this was liable to be whipped for presumption and sent supperless to bed. Hridnaya had had to dry little Lindet's tears, some years ago.

This afternoon tables had been set up against one wall, benches dragged in, and plates piled with sliced meat, fruit, cheese and cake. Cold and plain and dry food, for there was only one servant to wait on and assist over thirty people. Only the Voiceless, of course, could overhear these conversations.

Hridnaya was greatly honoured, dah dah dah - and also tense. She was willing as always to be interested in the powerful and their worries, but today she wanted something more. *Tell me about the b'Shen.*

The Family filled plates with food, and sat together in little clumps, and they didn't discuss how the choice had been made, but only the result.

"The problem with the b'Shen is *loyalty,* let's be frank. They've always had a sprinkling of reckless youngsters, and they're too interested in the West. I don't trust them."

"Are you saying, then," Jeruma said tartly, "that anyone whose grandmother's ever travelled outside Ricossa is a traitor?"

"Of course not, fool niece. But Jeriet b'Shen's been boasting about that journey to Vach-roysh for twenty years – praising the Haymonese and the Jaryari. I call that disloyalty."

"You're exaggerating."

Hridnaya was beckoned to pour wine further along the table.

"The border incidents are getting worse. Ever since they united Jaryar and Marod twenty years back Aigith's wanted at the very least to stamp his foot and scare Nerranya out of her smock, and his Chamberlain and the other b'Iri and the b'Met encourage him."

"Brechad b'Iri and his uncle think a war in the north will give them more land – that's all they want."

"Yes. I allow Rommi's unknown and untested, but at least the b'Shen have an interest in learning. They had a lad studying -"

"And look how well that ended up."

Jeruma raised her voice again. "No, the b'Shen aren't disloyal, but Aigith will believe they are, so she'll have even less chance of influencing him than Zinial, and we all know she did nothing."

"If it must be b'Shen, maybe Rommi's not the worst choice." Uncle Feodor was shifting ground to oppose Jeruma as usual. "Know nothing bad of her. Know *nothing* of her."

"Aye, quiet and dull as moss on a wall. We need someone tough-boned! Someone *strong,* someone who can tell Aigith *No.* Who else can, except the Queen?" Jeruma flicked a nervous glance up and down, even in this safe gathering.

"He has Councils to do that," said her uncle. "The Morning has other duties, and doesn't interfere with the Evening. And we're not truly likely to be going to war with Jaryar."

"War with Jaryar is what he wants. He chooses the King's Council, and they're all his creatures. I'm on the Council of the Families, and so is Father. We look at each other and at the b'Olim and b'Trai, even the b'Astith, when he and Brechad start rambling about Evil Beyond the Mountains, and we shiver. No one dares stand alone against him."

"At least she's not her sister," Lindet was saying further down. With a giggle, "Think of having Eyanda as Queen!"

"Is Eyanda the one with a foreign-born lover?" asked someone.

"No, Nadya b'Astith's not foreign-born. She merely has kin in Jaryar."

"Well, but isn't one of them coming to see her, Nadya, any day now? May be here already. Some ladyling from Makkera, to get us all in trouble."

"To put spells on us," said Lindet, waggling her fingers only half in jest, and Hridnaya saw several people cross themselves.

"That is absurd, Lindet." Lady b'Nida issued a majestic rebuke to her daughter. "In *this* Family we are not superstitious about the West. The woman is coming by invitation to City Qayn and then to the College, to deliver a priceless manuscript for our doctors to study. I am preparing a feast for her in a few weeks' time."

"I daresay that's all good, sister," said Feodor. "But what will the King think? Jaryari spying for that Queen Nerranya, he'll say, right here in City Qayn."

What was it Lord b'Nida had said to his wife and Jeruma after the Queen died? "She seemed to think Mobira may make trouble when the Jaryari visitor comes. Mobira! If we could only get rid of her." Lady b'Nida had pursed her lips, and Jeruma had coughed, even in the safe company of the Voiceless.

But just then Jeruma's unlikeable husband said loudly, "Eyanda b'Shen's fucking a *woman?* How do they do that, exactly?"

"Bortoi, must you be both stupid and coarse?"

"Wasn't it her son – Eyanda's – who knocked down the pauper a few weeks ago, and killed him? The flower-man?"

"Ha, is that right? Mad old Flower-in-Hood? Maybe the b'Shen aren't as useless as we thought."

"Bortoi," said Lord b'Nida suddenly from the next group, quieting the whole table, "killing harmless commoners is not something to be praised. The unfortunate man has kindred in this room."

In this room? Nobody said the words, but Hridnaya, trembling, felt them thinking it. Her master gestured towards her, and surprised eyes followed his hand. She stood still, enduring the stares, trying to look insignificant but unashamed. It had plainly never occurred to Bortoi that servants might have relatives. He cleared his throat in a "well, well" manner.

After a pause it was Jeruma who said, "Rommi b'Shen is a thoughtful woman who listens, and doesn't rush into action. She has more steel than sometimes appears. This is good."

Everybody nodded. "And I imagine she will find no

difficulty casting off her family, as law demands," Lord b'Nida added. "She's not been happy with them for many years."

Curious faces turned to him, and he smiled a sad smile. "Old gossip fades, I see."

But then, to Hridnaya's extreme frustration, he changed the subject.

*

Rorash b'Shen had had to be asked to speak up.

I'd seen the man before – never in Sapientia. I'd never spoken to him. That is, I don't remember ever doing so. No one asked me, or told me, to follow him or hurt him; absolutely not. I've been at the College since last September. The last time I was in City Qayn was three nights at Easter.

What the tavern-keeper - and my cousin - said is what happened. I didn't mean to hurt him. I must have been more drunk than I thought.

I was very angry with that woman. I felt she was insulting me, but not just me – the Ten, the College, my Family, my mother, everything I love. I went towards her – and he was in the way.

The Judge: You were angry with her, not him. Look what you did to him. What would you have done to her, if you'd reached her?

I don't know.

*

The new Queen had taken her oaths, and all the visitors could leave. There was a mound of linen to wash, but otherwise a sense of relief descended on the b'Nida household. When supper was over, Housemother Narrim stood up and said, "It's a fine night. Shall we take the dishes outside?" and the party, plainly approved beforehand by the Lord and Lady, began.

A cask of ale was rolled out of the front door and down the steps. Benches and stools and a brazier of coals, carried with

75

great care, followed. Soon some two dozen people, almost all the servants of the house, were sitting or squatting, or leaning back against the wall - nodding to the few passers-by, chatting and busying themselves with pleasant little things, waiting for the light to fade. Attar the nightguard helped the scullery-boy scour the pots, and others mended clothes, wove willow baskets or whittled pegs. Two of the maids set up a chess board.

Hridnaya normally felt uncomfortable at such events. *Nobody knows whether to feel sorry for me, or to resent me for having more money than they do,* she'd often told Balki. *And many people are – not scared precisely, but uneasy about us.* "She could be thinking anything at all," someone had muttered suspiciously of her once, not realising apparently that the Voiceless could still hear.

But tonight she was eager for useful gossip, so she approached Narrim sitting against the wall, and offered with gestures to help with the never-ending darning of the children's hose.

"Thank you," said Narrim. She was a thin woman with a face the warm colour of bread-crust, and black curly hair that never seemed to grow long, but was beginning to grey. She peered short-sightedly at her needle, and Hridnaya threaded it for her before finding one for herself. Narrim knew a lot that wasn't quite secret, and liked talking about people, but she'd be quiet at first, not wanting to intimidate the lesser folk. Off to the right, Jantorad the short bony cook strummed his lute. The great b'Nida banner flapped gently above the door.

There was a laughing argument to one side about which of the visiting servants had snored the loudest. On the other, the nurse Kara was suckling the youngest b'Nida grandchild, and complaining about the pranks of his older sibling.

Talk about pranks of the b'Shen, Hridnaya wished

uselessly, but the chance of hearing anything had been small. It would always be small.

Jantorad brought whatever he was playing to a conclusion. A tall man passing down the street joined in the applause and said, "Now sing something."

All other conversation stopped, and some dipped their chins to hide amusement. They did this cautiously, for Jantorad, like Narrim, was a power in the house. But he said mildly, "I cannot sing, sir, anyone here will tell you that," and handed his lute to the groom sitting cross-legged on a folded blanket beside him.

The passer-by moved on, but left behind a united unspoken desire to watch or listen to a performance of some kind. Jantorad turned to the family priest, and said quite loudly, "You went to the Crowning. It must have been magnificent." As Sister Judith was about to answer, he went on, "I wonder if our Lady or our Lord wished it had been them taking the crown. I wouldn't have wanted to lose them, but *they -*"

"Queen Irramatti? I don't think so, sir," said Kara, laughing. "Queens have to talk to people."

There were more chuckles, but "Speak with respect," said Sister Judith, before Narrim could.

"Is it lacking in respect to say that she is a wise and dignified lady who cares for nothing but her parchments and her College? She didn't even want to go to the Crowning – she's too busy with this grand feast she's arranging for that foreigner."

Lady b'Nida spent at least half her time at the College, as its Chancellor; and nobody in Scholars' Street missed her while she was gone, not even her husband and children.

"Perhaps you're right," said Narrim. "And although our master can talk graciously to everyonel, he also would not, I think, you know, have wished to set aside his work. Who else cares for the College as he and she do? And he loves his kin, his children and grandchildren and all, and wouldn't want to lose them."

"Ah, it was a sad moment, that," said Sister Judith, shaking her head. "When the new Queen stood before the altar surrounded by the b'Shen, Family and servants – and she had to swear to renounce them for the sake of the realm, and they all walked away from her, until she was alone. She had children, oh I'd judge not ten years old."

Narrim sniffed, perhaps remembering other children long dead, and said firmly, "Queen Rommi had some good relatives. But she'll not be sorry to lose a few of them, I think."

Ah! Go on! Please.

"Why not? Is that a story?" asked the youngest kitchen-boy eagerly. "Please, madam! A tale under the moon."

Faces glanced up, and saw he was right. Above the banner, above the roofs, hung a half-moon, a faint slice of lemon against blue.

Narrim was silent.

"Once there was a woman -" Jantorad nudged.

The Housemother lifted a finger from her sewing, and wiped her cheek. She cleared her throat. "Well, then. Once there were two sisters. Once, and not so long ago. Rommi and Eyanda b'Shen.

"They had an elder brother, too, you know, I cannot recall his name. He married, but he died before there were any grandchildren. And so - someone once said to me, one of our Family said, 'What's the difference, Narrim, between me, a b'Nida, and a good respectable common person like yourself?' I said, 'There are many differences,' and *she* said, 'Yes, but what I'm thinking is that you don't need to marry, and I do.'"

Perhaps some thought she was straying from her story, not uncommon for Narrim.

"Ricossa needs many of us common folk to marry and have children, to be soldiers and servants and farmers. But no one of us *must*. Marriage is a blessing, but one that we don't have to accept. It's different for them. The Ten Families need heirs.

"So after their brother died, you see, it was more than ever important that Rommi and Eyanda should be married. Rommi was a very quiet well-thought-of sensible girl, and she waited for her parents to choose her a husband. But Eyanda was wild, there'd always been tales – and she told them she wouldn't have anyone of their choice, she had an unsuitable sweetheart already, and indeed, oh *dear*, she was carrying their child."

Chuckles up and down the street.

"There were great rows, so it was said, and to make matters worse, she then quarrelled with the sweetheart, or he with her, and he disappeared. Her parents told Eyanda she could still do her duty, some men will be good to another's bastard, or else she could send the baby away, but she refused to do either. She had her child, she kept him, nursed him herself, and refused all other men. The family sent her to the country for a few years, but they could hardly beat her or starve her when she'd just given birth, and so she stayed unmarried, and she still is."

Hridnaya remembered words spoken upstairs about Eyanda b'Shen and one Nadya, the woman who had foreign kin visiting from over the mountains.

"So the b'Shen turned to Rommi, and they looked around, perhaps a bit too hurriedly, you know, and they found a young man called Gaddasor, one of the b'Asa, not the highest of their branches, but the richest. Rommi was dutiful, as I said, but she clearly didn't like him, and I did hear that she begged them to choose someone else, anyone else, but both her parents and his insisted. They were married, oh, about twenty-five years ago, and he was brought into the b'Shen, and they had a baby daughter, she's now grown up and married. All seemed well on the skim of the porridge, but they said, of course I don't know, but I remember rumours at the time that neither Rommi nor Gaddasor seemed at ease together, and their servants fought.

"Then one night, Rommi asked one of her maids to hide in their bedroom, in the great wardrobe, and placed a priest just outside the door, and – well, there was screaming. It all came out, that Gaddasor hit his wife when he was drunk, and had even raped her more than once. He would've done so that night, but that she'd prepared witnesses, so there could be no doubting her word."

"Ugh," said Sister Judith, as everyone saw horrid pictures in their heads.

"Did they hang him?" asked Jantorad, after a suitable pause.

"No. Some felt they should have done, but it's said the b'Shen were short of money, and his people paid them and the judges for clemency. I don't know that," said Narrim, instantly regretting (Hridnaya thought) her criticism of such high people. "He was gelded and divorced, and sent away north-east, for the b'Asa to keep him out of more trouble, and she would've been free of him, but she was already pregnant again. A child conceived against her will.

"The b'Shen needed lawful heirs, but they gave her the choice, much as they'd given Eyanda. To renounce the child when it was born, have it sent away to be adopted by someone under their banner, but out of the line of inheritance. Well, maybe she thought of what her sister had done with her baby, who knows? She got a wet-nurse to feed him – it was a boy - but she acknowledged him, and brought him up. Mejorad. He's full-grown now.

"She did her duty by him, but she could never bear to

touch him, they say. It was all very awkward for the b'Shen, and there was strain between Rommi and her parents for years, but there's a better ending. No one dared to choose for her again, and in time she found herself another husband, Skandar of the b'Oto, and they lived together extremely well, until he died a few years ago." Narrim paused, and her voice lowered. "There were two more children, as you said, Sister, whom someone else will now have to care for."

"So that's our new Queen. May God preserve her."

There was a ragged chorus of "Amens", and then silence. The dishes were long done and stacked. It was growing dark, and now they needed the torches in their brackets by the doorway to light their faces and their work. Flames snapped and leapt cheerfully, drawing eyes to them, and on up to the banner above the door.

Purple background, with pictures of a boar and a sun. *(But that's another tale.)*

The banner that meant b'Nida.

*

Mejorad had been summoned to the Small Meeting-Room on the third floor, to speak to his mother. His new mother. *This is going to be odd,* he supposed, as the servant outside knocked for him.

He walked in, took four paces forward and bowed, the moderate bow suitable for an adult child to a parent.

He remembered a day in this room many years ago. He and Rorash were being sent off to visit someone for a few weeks. Neither boy had a father, and nurses had brought them in for their mothers' farewell blessing. Rommi and Eyanda had each laid a hand on their son's head and spoken the words, but then Eyanda swept Rorash up into her arms to squeeze him, and touch his nose with her own. Rorash was his mother's joy, but he was also nine years old, and he stiffened. But Mej, his mother's problem, was five, and he remembered thinking, *Why can't Aunt Eyanda be my mother?*

And now she was.

She was sitting behind a large table, her ringed hands resting on a few papers.

"Greetings, my son," she said, and waited.

Absurdly, for a moment, he couldn't say it. "Greetings, mother."

"Sit down."

He sat.

"Mejorad. This is strange for both of us." Her shoulders were tense, and her forearms stiff on the table. Her hair swept back to the clasp behind her neck without a single stray, and there was no softness in her face. The room was full of prickle.

He was missing Rorash too, and he felt sorry for her. But he was also annoyed to see the other person – That Woman Nadya – standing by the window, her tall figure failing to look inconspicuous. *What's she doing here? Am I kin to her now as well?*

He looked back at Eyanda.

"I'm sure you share my concern for your little sisters," she said. "The change is hardest for them. In the next few weeks, you'll please spend as much time as you can with them."

Yes. His half-sisters from Rommi's second marriage were eight and six years old. They'd clung to his hands during the coronation and anointing in the Cathedral, stifling down sobs, unable to understand why their mother was no longer to be their mother. Mej had ached for them.

But why "the next few weeks"?

"What should I do?"

She shrugged quickly. "Walk with them – visit the nursery when they're at supper – make time for a game or two. Surely you're not too busy for that?"

"No."

"And prepare them for your departure."

"I don't understand."

"In three weeks at most you'll be leaving for Vachansha for your training. Isn't that the plan?"

He'd known this was coming some time, but not yet! *Please!*

"No! No, it wasn't arranged!"

"Queen Rommi and Uncle Yettrid tell me you're to be a priest. You said so yourself, at the trial. I can't see that you've anything else to do. How long since you came back from serving in the army? Four months? You've done nothing but gamble and drink and cause trouble. Now it's time for work."

"Can't you send me back to be a soldier?" he thought of saying. He'd wondered this many times. But on the other hand – *soldiers spend too many nights lying on the cold earth, and too many days bored and rained-on – and once they're promoted they've other people's lives in their hands –*

Priests have warm houses, but there's little else to like in the life -

"*No,* I – it was spoken of, but not yet. I don't wish to do this -"

"You don't wish? You'll do what the Family tells you, as we all have to do."

Her voice was *evil,* he thought. "*As we all have to do*" – Eyanda had been as troublesome a b'Shen daughter as any in her day!

"Abbess Priscilla is old, and cannot travel or think clearly. We need another high-born priest to look to our interests in the Church. This isn't my decision; it's your great-grandmother's and your uncle's, and it was made long ago. You agreed then."

When I was twelve. "I'm not suitable."

She looked down dismissingly at her papers. "Why not? You can read and write Latin, no sign of heresy, you're not vicious. You got through your military without disgrace. Everything else the training will provide."

Training in Defardu, land of priests and penitents. And now Rorash.

"Priests are not to be made unwilling," he quoted from somewhere.

"Then you'll have to become willing, won't you? I'll arrange for a retreat for prayer and contemplation."

Mej stared aghast at these terrible words. He saw himself locked in a tiny cell until he surrendered, without food – perhaps even *walled in*. His vision must have shown in his face.

"What kind of fool are you? A *retreat* – a stay in a comfortable monastery. I've been on one. Your moth - the Queen has done several. Be assured they'll treat you more kindly than you deserve." Then he felt her mood change, and heard a tiny gasp. "Much more kindly. Don't cause me extra trouble, Mej. You've already done what I can never forgive."

"What – I didn't -"

"You took him to that place, without servants to keep things safe. You got him drunk. Make what excuses you please, but I will always blame you! Rorash is the flower of our Family – he's never wronged anyone – he was just starting to study as he longed to do - as God was *calling* him to do - and then you take him to a tavern, and get him exiled."

Utterly unfair! But the bitterness made him shiver. He heard her swallow in sudden quiet. The woman by the window fidgeted with her gown.

"I'll arrange a retreat." Eyanda was blinking angrily. "I suppose you couldn't endure more than three days. Well. Be kind to your sisters. And there's one more thing." She turned. "You know my companion Nadya b'Astith?"

One of the most obscure of that Family. So she's here for a reason, after all, not just to hold your hand. He also turned, and made his face polite, and Nadya, thin, bent-beak-nosed and with thick coiled not-quite-black hair, stepped forward.

"I have a favour to ask of you, sir." Her voice was gentle. Mej remembered that Rorash liked her, *and I'm not a barbarian oaf. Who Aunt Eyanda loves is her own concern.*

"How may I serve?" he asked, trying to cover crossness.

"I have a kinswoman visiting me from Makkera, a woman called Kelji."

"Makkera?"

"It's the chief city of Jaryar," said Eyanda.

I bloody well know that!

"Yes. She's come with a gift from their Queen, a learned holy book for the doctors at the College to study. In a week or two she'll be going along the Lake-shore to deliver it, but in the meanwhile she's here. I've seen and been told that she's had great trouble at home, so I want her time with us to be as pleasant as it can be. Before you withdraw to seek God's guidance -" she smiled in a way he couldn't dislike - "can you escort her to a few of the sights; dance with her after dinners, that sort of thing?"

"If it pleases you and my mother," he said formally, but he felt dubious. How young and wealthy was this woman?

"Don't fear, no one is selecting a wife for you," said Nadya. "She's married already, back home in Jaryar."

Then why isn't her husband here to dance with her, or whatever she needs? Is her husband her trouble, like-? What does the bloody College want with a foreign book, anyway? But he couldn't say these things.

"I'll be very happy."

Hridnaya sat on the floor between the bed and the wall, hugging her knees. Against her back pressed the chest where she kept her clothes, a plain wooden box supplied to all the servants. On her lap was a much smaller box, lockable, which was hers alone.

A few paces in front of her was the door out to the Women's Passage. One small sleeping-and-storing room for Hridnaya; another for the Housemother; a larger one for all the other women. (The men slept on the floor below.) Each door had a square hole cut in front, and a little black cloth to cover it. This flapped and let in the draught, but it allowed Narrim to spy in if needed, to check if anyone was sick, or up to something bad.

Over the years, Hridnaya had grown tired of that black cloth. She'd spent money on four linen sheets big enough to cover the whole of her door in a series of bright colours – white in winter-time, then green, then blue for a sun-blessed sky, and berry-red. "Hridnaya's changed her curtain, so it must be summer," she'd heard one of the kitchen-girls say once, and it made her feel happy, and *placed*.

Provided she kept the room tidy and clean, and wasn't ill, no one else would come in. It was hers.

Another, slightly less busy, day had passed, and it was time for bed. Above her head was darkness; beside her on the floor a candle flickered. Balki squatted on the green-and-blue-striped patch of carpet, one winter's great extravagance, and they stared at each other.

The little box in her lap had a painting of a girl-child on the lid. Such things were sold in pairs, the Girl-Box and the Boy-Box, popular gifts for the baptism of twins, or at weddings. Brin and Lulet kept cooking spices in his, and the box made her think of him, every time.

Hridnaya stroked it, and then turned the key and opened the lid on her private things - mostly money, and her collection of buttons. There are so many games you can play with buttons. She stared down, and in her head where only Balki and God could see she opened the other box, the invisible one, the Box of My Questions and Answers.

"Is this still Question 34? 'Do the poor get as good justice as the rich?'"

No. But it's connected. She yawned, and rubbed her face hard. *Question 35. What do I know about Uncle's death?*

Balki was silent, perhaps nervous. Hridnaya took out a button, the shiny one, and polished it on her sleeve. She laid the box aside, shifted forward onto her knees, and put the button down on the carpet.

Imprimis. Balki raised her eyebrows mockingly at the Lady b'Nida word.

Uncle Gridor wanted to persuade people not to demand Voiceless servants. He talked to some of the Ten, he got a letter written to the Bishop. I don't know what happened to that letter. He annoyed
people. He did this for eighteen years, without telling me, or expecting any thanks. Nobody asked him to.

I didn't ask him to. She paused, a little cross (*God forgive me.*) Yet her eyes were unbearably painful, and she couldn't see.

So. Item. She put down a strokable brown button, made of felt. *A few times, two or three I think, he was beaten or dismissed for this. I don't know who by – maybe not always the same*
people or their servants. It might have been the King's Cousins, who scared Sister Felicity. (Which means someone powerful.)

"Who are -" prompted Balki.

Leave that for now. He was beaten, but not recently.

Nothing happened for years, so far as I know, not since Brin and Lulet were married.

Item. A cool pale button that felt like bone. *Then things did happen, two things. He was being watched. This is fact. He told Miya and Brin, and both of them also saw people. A limping man, a*

fair-haired woman, another man. That's a lot of people to spy on one

person, one ordinary person. Perhaps they worked in shifts, or perhaps they came from separate masters. She looked up at Balki, and they both shrugged.

And he went to see this Doctor Dirria, at the College, in Sapientia. That's how far? A day, two days' journey? She summoned him. Why? How? He was pleased, and thought it worth going to a lot of trouble. Time away from work, and the waggoner's fee, would all be costly. Poor Miya.

I don't see why a College doctor would be interested – why anybody would be. He was going to talk to her about the Voiceless. Did somebody want to prevent this?

Abruptly, *He might have met this doctor before he went to the tavern! Suppose he met her, and he angered her, and she sent killers after him?*

No, that's not it, he asked the landlady for directions. He hadn't seen Dirria yet.

Dirria, and the watchers. Which came first? Which caused the other?

"Maybe they weren't connected."

But that makes no sense. They must be. Balki shook her head agreeingly.

Item. A very small button. *He went there, and he died. He had a cloth in his satchel, with lettering, that someone must have given him. A name, an address, a warning, a promise?* She screwed up her face, temples throbbing. *They said he went in the tavern, and the young men came in afterwards, and that Rorash quarrelled with someone else, and he was knocked aside by chance. The Judge seemed* fair, *and she called it an accident, not meant. But she knows no more than – she only knows the same as what* I *know, what people said.*

So this is the problem. Brin thinks it wasn't chance. Because it's too much chance.

And the Judge didn't know what Sister Felicity said. Item. The King's Cousins told her to be quiet. They told her later, after *the trial. The Cousins take orders from the Evening King's Chamberlain, so people say. They search out anyone he thinks is a trouble-maker, and beat them about, threaten them, break legs. Like when Lindet's friend was insulted by a young priest, and the priest was beaten and had shit smeared on his face and clothes, and Lindet said it was them. They're shadowy people, not city Guards, and we all fear them. But I thought they act on orders, and they don't usually do more than that sort of stuff. Why would they, or anyone, want to kill Uncle?*

Unless it wasn't meant to cause death. It was meant to be a warning, but he died.

"That could be."

Yes - but the Cousins aren't people like this Rorash. They're low ruffians. He's the son of Eyanda b'Shen.

The tavern-keeper said Uncle mentioned someone behind him in the street. Cold touched her spine. *Those b'Shen students could have been following him. But still how could they plan the quarrel? Did someone tell him to go there; did they place the woman Shina? Did she come in after him – I thought she was already there?*

Why would anyone commit a murder like that – he might

not have died at all? Robbers stab people in alleys; that's how murders are done.

("'Alley' is a dangerous word," she remembered Uncle Gridor teasing. "Never go down an alley, children – always make sure you call it a 'lane.'")

Or perhaps all the witnesses are lying – the tavern-keeper and all. Maybe he was never in The Morning Dream. Maybe there's no such
place.

"Steady your soul, Hridna." Sometimes she needed Balki to say that.

None of this seems likely! None of it.

She dug her fingers into the carpet softness, kneading. The buttons slid together.

"Have you any more Items?" Balki turned a somersault, almost singeing herself in the candle flame.

Hridnaya paused. Then slowly she took out another button, and it was the one her aunt had given her, from his cloak.

Item. One of those two young men – or both – were lying. I'm sure they were. Perhaps not everything they said, but about something.

"You can't accuse great people of lying!"

Why not? Higher-born is higher-born; that's all. They're just
people. Young men sometimes lie, I've heard them.

"How d'you know?"

I don't know. But – she screwed up her eyes. *When Rorash said – he said, "What the tavern-keeper - and my cousin - said is what happened." The way he said it, and looked over at the other one. It sounded false to me.*

"He's a bastard."

That doesn't make him evil. The other, Mejorad – his

father was bad, very bad, Narrim said. He might be bad too.

Those are the facts. She took a deep breath. *So, then. Question 35. What do I know about Uncle's death? Answer: That he died far from home, and before his time. He shouldn't have died. That there must be a connection – there must – between the watchers – three*

people! – and this Dirria's summons – and the writing on that cloth. That I think the b'Shen lied.

That's what I know. Question 36, she told Balki. *What does it all mean?*

Contradictory thoughts swirled. How unfair of her uncle to leave her such a problem! "Hridnaya," said Balki with sternness, and she smiled ruefully.

It does look like an accident. But it also feels to be too much chance. And if nothing is wrong, why did the Cousins visit Sister Felicity afterwards? Did someone see her talking to us after the trial? Were we watched? She thought of their little family clump; imagined a calculating pair of eyes in a ruthless story-villain face. *If there's nothing to hide, why do that?*

Narrim would say that the Judge must know best. *She seemed fair and wise.* "The Ten Families know everything. Our place is to trust them, and obey. Trust, obey and do not question." So everyone said: parents and employers and priests and most stories. But Question 11 in Hridnaya's Box, years ago, had been: Are the Families always wiser than us, as we're told they are? Answer: No.

The darkness hovered around and above the still candle flame. Balki waited. The whole b'Nida house waited. *Brin is so angry. My dearest Brin. Is he inspired, or is he mad? Or not mad, but just wrong?*

Slowly, *If it was planned, God help me, I am angry too. I want justice. But I could forget it. I don't care so much. Perhaps* because I'm a servant, I don't have a life of my own, so I don't feel deeply about, hmm, about anything really –

She thought of her uncle shouting downstairs long ago - of Brin glowering.

"It'll be sorted out on Judgment Day. There's nothing you can do." Balki made these obvious points, and walked away, running up onto the bed and beginning to bounce like a child.

But another thought was growing. *Even if he wasn't murdered, I'd still like to know. About Dirria. I am curious.*

Mid-bounce, Balki turned on her. "Dirria! You can't! She lives miles away! Miles and miles!"

Lady b'Nida must know her. Maybe not well, or I'd remember the name.

They were both silent, pondering the impossibility of getting help from the Chancellor of the College.

Remake Question 36. I don't know what it means. Can I find out?

I can't involve Brin. I can't ask questions. I can only be in the right place to listen. But what is the right place? I can't go back to Sister Felicity. I can't read the word on the cloth. I can't go to Sapientia, unless Lady b'Nida – Leave that. I can't go to Defardu.

If it was a b'Shen plot, all of it – maybe Rorash didn't go to Defardu at all! Maybe he's still here! Could I find out more about him, about them?

"What are you thinking?"

I know where the b'Shen live.

She felt Balki's horror, which meant the horror of everyone sensible she knew. "You want to rob their mansion? Call at their door?"

I want to know more about Mejorad b'Shen. He's to be a priest, so – he might be going to Defardu also – but he'll surely attend some church until he does. They don't go to ours, but there can't be many other places fine enough for the Families – and rich people stand around afterwards on Sundays and talk – and I'm usually free after Mass –

"You are mad. It was chance. Remember the Cousins."

Jesus, you are the Word of Truth. Help me, what do I do? How do I decide?

A memory came, from years ago. *When we were small,* she told Balki, *Uncle Gridor would tell us stories, Brin and me, and in the middle he'd take out a penny and tell us to toss it. Heads, they win the battle. Crosses, they lose. Or whatever it might be. I could do that.* She scrabbled in her box and brought out a silver piece. *Heads, it was chance and I leave well alone. Crosses, it was murder, and I try to do something?*

"And then we go to bed?"

Heads or Crosses? Shall I try this way?

"Mad old Flower-in-Hood?" the nastiest of the b'Nida had said. "Maybe the b'Shen aren't as useless as we thought."

"Killing harmless commoners is not something to be praised."

Heads or Crosses?

No. I will make this choice myself.

The Voiceless didn't often make choices. But eighteen years ago, she'd walked away from her uncle and chosen her life.

She clutched the coin for a moment. Then she put it back in the box and locked it, blew out the candle and got into bed. It seemed a long time before she was warm.

*

Mej spent Mass that Sunday glaring at the priest moving between altar and pulpit. That was where his Family wanted to put *him.* There was the familiar sermon telling the commoners to respect their betters and rejoice in being Ricossan – made more topical by

93

last week's coronation – and then the liturgy of the Eucharist. His elder sister had told him once that this most holy of all prayers must be said word-perfect, or the priest was eternally damned. "I don't think that can be right," Rorash had said slowly. Mej certainly hoped it wasn't.

His little sister Firi leaned against him, pulling at his fingers, and picturing what all the respectable tiresome tall people would look like naked. At least that was what he'd suggested to her when she'd whispered of being bored.

It was over at last, and everyone was stretching stiff limbs in the Cathedral churchgarden – commoners hurrying home, and the better sort looking for people of influence to talk to. "Mejorad, may I -?" It was tall friendly almost-kin-to-me Nadya.

He gave Firi back to her nurse, and he and his manservant edged past all the not-naked people, following Eyanda's lover towards a woman standing sedately by the wall.

"Mejorad, may I present to you Kelji, daughter of Shanell?"

So this was her, the famous cousin from Jaryar. She looked very foreign. She wore a gown with sleeves that were the same blue as the rest, like a *commoner*, but with gems round the bodice. And her head! A stiff band of cloth crossed her forehead, showing only a few black wisps, and all her back hair, if indeed she had any, was bundled up into some kind of white bag. A hat, he believed such things were called. People were staring, he saw, and no wonder.

"I am honoured," he said, bowing.

She curtsied in response, very low, and staying down for a moment longer than he expected. "The honour is *mine*," she said as she rose again, nearly his height, rather over his age. Possibly as much as thirty. "You are being the distinguished Mejorad b'Shen, son of my second cousin once removed's friend

Eyanda?"

"Er, yes."

"I've been very eager to meet you, sir. Nadya barely stops talking of you. She swears your horsemanship and charming conversation are only matched by your musical talent and skills with a blade."

One of the women was teasing him, perhaps both. He was cross and hungry. "She exaggerates," he began, but Kelji went on smoothly.

"But of course I won't need the protection of your sword, for no one would make violence in this fine capital. City Qayn, magnificent and orderly and devout. I've been hearing so much, and am hoping you can show me some of its glories."

Her chin seemed to stick out forward from her plain brown face, as if eager to bite someone. Her voice was sweet, and her words courteous, but that chin was neither.

"I'll be very happy," he managed to say unwittily. Remembering that he wanted to please Nadya and Eyanda, "Can I escort you to -"

"To your own home, if you'd be so kind. I am privileged to be dining with you and your mother today." She let him take her arm, and they began to stroll towards the street, Nadya a little to one side, with her servant, and his, and a hatted maid who must belong to Kelji. How very fine-folk-at-Sunday-ease they were being.

"Will you be in the city long?"

"Oh, I hope *many* days, if Nadya permits. But I'm awaiting a call to perform my errand. My Queen sent me to bring a book to your College in Sapientia."

I remember. Rorash would have been fascinated. But I'm not. "A long journey."

"Yes, we were seven weeks on the road. So now I'm

resting in your beautiful city."

Suddenly he imagined himself talking in a tavern a few years hence – *My first time was with a foreigner – a cousin of a cousin on a visit from Makkera without her husband. And I can tell you it's all true what they say about the Jaryari in the bedroom –*

Deep inside him there was cold. He took several breaths.

"Will I be granted the honour of meeting the head of your Family?" she asked into the pause.

"You'll meet my great-uncle Yettrid. Lady b'Shen is my great-grandmother, but she doesn't meet guests – that is, usually. She's eighty-one years old."

"Oh?" As if this were very surprising. "And who else will be there – do you have siblings?"

"My elder sister lives near the Gate with her husband and baby. The little ones will eat in the nursery." He thought she looked pleased by this. Bored but courteous, he continued, "And how are your family, madam? I hope you left them well?"

Had he imagined her little gasp, almost a shudder? She'd stopped walking, at any rate. Then her chin jutted again, and she said clearly, "My uncle is the Duke of Vard."

What the hell has that to do with anything? What's a Duke? She added nothing helpful, and he thought Nadya was also puzzled, so he said, "And that is a high position?"

She twisted her mouth, perhaps at his ignorance, the bitch.

"I believe," Nadya said, "that a Duke in Jaryar is like a Lord or Lady here."

"Yes. Jaryar has nine provinces, or had before Marod was united to us in the north. Vard is the fifth largest, but the second richest and most renowned. My grandfather Massin Mardai was the first Lord to be named a Duke, sixty years ago, but when my cousin Nerranya became Queen in the south in 620, she lifted all the lords and ladies of provinces to the title." At the conclusion of this recitation, there was silence, unimpressed on Mej's side, until they came round a corner into a wide space. Kelji said, "Yes, well, they are all in good health. Is this the famous Square of Silent Remembrance, with your Family pillars?"

Obviously it is. "Indeed, the pillars to commemorate the fallen."

"I see." She stopped by one of the pillars – was it b'Asa? – stretched out to almost touch it, and lifted her head slowly to run her eyes up its full height, and then to and fro along the list of names carved all around the column.

Bored, Mej let his eyes wander. The Square was almost empty. Pigeons strutted. A small drab woman in grey was standing alone not far off, staring at another pillar.

Kelji said, "These are the people who died in the War of the Throne?"

"We call it the War that Must Never Happen Again. The names of those from the Ten Families. Many more died, of course, commoners and slaves."

Her eyes abruptly stopped tracing letters. "You have slaves in Ricossa?"

"Not now! They were all freed at the end of the War, part of the New Governance." *Please don't ask any more about it – I hate history, and that's all I know.* "They'll be carving the meat," he hinted.

"Oh, how rude of me to delay you. I'm sure you're so hungry, as I am," and she took his arm again, and started walking very fast. They had indeed fallen behind, and there were only themselves and their two servants as they crossed into the Street of Holly, where the b'Shen mansion was built, opposite the inconvenient but probably symbolic row of spiky bushes growing against a plain wall.

The others were waiting for them. "Thank you, Mejorad. I am in your debt," Nadya murmured. She was possibly grateful herself for an invitation from the b'Shen, suggesting acceptance by Eyanda's relatives at last. And it occurred to Mej that My-Uncle-Is-The-Duke-of-Vard-and-My-Cousin-Is-The-Queen Kelji might not be the most comfortable guest to spend time with.

Are the stories they tell of Queen Nerranya true? Even the really filthy ones?

After all, nothing good comes from the West but Tell wines and Marodi wool. So they say.

*

Brin greeted her with a beaming smile, a blanket-wrap hug, and the words, "Oh, calamity." He pulled her into the room, which today smelt strongly of cabbage.

"God's blessing, Hridna!" Lulet looked up from cutting chunks of rye bread. "You've come for dinner, I hope?" To her husband, unworriedly, "What's the calamity?"

"Auntie, auntie!" Two-year-old Jof scrambled up and ran over to be lifted and hugged. His older sister was staggering to the table with an earthenware jug. She stuck her tongue between her teeth, lifted it to its place with care, and then curtsied. Very distinctly, "Welcome, and good morrow to you, honoured guest, Aunt Hridnaya, daughter of Haidi."

Hridnaya exchanged an amused look with her brother, and nodded Minna as formal a reply as she could manage with Jof twirling fingers in her hair. Her heart was still thudding. *I've become a spy. I watched the b'Shen after Mass. I didn't learn much.*

Lulet asked again, "What's the calamity?"

"A customer has arrived, and her order isn't ready."

"You fool," and she rolled her eyes, smiling. "A cup of ale?

You'll join us, I hope? Dinner is almost done, though your cloak isn't," to her sister-in-law.

"This is how far I've got," Brin said, and he laid it over the back of the chair. "Is it what you meant? I wish you'd let it be a gift."

A gift would have to be made in your own time. If I pay, your master will let you sew it in the day, at his shop – quicker, more

profitable, and better for your eyes. And I have the money.

The cloak was brown, of good weave, and with the decoration she'd requested by gesture and drawing on the back. Petals in blue and yellow and red grew all across the shoulders. It wasn't quite finished, but nearly, and she wondered how much of his own time he'd spent on it after all. It was going to be perfect. Wearing this, she would remember, other people would remember, Flower-in-Hood. She stroked it, and looked up at him, and found he had tears in his eyes.

"Pretty!" said Jof.

"Dinner's ready," said Lulet.

The cloak was folded away, Jof was tied into the chair, and the others squeezed onto benches. Lulet served out cabbage broth and bread, and opened the pot of mizzum for the guest, and they ate. Six-year-old Minna was questioned about the sermon at church – for there had to be conversation, after all, and Lulet wanted to cover the fact that their guest couldn't contribute. Eating without a tongue, even mizzum, was a difficult and unpretty process, and she hated being watched, and Brin knew she hated it, and yet he kept glancing at her and then away. Minna couldn't make herself not stare, and was probably going to be told off for it soon. But plainly Brin was upset by something.

After the meal was over, her sister-in-law carried Jof away to an afternoon nap in the corner, and Minna was gathering the plates, when "We could finish it now," Brin said.

So Lulet knelt on the floor to wash the dishes, while the twins sat together at the table, and sewed, and little Minna whirled round to help both tasks – putting away a cup and then bending to bite off a thread or pick up a dropped pin – swishing her skirt with dancerly swirls each time she moved. And all was pleasant and quiet.

Brin worked hard, and kept his home clean and tidy, and the curtains he'd made for the beds were things of beauty. But it was his wife who made this the happiest place Hridnaya knew. Six months ago Lulet had managed to wrap four washed egg-shells in scraps of cloth, draw faces on them, and dangle them on a string by the fire, all without breaking them, and all to entertain her children. Four little bobbing people to name and talk to. "I think that's rather pagan," Aunt Miya had said. "No more than a doll, surely?" had been Uncle Gridor.

Now Aunt Miya was living alone - husband dead, one of her children settled at the monastery, and the other at the docks - she might have more sympathy for an imaginary friend.

Lulet hummed gently, grimacing to make Minna giggle now and then. "Why, it's nearly done. If you can stay another half hour, Hridna, you can take it with you."

"Fa – oo," and she meant it.

But Brin was silent.

He didn't speak until she'd paid him the money, and folded the cloak away in her satchel. She kissed Lulet and Minna good-evening, wondering when she'd see them again. It wasn't possible or appropriate to visit every Sunday. Then her brother took her arm, and pulled her to the corner by the bed. His mouth twitched a few times, as he tried to think what to say. *What's wrong?*

At last, "Why d'you want it, Hridna? Why a cloak like that?

Is it just to remember him?"

She looked away, unwilling to deceive.

"Think of his kindness, and his stories. Uncle's were the best." *(Him with his story-telling penny.)* "Don't - don't remember his death, Hridna. We can't. It could be dangerous. The limping man, or those b'Shen -"

Hridnaya gave him a puzzled look, and then the arrow struck her that maybe Someone, the King's Cousins, had talked to him also. Her fury showed on her face.

He went on, "But that's not all. I told you I was angry, I blamed all the rich, which is unjust. I said a lot of foolish things, but it doesn't matter anyway what I think. Who am I?" His voice slowed. "Last week, every stitch I put into this -" he gestured – "I was wondering, why does she want it, what is she thinking? What's she going to do?

"I kept thinking of the Slaves of Baragaida."

She stared.

"Lulet says I'm a fool. I hope I am. However much I hate them, I can't do anything. You're different, you live with them. I don't know how close the Lord and Lady let you come to them, to their food – yes, it's absurd," he said awkwardly, trying to smile, "and your Family aren't like the b'Shen, but if you let yourself get too angry - you took an oath, Hridna."

And at last she understood. *Baragaida was a tale of rebellion and murder. I'm not a slave, but I swore loyalty to b'Nida. If I attacked them or betrayed them, it would be petty treason, and I'd be burned alive - as those slaves were, one at a time.*

But of course I'm not going to do that! What does Brin think of me? She squeezed his hand and smiled reassuringly.

But she was rather shocked.

He was so afraid for her, because he loved her, as he'd

loved Uncle Gridor. And he must love Lulet and his children even more.

Hridnaya didn't love anyone that much. Perhaps all the Voiceless felt that way, or all servants - or perhaps it was only she that was hard of heart.

*

Despite Brin's warnings, then, for the second Sunday she made sure she was closest to the door when the b'Nida household filed into the Church of the Fear of the Lord, and managed to draw Narrim's attention to the fact that she was obediently present. But as soon as Mass was over, she scurried out, pulling off and tucking away her revealing b'Nida tabard, and chanting to herself the route she'd learned in another nerve-jangling night-time visit to the study. With luck and God's favour the unbusy rich would again be standing around the Cathedral as they did, talking gossip or business or love.

The Cathedral, the tallest thing in the city, stood assured and lordly in a half-acre of grass. As she arrived at a fast walk, the grass was empty, the service still not finished. *No one would dare tell a Bishop to hurry herself.* Hridnaya grinned.

She crept in, crossing herself meekly, and allocating a single glance at windows glorious with stories in purple and green and gold glass. She was just in time to watch the procession out of choir and clergy. The space around and above filled with their singing – words that one couldn't follow because the singers chimed against and interrupted each other, grand but incomprehensible. Jantorad or Lindet would have loved it, but Hridnaya had no ear for music. They stalked out, and other people began to straggle after them, the great ones first of course, and Hridnaya flicked her eyes around and about, looking for the dark-skinned b'Shen. The rich stood in bunches, mixing their Families confusingly.

Why wouldn't they? They're not here for my convenience. She grinned.

"It's not likely you'll learn any more than last week. Which is nothing," Balki warned.

I know, unhelpful creature. Last time I learned that – well, that Rorash wasn't with them, so I suppose he did go to Defardu – and Mejorad was talking to that foreign woman that Lady b'Nida's going to meet soon – there they are again! She crept out with the itchingly slow crowd, and sidled innocently towards them.

There was general talk, some of it holy, some less so.

"I don't care how high her prices are, I won't buy shoes from anyone but Sali." Hridnaya edged by.

Mejorad, and the woman with the hat, and another highborn lady, and one servant for each of the three; six people. They were again meandering along away, and Hridnaya followed. She picked up a little dust to smear on her face, and held out a bowl she'd borrowed from the b'Nida kitchen, as an excuse for dawdling about. *If anyone gives me anything, I'll pass it to a real beggar.*

"The Bishop's words were uncalled for, I think," said the older lady with lots of brown hair. "I'm certain they were not meant personally."

"Was she being rude about my country, Nadya? I was warned to expect that. 'The Ricossans are dripping with courtesy on all subjects but one,' I was told." The foreign woman spoke lightly, with her nose in the air, not looking at either of her companions. "Don't fear. I am not a woman who listens to sermons, in any land."

Mejorad b'Shen laughed. Which was either very polite of him, or rather unpriestly.

"In any case I've only to sit through two more here," the

Jaryari woman was saying. "Two weeks from Thursday I'll be leaving for Sapientia. Your College has called on me at last to perform my errand."

"Indeed, to deliver your book?"

"It's not mine. A monk wrote it, 'On the Blessings of Poverty'. One of our Library's most significant works, or at least the most expensive. So on Friday 24th I am to give it into the hands of Doctor Bekonin, and be free of the responsibility. And in the evening I'll wear my best gown and be privileged to meet and dine and dance with all your College's doctors, who know everything about everything."

"Or so they like to think," Mejorad was saying, but Hridnaya couldn't hear more. The Square went blank before her eyes, and she stood statue-like, while inside her head bells swung. *Two weeks from Thursday.*

"Dine with the doctors!" She means the great feast! Lady b'Nida's been talking about it and planning it for weeks, and I didn't realise – All the doctors! Dirria will be there! Dirria and my Lady will be in the same room on Friday 24th August. If only I could be there also, if only – it must be possible – it must –

"Hey, *you*." A man bumped into her shoulder – hard enough to jerk her back to reality. He was grey-jacketed with the b'Shen green tabard. He'd hit her on purpose. "What're you doing? Who're you spying for?" He punched her on the other side.

Fear flooding her, she tried to make innocent gestures and sounds, waving her empty bowl.

"Oh, you're looking for charity? Begging's *work*. Don't you know what day it is?" He punched lower, and harder, in the stomach; she cried out and bent forward, and the bowl fell and cracked.

"Tor? What're you doing?" someone called.

"Don't run," and he grabbed her, holding her in front of

him like a shield. "Sir, this woman's been watching you and the ladies, staring at you last week and today. Spying for someone, the b'Iri or the b'Met, I'd guess."

"Oh – oh." She shook her head. Mejorad b'Shen and the two women (and their maids), such high people, looked her up and down.

"Who are you?" demanded the older woman. Hridnaya managed to lift a trembling finger to gesture.

"Voiceless?" said Mejorad.

"A Voiceless *begging?* How unusual."

"Breaking the Sabbath," said the servant Tor, tightening his hold. One hand was on her breast, squeezing, reminding her – She was sick with terror.

"Two Sundays? *Were* you watching us? Which of us?"

"Is she really dumb, Nadya?" asked the Jaryari with interest. Then, eyes narrowing, "Were you watching *me?* Could we be making her write down -"

"She can't write," said the other woman. To Mejorad, "Tell him to take his hands off her – he's making me sick." Mejorad gestured, and the man slid his hand over her stomach, and away. He was still standing behind her and gripping her arm, so she couldn't escape.

"We weren't speaking secrets," Mejorad said. "All she's done is be in the Square, you think, two weeks running."

"Mej." The older woman beckoned him two steps aside. Tor still held her. The Jaryari stared at Hridnaya, head on one side, looking like a cat considering a pounce.

"You really can't talk?" She made an interested-in-the-grotesque face. "Have you never been tempted to learn to write? It's not so hard, and it's useful. I teach all my maids."

Hridnaya shook her head with frantic virtue, and heard the man say heavily, "It is forbidden for such as her, madam."

The other two were looking back, and the woman Nadya (*Nadya b'Astith, isn't it?*) said, "Well, I see you've broken your bowl. That'll teach you to keep the Sabbath in future. Run along now. Kelji?" she said to her friend.

Hridnaya bobbed a frightened curtsey.

"I don't want to see you again," hissed Tor, and as she came up to meet his eyes, she saw rape. Or maybe she didn't, but –

Two street-turns away, out of their sight, she leant against a wall, feeling her legs shake. What could they do to her, the Families, and their servants? They could do almost anything. How much would the b'Nida banner protect her, if at all?

(Question 21, from the Box: Was it rape, what Sinavid did to me? Even though I didn't cry out, or fight? Answer: Yes, Narrim's right, it was, because he made you too frightened to protest. I could complain, try to get him hanged, but it would be so hard because I can't talk, and he's so high – and it would humiliate the Family.)

And that time I wasn't even in the wrong.

"You must stop this! It's dangerous," said Balki.

Uncle Gridor didn't stop.

And surely she needn't see him, Tor, again.

For suddenly she wasn't interested in the b'Shen. She might be in the future. But Dirria would be at the great dinner! "The feast for that Kelji woman," Lady b'Nida had called it. Or almost certainly she would. *Can I find out for sure? There are plans in the study, lists of dishes and guests – I can't read, but I could copy the shapes of letters on a list perhaps. If it wasn't too long. Would someone read it for me? Not Sister Felicity, but our priest, or even Narrim? Probably not Narrim.*

How many risks should a spy take? Question 37. She shakily smiled.

And if – Lady b'Nida could take me instead of her own maid! If I could ask, if they were willing, if I could only explain –

There must be a way to get to that dinner.

"Hridnaya, daughter of Haidi, you are insane."

*

The rest of that Sunday afternoon Hridnaya spent practising the letters she knew the shapes of, even if she didn't know their sound, scribbling in charcoal on one of her moontime rags. Going to the Cathedral had been enough excitement however, so she did nothing else that night. The next evening Lindet kept her up late to brush her hair and listen to her complaints about all the young men she knew ("Mmm, mhm, mm," said Hridnaya, nodding, and in her head pondering the other person's point of view, and feeling sorry for the young men.)

So it wasn't till Tuesday was over that she woke herself up with her shoe in the middle of the night, and again lit a candle in her master's study. "You'll be tired tomorrow," Balki said, but she ignored this wisdom.

All that cabinet is old College administration. The current year-book with plans is the one with the blue ribbon.

She laid a fairly clean cloth out on the desk, holding it down with a candle, and opened the book to the most recent writing – yes, a list with a date at the top. She knew numbers – "24th – some word that might be August - 641."

Her stomach tingled. Deep breath. She started to copy the shapes on the list carefully, thankful for her mistress's neat handwriting. She wasn't used to using a pen, and there were smudges. But she did it.

Since I'm here – there must be a map of Sapientia, or the College? I suppose the feast will be in what they call the Refectory.

She'd just found what she thought was the right parchment, and was spreading it on the desk, when she heard a noise, and looked up to the left.

The door finished opening on Narrim and Attar, the night guard.

"You see," said Attar.

A heart-beat. "Hridnaya," said Narrim. Her voice changed. "Put your hands flat on the desk." Another heart-beat. "Now!"

She'd not for years seen Narrim in her nightgown, her feet bare. The Housemother padded to the desk, and looked from the map to the not-yet-replaced blue book to the marks on the linen. "You treacherous little -" and she slapped Hridnaya hard on the cheek. To Attar, "Fetch the Lord and Lady. Wake them."

He went out. There was silence. *Oh God help me*. Every other thought was scattered, like spilt flour.

Lord and Lady b'Nida were in the doorway, night-cloaks thrown around them. She squeaked, and darted forward. He said, "My books!"

Narrim stepped aside, waving a hand at the evidence. The Lord looked at it, and then he looked at Hridnaya. His face made her think of dead things.

"How dare you?" cried his wife, in her shrill voice. "You'll get the worst whipping of your life!"

Lord b'Nida said, "No."

*

They took her down to the front hall, the long room off which doors and stairs opened. Narrim lit a candle. They left her sitting on the floor, with Attar standing two paces before her, sword drawn. Silent time passed. It grew lighter. She was only wearing a smock, and she shivered.

Hridnaya had been a well-behaved child on the whole, and an obedient servant. She wasn't used to being in trouble, awaiting her fate.

Around the time (she guessed) when fires should be lit

and breakfast begun, Narrim came out of the kitchen and walked straight past her and upstairs. There were voices, doors opening and shutting. People, hastily clothed, hurried down, staring and whispering.

"But what's she -"

"Wait."

Jantorad; Jeruma and her husband; Lindet; giggly Kara. Narrim. More and more people.

The Lord and Lady walked into the hall. Hridnaya dared not move or look up, but saw the bottom of green dress and blue hose, and sensed her fellow-servants bowing. Her master and mistress were given chairs, and they sat facing her. Everyone else stood round the walls.

"Hridnaya. Look at me.

"You were caught in our study, copying out one of our documents. You, one of the most privileged and trusted people in this house." His slow voice paused. "I thought we'd treated you well for eighteen years."

You did. You do.

"You cannot read, so you must have been copying it for someone else. Betraying us to our rivals, or our enemies. It will count somewhat in your favour if you are frank now. Nod when I say the name. The b'Iri. The b'Asa. The b'Shen."

She kept shaking her head. She lifted her hands and lowered them again. Contemptuous eyes burned her.

"Are you going to tell us?"

I can't. There's no one.

He nodded to Jantorad, who hit her.

"Who? You're refusing to tell?"

"There's no one, no one! I wasn't betraying you, I never would! I only wanted to know about the College feast for the foreigner – my uncle was going to meet Doctor Dirria, and he was murdered – I meant no treason! Please, I never would, please!"

This was what she tried to say then, knowing it was useless, hearing the mangled sounds that no one could understand. She went on and on trying, for an age it seemed, and at last she started to cry.

"I want the name," said Lord b'Nida.

"My lord, we can make her tell," said Jantorad shyly. "I could get knives from the kitchen, or there's hot coal."

Someone hissed excitedly.

"No. I've never tortured a servant, and I'm not starting now." He exchanged a look with his wife, and turned to Narrim. "Bring down everything she owns. Search the room thoroughly. We don't know what she may have stolen." Narrim and two maids went upstairs.

There was more silence. Hridnaya couldn't think. All these people stared at her, people whom she hadn't made into friends – but it wouldn't have made any difference if she had.

She wiped her slobbered face with the back of her hand, but more tears kept sliding down.

At last the three returned, arms full. Narrim dropped Hridnaya's shoes, cloak and little carpet in front of her, and then her blue summer door-curtain on top. Judi and Salamat laid down her clothes chest. "That belongs to us," said the Lady, so they tipped it open, spilling clothes onto the pile, and Narrim picked out the bedding that was b'Nida property.

"Give me that." The Lord took her small box, and shook it. "The key," he said to Hridnaya.

"It's hers, my lord," Narrim murmured.

"The box is hers. For all I know, everything in it may be mine. The key."

It was on a string round her neck. She watched him open

the box, and rummage through her money, her buttons, her keepsakes (dead Siri's hair.) He locked it again without removing anything, and tossed it onto the pile.

"Look at me, Hridnaya. You still refuse to tell us who you're spying for. It doesn't matter. I'll make it my business to find out.

"Get dressed."

Under the eyes of the household, she pulled on her underhose and kirtle, and her shoes.

"You will leave now. No one will employ you, a woman with no tongue, and a name for treachery. You've enough money to live on for a while. When that's finished," he shrugged, "you can go and burden your family, or you can beg, or thieve, or whore yourself in the streets, or starve.

"Ah, but you're thinking the people you're working for will help you." He stepped deliberately forward, squatted down, and grabbed her chin, pulling her eyes to meet his. "Perhaps they will. And then I'll find out where you've gone, and who they are. So that we can take you to the Hall of Justice, and see you hanged, as you deserve."

Releasing her, he stood up, wiping his hand on his gown. "You are no longer under the protection of our banner," he said formally, and turned to Attar. "Put her out."

So the last time Hridnaya left the b'Nida house, it was by the front door, and all her possessions that she couldn't carry in her arms were thrown out after her.

The Declaration ending the War of the Throne

(commonly called the New Governance)

WE, the undersigned of the Ten Families and the ministers of GOD in Ricossa, declare this 14th day of October 575 After Landing, that we have MADE PEACE, and that in order that by God's grace such a strife may never occur again, HAVE AGREED the following matters relating to the future governance of the Realm:

IMPRIMIS. The land shall be ruled by two monarchs, one styled for the EVENING, to order matters of war and diplomacy and justice, and one styled for the MORNING, to order matters of faith, agriculture, commerce and art. The Council of the Families shall continue as before, and all taxes shall require its approval, but each monarch shall in addition maintain their own Council for advice, to whom they may appoint whom they will.

Selection of the monarchs shall be by a Conclave in City Qayn. Ten persons shall be chosen by and from each Family, and when a selection is needed these persons shall be summoned with notice given of not more than four nor less than two weeks. One Family shall then be selected by lot, and the representatives of that Family shall select from their own kin one to rule.

The Kings and Queens thus selected shall take the most solemn oath not to lift hand or power against, nor interfere with, the other, and they and their spouses shall renounce forever all previous loyalty and ties to their kin. They shall serve GOD and the realm only. Their children shall be adopted within the previous Family. Each shall serve for life, and shall act independently, save that neither may declare war or levy tax without the consent of the other. War may also not be declared without the consent of the Council of the Families. The proceedings of the Conclave shall be kept secret from all save those appointed to it.

SECONDLY, one month from this date, all slaves within Ricossa or owned by Ricossans are declared FREE PEOPLE, and it shall be forever forbidden to make anyone a slave. The former slaves may remain as waged servants of their previous owners if they choose, but if they do not choose these owners shall pay each one a bounty of five silver pieces. The children of slaves up to the age of fifteen years shall remain with their parents. In order that the Families may retain trust and secrecy, they may hire servants whose secrecy is enforced by removal of the tongue, but no one is to be made Voiceless without their consent, nor shall any such be dismissed during their lifetime without good cause.

THIRDLY, the first Morning King or Queen shall establish and provide a COLLEGE of learning, to be erected on the grounds of the former Shore Palace, and here men and women of good parts shall be encouraged to learn and develop all lawful kinds of knowledge and skill to the benefit of the Realm and the glory of GOD. The management of this College shall be in accordance with laws to be drawn up within the next twelve-month following this date and shall be funded by a levy on all foreign-imported items and visitors. Study at the College need not be restricted to those within the Ten Families, if students with aptitude are found.

LASTLY, we who have agreed these terms acknowledge and confess before GOD that this nation has sinned grievously in allowing sibling, cousin, neighbour and friend to make so terrible and great slaughter on each other, and also in numerous acts of murder, rape, cruelty, deceit and pillage which accompanied the War. There can be no peace without a renunciation of bloodfeud, and yet innocent blood has been shed and cries out to GOD for retribution.

THEREFORE each of the Families shall select by lot one

household in the land to be surrendered to death. All members of this household, young and old, slave and free, shall be killed, and their bodies burned in their house, and its ruins shall be sown with salt and unbuilt on forever. No further acts of bloodfeud following the War shall be permitted, and any such committed shall be treated as murder. And in the Square formerly called Monday Market pillars shall be erected with the names of the Fallen. And the 14th day of October every year shall be declared a day of fasting and sorrow throughout Ricossa forever.

May GOD graciously approve this solemn Declaration.

"Blessed are the peacemakers, for they shall be called children of GOD."

Signed

Jeremiah Dniren, Archbishop of Ricossa

Pariet b'Met

Dindikaris b'Iri

Otto b'Shen

Feodor b'Asa

Yadiana b'Olim

Ardinshor b'Trai

Joa b'Lan

Githri b'Astith

Tren b'Oto

Minna b'Nida

and forty-two other names.

This document formed the basis of the government of Ricossa. The bulk of it was learned, recited and revered throughout the land, although the parts relating to the Conclave procedures remained secret.

Part Two

The Foreigner's Book

Rommi, Queen for the Morning, woke up in the bed where her predecessor had died.

The hangings had been left open in the warm weather, so as she rolled over she could see the whole too-magnificent room. Wood panelling gleamed on one wall; a huge tapestry, The Making of the Peace, covered another. Shelves creaked under the weight of wise oppressive books. In one corner stood a smaller bed, where her personal maid lay asleep, face to wall. There were two doors - one to the Queen's private chapel, and the other to the frightening outside.

The sun shone through the coloured glass window, tinting everything with unreality.

Rommi waited, listening to the other woman's breathing, and trying to gather strength for the day; alone.

She slid out of bed, and her bare feet touched softness. Her life had always been wealthy, compared to most, but now she lived in a place where people spent a fortune on elegant carpet - and then put it casually on the floor and trod on it, rather than hanging it on a wall to be admired. *I will get rid of it. Someday soon.* Her night-cloak waited slung on a chair whose back was dovetailed out of three colours of wood. She pulled it on, and turned to the inner door, the safe one, into the chapel.

There were pictures here also, and the cross on the altar was peppered with gems, but at least the floor was bare. She knelt, and then lay flat, stretching out her arms, and recited the Gloria.

She'd been Queen for three weeks. There was no training;

there couldn't be any. All she'd had were two words of advice.

Her Uncle Yettrid: "We've chosen you because you think. Thinking is better than talking."

And her grandmother: "They'll give you dozens of servants, all eager to please you. Remember that at least half of them will be reporting to Aigith and Brechad."

The current King for the Evening had ruled for twenty-nine years. Every Saturday, the two of them met for formal discussion. King Aigith was smilingly conversational – and every now and again his eyes would slide away, as if she were an irrelevance. A child. His Chamberlain looked at her with almost open contempt, but somehow the King was more frightening, and Rommi had always been easy to frighten.

How old is he? Seventy, eighty? He was born before the War, when everything was different.

Her grandmother's words had given her her first problem, and she still wasn't sure how to solve it. She'd been provided with a chaplain and steward; guards and maids. Her own Chamberlain was Krothon b'Trai, as he'd been Queen Zinial's; and he guided her through her duties with meticulous smiles, and had no opinions on anything - except, she'd learned, poetry. She didn't dare speak honestly to him, to any of them.

The Conclave had permitted her to bring only one maid and one guard of her own. All else was left behind, along with the name b'Shen.

Still her eyes pricked at the thought of her children. Darling Aladim and Firi. Anamet. Mejorad.

Mejorad.

Somewhere a bell chimed. Today she was to meet her wardrobe mistress, and to study papers about repairs to the north wall of the Cathedral. And later she'd arranged to share dinner with the leaders of the b'Met Family. She was working round all the Ten. ("But why?" Krothon had asked. "I need to understand and share all their concerns." "I see, how conscientious.") The b'Met and the b'Shen had never been allies, and he wasn't the only one to raise eyebrows. Her invitation to the b'Iri had raised more.

And the b'Oto were on the 24th, which meant she couldn't attend that presentation and feast with the Jaryari envoy in Sapientia, which was probably a mistake, possibly a bad one.

She lay still, waiting for the day, reminding herself of her call. She was chosen to be Queen. Divinely appointed, and therefore, she must believe, divinely equipped.

"Almighty Father," she prayed, "help me not to show fear. And in Your great mercy, prevent me from doing anything completely stupid today."

*

Hridnaya had been staying at St Ansha's for two days and nights. On the third day she stepped out onto the street, trembling but freshly washed and brushed, and wearing her lovely new cloak. Its defiant flower design danced out from her shoulders as she turned very deliberately in the doorway, and hung her satchel over her shoulder.

Jesus, Word of Truth, help me to do this.

"Is anyone there? Yes, I see him. Definitely Gabo," said Balki. The b'Nida kitchen lad, long-legged and curly-haired, was pretending to study the pie-shop opposite. He wasn't wearing the tabard that all Family servants ought to wear when out of the house. He was a spy. Hridnaya twirled again, slowly, letting him notice the cloak, and then started walking, not too fast.

As she strolled down Kitten Street, she occupied her mind explaining to Balki that only high and holy people called the place by its proper name, St Ansha's House for Rest and Refreshment. *To everyone else, it's Stansha's Inn. The landlady even answers to the name Stansha.* "Yes, you told me before," said Balki.

The sun was hidden, but brightness seeped through cracks in cloud. "The Cathedral's round the next corner, isn't it?" asked Balki, earning her keep, "oh, and there are the bells for Matins."

I have ears.

Devout or unemployed people were arriving for daily service. Decked in cloak and satchel, Hridnaya walked slowishly in among them.

Now! Into the quietest side-chapel – no one here. Get behind a pillar. Cloak off and into satchel. Pin on the holly-green tabard she'd sewn yesterday, put satchel back on, cover it up with her other cloak, unbleached homespun.

She sidled down the right-hand aisle to the Cathedral's south door, and *out.* Over the road, round the corner, *pause.*

There was no sign of Gabo. "Either he didn't follow you, or we've lost him."

He followed. Now to the wine-shop.

They'd argued over what gift to buy a rich foreign traveller who probably had everything she needed already, and Balki had won. She was a tipsier soul than Hridnaya. Once in Merry Mic's shop and safely out of sight from the street, they selected a bottle, and then went to the market for a basket to put it in, and fresh flowers to arrange round it. Altogether it made a pretty thing, Hridnaya thought, and laid a green cloth on top.

Green for b'Shen.

Two nuns were strolling ahead of her, as she and Balki passed the House of the Exile, crossed the Great Passage, and entered the Second Quarter. An errand-boy dashed past. "He's in a hurry," Balki commented. The lad was wearing a similar tabard to hers, but b'Iri red.

"Are you sure you know the way?"

Up until yesterday, the answer would've been *No*. The Second Quarter was where the not-quite-greatest but still high people lived, and Hridnaya had almost never had cause to go there.

("Isn't one of the Jaryari coming to see her, Nadya, any day now?" someone had said. "May be here already. Some ladyling from Makkera, on an errand to the College to get us all in trouble.")

Hridnaya was guessing that if this Nadya had her own visitors, she must also have her own house, and thus wasn't the top rank of the b'Astith. So her other task yesterday had been wandering the Quarter, trying not to look lost and aimless, feet growing sore. She'd been rewarded at last. The four just-familiar women, two marked out as foreign mistress and maid by embroidered caps, walking up to a house with a blue door, which they entered as if they lived there. Not their Family mansion, but still b'Astith blue.

And here it was again.

I'm going to do this. Help me.

Balki was banished from her thoughts, probably glad to go. She kept her steps even as she walked up to the door, and rapped. The noise made her heart jump. There was no guard outside – the street was almost empty – but she'd seen a flicker of moving gown at a window.

If she were very lucky, or blessed, Kelji from Makkera would be within, and willing to see her.

"Are the Westerners all evil, a different kind of folk, as some say?" That had been Question 10 some years ago, and she clung now to her answer: "No. All people are people. 'There is neither Jew nor Greek, slave nor free, male nor female, Ricossan nor Jaryari', St Paul might have said."

The door opened, and a thin woman, a foreign woman, stood there, the maid in the cap. Hridnaya curtsied, not too low. She held out her basket, just enough to draw attention to it; not enough to be handing it over, and made the sound, "Kheh-ih."

"*Eh?* What are you meaning?"

She tapped the green tabard. "Faw Kheh-ih."

The maid looked her up and down. "Are you telling me you have a gift for Kelji, daughter of Shanell? You may step inside."

It wasn't like the b'Nida hall. This was a room with a candle-lit desk and stool, a cabinet, and two paintings opposite the door. Blue-painted inner doors led off each side. A single guard stared boredly ahead.

"Wait here, please." The maid disappeared to the left, and Hridnaya had time to decide that one picture showed a large church or perhaps abbey in the countryside, and the other a prancing horse. This must be where Nadya b'Astith did business (whatever her business was) but the businesswoman herself wasn't there. She'd hardly dared even to pray for such fortune.

"This way."

The left-hand room was plainly more private. There was a long table with a lute lying on it, a spinning-wheel, benches and chairs, and a tabby cat sleeping before the unlit fireplace. And a window onto the street.

The woman Kelji was sitting by this window, slumped-idle and frowning, a piece of embroidery dangling from her hands. She was wearing a red-brown gown that was all one colour, but with edges of rose-pink undergown visible at bodice and cuffs. This must be Jaryari style. A pink cap half-covered her coiled-up black hair. Somehow sitting here in a proper house she looked stranger than she had in the street or churchgarden. And her expression was also strange – she was staring ahead of her at

- at darkness, Hridnaya thought.

Jaryar, over the western mountains, where they hate us.

But when the noise roused Kelji, she looked up and smiled, and although her chin jutted forward in a fighting manner, it was the smile of a sweet-natured queen, or St Mary-Christ's-Mother – a smile without recognition. "The b'Shen Family have sent something for me? I'm honoured." Hridnaya curtsied neatly, and handed over the basket. As Kelji lifted the cloth (oh, the scent of the flowers!) she realised suddenly that it wasn't just that *she* didn't know what kind of gift to give, but the other also might think this a confusing Ricossan custom, and wonder about the correct response. Whatever the correct response was. She might think it some kind of courtship. Mad laughter bubbled in her, and she quashed it.

"This is being very kind, but who precisely is it from? Is there a message?"

Hridnaya bowed her head, put one hand on her breast, and then jerked her head just faintly towards the maid standing at her shoulder. It was a gesture she'd learned from great people at home, when privacy was wanted, and Kelji understood it.

"You can wait outside. Find something to do," she said, looking rather less like St Mary, and the maid left with a cross curtsey.

"Well? Is it a private message from Mejorad or Eyanda?"

Hridnaya's heart thudded like running footsteps. Very deliberately she shook her head, took off the cloak and tabard, and dropped them onto the floor. Kelji's eyes followed them down.

"Not from the b'Shen? Who then?"

With both hands on her breast, she curtsied low, and prayed.

"Not from anyone? The b'Shen didn't send you - you

were lying at the door? Who are you? Wait -" Kelji peered forward. "I've seen you before. Last Sunday. You're the woman he said was watching us – who definitely isn't a beggar." Her face was eager and hard – but interested at least. "Spying on me for King Aigith?"

No – no – no!

"For someone else – what's-the-name - b'Iri?"

No.

"Then who sent you? No one sent you? How very – strange. I think you're fortunate that I'm bored today. If you're meaning me harm, I have servants within call, and I know how to use this." She tapped the knife at her belt. "Explain yourself."

Now. Hridnaya passed over the white cloth Brinnon had given her.

"Did you sew this?" Kelji stared down. "Not very neatly, if so. It says Ittrad. What does that mean?"

Ittrad. Not Dirria? Who or what is Ittrad? A man's name – or perhaps a place? A man in Sapientia?

She curtsied again, said, "Fa – oo," and took it back.

"I don't know who this is. If it's a name, it's not Jaryari. You lied your way in here so that I could read a word?" Kelji's voice was incredulous.

Yes. And now –

She'd bought a piece of parchment, and borrowed a chunk of charcoal from the inn. She carried them to the table, and began to draw, the top of her head dizzy and her face hot, feeling Kelji's eyes on her back, hearing steps behind her –

"What in creation are you doing? A road, is that it? A cart? I travelled along a road, yes, but not by cart. We rode. What do you *want?*" Kelji took her quite gently by the shoulders, and twisted her round. "You can't be anyone's messenger, or you'd have it ready written for me, have it clear. Tell me, not-beggar-woman, why you're here, what you want!"

I want to go to Sapientia. "Sa," she said, hopelessly. *Why did I come? It's no use; I was mad.*

"Do I have to – *yich!*" Kelji was the taller. She took Hridnaya's chin in hers, and lifted it a little to stare into her eyes, as Lord b'Nida had done. People rarely touched the Voiceless, and Hridnaya almost shuddered. Slowly, "You truly can't talk, can't explain."

There was a silence.

She was released, and Kelji moved and spoke fast. "Look, you." She pulled the parchment across, and picked up something from the table. It was a pen, like the b'Nidas had. With it she drew a shape, one Hridnaya knew but couldn't interpret. "My hostess is out visiting her high friends this morning for an hour or so. This is the letter Y. It sounds 'yuh.' For Yes. And here's N. The sound 'nuh,' for No. Shall I teach you some more letters, so that I can understand you?"

What? Hridnaya stared.

It is forbidden for Voiceless servants to read and write. Of course it is.

What kind of person is she, this Kelji? Why is she here? Narrim would be suspicious. What does she think of me? I cleaned up as well as I could.

Y for Yes. N for No.

HridNaYa.

It is forbidden.

"Well? Yes or No? If you can't tell me what you want, you can go away."

I'm no longer their servant. I was cast out.

The air tingled. Hridnaya reached out and touched the Y.

"You want to learn to read, mystery woman?"

And then Kelji grinned, a huge grin. "Excellent! Sit on that stool." She strode fast to the door – her red gown whirled. "Imadal! Bring more candles, and ale. And parchment."

So they began.

*

Two days ago, Hridnaya had been sitting in the middle of Scholars' Street, too shocked to cry any more, aware only of Attar standing above and behind her on the stairs with contemptuous eyes. She couldn't sit there for ever, so she'd somehow dragged her belongings to the corner, and paid a passing young man to help carry them. "Where to?" he'd asked, and she'd almost screamed, but guided him to the second-nearest inn. *The one thing the Voiceless have enough of is money.* And some inner voice was telling her not to go to Brin, not to give him another reason to be angry.

So she'd arranged herself a bed upstairs by gesture, and got mizzum and ale and a place in the common room to sit, and still the tears didn't come. She sat for a long time, considering the nothing, the *unperson,* she was now, and she rocked a little, and thought, "Oh, God," and finally understood that this was a prayer.

If she was praying, she was still alive. If she was still alive, there would be a tomorrow, for her to wake up to and go through.

She had a few relatives and some money; a dead uncle, and a list of questions; and no proper future.

"You can go and burden your family, or you can beg, or thieve, or whore yourself in the streets, or starve."

What can I do? What can I do?

She took deep breaths, and stared ahead. She stared at the work available in City Qayn for someone who couldn't talk, whose presence already made people uncomfortable, and who was in disgrace with one of the Families. Not much at all.

I could go to Brin, but what good is that? Worry them,

anger them, be a useless extra person in their house–

She stared, then, at her elder brother, Gardyish; at the village she'd never been to some way south, where he lived with his family and their mother. She probably had enough money to pay her journey there. She could sew fairly well, and look after children. *Gardyish would be kind*, she thought. But once her money was spent she'd still be a burden. He'd grow to hate her; she'd grow to hate herself.

And I'll – I'd have to forget about Uncle Gridor. There's a feast for all the doctors two weeks from Friday, and I had a list of names!

Narrim had taken the list, and the remembered shapes were fading.

"What are you thinking? You have to give all that nonsense up! You have to go to Gardyish!"

Maybe.

Among her belongings, now dumped upstairs, was the cloak she'd ordered from Brinnon, with the flowers embroidered on the shoulders. In her mind she stroked it.

If I can pay passage to Gardyish's, I can pay passage to Sapientia. But that won't get me in to the feast.

How can I –

And then she remembered. "In the evening I'll wear my best gown and be privileged to meet and dine with all your College's doctors, who know everything about everything." Kelji.

*

"A little space between every word. And at the end of a sentence – a set of words that makes sense together – you put a dot. Like this."

Hridnaya nodded and looked up, and their eyes met shining.

It had been an hour, an astonishing hour. Kelji looked

strange, and talked strange, but she was a good teacher, better than any the b'Nida had paid to instruct their children. She'd been surprised at how much Hridnaya already knew - all the shapes, just not the sounds that matched them. Now -

I know the letters! If I opened a book, I could understand it, or begin to! She felt dizzy.

"Nadya b'Astith, whose house this is, will be back soon, I think," said Kelji. She paused. The lesson was over, and the air in the room changed. She put a hand on Hridnaya's arm. "So now you can explain why you're here. What you want."

Please don't interrupt me; I'm learning –

The hand squeezed, hard enough to pinch. "Explain."

So she took the pen, and stared at the parchment, and as Kelji watched, she made shapes.

tu go plez god tuo sape entea

Kelji looked at this, and at last said, "Sapientia? You – were we talking about it on Sunday in the Square? Yes, we were. That's why you were listening! You want to go to Sapientia. Why? Are you wanting to see someone there?"

Yes.

Kelji got up, and walked around the room. *Please –*

Turning by the window, she said, "Listen to me, you. I'm a foreigner, but I mean no harm to your College, or your King or Queen. If that's what you're here for, you'll regret it. To go to Sapientia to meet someone, and you can't go alone? Well." She put her head on one side. "You need more lessons. Spelling rules and so on." *Yes!* "Do you – I suppose you don't know how to wait on a lady, do hair, serve at dinners, that kind of thing?"

Yes, yes, yes!

"I'm going to Sapientia on the 23rd. If you wish, you can come as my maid, and I'll leave Imadal here. It might be entertaining."

*

Twenty-six letters (only twenty-six, for "A" is just the important-word-beginning form of "a" – a wonderful discovery – *only twenty-six!*) were in her head with their sounds.

She walked and didn't pause, because her legs were shaking, and if she stopped she might fall down.

In her head she stared at the letters Kelji had written and she had copied. *(I must buy some more parchment, and a pen of my own, and an inkhorn.)* A a apple; B b basket. One by one, she again matched shapes to sounds. Yes, she knew them, and she was willing to believe that there was more to learn, but she'd made the first mile. And now, now, in two weeks -! Balki capered around her, up and down street walls in the dazzling sunshine.

She remembered just in time to slip into the Cathedral, so she could return to Stansha's Inn wearing the recognisable flowery cloak. When she got there she found a corner of the empty common room, and sat very tidily, just breathing.

*

On Thursday 23rd August, Mej said a solemn farewell to his mother, and an affectionate one to his sisters, and then he led Wind's Son off down the Street of Holly, his servant Tor with another horse just behind. And he managed to keep the smirk off his face until they were round the corner.

It was too early to be bustling, but still the beasts tossed heads, and common people eyed them nervously, and kept a clear twelve inches out of their way. But close enough for him to smell rancid fish on one woman's kirtle, and tanning stink on another man's jacket and hands. The open spaces called him urgently.

Tor was of course silent (when was he not?) and Mej resisted the urge to say, "You're quite clear what you've to do?"

127

like a nervous steward before a dinner party. It was all arranged. Patterings of glee swarmed through him. And it was a beautiful day, sun warm on his forehead and arms, and only a little cloud between roof-tops. Gulls called and swooped, crossing all the way, north to south from water to water, across City Qayn.

But Mej and Tor rode to the Friendship Gate, and were nodded through and under, riding east off the peninsula and out of the city proper. They turned right, and arrived at Darbon's stables, where he'd agreed to meet Kelji. At the door, he paused and handed Tor a gold coin. *Quite a moment,* he thought – *has he ever owned a whole one before?* "There'll be another for you afterwards, if all goes well."

Tor nodded, not actually saying, "Thank you." He was a miserable curmudgeon, but efficient. "Fare well, sir," he said, mounted, and rode off. *Gone, gone, gone.*

Mej walked into the stable yard, and there were Kelji and her servants, dressed for riding. He hadn't seen her in jacket and hose before. They had two horses and two mules, and the groom (he supposed) was fiddling with baggage.

"Ah, good morning, this is most kind," said Kelji. To her people, "Are we ready?" She didn't introduce them to him, he noticed, mannerless woman.

The groom lifted the maid onto one of the mules. It seemed more padded and high-saddled than customary – was that Jaryari, or could the woman not ride properly? She gripped the saddle with pale knuckles, looking oddly nervous for someone who'd ridden all the way from Makkera.

He bowed, smiling, to Kelji, and they both mounted.

The four rode out of the yard, down the alley and another street. Mej nodded pleasantly to the people getting out of their way. He found himself whistling. The song was "Nerranya's Nineteenth Lover", which his tuneful friend Narod had been singing in The Dog and Boot last night. Abruptly it occurred that Kelji might not like the words of that at all, and he tactfully stopped before she could ask any questions. But in fact she was ignoring him, looking around with a superior visitor's air. People stared back. It was the hat.

But the maid wasn't wearing one. That also was strange. And when he glanced back, she looked familiar, but familiar in the wrong way. *That's not the maid she brings to church.* Kelji must have borrowed someone else from Nadya for the trip.

They found themselves riding behind a small group of boring-looking clerics. It was apparently some bishop with his entourage, probably returning home from the Conclave and Crowning. A woman riding at the episcopal shoulder was reading aloud something about tongues being like horses' bridles – Scripture, presumably. This kept them slow, and Mej saw his companion tap cross fingers on her saddle. At another time, he would've shared her impatience, but the delay was no problem, and he was too happy for annoyance. He imagined the wind lifting all these pompous people out of their saddles, and whirling their stern black gowns around.

*

This would be his sixth conversation with Kelji, but most of the others had been passing twitter at dinners. He knew some of her tastes in food, architecture and music – the latter pleasingly similar to his own – but not much more. He'd watched her smile and coo graciously, but that smile could also cut like a knife. Potential hours of silence stretched ahead as he watched her rhythmically turning her head from side to side, smiling the same cool smile at him, at the fields, and beyond. Anyway, she was a thousand times better than a monastery.

And after a little while, happily, she broke the silence with, "Are you being familiar with the College of Sapientia, sir?"

"Oh, indeed. I've never studied there myself, but my relatives and friends have, and I've visited them. What would you like to know?"

She shrugged, but quite friendlily.

"Um, the College is a separate part of the town, uphill. It's all built in squares – Quadrangles. The students live in tiny holes, like cages or monks' cells. The people who teach are called Doctors, and they rule very strictly."

("You have to sit at commoners' feet? On the *floor?* Just because they've read more books than you? And they don't let you keep your sword?" he'd asked in horror. "Don't they know who you are?"

"It's to teach humility," said Rorash, his smile twisted.)

With honey, Kelji replied, "We're all aware that stern virtue prevails throughout Ricossa." *Unlike your homeland, if the stories are true.* "And what do they learn?"

"Several things at once – my cousin in his first year was studying Latin and History and Natural Philosophy - which means plants and rivers and different kinds of stone and such - Poetry – I can't remember what else. And Combat, of course. Then he'd have done other courses next year. Most students stay for two years – some do longer."

"And others train in the military instead?"

"Not instead, no, you can do both. Rorash – my cousin – did. 'There are many ways to keep youngsters out of trouble'," he quoted, and then remembered the trouble Rorash had got into anyway. He scowled. *Get out of my head, foolish old man!* "Do you in Jaryar not do time in the army?"

"No, but many of us are serving seven years as squires, which may provide similar training. I did, and so did my -" She stopped.

'*My husband,*' guessed Mej. Kelji wore a ring on her

fourth finger, but from her conversation he wouldn't have known such a man existed.

The word "squire" was much more interesting. Squires and masters, the adventures of the Queen's Thirty, tales of heroism and barbaric loyalty. That was what he wanted to hear about the West. But before he could phrase a question, she said, "And where were you stationed when it was your turn to fight? How many of my countrymen did you kill?"

We didn't do much bloodletting. We were more occupied keeping cattle on our side of the border. "I was down in the south – b'Met lands. Over from your – er – province of Lefayr, I think."

"Oh, how fortunate I know no one down there." Again her sweet hard smile. They were passing a family pushing a cart along the road. Kelji nodded graciously to them, like a Queen's cousin. Two of the children pointed and giggled together. *Discourteous,* Mej thought, but *if you must look so different, what d'you expect?*

Kindness vanished from her face, and she jerked her eyes away. Haughtily, "How they stare. From bishops to babies, you all hate us."

"Indeed not; we don't hate you. But we know so little of you. And there are stories, perhaps exaggerated -"

Irreligious, immoral, uncivil, unchaste – and unteachable. That is Jaryar.

"Oh yes. We also have stories."

*

Hridnaya was learning to read. She was riding to Sapientia, to the College, that place of awe. She was travelling with Mejorad b'Shen, the witness, accomplice to murder, whatever he was. ("A young man will put us on the right road," Kelji had told her. She should've guessed which young man.)

131

I need to listen to him talk – but the mule and the sky wouldn't let her. Everything was too strange. The mule's rolling movement, its disconcerting aliveness underneath, made her nervous: surely she'd slide off these blankets and bags soon, and it was far enough down to hurt. She didn't dare shift even a little. It took time to grow precariously accustomed to the ride, and by then the people in front had turned off another way, and they four were out from the buildings, speeding up.

Under the sky.

Once or twice long ago, her father had taken the twins to the wharves, and pointed across the miles of slapping water to a dark distant line, that might be the further shore and might not - and above at the grey up, up for ever.

But that was over twenty years past. Since she'd gone to work in Scholars' Street, she'd almost never been able to see further than an opposite wall. Now she looked up, and instead of the usual road of blue or white between roofs was an endless upwards-and-around that turned her into an insect. Blue with faint white cloud-stripes. *Think – lots of ways the sky can look, and lots of things the weather can do: all of them a huge ceiling up above!* she marvelled to Balki, and shivered. The patterns and colours filled everything up to God.

Left and right below was almost as empty. There were yellow crops in wide strips. ("Is that corn or oats, I wonder?" asked Balki, sharing ignorance.) In some fields people were bending over, working, swinging arms with blades that gleamed in the sun: it was harvest time. Or there was green with large animals staring at them and flicking tails, munching grass with sharp-sounding bites. "Are they cattle or sheep?" *I don't know. They're not pigs or horses – what about deer, or do they only live in the forest? What animals are there?* They passed a few buildings. There were harsh and sweet new smells, dizzying.

How long will it take? She said more than a day to reach Sapientia.

And how long will that lad be here? What's he saying? But in any case Kelji and Mejorad rode a horse-length ahead. They talked, and sometimes he laughed. The groom – Kelji hadn't mentioned his name – rode a horse behind Hridnaya, leading the second mule, several sets of hooves somehow comforting, a wrapping-around sound. He would at least notice, if not catch her, if she fell off. Occasionally he asked cursorily, "Madam, are you all right?" and Hridnaya nodded.

Then there were strangers ahead again, and they had to slow. "We're nearly at the Crossing," she heard Mejorad say louder.

She thought she'd heard of the Allways Crossing. A few dozen paces ahead was a patch of dust where five roads came together, and a lot of traffic: riders, wagons, carts and walkers. Travellers paused at the head of their line until they were plainly the most distinguished party, with priority to go. Then they rode across, dignified under the crowd's eyes, and down the road of their choice; and the next group could move up.

To the left, as they slowed and waited, was a space with lines of wooden posts – gibbets - surrounded by a low stone wall. *Don't look if it'll make you sick. I should have remembered.* The bodies of those executed in the Great Square were brought here to dangle as warnings – they had to go somewhere, for no one wanted carrion birds haunting the City's markets. Kelji's head jerked away, and so did her horse's, perhaps from the smell, which was making Hridnaya gasp and swallow also.

The very hungriest people came here to catch the ravens, she remembered. Uncle Gridor had had a gruesome story.

Most of the travellers, sensibly, didn't look. But further on, around the edge of the Crossing itself, some chose to pause.

Wagons were drawn to the side (but still rather in the way) and a few people crowded laughing and talking round a large horse-trough, and a stall selling bread and cheese, pies and ale. That ale would surely soon be undrinkable in this weather (Narrim would have complained.) The horses didn't like standing near so many people, snorting and shaking themselves like sneezes.

"So which way do we take?" she heard Kelji ask, perhaps both teasing and impatient, as they waited their turn behind a small party – two Family members, it looked like, youngish, with three servants.

"South-west." Mejorad indicated the road to the right, edged with pleasant-enough houses, that looked as if it curved quite soon. Perhaps deciding to be the charming guide, he went on, "This is the Allways Crossing. The City Way is the way we've come. The Holy Way is straight on east to the coast, where the saints landed: the saying is that you go that way to pray." Hridnaya wondered at his abruptly gleeful smile. "The Country Way takes you south to where food is grown, and the people work. And there are two roads round the Lake – the northern one up to the left is rather dull, and doesn't have a name. You go that way to sleep. But our road's down there – it used to be Palace Way, but the Shore Palace was burned in the War, and they built the College instead. It's the Way of Wisdom now. Or 'the Way of Drunken Students,' if you don't want to be formal." He grinned at Kelji, and one of the people in front looked round and laughed.

*

Soon after they'd left the Crossing behind, they were alone again. How long it was she didn't know, but at last the packed earth road curved a little, and there was a thick line of sparkle. The Great Lake. They rode closer and closer, until between them and the water on their right was only one green field and a little yellow beyond, scattered with grey humps of rock. And then the

134

dark glittering water, rolling to and fro, never ever still. Hridnaya could see coloured objects that bobbed, fishing craft she thought. *Oh my. I want to be closer.*

Everyone else was looking straight along the road. "D'you see that dark place by the shore, just below the forest line?" asked Mejorad, pointing.

"No – oh, perhaps, yes, sir."

"There's a village there with an inn. A good place to stop tonight. If we move a little faster, we'll get there in time for supper, and then be in Sapientia before noon tomorrow. Does that please you?" Hridnaya caught a glimpse of his courtly smile.

"Wait," said Kelji, not courtly. "Did you say 'we'?"

"Indeed, madam." He was trying to look confident, and failing.

"We agreed that you come and point me in the right direction, and you've done so. It was most helpful, I thank you. We follow the coast road straight west, and cannot miss."

He took a breath. "But I'll accompany you to Sapientia."

Ah, thought Hridnaya, puzzled, pleased and nervous.

"There's no necessity for that," said Kelji.

"I thought, madam, that you might like company or protection on the road." He smiled again.

"No, I need neither." And she knee-nudged her horse to start walking again, looking away from him, straight ahead.

Hridnaya had almost never heard an adult speak so rudely. *These foreigners.*

Mejorad stared. He motioned his own mount to follow. "Madam, it – it's a long way. You have no one to talk to – to explain -"

"I have my servants, if I wish conversation. This is a safe country, and we all speak the same language. I can hire a guide, and Vaddras will help me fight off any robbers." *Vaddras, he must be the groom.* "So, sir, farewell."

"Madam, that's absurd. You converse with equals, not servants. It's a free road!" he added suddenly.

"Are you stealing yourself a holiday, sir, or running away from home? You know I'm to be away from the city for three nights at least."

"Yes. And I'm to be away for five. I – my mother thinks I'm going to St Antonius' Monastery for a holy retreat."

Kelji barked a laugh. "I see. Why?"

Hridnaya was fascinated. He was a highborn noble of the b'Shen; he might be a murderer's accomplice; but he was also a silly youngish man, and the b'Nida had their share of such.

The horses had stopped again, twitching their ears.

"Why?" He was fiddling with the mane – he looked at the water, and then back. Grumpily, "I'm to be a priest someday, may it be long delayed, and so they want to send me to Defardu, and I objected, so she – my mother – wants me to go and pray until I'm meek and good. Kelji, madam," he said suddenly, "you've ridden all the way here from Makkera. Would you want to sit in a cell for three days, talking to God?"

A pause. Then, "I sat in my chamber for a month, talking to no one," said Kelji. "I shut the door on all the world."

"Wh -" and he plainly glimpsed her face, and decided not to ask.

The groom Vaddras had come up next to Hridnaya, and gave her a these-mad-rich-folk look. She just managed to give him one back before he looked away.

"Well," said Kelji then. "It's a free road. I'm talking to whom I choose, and I'm doing what I choose in Sapientia."

"Of course," he said, relief saturating his voice.

They moved on. *So I have three days to listen to him!* But Kelji hadn't finished. "One more thing. A free road, and a free inn.

I don't know what your customs are in Ricossa, but you do not touch me. Or her - them," she added, jerking her head back towards Hridnaya and Vaddras.

Embarrassment poured from the young man. "No, of course not! Eyanda told me – I know you have a husband back home."

"I have a husband."

I haven't, thought Hridnaya, and knew fear. (Sinavid b'Olim.) *I can't talk, but I can scream. But surely he'll obey her.*

They rode on.

*

It was a long time before Mej's cheeks were cool. Could she see inside his brain?

Yes, he'd tried a few thought-games on her, the kind he used to play with pretty women in the market or at church. In his imagination he'd said, as he'd heard other men say, "Even sweeter *under* her clothes, I assure you. One of my very best nights," and had pictured himself slipping his hand into Kelji's bodice, kissing her nose while unfastening – something –

It was never any good. Only the coldness deep inside, distaste and boredom. *Why do people want to do that? "Putting it where we both want it put," as they say? To get children, but why else?*

Rorash had been fifteen and Mej eleven, when they got confidential one evening about sin, sitting in a shadowy corner of the b'Shen hall with wine and dried fruits. Mej confessed to squashing a fat worm between the pages of his tutor's prayer-book, and Rorash laughed. "When you're my age, it's all about fornication. Or wanting to. Iggerd says it's the young man's curse." He looked away with an awkward smile. "I think about women's breasts all the time. Uh, not all, but a lot. You will too, one day."

"Ugh," said Mej, grinning.

Years passed, and he waited to become enraptured and obsessed, but it never happened, and he still thought, "Ugh."

More years, and he learned that some people, like Eyanda, preferred bedding with their own sex. Perhaps that was it, and he tried his thoughts on men: even on Rorash, who was perhaps dearer to him than anyone else. But there was still nothing. Fucking was married people's duty, and most people's pleasure, but not his, and he could never tell a soul.

*

At last Kelji turned her head back to her servants and said, "This would be a good place to rest. Do you think, sir?" to Mej. He agreed, and so it was. Green under trees on the left provided a shady place to sit. The animals, all five of them, needed water, and Mej decided to be helpful and assisted the groom to lead them down a path to the Lake.

The sand shifted under his feet. He stood listening to the beasts' splashing gulps, and watching sun sparkling on the water, and the Lake stroking the sand. His stomach bubbled at his success so far. And he looked over, far away –

Try as he might, he couldn't see the further shore. One almost never could. Up there, Beyond, was the north of Ricossa, lands of b'Iri and b'Asa, who raided each other when they weren't both busy keeping the foreigners behind their border. But beyond Beyond – Mej grinned. Through a mountain pass into the north-east portion of Jaryar, the part once called Marod, home of heroes.

"Barbarian heroes," most people said. But barbarian or no, who wouldn't dream of being named to Marod's Queen's Thirty, the warriors, judges, bodyguards of legend? Stories of their adventures were told all over Ragaris - the Oath branded on their shoulders, their unshakable comradeship and their undying loyalty –

The fights he and Rorash had had about them with that bully Martad b'Iri – all of them lost and painful, for Martad was bigger and stronger, and had lots of friends.

But Mej had been all of twelve before he'd finally admitted to himself that he would never be Mejorad Queensbrother.

Kelji might even know some of them.

"Ready, sir?" said the groom, and they walked back up the beach.

The two women had spread out a cloth to sit on, and produced linen-wrapped bread, cheese and dried fruit. *Is Nadya's kitchen always as dull as this, or is it Jaryari taste?* And the maid was reaching into one of the satchels for a jar of that disgusting stuff that babies and toothless ancients and the Voiceless ate. *I didn't know they had Voiceless in Jaryar.*

Then, *The Square, the other day!* The shock was sudden ice in the sunshine. *I knew I recognised her! But what –*

Kelji jumped him out of his bafflement. "You can give thanks to God for us. Since you're to be a holy man soon."

So he muttered a few standard words of prayer, and then opened his own satchel, and said with some smugness, "Can I offer you some cold goose, and apple? My sister taught me to take delicacies on a journey, and then eat them at the first stop while they're still fresh. And I have wine."

He was rewarded with Kelji's gracious-queen look. "I thank you, very much. Is there enough for us all?"

Her groom, whose name was Vaddras, stared watchfully towards the animals as they ate, but the four of them sat together in the sun almost like friends, a light breeze untucking the ends of Kelji's veil, and flapping Mej's hair round his face.

He tried not to look as the servant dipped into the jar,

and then into her mouth, pushing the food back with a finger as they had to. The groom stared in a frank way that Mej could see the woman didn't like; no one would. *So he doesn't seem to know her.*

She was in the Square, watching us. What's she doing here? Does she know Kelji, or is she spying on her, as Tor thought? Or even guarding her, without Nadya's knowledge? That makes no sense. Who's scheming here – is she working for one of the Families? Or the King's Cousins? Against whom? Or is this some Jaryari plot?

Kelji surprised him again. She slapped crumbs briskly off her hands, and brought out a piece of parchment. "Here is a pen," she said to the woman. "You need spelling. Write the first part of the Our Father prayer, as you guess it to be. I suppose you know it." And Vaddras was surprised by the suggestion, but the woman wasn't. She took the pen clumsily, and bent forward.

"May I ask, madam, what you are doing?" Mej asked politely.

"She can't talk, so I'm teaching her to read and write." He wasn't sure whether to say it out loud, but Kelji guessed. "Yes, she's the one we saw in the Square the other day, whom your man didn't like. I met her again, and this amuses me, and I hope will be of use to her, so I left my own woman back at Nadya's. She has plenty to do there." She leaned forward to correct the letters of "who". "You're doing well."

What the hell? Mej kept thinking, but he didn't get much further than that.

Another thought. *The Voiceless don't write. So maybe she's not – she could've lost her tongue another way, for blasphemy or perjury; something like that. She can't be the respectable mouse she's trying to appear.*

Should he warn Kelji? But warn her of what? He didn't

want to face her glare again – it was much too like Eyanda's. Twisting his mind more pleasantly, he pictured himself leaping up to save her from a murderous knife-attack – but in the sunshine it didn't feel likely. He lay back and squinted at the bright leaves above him.

*

Some years before, the b'Oto family had had a Voiceless servant, his head six feet off the ground, and always wearing a superior smile. Hridnaya hadn't liked him much, and never learned for sure if his name was Vidder or Fidder, but she saw him a few times at meetings and dinners. The b'Oto valued him highly, and when some of them arranged a pilgrimage to Saints' Landing, this man was chosen to accompany them. It was a reward for years of faithful service, a journey to see a bit of the world. The pilgrimage had been (it was said afterwards) a blessed and trouble-free fortnight, which he'd apparently enjoyed. Two days after their return, he'd hanged himself.

No one knew why. Hridnaya had always wondered, shuddering. This morning she'd thought, *Maybe it was too much sky. Too much space around. It's everywhere, I'm used to a box, a house.*

But after a few hours, she was fairly accustomed to the sky – and he'd had two weeks. And once he was back home he needn't ever have looked up again if he didn't wish to.

They packed away and remounted, and now they rode closer together, and she could hear what was said.

"So, tell me more of yourself, sir," Kelji ordered Mejorad with a smile. "Your noble family, and how you live when you are not praying at a monastery?"

He laughed, and Hridnaya felt hopeful, and prepared to listen hard.

But of course what he told was not what she wanted to

141

hear. He had an elder sister, with a brother-in-law and small nephew, and two little half-sisters. He'd spent much of his childhood on the b'Shen lands in the east, but was familiar with the City from annual visits. He'd returned six months ago from his year's military service. He enjoyed hunting and dancing, and said he played the rebec badly. It was all very normal.

"And Eyanda's sister – the new Queen – am I permitted to say that she was once your mother? That is a strange thing to me. Was she no kin at all to the previous Queen?"

"None. She was Chosen. Like your Queen Nerranya, I think?"

From his expression, he was quite pleased with himself for making this connection.

"I don't think it's the same. There was a dispute twenty years ago as to which of King Osgar's cousins should succeed him when he eventually died. My Uncle Haras was the other claimant. He and his friends went to the Great Council in Haymon, and Queen Nerranya sent her people also, and they talked and talked, and there was a vote, and our nobility selected her. But that's not the usual way in Jaryar, and Prince Gaskor Achad will inherit from her when she dies. Were you having such a discussion for Queen Rommi?"

"Ah, that's the Ricossan Secret. I know it, of course, but I'm sworn not to tell."

If you know it, the b'Shen are very careless, Hridnaya was diverted into thinking. *I doubt you're on their Conclave list.*

"I'll not ask, then. So you say you're to train for the priesthood?"

His face dropped, and he said, "Some day. I hope I can delay my departure till after the hunting season."

"Next spring?" said Kelji drily.

"What does your uncle think about the choice? When he

didn't win the throne?" he dared to ask.

Kelji looked at him, long enough to make his face awkward, but at last she answered, "It was long ago. Other people say it wasn't his most glorious hour, but he doesn't talk about it. He does his duty as Duke, but he only cares for -" there was an odd pause – "coddling his children - and hunting, like you."

They were quiet for a little, and then Mejorad said, "The other night you said you rode through Defardu to get here?"

"Yes. I was sent with two copies of the book, one for Prelate Susanna, and one for the Doctors. So I went to Vachansha first."

He didn't seem impressed that Kelji had met the Prelate herself, the head of all the church in Ragaris, but Hridnaya was. "What's the mountain city like?" he asked idly.

"Full of churches. The bells ring constantly and make your head ache," she said, not as if she were eager to go back.

"And at home – have you always lived in Makkera?"

"In Jaryar," she said, and her voice was suddenly hard again, "it is impertinent to ask too many questions."

"You were asking me!"

"You're Ricossan." *That doesn't make sense*, Mejorad was perhaps going to reply, when she spoke again. "Uncle Haras' home is in Vard-town, but I live in Makkera and serve the Queen there. I have two brothers and a husband. That is all you need to know."

She looked away, rude and silent again. *She avoids all private questions*, Hridnaya thought, almost feeling sorry for Mejorad. Her mule happened to shake its ears and twitch its head, and she jerked nervously. The man Vaddras put out a hand to stroke and steady it. He met her eyes and murmured softly, "Someone had to bring these books, and I'd swear they chose her to get her out of the city. None of our household could endure her temper any more."

Hridnaya smiled a little back at him, grateful for the confidence, but guilty also. Thus far, Kelji had been kind to her.

Very, strangely, kind.

It was going well, too well perhaps. As Kelji's maid, she'd be at tomorrow's feast, putting herself where surely someone would mention the name Dirria, and then, who knew? The blankness of that future made her uneasy – excited but a little sick.

"But she is a foreigner." Balki, posing as her conscience – or was it the other way round? – had questions. "She's been kind, yes. What will she expect in exchange? B'Nida secrets, or even Ricossan ones?"

I know very few of those, and I'll tell her none. I wish I could
pay for the lessons – I have money, after all. Then I wouldn't be so much in her debt.

"You do realise that Lady and Lord b'Nida will be at the feast also, and will see you there? They already think you're a spy. Will they decide you're working for the Jaryari, or the b'Astith?"

A convicted spy for Jaryar would be ripped apart, or worse. *But she's only just come here – how could anyone think she'd recruited me? And now I can write, I can explain.* The thought brought tears to her eyes.

"If they listen."

Shut mouth, Balki.

Truly they are very kind in Jaryar. Or – at least – Kelji has been kind to me. Perhaps on a whim. She isn't so courteous to Mejorad, or to her own maid.

An odd thought came to her then. *She's been very kind. But she hasn't asked my name.*

"God's greetings, madam. We're seeking rooms, stabling, supper and breakfast. One man, one woman, separately, two servants, five animals. Can you assist us?" Mejorad's tone, as he walked up to the innkeeper, had the confidence of his Family upbringing, mixed with the nervousness of a youngster eager to impress an older female. Or so Hridnaya thought.

A bent and wrinkled woman with pure white hair tied back, bobbed to him politely. "Most certainly, sir, we should be honoured. May I guess that you belong to the b'Shen?"

"Indeed. Mejorad b'Shen. This is Kelji, who is kin to the b'Astith, and we're travelling to the College."

Unlike Stansha's Inn, Rest After the Storm was a house set alone except for stables. It was only two storeys high, the roof was thatched and the windows were made of horn. There were rush mats on the floor of the common room, where benches gathered around a huge fireplace with a small summer fire. Candles stuck to the most basic of iron holders jutted out between bricks, seemingly at random. Hridnaya had never been in a place like this before, and felt a childish excitement. It was like somewhere out of Uncle Gridor's tales, and she almost expected an ancient hero or heroine – Dark Defani, say, or St Ansha-of-the-Sword-and-Cross - to leap through a door and start talking about dragons.

"You take our baggage upstairs. I'll help with the horses," Kelji said, brusquely – but perhaps brusqueness was the Jaryari way, and it was true Hridnaya was unused to stabling.

The white-haired innkeeper showed her upstairs to a room under the eaves, with three beds. Two were already claimed, to judge by the strewn possessions, including a white gown laid out in state. Hridnaya wondered if she would be sharing a bed with Kelji – if that was what grand folks in Jaryar did.

She hadn't slept in a bed with anyone else since her first
night with the b'Nida. Looking back, she saw her terrified child-
self, mouth seared with pain, and felt an ancient gratitude to
Narrim, who'd taken her into bed, and cuddled her kindly all
night.

It hurt to think of Narrim.

They weren't on a country frolic any more, so Kelji and
Mejorad sat at the long table for supper, and the others waited on
them. There were three more guests, a husband and wife who
had a chamber to themselves, their servants and their daughter on
her way to her wedding ("Ah, the white gown," said Balki.) The
innkeeper was assisted by a younger couple, plainly her children
or children-in-law, and occasionally a grandchild's face (five years
old or so) peeped round the kitchen door. Hridnaya thought Kelji
frowned at the sight.

Polite conversation was made during the meal, and then
the wedding party went out for a stroll, and there was a not-
bedtime-yet pause. "Are you wishing to see the Queen's gift to
your College before I deliver it?" Kelji asked Mejorad courteously;
and he of course answered, "I'd be delighted."

To Hridnaya, "Fetch my satchel."

Again, one of the b'Nida would have added, "if you
please."

As she came back down, she saw two heads bent
towards each other across the table, and heard "Nadya said
people are sometimes paid to watch for information."

"Yes, so she told me afterwards, but not this one, I think.
She has a lover or someone she's seeking in Sapientia." She
stretched out her hand for the satchel.

Probably all three had seen books before – Vaddras on
the journey, and the other two in Family libraries - but Hridnaya

tried to look duly impressed. And it was a handsome one: gleaming new leather, and lettering of inset gold on the front, and tiny beaded jewels.

"Pearls from the Bay of Marod?" asked Mejorad, touching gently.

"Yes. 'Of the Blessings of Poverty'," Kelji said. She opened it, not to the first page, but somewhere in the middle, where writing covered both sides. Hridnaya itched to test her new magic, practised over hours at Stansha's, and turn the scratches into meaning. "Try," said Kelji, pointing with a smile.

"For God did not" – she'd got as far as this, when Kelji read smoothly, *"For God did not merely die for us, but for our sakes became poor."* That was out of the Scriptures, Hridnaya thought. Something was glowing inside her that she didn't understand.

Kelji turned back to the beginning, a page where the letters were bigger, and there was a picture of a woman and man, Jaryari-clothed and crowned, on magnificent chairs. She read aloud, *"To the most wise and virtuous Nerranya Marial, and the most honourable Barad, Queen and King of the United Crowns of Jaryar and Marod –"*

Mejorad said, "A very holy book," not concealing boredom.

"You should be civil." Kelji glanced up at him. "Unless you wish me to inform Eyanda b'Shen where you didn't go today."

Hridnaya thought she was teasing, but Mejorad looked daunted, and improved his manners. "Who wrote it?"

"A most holy abbot from the north of my country, Paul of Lintoll. He was one of my Queen's delegates to the Council we were talking about, but he's been dead for years." She flicked slowly through the pages – thousands of words in black and occasionally red – and here and there a brilliant-coloured picture. Hridnaya's body leant forwards without meaning to.

Then the kitchen door burst open, and two small children ran in shouting. One was the boy Hridnaya'd seen earlier, and he was chasing a younger girl.

"Give it back!"

She was holding a cloth doll as far out of his reach as she could. "Ask with courtesy!" she said, in an adult-imitating voice.

"It's mine!" He was taller and stronger, and he twisted her wrist so that she let go, and squealed.

"I hate you, Dorrid!" She put her head down and butted him in the midriff, and they both fell over into an angry rolling fight. Doubtless an ashamed parent would appear at any moment, thought Hridnaya, hiding amusement – but Kelji jumped up with a gasp, slammed the book shut, and ran out of the room, up the stairs and away.

"What's wrong?" asked Mejorad.

Vaddras stood up. He seized one child's collar in each hand, tore them apart and tossed them into the kitchen, shoving the door open with his shoulder. Then he walked back over, and tapped the book with one finger. "She had a young daughter who died last year, and she ran mad. You'd think no one'd ever lost a child before. Screamed for a week, and locked herself up for nearly a month – quarrelled with her husband, dismissed half the servants."

"Oh," said Mejorad.

Vaddras gave a little snort, and turned away. "A good night to you, sir." He marched upstairs.

Hridnaya thought of Lulet, whose second child had breathed only for a day, and of her own dead sister Siri. Pity stirred in her.

But now she was sitting at a table with a man she wanted,

impossibly, to question – a man who might himself have questions about her – and a book. She peeped daringly at him, and he wasn't looking at her, but his face was suddenly ugly.

"What fools some mothers are," he said, flipping the volume open again. "Hmm." This page was partly writing, and partly illumination; it looked like the miracle of the loaves and fishes. He peered at the picture; Hridnaya peered at the words, and then remembered her place, and sat back meekly. "The most wise and virtuous Nerranya Marial," he quoted, staring down again. "Of course you know what they say of the Jaryari Queen. The Exile says, and he knows. Five children, and none of them by her husband, because he can't -" He stopped.

That's what that man tells us; what we want to hear.

Mejorad jerked the book towards him, and reached roughly to turn the page. He knocked Kelji's half-drunk cup -

They both watched crimson wine spill over the writing, bottom to top.

"Shit," he said. There was a pause, for nothing to happen. Then he grabbed the book away from the rest of the pool, and Hridnaya snatched up a napkin for the table.

They did their best. The page was wiped and gently scrubbed, and dried before the fire – but nothing could remove the purple stain from the cream, or smooth it soft. Mejorad pushed it across to her. "Put it back in the satchel. I wish you a good night." She heard his banging feet, as he disappeared upstairs.

So she packed it away, feeling sorrow that such a lovely thing had been spoilt. What would Kelji – or the College doctors – say?

Upstairs, Kelji seemed to have an embroidered garment to wear instead of sleeping in her smock or naked, as servants did. She gestured for the satchel to be pushed under the bed.

"Brush my hair."

So Hridnaya brushed, as she'd done for her employers so many times before (but Lindet would have said "thank you") and then she took off her outer clothes, knelt beside the other woman to pray, and got into bed with Kelji, back to back. She had been spoilt by having a bed of her own for years, and found it difficult to lie undisturbingly still.

*

It was morning, early. Birds were twittering not far above her head, and a dog barking outside. Her mistress lay curled, taking up most of the space. It was easy to half-slide, half-fall out onto the wooden floor. The room's other occupants were still asleep, the bride breathing noisily with her mouth open.

Hridnaya rubbed her face and washed it in the bowl provided, and then – was there really a reason not to? – slid the satchel out from under the bed. The book tingled under her hand. She carried it over to the small window and pushed the shutter a little apart to give her light.

Very, very carefully she turned to the first page, and the mysterious shapes obediently shifted for her.

"To the most wise and vir – virtuous Nerranya Marial, and the most –" Lots of long words.

"Do all books start like that, with queens and kings?" Balki wondered. Hridnaya shrugged, and turned the page.

There was a gorgeously-coloured picture of a building – one with no walls, as she knew was artists' convention, and a monk sitting writing at a desk inside. Outside, a rich-looking person in foreign clothes was giving money to obvious beggars, and more poor people were doing something with crops in the background. Angels reclined across the sky, pointing downwards.

She stroked the page very gently, and turned back to the

beginning, looking for short words that were easy to read.

"it seems plain that every man and woman has a duty to look around the place God has put them, and ask for what purpose they are sent?"

Ah!

Painfully, her eyes were full of tears.

It had been her secret belief for so long. *I don't just walk and eat and obey – I should, I can, wonder and ask.* Across the miles and years this Paul of Lintoll reached out to share the thought.

That's what books are for! Of course! So that people in all lands can search for knowledge and truth together. And now I can do this too!

She blinked and looked down again at the marks that were no longer merely magical, but miraculous. Breathing in joy. Breathing in a new life.

"That is not yours," said Kelji sternly, from behind her. She reached out, closed the book, and took it away. Hridnaya curtsied and wiped a tear off her cheek, aware of the other woman's suspicious look.

"Help me dress."

So they both dressed, and combed their hair – so much for the old tale that Westerners wore hats because they were all bald as eggs – and then went downstairs, and Hridnaya's head buzzed with almost too much excitement. Today she'd be in Sapientia. She might be able to learn about Uncle Gridor's visit. And *from now on* she was somehow going to use books to explore God and the world and justice, and what all of them meant.

She and Vaddras waited on their betters, and then ate themselves, quickly, while Mejorad stood around flexing his shoulders and toes, and Kelji paid the account, and looked again through her possessions.

There was a long angry gasp. Hridnaya looked up just in time to see the fury; and then Kelji hit her arm, harder than she'd ever been hit before. She gasped and fell against a bench.

"You insect! What have you *done?*" Kelji hauled her up to slap her cheek.

"What -" said Mejorad.

"Are you knowing what this is? Are you?" She shook Hridnaya's shoulders hard, and then threw her down to the ground. "It's a gift from the *Queen of Jaryar* to the Great College! It cost two years' wages to make! And you pick it up and ruin it – how can I explain this? I should whip the back off you!"

"Madam -"

"She was spying at the book this morning, and last night, and she's spilt something on it, wine or worse, damaged it – this can't be repaired! What can I say to the Doctors, and to my family, to the *Queen?* She trusted me! I'm shamed, and Jaryar is disgraced, thanks to you." She dragged Hridnaya halfway up, to slap her again. "I helped you! I was *sorry* for you, and I *helped* you, and this is how -"

"Don't, madam, it was an accident," said Mejorad.

Oh God, thank you!

"I mean, it must have been an accident," he said.

"I'm sure it was being a bloody accident! She'd no sense of its value, it didn't matter, just a lady's plaything! *Get up,*" she said.

Hridnaya got shakily to her feet. "*I didn't*" – *but he'll lie –* She barely glanced at him, and then back at Kelji.

"And you didn't have the courage to show me. I'd throw you out here and now, and let you walk back to the City, but I need a maid." She paused, slightly calmer, considering; then hit

Hridnaya once more, and turned away. "Get the horses," she ordered Vaddras.

"You fool," he muttered as he passed. Mejorad went out with him.

Hridnaya's head was ringing.

Woe to the rich, she thought. *Woe to the bloody rich.*

*

All the way to Sapientia Kelji fumed, and no one dared address her. Hridnaya's head was too full of confused feelings to bear. The Lake was no longer beautiful.

Once or twice Mejorad timidly pointed out a landmark. "Up that way to the left's called the Haunted Pool. I've never been there."

Hridnaya had heard of the Pool, something to do with the troublesome woman Mobira, but she didn't look up.

Slowly buildings became more frequent, and at last, almost noon, they were riding towards a high round tower by the left side of the road. Mounted people waited outside it, some of them in full-length gowns, College gowns. They must be College people.

The one in front was Lady b'Nida.

Hridnaya went cold and ducked her head down. *Don't notice me, don't see me, I'm just a foreigner's servant –*

"Kelji of Makkera? Be welcome, in God's Name." The front panel of Lady b'Nida's otherwise grey gown was chess-boarded with black and white squares. Hridnaya had never seen her wear this in City Qayn. "I am Irramatti, Lady b'Nida, Chancellor of the Great College. We are honoured by your presence, and your Queen's gift. Many of our Doctors have been eager to meet you, and to study the book. Please follow me, with your companions, to the apartment prepared." She spoke in her usual precise uninterested tones, and raised eyebrows not

153

towards Hridnaya, but Mejorad. Perhaps she was wondering what kind of companion he was - obviously neither servant nor foreigner.

"I thank your ladyship," said Kelji in her sweetest voice.

The Chancellor introduced some of her companions, but none of them was called Dirria or Ittrad. Hridnaya began to breathe. Then they rode together past buildings on both sides, tall and small, grand and lowly; turned left up a steep but smoothly-paved road with a few people watching, and passed through an arch that was almost a little tunnel.

Beyond was a square of uninterrupted building, set round a space of laid-out paths, low hedges and flowers. In its centre towered a pillar, like the ones in the Square in City Qayn. A clump of five or so youngsters was chattering and laughing together nearby. One of them tossed a money-pouch high in the air, and just missed catching it, to more laughter. Lady b'Nida tutted, and one of her companions strode towards them with a stern "Proper behaviour in the Quadrangle!" - so they bowed, smiling, broke into a two and a three, and strolled towards other doors. *Students,* thought Hridnaya. *These are the young people who study History and Latin and all that he said, whose conduct my Lady complains of.*

Lady b'Nida was being helped off her horse. "Your beasts will be stabled behind that side," she said, waving to the right, "and the guesthouse is over here. Krandether, show them, please."

"You go with the animals," Kelji ordered Vaddras.

The other three turned left, leaving the Lady behind, *thank you, Lord,* following a servant with a black-and-white tabard to an arch in the centre of the left-hand building. A magical staircase set within the wall led to a pleasant airy room, with bread and fruit and wine on a table. "If you wish to refresh yourselves, there are baths ready downstairs," said the man. Since they'd all ridden a long way in the heat, Hridnaya found time to wonder at his "if". "For anything else, please ask me or any other in this livery. The Doctors will soon be gathering for the presentation. Shall I come to escort you in two hours? There is a banquet afterwards."

"Thank you."

And so he left, and three of them stood in a rather empty room with a tapestry on one wall, and two carved chairs, and doors opening off. Mejorad opened them, and revealed, not surprisingly, bedchambers.

"You're still with me," Kelji observed, questioning.

"I'd be eager to escort you to the ceremony, if you're willing, madam," he said hopefully. "My – my cousin studied at the College, and I'd like to see it."

Your cousin Rorash, Hridnaya thought with hate.

Kelji shrugged, apparently an assent. Sweeping across to one of the doors, she jerked a furiously beckoning hand. She pushed Hridnaya into the inner room (two beds, a large window, a chest for linen). "You'll stay here until we leave tomorrow," she said. "This is an important day, and I don't trust you not to cause even more trouble than you already have. Vaddras will watch to ensure you don't damage anything of mine this evening." The door was shut.

The wonderful book which was to be presented today remained with her. Hridnaya would never see it again. Dirria would be at the feast, but she would not be. All her half-plans had depended on being in Kelji's favour.

There was a window to the room, a large one without glass, but it was upstairs and looked down on the main square (*Quadrangle.*) Looking out, she saw that there were constantly people passing through – not many, but always some.

She had some money, but not enough to bribe Vaddras. She had some parchment.

Hmm.

Perhaps an hour passed, perhaps more. Kelji came in, freshly bathed, to close the shutters, and be dressed in what must be her best gown, light blue on top of an undergown of purple, with embroidery round the neckline, and pearls on the little cap that was also purple. She went out again. Hridnaya heard the three others eat and drink in the outer room, fed herself water and mizzum from her own satchel, and waited.

At last she heard Kelji and Mejorad leave. Vaddras opened the door, glared at her, and closed it again. She thought she heard him walk to the other side of the room.

I'm thirty years old. I've had most of my life anyway.

She moved to the window. Outside was merry sunlight. There were a few people in the garden – one standing at a corner, two in the centre talking, another striding through. Hridnaya fluffed her thick still-short hair, to make it youthfully untidy. Then, cautiously, one leg first and then the other, she sat herself on the windowsill with her feet outside, and her satchel beside her.

It wasn't possible to get out without being seen, so she had to be seen but unsuspicious.

The ground looked a long way away.

I am a foolish playful student, she said to Balki. *Watch me play.*

Balki said, "You are a madwoman. You'll be killed."

Hridnaya twisted to look back into the room, made herself lift one hand in a happy gesture (the other clutching hard to the sill), and laughed aloud to Balki or some other unseen companion. She swung her legs carelessly. She knocked her satchel off the sill. "Oh!" *Not too loud.* Someone looked over. She turned back again, and mimed brief words. Then – *I can't, Lord help me* – she swung round, clutched the sill, hung by her hands, and dropped.

She landed hard, and rolled on stone paving. *Oww.* Someone laughed, not unkindly. She made herself get dizzily up, grabbed the satchel, and waved it in pretend triumph to the window above. And then walked as calmly as she could – but her legs were shaking – back into the tunnel. There was more laughter behind her, but no footsteps. No sound from Vaddras upstairs.

She paused just long enough to smooth her hair – arms trembling as well – and walked on through into the next Quadrangle. The College was made up of them, it seemed. *Remember how to get back.* This one had no hedges or pillar, only an empty paved centre. There were doors at each corner, and at the centre of each wall. At most (not all) of the doors a person sat or stood – servant or porter or guard, must be.

One of these people surely knew where to find Doctor Dirria.

*

Since they'd left Vaddras behind on guard, Mej wondered if he ought to offer to carry the precious book in its satchel, but Kelji kept it close to her side. They followed the College servant down the stair, out, and across the Quadrangle. Where Rorash might have been wandering, a few weeks ago.

His uneasiness about the maid had been prickling him. Perhaps he should slip her some money as compensation. And thinking of money –

"I owe you the cost of last night's room," he said.

"Yes, you do. I wondered if you'd remember that," said Kelji. His face burned. *Everyone knows they have no manners in Jaryar.*

Several people, old and young, turned to stare as they walked briskly by. There were a few whispers.

Still annoyed, he said, "Did you ever think of wearing our clothes while you're here? I'm sure Nadya could have found some."

She looked scornfully sideways. "You don't know your own laws. 'All foreigners in Ricossa must dress openly in their home style.' So they can be marked out as strange and untrustworthy. They were careful to tell me at the border. The penalties are severe."

"I didn't know."

They came to a dark doorway in the middle of the Quadrangle's side. The Chancellor, who looked ill at ease (she always did, he seemed to remember) was waiting for them with her maid.

"Will you come up, madam, and your companion of the b'Shen also?"

Kelji curtsied. She opened her satchel, and took out the book. No one would have known it was damaged. She had a wooden board the same size, so she could carry it flat, like a tray of meat, without her fingers touching the gleaming leather. The satchel she handed casually to the servant. "Thank you, my lady. I'm ready," she said.

So they were led up a dimly-lit stair. On the first landing, someone opened a door from within. As Lady b'Nida paused on the threshold, a voice cried, "Loose!" and two flights of arrows flashed across the entrance in opposite directions. Kelji and Mej gasped, but their hostess walked in calmly. They followed, and the servant came last; and as soon as all were inside - "Loose!" and another flight passed behind them. Mej turned, and saw three archers standing by the wall on each side, next to three targets. Arrows had landed in the exact centre of each.

Music was playing softly.

It was a long room, with large windows, and there were quite a lot of people in it, busy at various activities. A tall man whom Mej faintly recognised bowed. "My husband, Riodran, Lord b'Nida."

"I am honoured," said Kelji.

"The honour is ours. This is the Hall of Remembered Sorrow. On this site seventy-three years ago the Princess Ramielli was murdered and her home burned, leading to our most terrible war, which you have doubtless heard of."

Kelji nodded. "The War That Must Never Happen Again."

I told you that! He felt pride.

"Yes. Now it has a happier purpose. These are a few of the College students at practical study," said Lord b'Nida, and he also sounded proud. *It's your wife who's the Chancellor, isn't it, not you? But Uncle Yettrid says the College is the b'Nida obsession, and you certainly talk better than she does.*

The b'Nida couple led them straight down the middle. A dozen men and women were practising swordplay to right and left – very skilled, very fast. Mej reminded himself guiltily that he should practise more. Then on one side they saw an artist with her back to them painting at an easel, and on the other a table with something lying on it, and a group standing around -

"May I?" asked Kelji, and she stepped aside to look more closely at the table. *Ugh,* thought Mej as he followed. A newly dead person lay there, naked except around the loins, and a Doctor with rolled-up sleeves and a long knife had peeled off the skin from the arm. "Here are the muscles," she was saying, and young people nodded seriously.

"A great deal of skill," said Kelji.

"As you see, madam." Lord b'Nida.

Mej realised that these activities had been chosen from

different Schools. Was it all a show for Kelji to report to her Queen? It seemed so. They walked on past a large map of the stars, and towards the source of the gentle music, a lute and a rebec being played on either side of the far door.

For a moment he almost understood why Rorash had wanted to come.

Lord b'Nida leant towards his wife. He murmured very quietly, "Mobira is here." It seemed to Mej that the two shared an angry look, but their faces were blank almost at once. *Who's Mobira?* Then the guards opened the door, and they walked through to a room that was smaller, and less full.

In fact, his first thought was that there really weren't many people to greet them at all. A few miscellaneous servants round the walls, three – no, four – people in gowns, and two great chairs for the Chancellor and her husband.

This was going to be the tedious bit.

Lady b'Nida recited names, none of which was Mobira. (Bow, bow, bow.) Then she stepped aside for someone called Bekonin, First Doctor of Divinity. He was tall and thin, with eager protruding eyes in his brown face.

"I – ah – we – we -" Bekonin seemed to sense impatience. He drew up breath and height. "Madam, we of the School of Divinity are most ah, delighted to welcome you, and to receive this gift. Truly the actual words of Paul of Lintoll?" He wriggled a little. "We already have some letters of his, sent to my predecessor, but this is a very generous addition to our Library. We are most grateful to you, and to your Queen." He smiled broadly and joyously, and somehow the air around Mej and Kelji seemed to lift.

"It's my pleasure to be here," said Kelji. She held out her book. "'On the Blessings of Poverty', a work the Abbot started in the year 618 and finished in 625, two years before his death."

The Doctor stretched out eager hands and stepped forward, but someone else intruded from beside him. It was a youngish woman with hair scraped severely back from her narrow face. "As my elder Bekonin b'Olim says, it gives all of us at the College *great* pleasure to acknowledge the learning of one so unique, so rare as the Abbot. Here *at least* his words will be valued and studied, contemplated and revered. It rejoices us to see that even in the remotest north of Ragaris, *some few* have turned their thoughts to holy and deep matters. He deserves great honour." Her voice rang musically. Mej saw Doctor Bekonin almost frown.

"Thank you," said Kelji very very sweetly.

"You will privilege us by reading a passage? We'd all benefit from his words."

There was something wrong with the room, with the way it felt. It came to Mej abruptly that this pompous none-of-you-in-Jaryar-appreciate-learning doctor might think that Kelji couldn't read. Or might hope she couldn't, and that was the point of asking her. He was reminded of bullying captains in the military, and of worse memories (Martad and others) from childhood.

"As you wish, madam," said Kelji. She opened the book, a little awkwardly as it was still resting on a board, and read, as she'd read the night before, "*To the most wise and virtuous Nerranya Marial and the most honourable Barad -*" She turned several pages, and continued, "*Our Lord declared the poor to be blessed, and many have debated in what way -*"

She read smoothly, certainly as well as Mej could have done, and then she closed the book, and handed it to Doctor Bekonin.

"I thank you, we all thank you." His smile was warm.

"Yes," said Lady b'Nida, and hers was less so. She didn't

seem to know what to do next, but her husband said, "And you
also visited Vachansha? I envy you the sight of the holy city. We
can speak more of this at feast, I hope. Be welcome to the
College. And welcome also, Mejorad b'Shen."

Lady b'Nida gestured courteously to Kelji. They led the
procession, Lord b'Nida and Doctor Bekonin behind them, and
Mej with the unpleasant young woman.

They passed the showing-off students, to a grandly-
painted room across the stair.

I am actually starving. Food at last.

*

For the fourth time Hridnaya presented her parchment **I
SEEK DOKTOR DIRRIA** to a bored face. This was a plump
woman on a stool, patching a sheet - the dullest sewing. "Dirria?
Down the passage, first door. But why? Who are you?"

Hridnaya smiled as charmingly as she could, touching her
mouth. *Does she need a bribe?* But the other woman just
shrugged with the familiar look of slight distaste, so she stepped
out of brightness into yet another tunnel between Quadrangles,
past a stairway. There were two doors on the left of the tunnel. A
burly man leaning on a stick limped out of one and entered the
other. *Dirria is a woman's name,* she told herself, and knocked at
the door he'd left.

"Enter, please," said a courteous elderly voice.

It was another square room with narrow windows, but
her eye jumped to two whole shelves of books on the far wall.
There were cushions on the floor, an unlit brazier, and a tall desk.

The woman sitting at the desk and looking across at her
must have been beautiful once, and was elegant now. She was
tall and very thin, with fine features and smooth brown skin
beginning to wrinkle. Her hands were long-fingered. She wore

another of those long grey gowns, this one without a chess pattern.

"Be welcome. What is it?" she said, stepping away from the desk.

This is what I've come for. At last. What happens now?

Hridnaya curtsied as smoothly as she could, and handed over her second parchment. She watched the woman unfold it and start reading. She could hardly breathe.

What does happen now?

Hridnaya dawtar of Haidi begs to greet Doktor Dirria of the Grayt Collej. I am the nees of Gridor son of Arro sum times cawled flower in hood. I have lerned that you sawt to meet him and I seek your favour to tawk of wy that was and how he dyed. My unworthy prayrs and good wishes are yours.

"Aah!" It was a shrill croak. "No – go away!"

The Doctor was gasping, clutching her throat with one hand, and waving the parchment with the other. As Hridnaya watched in confusion, she stumbled across the room to bang twice on the wall. "Go – you – go away. There's nothing -"

As the man who'd just left the room limped briskly back in, she thrust the parchment at him. "Get her – get her out." She could barely speak for heaving gasps, and tears poured down her face.

The man gave Hridnaya a stern look, before putting one arm round the woman, and guiding her to her seat. "Breathe, madam. I will deal with this." He found her a cup and poured wine into it. She sipped, gasping less.

Hridnaya stood scared and wondering.

The man stepped between her and the crying Doctor. He put one hand on Hridnaya's shoulder, and with the other managed to hold her parchment as well as his stick. Like the Doctor, like the Lord and Lady, he could read without moving his lips. Then, "You will leave," he said sternly. "This was ill-done, to scare her." She found herself being pushed lurchingly out of the door, back into the dim passage between two places of light.

"The Doctor's done nothing wrong. Do not come back. Ill-done," he said again, slowly, "to harass her without warning or reason. You have no appointment, or introduction or token of goodwill. Leave her alone. Go now."

But.

"Go."

She turned, and wandered a few steps the other way, avoiding the sewing woman.

Why? What's so wrong?

So it stops here. I can do nothing more.

Please, no.

"*Without warning or - what did he say? No 'token of goodwill?'*"

She'd gone a few paces. Now she spun and ran back, like a child. The man was still opening a door when she reached him and went down on her knees. She flung open her satchel and searched desperately.

"What are you doing?" he said, unimpressed.

Hridnaya thrust the napkin Brinnon had given her up at him. The one saying Ittrad.

A few heart-beats passed.

Then, clearly and loudly, "I am not interested in your tales of woe. Many people are far worse off. I can spare you a penny, but do not come back here again. Get up."

As she rose, he was fiddling in his pouch for the penny. He shifted to block the portress' view, and said low, "Go out of the College – there's a tavern two right turns away, Singing Frogs.

In one hour." Louder, "Here you are. Now *go.*"

*

Today, very unusually, Mej was going to be one of the people who process into a feast while everyone else stands up in dutiful respect. He was looking forward to this. Fortunately he'd thought to bring his decent green gown with cream sleeves. His time in the military had taken off some weight, so that the garment now had more space across the shoulders, and the swing of cloth round his knees was pleasant.

Before the procession, however, there was another immensely tedious time in an upstairs chamber, when Kelji was presented to every one (it seemed) of the College doctors – First Doctor of History, Second Doctor of This, Third and Least Significant Doctor of That, and so on and on. Kelji curtsied over and over, and smiled her sweet smile. The Doctors bowed or curtsied back, some looking more sincere than others. A few stared openly. Only about half of them were Family members; the rest commoners. Almost all were oldish, dullish people. Mej – and possibly Kelji also – listened carefully for the name Mobira that had unsettled the b'Nidas, but it was not spoken. And then Lord b'Nida gave Kelji his arm, a steward arranged everyone in couples, and they all walked downstairs, into a huge hall.

It must have occupied the whole of one side of the Quadrangle, and it had an open arch two-thirds of the way down to hold the roof up. Dozens and scores of students stood in rows by tables, glancing up from meat that they daren't yet touch as the great ones swept by. Mej grinned to himself. Beyond the arch, the tables were polished and laid with cloths and silverware – and set out in a large rectangle, so that the thirty or so higher guests could look at each other while eating.

Mej was walking again with the woman who'd made Kelji read, the Second Doctor of Divinity, whose name he'd learned was Akraib. Just as the last person found his chair, he saw her bend towards Kelji opposite, and heard her say, not as quietly as one might have expected, "Did you not bring your own maid, then?" A question that could have been asked in private, any time in the last half-hour.

"No."

"Ah? We can provide." Servants were waiting all round the walls, of course. Lady b'Nida put on a holy expression, and prayed a loud prayer, and throughout the hall everyone sat down.

Mej didn't remember much about the feast afterwards. It wasn't an entertaining event. Musicians stood in the far corner and played, so quietly they were a faint irritation rather than a pleasure. The plates gleamed and the service was flawless, but the food itself only mediocre, and lukewarm. The raised pigeon pies had almost dried up. As for the wine, it fell far below the standards of The Dog and Boot. He saw Kelji's face as she tasted it, and almost laughed.

Perhaps it was boredom that made her say suddenly, "Is there not a Doctor Madrasun here? I understood it was he who wrote to my Queen to invite me? I was hoping to pass on her good wishes."

Someone in the hall, or more than one person, jerked a little. A voice said, "There was -" but Lord b'Nida, next to Kelji, took it on himself to interrupt.

"Madrasun b'Olim sadly died last autumn. He was the second Doctor of Law, a post now held by Dirria here." (Courteous nods along the table between Kelji and presumably this Dirria.)

Bekonin said, "He handled all our correspondence with Makkera. I think it was Madrasun's dream to have such a visit as this, and such a gift. We miss him sorely."

There were agreeing insincere murmurs of the kind that

Mej knew well. After a pause, a fat man asked yet another question about the weather in the Defardi mountains; and it all became so dull that Mej stopped listening to the words, and just watched faces.

Doctor Bekonin glowed with excitement, and almost forgot to eat, but he was the only one. Lord and Lady b'Nida looked very determinedly calm, he thought, as if waiting for someone to drop something. Akraib watched the guest with a maliciously superior smile. Some people were mainly interested in the food; others looked nervous. And one or two seemed to be catching each other's eyes, exchanging smirks. What was that about?

He caught himself wondering if he should put a cake or two in his pocket for Nameless Woman and Vaddras, as he would've done for his sisters, but that was absurd. They were adults: someone would feed them. And he needed to plan what he was doing next. He had at least one day and night to fill while Eyanda expected him to be praying. And what after that? *How much longer can I keep Defardu at bay? Would they take me back to the army anyway?*

Familiar questions.

Someone placed a dish of custard and strawberries before him. "I thank you." And Akraib was saying, "Our library does have a half dozen other books from the West, but no more than that. Do any people in Jaryar read?"

Nasty, Mej thought.

"In Jaryar," said Kelji, "some people read a great deal, others a little; and most not at all. Is it not the same here?"

"The common people don't read in any land, I think," Lord b'Nida agreed, and Mej caught himself feeling gratitude - pompous broom-handle though the man was.

Again his eyes caught a smirk from the far corner, and

Akraib, he thought, was smirking back. Like – yes, like children or servants who know that one of their number, not them, is about to be in great and painful trouble. Probably it was just one of the cooks.

He enjoyed the strawberries, and went back to his own thoughts.

*

Hridnaya found Singing Frogs at last, but it wasn't two rights. Right, *left*, cross over the road and right again. She wasn't sure if the discrepancy reassured or alarmed her. Having found it, she had time to wander back to a small shop and buy herself more mizzum; then back to the Frogs.

Ordinary-looking people, some perhaps students, were sitting outside on sunny benches, but she walked in out of the public light. She wasn't used to taverns, but Brin and Lindet b'Nida visited them, and Aunt Miya worked at one. She bought a cup of ale from the dark-skinned man at the table with barrels, and found a place to sit and wait, back to the wall.

What now? What this evening, tomorrow, next year? *I've had more than half my life*, she told Balki again. *It doesn't really matter if I die soon.* But her heart seemed to thud in her throat, and Balki raised a sceptical eyebrow.

There were uneven footsteps, and then he was standing looking down. He was broad-shouldered and thick-armed; round-faced, with a curly black beard hugging his cheeks and chin, and hair tied untidily back. His jacket and hose were plain and old, but he wasn't wearing a College tabard. So was he Dirria's servant or not? Could he be one of the Cousins?

"I gave you bad instructions. I'm sorry." He pulled out a chair. "And this is a discourteous question, but would you open your mouth?"

It was very discourteous, and she stared. He twisted

round with a soft grunt to pull over a lit candle from another table. "Or I can leave."

So she opened her mouth, and he held the light to peer in, satisfying himself that she was indeed tongueless. "I read your document. You wanted to talk to the Doctor about Flower-in-Hood?"

She nodded.

"And your name is Hid - Hridnaya? You showed me a cloth. Where did you get it from? Can you write?" he added.

She wanted to slap him or cry. Of course she did neither, but scrabbled for pen and ink. He waited in horrible silence while she wrote **My ant found it in my uncles sachel after he dyd**.

"I see." The man leant back. She dared to meet his eyes. He said slowly, "I'm Ittrad, son of Ambario, and I gave that to Gridor to use as a password. Now I think I've asked enough questions, and it's your turn. But first. First. I should warn you that Dirria sent a message to tell – someone - about your visit."

Who? Kelji, or Lady b'Nida?

He was standing up.

"Second, I'm getting something to eat. You're my guest – er, a bowl of porridge, or a meat pasty?" He spread out one hand for each option, so she only had to nod an indication. Porridge should be possible. The order was given, and Ittrad manoeuvred himself down again. He took a piece of parchment from his belt, and a pen from his pouch, and pushed them towards her.

"Your turn."

She sat baffled; then slowly,

How did you and Doktor Dirria no about my uncle.

Faster, **Wy did he come to see her and wat did she tell him.**

Wy did she send me away. Wat do you no about his deth.

Almost she added, **Can I trust you**, but there was no point.

He read the words, pulling in his lips thoughtfully. At that moment a tray arrived, porridge for her, broth, bread, ale, and a hunk of cheese for him.

"Blessed be this food to us, and blessed be Thou for the gift." Ittrad took two rapid spoonfuls, tore off a piece of bread and said carefully, "Your uncle. I was sent to talk to him – I should start earlier. I don't know how much you know about the way the College works." *More than you think.* "Dirria, daughter of Serada, is the Second Doctor of Law. She hasn't held that post long. When she was appointed, she was looking through papers left behind by the Doctor before her, and there was a letter." He paused to bite, and check with a glance that she understood what a letter was. "It was written last year by some priest in the City, addressed to the Bishop. The priest wrote on behalf of a man who had questions, Gridor. He'd asked whether -" he looked across at her, and took a breath – "whether the Families and the realm have a good enough reason for what the Voiceless have to endure."

Hridnaya's eyes stung.

"The Bishop hadn't been interested in this letter herself, and passed it to the former Doctor of Law, Doctor Madrasun, her cousin, and he wasn't interested either, so nothing happened till it came to Dirria, at the beginning of this year. She was curious about the man Gridor and his questions, and she sent me to find him and arrange a meeting if I could. In private, of course. Questioning anything about the New Governance may be unwise. So I got a ride to City Qayn, and spoke to the priest, and she told me where your uncle worked, and I found him and followed him home."

Ah. At long long last, something was beginning to fit

together. ("He walked with a limp, he had a stick, but I think he was quite young, not thin," Brin had said.)

"Your uncle didn't want to worry his wife, so we went to a tavern. He was eager to see Doctor Dirria, but he'd need time to arrange to come to the College, so I gave him the token. In case he needed help finding me, and to prove to the Doctor who he was, if I wasn't there when he arrived. Then I came back here, and we waited."

He took another spoonful. So did she, watching him. "I know he died here, and I suppose he must have been trying to reach Dirria, but we never saw him – I certainly didn't. But *then -*" He paused. "A woman, a woman who watches people here, came to see Dirria, and told her a man called Flower-in-Hood had died in a tavern, and she should be warned by his fate to stay out of such matters. And everyone was already talking about the student arrested for manslaughter or murder. So Dirria was very frightened. And puzzled.

"You may not believe me, but I swear," he waved his arm about vaguely, "we, at least I, had never seen Gridor after that once. So I've answered your questions."

She had more, and reached for the parchment, but he put a finger on it. "My turn. It's weeks since he died. Why are you here, madam? What do you want?"

He went back to his broth.

She wrote slowly, **I want to no the truth. And I want justiss**. Then she waited while he thought.

"Don't you have that already? Rorash b'Shen's a harmless fellow; he didn't mean to kill, and he was sent to Defardu."

Not enouf. You said a woman scared the doctor and I think some one scared the preest. Wy woud they do that if

theres no secret.

Ittrad pushed his bowl away, looking at the wall. Then he leaned forward, fingering his piece of bread. "It's true, that looks odd. People spy in the College, of course. This woman who came spies for King Aigith and his Cousins. 'Gathers information', I should say, not 'spies'. She used your uncle's death as a threat, and she did seem to know about it very quickly, as if she was keeping track of him – but that doesn't mean it was murder. I see no reason to kill him, or how: It was just a tavern fight, they said. I don't know the details. Do you?"

I no wat they said at the tryl. I was there. They said it was a brawl but I think sum one was lying.

Ittrad lifted his spoon and twirled it round the bottom of the empty bowl. "I don't know how I can help you. Dirria can't."

Daren't.

Hridnaya put her fingers to her forehead, and tried to think. He waited while she did, picking up all the crumbs with a fat forefinger, and eating them.

You folowed him to his hows. Was he alone.

"No, there was another man with him, but your uncle was distinctive, with his flower."

That was my bruther. He saw you. How offen and wen. Plees, she added politely.

"Just once. It was the Thursday after Easter. The College has a week's holiday."

Other peopil were waching him to. He told his wife. A man and a woman. She had a thought. **Hoo was the woman hoo threttened the doctor.**

Ittrad didn't speak. He took the pen from her, and wrote,

Her name is Mobira. Hridnaya had already guessed. **And she's the one Dirria sent to after you came today.** He watched her read this, and then he scratched the words out.

(*Mobira. Venomous Mobira, whose very name makes Lady b'Nida scowl.*)

Uncle Gridor's death is connected to her? How?

The people Brin and Miya said watched him -

Wat does she look like. ("Middle years, and very pale, and fair-haired, not grey but like straw," Aunt Miya said.)

"Like anyone else. Plumpish, brown. Younger than you or I, maybe twenty-five at most." Then he asked, "What are you doing here? Have you no employment? And writing?"

I werked for a family. They fowned me looking at books and thowt I was a spy. Im here with a woman with an errand. Suddenly she was enormously tired. With a great effort, she wrote, **Hoo is Rorash bshen. Wat is he lyk.**

"Rorash? The one who killed your uncle." Ittrad sat back. "I didn't know him well. Students study here for two years, you know, or else for seven. Most of the ones from the Families, like him, come for two, and they don't have to pay. I'm in my fifth year, and my lectures aren't free, so I serve the Doctor to pay my dues." Hridnaya nodded, placing him at last. He was a servitor. It was restful to be told things she already understood, and she needed something to be restful.

"So you see, every year new high people from the Families come, and they find it strange. Suddenly they can't have servants and swords, and there are rules. And they have to mix with lowly folk, like us. We watch them, see how they manage." His solemn face smiled at Hridnaya. "Rorash had rather expensive clothes – so people told me; I know naught about dress – and he didn't like sitting in the dust at the Doctors' feet. But otherwise he settled well. He wasn't arrogant; he seemed eager to learn. I had no classes with him. I do remember his mother came to visit him, and afterwards I heard he told someone it was very kind of her, but he'd rather have seen his daughter." Hridnaya's face must have shown surprise. "Yes, the gossip was he was missing his former lover, and their child.

"He didn't like being a bastard, that everyone knew. He'd always give his name in full, Rorash Adam – and glare. But there was nothing to dislike. I can't believe he'd -" his voice slowed – "that is, I wouldn't expect him to commit murder, and not for the King's Cousins. And they don't kill people anyway. I'm still hungry. D'you want anything more?"

Hridnaya shook her head, and watched him order himself a second bowl of broth.

It disappeared fast. When it was gone, he said, "You seek truth. The truth is that someone, or some people, were watching Gridor, and used his death as a threat, but none of that proves it was intended. I don't know what else you could do – talk to the tavern owner?" The word "talk" seemed to strike them both at the same time. "I've been to The Morning Dream once or twice. I doubt Bada'd be able to read a message. Hridnaya," he said abruptly, "if you lost your place, how did you get here? D'you have somewhere to sleep tonight? I'm, I'm not permitted to have guests."

I have a playse. Perhaps she still did, and the streets weren't cold.

"I should go. I'm sorry I wasn't more help. Can you think of anything else?"

She shook her head, and they both stood up and bowed;

a small bow only, since neither was a great person.

"Gridor talked of you, his niece." He paused awkwardly. "Madam. I – haven't yet given you my, my small share of your sorrow. What your uncle was trying to do - it was astonishing. I don't know if Dirria would've been able to help. The College has very little influence on law. But he deserved better than he got.

"Be careful. I've never lived in the capital, but Sapientia isn't as pretty as it looks. The King – God save him – thinks he may have enemies here. Some people twist anything, and report it where it does harm. It's quite hard to keep honest."

I've known dishonest people, thought Hridnaya bitterly. Then, *I've become dishonest myself.*

"Oh, and, forgive me, but next time you're writing -" Ittrad reached out for the parchment and drew a squiggle and a dot. "This means your sentence is a question." He smiled quickly, and walked away.

*

He was gone.

Hridnaya sat back down, hands cradling her mug.

Can I trust him? How much – or how little – have I learned?

She wondered what happened next. Somehow over the last few days she'd become a person who jumped from reckless action to reckless action, with no firm ground to settle on; and no proper place to sleep. She didn't like turning into that person, and yet she couldn't seem to stop.

And she was so tired. This day had been one strange event, one unexpected feeling, after another, and nothing familiar anywhere. She stroked the hard wooden table with a finger, wishing she could put her head down on it and go to sleep. "Are you going back to Kelji?" asked Balki. *Where else can I go?* She'd left a note: **You have an errand. I have one to. You can hit me**

wen I come bak.

Was there anywhere else for more information? The Morning Dream, and the quarrelsome customer there? Or the wagoners who carried people along the Lake road for money? They might be able to tell her when Uncle Gridor'd arrived, and what he'd talked about on the way. But none of these people would be able to read. She could ask them nothing.

Perhaps it's time to say, "I'm at the end. Yes, all the rich people are right. Dirria never saw him. No one planned to kill him. It was an accident"?

But why Mobira? And he said in the tavern that he was being

followed, not just sometimes, but that very night.

She'd put the parchment away, but she lifted a finger and traced on the table, **Almytee God I pray that I will not giv up.** Then she sat and looked at the invisible words.

And went on looking, thinking of less and less, until a woman shook her shoulder and said, "I fear you can't sleep here, madam. Do you wish to buy another drink, or is it time to find your home?"

She owed it to Kelji not to disappear.

*

Mej and Kelji were escorted back to the guesthouse by the silent servant Krandether. Lights in windows looked friendly as the sky dimmed.

Softened by food, even unimpressive food, and glad to be away from Doctor Akraib and the b'Nidas, he looked more kindly at his companion. "What are you thinking?"

"That it's over," said Kelji. She didn't smile or look softened at all. He wondered again about this odd-humoured creature, with her faraway unmentionable husband - and her

176

dead child – and her mission that surely anyone else could have done.

They walked into the tunnel between Quadrangles, lit now by torchlight bouncing in a cresset. Mej saw a black-and-grey jacketed woman Guard standing at the foot of their staircase. She bowed in response to his gracious smile. Krandether left them.

The two went silently up the stairs. A dull evening they were going to have – *maybe I can slip out to a tavern for a game of dice?* He pushed open the door to their set of rooms.

Several tall candles had been lit. Vaddras was there, and three strangers.

Two were more Guards, either side of the door. And they also wore grey jackets with black sleeves – these were the King's people, not the College's. Sitting opposite was a woman in single-colour dark green jacket and hose, middling size, Kelji's age or younger.

"God give you good evening, madam and sir," she said.

Kelji and Mej blinked. "And to you," said Kelji. Then, "The Chancellor allocated us these rooms. Are we being asked to share them?"

"No, madam. I have come to talk. You may remember seeing me before dinner, when you met the Doctors, and gave Bekonin your book?"

Yes, Mej thought, *she was there, silent and not introduced.* He was puzzled – her arrogant manner was out of keeping with her plain clothes. She wore no jewellery, not even a circlet on her head. Her light-brown face, broad at the hairline, and pointing down like a triangle, was very ordinary.

Suddenly he thought, *This is Mobira.*

"Who are you?" asked Kelji.

"I serve King Aigith. And you, of course, are Kelji the

Foreigner." She put her head on one side, as if to charm away the rudeness of the words.

Kelji smiled almost as sweetly. "My name is Kelji, daughter of Shanell. I was sent here by the Queen of Jaryar, my cousin, and I come from Makkera, the finest city in Ragaris."

"The proudest, certainly. Who did you bring with you to Sapientia?"

Confused, Mej supposed she meant him, although her gaze didn't waver from Kelji's face. "I'm Mejorad b'Shen, accompanying the lady on my Family's behalf. She's the guest of one of my mother's friends."

"Charming." She barely looked at him. "What servants are with you?"

"I see no reason to answer these questions until you explain who you are, and what you're doing here," said Kelji. She took off her cloak and waved it imperiously for Vaddras to take. But his face, Mej saw, was screwed up with a message he couldn't deliver out loud.

"I'm sorry you don't wish to co-operate with the King's courteous enquiries," said the woman. Her smile was now even less pleasant than Doctor Akraib's.

Kelji shrugged. "I brought a groom and a maid to Sapientia. This is the groom, and the maid's in there." She waved, and started to move towards a chair.

"Is she?"

"Madam," said Vaddras, "she – she got out."

Kelji strode to the inner door, and flung it open. There was no one. She turned back, fury-faced. "Well, then, she's dismissed."

"A little harsh," said the strange woman, "considering she went out on your work."

"What nonsense."

"Queen Nerranya sent you to spy, and you bribed that rat to assist you."

What?

He thought he felt Kelji's shock, but she said firmly, "That isn't true, and you will leave this room."

The woman sat back comfortably. "The room belongs to the College, not to you. Contrary to what you may have thought, Doctor Dirria is loyal to the Evening King."

"Who is Doctor Dirria?"

"Perhaps your maid, your *agent*, can remind you, when she returns - if she does. And tomorrow I will accompany you back to City Qayn. You were travelling back to the b'Astith's in any case, were you not?"

Kelji said firmly, "I am a guest in this land, and I'm not a spy."

"You can try to prove that at your trial."

"I've done nothing to be tried for! What are you accusing me of?"

"I don't make accusations. That'll be for other servants of the Evening King, in due time."

The two women stared at each other, both (Mej thought) accustomed to winning glare-battles. But it was Kelji who looked away, and moved to sit down.

Bewildered, Mej wondered in the quiet what to do. He was here with Kelji – but he didn't have to be – his loyalty had to be to the King – *could* she be a spy, and the Voiceless woman her assistant? Kelji had seemed very angry about the book this morning, not as if they were working together. *And how can someone without a tongue spy?*

He could walk out now, and find that tavern. Eyanda would want him to support Nadya's guest. The most important thing was not to bring any danger or disgrace on the b'Shen.

He decided for the moment to stay, and wandered over to the window. He had to force his legs to move again, and the sound of his shoes was loud.

Kelji said to Vaddras, "What d'you mean, 'she got out'?"

"I thought she'd been very quiet, madam, and about a half hour ago I looked in, and she was gone. She's taken her satchel. She must have climbed out of the window."

"Ungrateful beggar!" said Kelji. "Give me some wine."

He poured for her and for Mej, and then caught his mistress' eye questioningly. "Yes, offer to all our guests." Mej admired the subtlety of the insult, putting the woman in the same category as the Guards by the door.

They all drank. Then there was a long pause. The sky was growing darker. Kelji sent Vaddras for her satchel, and drew out some embroidery. The Guards stood like blocks, but Vaddras fidgeted. The green-jacketed woman sat and smiled. Mej stroked the shutter.

Looking down after a time, he saw a small figure walking across the Quadrangle. It was her. She must have expected to be in trouble, but she probably didn't know how much, and he felt a pang of pity. She disappeared into the tunnel.

He waited for light steps. Perhaps she would pause before coming in. The way he used to stop outside his tutor's door, when he anticipated whipping.

But the steps did not come.

To the most wise and virtuous Nerranya Marial and the most honourable Barad, Queen and King of the United Crowns of Jaryar and Marod, this book is offered in humble duty by Paul Tommid, Brother of the Church and Abbot of Lintoll.

In these pages I will ask the meaning of Our Saviour's words "Blessed are the poor", which are found in the sixth chapter of the Gospel according to St Luke, and again "Blessed are the poor in spirit" which are found in the fifth chapter of the Gospel according to St Matthew.

It may rightly be asked why this most ignorant monk should presume to address such deep matters as are contained here. I am not competent to do so. But despite my inadequacy it seems plain that every man and woman has a duty to look around the place God has put them, and ask for what purpose they are sent? One may say: I am a Queen, and another: I am a beggar. But each is more than that. We have not only places to serve, and neighbours to love, although this is not little; but each has their own heart, soul, mind and strength, and each is called to serve God with all their being. I have known a warrior who was also a poet, a physician who was also a wrestler, and a milkmaid who was also a prophet.

Even a queen is not only a queen.

And so when thoughts came to me, even me, a great sinner and once a criminal, I made bold to write them down for the benefit it may be to others of God's people who read.

Part Three

How To Deal With Troublemakers

Lulet almost ran into the house. Friday evening, only one more day at the potter's till Sabbath, with its glorious rest.

"Mumma's home!" cried Minna, racing her brother over. "Mumma, that girl Hoka stole two nuts today! She did! Brovver Flip wouldn't b'lieve me!"

The priest who supervised the nearby childpen was surprisingly tolerant of Minna's righteous complaints.

"Broth-er Phil-ip. Tell me about it when I've rested. Now, Jof, look at that nose."

Minna giggled. "You can't look at your own nose, Mumma." She squinted in demonstration. Lulet searched for a clean cloth to wipe her son's face.

"Did your great lady customer approve what you'd done to her bowl?" Brin, smiling, poured chopped-small beans into the stew-pot over the fire. They smelt good.

"She made a lot of unimpressed faces," said his wife, who spent her long and eye-straining days mending other people's crockery and hiding the cracks, "but at last -"

Someone banged on the door, un-neighbourly loud. Lulet's heart thumped foolishly.

A tall thin woman in a long gown and a man with a pockmarked face swept in. *Who -? Haven't I seen you before, somewhere?*

Both wore purple tabards, so that meant – The man shut the door.

"God's blessings on this house," said the woman.

"Be – be welcome, my lady." Lulet curtseyed. Brin stood

up.

"I wish to talk to Hridnaya, daughter of Haidi. I am the Housemother of the b'Nida. Can you be kind enough to tell us when she'll be back?"

The Housemother! She came to bring us news when Hridna was ill that time. She was kind -

"I don't understand, madam," said Brin slowly.

"Hridanaya is your sister?"

"Yes, she is, but she doesn't live here. She lives with the Family – with you, madam, on Scholars' Street."

"When did you last see her?"

Husband and wife looked at each other. "She – she last visited us one Sunday – it was about three or four weeks ago." While Lulet was still speaking, the Housemother nodded to her companion, and he marched to the beds to pull open curtains. Lulet stared; so did the children.

"Three weeks ago?"

"What are you doing, sir – she's not here! Is she ill?" asked Brin.

The man pulled the bedclothes about roughly, very plainly ensuring that nobody was crouching behind them. One of the curtains fell down.

"Did she not tell you?" asked the b'Nida woman. Stared at, she marched across and lowered herself onto the chair. "Two Wednesdays past your sister was caught spying for one of our enemies, and was dismissed." Lulet felt her mouth fall open. "She took herself to an inn in Kitten Street, but yesterday evening she didn't go back there. She will be with the people paying her. It will be better for you and your family, and for her, if you tell us where to find her now."

"Please, madam, this doesn't make sense. Hridna would never do that!" Brin took one step forward, and then stopped.

"But she did."

Lulet said, "We haven't seen her since that Sunday, madam, my lady. She came to collect a cloak my husband made for her."

"She told you nothing? We are to believe that?" There was anger and contempt in her voice and face – and even hurt, Lulet thought. All for Hridnaya.

"She can't talk!" said Brin. "She – she looked unhappy, that's all. How can you have dismissed her? She's done nothing!"

"She was spying," said the man behind his shoulder, so that he jumped.

But he said, "Are you saying she's disappeared? What did your people do to her?"

The man hit the back of his head, and he staggered. "Watch your mouth."

Minna squeaked, and Lulet clutched the child's shoulders. "Ssh." Jof began to cry.

"When you see her again, you will report immediately to the b'Nida house. Not to anyone else. And you'll regret it if you're lying."

The Housemother was standing up, but Brin looked at her and said, "I don't believe this."

No, dearest, don't!

The man hit him again. Then he looked around, and stepped over to the fireplace. He tugged down the children's silly dangling egg-shells, and crushed them under his boot. The two walked out.

In trouble with one of the Families: every commoner's nightmare. *Gridor was bad enough, poor dear man, but what has she done?*

Both children clung to Lulet's legs, wetting and staining her skirt with snot and tears.

"Where is she?" Brin whispered. "What have they done to her?"

*

There was a Guard, a blank-looking sturdy woman, at the foot of the guesthouse stair. King's livery, not Palace. *Oh, Lord God!*

Hridnaya walked straight past her, just a servant, and wasn't stopped. A moment later she was through in another square, turning right for no reason. There were torches at the corners, but almost no people. The respectable were going to bed.

Guards meant someone was waiting for her - to arrest, torture, kill her. Who? Kelji, Dirria, Lord b'Nida? Or even Venomous Mobira, enemy of the College and (if she believed Ittrad) somehow involved? More trouble and danger, unbearably *more*. She had no friends, and nowhere to go.

It's too much, Lord God, please!

She needed a place to hide; a place where no one could look out from a window and spot her.

"What d'we know about the College?" Balki squeaked in her head.

Not much about its geography.

The College has cells and rooms for sleeping, and teaching - and large halls to eat and lecture in. It has a chapel and I suppose storerooms, and a library-scriptorium. No taverns or shops. Where can I hide? Where, where, where? Can I get out into the town, or will they be watching for me at the Gate?

She was half-way across the Quadrangle, and she needed to *decide* -

If anyone tried to talk to her, they'd know instantly. If they even came close, they'd hear the banging of her heart; wonder at her satchel and her lack of a tabard.

She kept walking, trying to look prompt and bustling. She

185

clutched her satchel in front of her as if it were something she'd been asked to deliver for someone else.

Through the Quadrangle into another unfamiliar square, but this one with with trees all along the far side.

And a memory came to her, like an answer to prayer. "We're having to prune back the Library Quad trees," Lady b'Nida had complained a while ago, and her husband had smiled an agreeing rueful smile. "No one's getting in at those windows a second time." It had been a scandalous tale, giggling-matter for Lindet and her friends - two students committing late-night fornication between shelves of knowledge and piety.

But now the word Library called her like a charm.

There was an empty doorway. Her footsteps tapped on the stairs, and her heart banged in rhythm. One flight up, there was a turn of the stair with a closed door off it, and here she paused. Ahead and above her, she dimly saw a carved arch and an open door; but before it on the landing sat a portress, an oldish thin woman, with short white hair. Of course the Library would be guarded. *Books are rarer than jewels.*

"Not such a good idea, after all. My feet are sore," whimpered Balki. "What now?"

The portress stirred slow bones. She rose and tapped on a little bell hanging by the door. "Make ready to leave, if you please, my friends," she called, and there was a shuffling of books and feet from inside.

Is it possible?

Hridnaya turned and lifted her hand to the door before her. She waited as if for a reply to a knock, while a few late-studying people clattered down past her. *Now I hope she'll go in to check they're all gone and left no mess – I would.*

"Mad again."

186

Mad but correct. As quiet as she knew how to be, she slipped into the Library a dozen steps behind the old woman.

It was long enough to have been a small church. Shelves stuck out on each side, making stalls more like a stable, but with windows instead of mangers. ("When were you ever in a stable?") Each shelf ended with a tall desk and stool. The portress walked right down the room, peering about. She picked up a book and replaced it. Then she walked back again, extinguishing lights as she went. The only candle now was outside by the bell. The woman walked towards it and out, not seeing Hridnaya pressed flat against a shelf in the nearest alcove to the door.

A key clicked in the lock. The Library was in darkness. All around her were books.

*

Mej wasn't going to spend a whole God-given evening watching the two trouts glaring at each other. And he had a point to make. So, "I will join you later," he said, striding towards the door, and Mobira said, "Of course, honoured sir."

His great-grandmother was Lady b'Shen, after all.

What the bloody hell is going on, and what has it to do with me? He really didn't want to think about it, and he probably didn't need to. *Some trouble for the tedious College; or for Kelji, who is rude and may be sinister; and for that runaway servant, who is gone -*

Give me fresh air. So he found his way out of the arrogant identical squares of the College, and wandered into only-slightly-more-friendly Sapientia town. Wetting his throat at The Golden Catch, he spotted a familiar Guard sitting quietly in a corner, staring.

Yes, I thought you were following me. That's enough of that, Mobira Whoever. Back out in the twilight, he eyed the ups and downs of walls as he strolled apparently at random. There was a corner with a tree next to a stable next to a flat roof. And *jump heave scramble*, he was away, up to the roof level, which is the best place to be in a city if it's not raining, and free of his follower.

Scamper, crouch, measure, leap, clutch. Run. And again. The pleasure of the game took him, and he wandered the roofs; sometimes of course having to retreat back or down, but up again; sheltered by darkness. And then he stopped to perch twenty feet above the street, wrap his cloak round him, and look about his kingdom.

A couple walking arm-in-arm, heads together. Candle-light and music from low windows. Two cats confronting each other on the neighbouring roof, arched backs and spitting faces. *That one is Mobira, and the long-tailed one Kelji.* From an upper room, an argument: "I'll not go there this Sunday! If you must eat at your brother's, you can go by yourself till he learns to behave!" "But, Palla -"

He looked up and grinned at the moon, two-thirds full. "Are you lonely, up there?" The moon was friendless. Tiny stars speckled around her would only be servants. ("Some in the College study the stars," Rorash had said, and Mej had snorted scornfully in his wine, making more mess than intended.)

He missed Rorash, the other fatherless b'Shen boy.

Tomorrow I can leave this mess behind; but where do I go?

The evening grew colder, and he found a place to slither down, scraping his hip painfully, and tearing his good hose. *You brought a second pair, Mejorad? That was well done,* he thought in his dead stepfather's voice.

That inn throwing out last customers: was it The Morning Dream?

No, it wasn't.

It took him some time to get back, and the porter at the College Gate gave him a strange look, but would have no authority to scold or question one of the Families. He stomped up the dark guesthouse stairs, brushing with courteous weary smile past the yawning Guard.

A College servant was leaving the room as he pushed in. Inside, all was quiet. The Guard who hadn't been sent after him stood by the door. Mobira was studying a message by the light of one candle. Everywhere else was dark, and Kelji and Vaddras were nowhere to be seen.

The woman nodded and raised eyebrows at him in a condescending welcome. He was reminded of the smirks at the feast, and wanted badly to read the parchment in her hand. But it wasn't for him to meddle with King Aigith's agent (or so she claimed), so he slouched into the second bedchamber, where Vaddras was lying on a pallet by the window. He peeled off his outer clothes and lay down, very aware that she was still out there, sitting.

*

Curled up on a bottom shelf from which she'd dared to remove fat volumes, Hridnaya slept a little, but not enough. Terror and despair and bafflement scampered painfully around her chest and throat, pricking her eyes, and sometimes making her gasp aloud. *What have I done? Why Guards? Can Doctor Dirria call Guards? Surely Kelji couldn't? Or did Lord b'Nida report me to the King? Why would the King care?*

What crime do they think I've committed? What have I committed? Is this about the wine on the book, or about Doctor Dirria? What else can it be?

Why? Why?

Except for her breathing, everywhere was silent. She huddled in her dark space, like a box. Her uncle had had a story

189

of a child hiding in a box while her siblings were murdered in the
room outside. Dear Uncle Gridor: she pictured his face, and tried
to calm herself by praying for his soul.

Cold and dawnlight - the windows were glazed and
unshuttered - woke her from a doze. She tidied up, and explored.
At the far end of the Library was a space without shelves, with
desks, a larger window, and a stack of parchment. This must be
the scriptorium section, where new books were made. *New
books!* There was also a door to a tiny storeroom for parchment,
binding materials, and suchlike. That was where she went to
crouch on the floor, eat and drink, and look at today.

There was no one in the Library yet, but there soon
would be. Servants have little place in Libraries, and a servant was
what the Guards would be looking for. *So that's what I'd better
not be.* She found and lit a candle, took off her jacket, and sewed
onto it false blue sleeves (like Aunt Miya's) that she'd bought in
City Qayn, and had almost left behind with her bulkier
possessions at Stansha's. *Will I ever see any of those things again:
my curtains, my buttons? Don't be so worldly, woman.*

So now the jacket and hose she'd worn for riding,
although still unbleached and plain, had bright arms and a
matching blue scarf tied loosely around her neck; and her hair
was finger-patted smooth. She might be a student, or a visitor - *if*
no one looked closely, and if she remembered to keep her head
up and not bow to everybody.

She might.

The portress – or another one – would come back, and if
she checked the storeroom, Doom. But she might not – might just
open up, and let people come in to study – and *those* people
would just think Hridnaya'd come early. Not a very elaborate plan,
but the best she had, to get her at least past one door. It was hard
to think further than that. Beyond that door, books and the rest of

her life waited.

She'd been listening, as light grew. Now there were noises outside the storeroom. *Please Lord, I have not deserved Your favour, but please –*

It was bound to come sometime. She pushed her satchel into a corner, and walked out, carrying some parchment. *I am a student.*

There were no accusing stares. Far off, the library door was open, and a male porter sat back with legs stretched wide. Two people were busy at desks already, a tousle-haired youth whose sleeves and collar were edged with gold thread, and who picked at his face; and an old woman bent close over her book so she could follow her finger along lines.

Hridnaya wandered past them and into one of the alcoves. Shelves each side of her, perhaps twenty books on a shelf. She made herself reckon up. This library might have more than five hundred volumes!

The most expensive and imposing were chained to the shelves. Even the spines of some were inlaid with gold or shimmery stuff. Hridnaya clenched her teeth to keep in her gasp of awe.

Most of the books, however, were plainer and unchained. She thought this strangely careless of the library. Anyone – herself for instance – could carry off a book under a cloak to keep or sell. But then she gently edged one out, and saw metal lettering set into the leather cover.

The Kings and Queens of Ricossa

Tim dom init sap.

The next one was "The Most Ill - Illus – something - Life of Anbar the Terr- Terrible and Just", but it also said "Tim dom init sap." Maybe they all did, and these words (whatever they meant) were like a brand on an animal, claiming the books for their owner. Maybe they were Latin or Greek.

A real student would know what she was looking for. Don't be random.

The third one was "Of the New Gov – Governance"?

Pictures formed in her head. The Pillars in the Square of Silent Remembrance – the Family marching out to the Conclave – gruesome tale-scenes from the War That Must Never Happen Again. The New Governance. Her toes tingled. She carried it over to a desk, and sat down.

"What are you *doing?*" wailed Balki.

She opened it in the middle, and for a few moments she sat there, happy.

I could stay here.

"No, you couldn't."

I'm tired of this. Yesterday was so horrible. I can't bear any more. They'll find me soon, but until they do, I'll just stay here. I'll read and learn more about the world before I die. I'll sit here and read until they come.

The peace of that thought laid itself down on her shoulders. Even in thought, even to Balki, she didn't say, "The books are my friends." But she stroked the page before her, and blinked.

What else is there for me, after all?

There's what I came to Sapientia to do.

"Almytee God I pray that I will not giv up."

There might be one other piece of information she could get. Sister Felicity had written a letter to the Bishop.

*

Mej woke next morning with a great and familiar sense of loneliness. Although he had spare hose and jacket, he knew the steward at home would have things to say about the green smears

on his best gown. *Indeed. They're used to that
from me anyway.*

"A blessed morning to you, honoured sir," said Mobira sweetly, gesturing to a table. "There is breakfast."

An hour later, she ushered Mej, Kelji and Vaddras down the stairs again, followed by her Guard, and two College servants who'd appeared from somewhere to carry their boxes and bags. Mej didn't like the angry inquisitive way they were looking at Kelji, and even him. There was still no sign of the runaway *(good luck to her)* and since the others didn't comment on this, he didn't either. Kelj was wordless, merely nodding whenever a "Good morning" or "Thank you" would've been appropriate. Occasionally he thought she looked scared, but she wiped that off and replaced it with haughty before Mobira could see. *Does scared mean guilty? Never trust a foreigner.*

A wagon pulled by two horses was surprisingly standing in the Quadrangle, half-blocking the arch. The driver bowed his head to them. Behind and beyond the wagon clustered the horses and mules they'd brought yesterday – and people. A lot of curious people.

"I will follow you, lady," said Mobira, with imitation politeness. It was barely more than a farmer's cart, but with benches across its body to sit on, and it seemed clean. Kelji climbed in. Such a clamber is hard to do with grace, and the sniggers around were unfair, he thought. The groom followed, sitting behind her, and then Mobira looked at Mej.

Making his point again, he said, "I see my horse is here. May you journey safely," and turned away. His eyes flitted over the crowd – at least two dozen adults – servants, students and miscellaneous – no children of course.

And then he saw a figure approaching with long smooth strides, someone who wasn't miscellaneous at all.

Riodran, Lord b'Nida, stopped by the horses' heads. "My lady," he said to Kelji, "I wish you a good morning." His eyes brushed across Mej. "Madam," severely to Mobira, "This lady is a guest, under the College's banner. You will need a very good reason to justify this conduct."

Mej felt their dislike taint the air.

"God give you a good morning also, my lord. She is a spy, suspected of carrying messages to possible traitors here."

Mej gasped, and so did the crowd. Lord b'Nida blinked, and looked at Kelji, and she looked back. "As you see, my lord, I am enjoying the fabled Ricossan hospitality. My Queen will hear about the College's treatment."

Heads turned, as people stared excitedly at each other. Mej heard someone hiss.

The Lord turned back to Mobira. "The lady brought a gift-"

"She came here yesterday with a holy book, yes. But it seems that was just a pretext, a most sacrilegious one."

"Nonsense!" Kelji's voice was higher than usual. To anyone listening, "I brought a servant, who ran away. Is that a crime? Your Doctors *invited* me, and I'm an emissary of Queen Nerranya."

"Your great cousin's name isn't popular here," said Mobira, smiling a thin smile. There were one or two titters. She looked at Lord b'Nida, and her smile grew broad. "All this matter must be fully investigated. The Lady Kelji has been residing in City Qayn as a guest of the b'Astith – as you pointed out, my lord, she's also a guest of the College. And she was accompanied here by the b'Shen. Why all these great people chose to sponsor and befriend a foreigner, I don't know. In Ricossa the rod of justice reaches even the highest." She seemed to be trying to conceal joy.

Mej was cold. *"Accompanied by the b'Shen"? What*

trouble is here for us? The Lord's eyes turned on him, very angry. "It's Mejorad, is it not? What have you to say about this? I'd heard you were at a monastery."

Family comes first. With sudden brilliance he said, "That was the tale given out, but I was sent here to accompany Kelji. To watch if she did anything suspicious."

"How wise of Lady b'Shen," said Mobira. She looked up impudently at Lord b'Nida, and shrugged. "To assist the enquiry, my lord, do you know of a servant called Hridnaya?"

Mej saw Lord b'Nida jerk, and his hand clench at his side. *Who's "Hridnaya"? What – that Voiceless woman was b'Nida's?*

Mobira went on, "It seems unlikely that Lady Kelji's servant 'ran away'. She sneaked out yesterday on a dubious errand for her employer. But the Doctor she was sent to is loyal to the King, and reported the matter to me."

"Hridnaya?" Slowly, "She was our Voiceless, whom we were forced to turn off earlier this month. Then she disappeared, so – If she's here, and suspected of crime, send her to me for questioning. I wrote asking my colleagues to do this if they saw her."

"Unfortunately, I didn't receive any message. I'm not one of your colleagues. Wherever she may be, King Aigith desires to talk to her."

"She will be brought to me first."

"Not first. No. And, my lord, was she dismissed, or not? Is she still under your banner, to command? If you wish to question her after the King has finished, it may be permitted. Good day to you. We have urgent business in City Qayn."

If you claim her, you share her guilt. If you've given up your claim, go away. Go away anyway. That was what she meant, and it shook Mej a little to see someone so ordinary and plain defeat one as great as Lord b'Nida. For although his face didn't change, he was defeated. Mobira tapped the driver's shoulder, and he slapped reins on the horses' backs. The wagon began to move. The tall man stepped out of the way.

Among the watchers, heads and feet shifted. "Good riddance, foreigner!" someone called – and then other voices were released. "Take your sins out of here!" "Heathen!" "Spy!" Kelji stared straight ahead. She looked like a noble statue – stern and angry, a queen of old.

What do I do now? The answer became plain. "Madam," he called, "I will report this to your hostess. Doubtless all can be explained." The wagon passed, and the back of Kelji's head didn't respond. He heard Mobira laugh, and hated her.

How dare you accuse us, you jumped-up busybody? And you, arrogant b'Nida stick? He didn't know what side he was on, or should be on. *Protect the Family.* So everyone would say. He saddled up, stared at by a few. But Lord b'Nida had turned away fast, and was talking to a chubby manservant, and others were disappearing back to work.

Mej rode out of the College. Wind's Son could go a lot faster than the wagon.

*

Students attended lectures on the hour, and those who were late were fined. So just as great bells thundered through the College to mark ten of the morning, Hridnaya walked rapidly out into the Third Quad with a worried face, clutching parchment. "Only cowards and children run," people said. "Latecomers walk very fast."

"You're mad. Dirria may not even be away lecturing. If she's in her room, she'll throw you out, or worse."

If she's there. I'm mad. I'll soon be dead.

Though they all looked similar, surely here was the entrance to Dirria's passage. *Knock – if there's an answer, run away like a naughty child.* Laughter bubbled inside - worrying her a little, for a sane woman should be trembling (and she was).

Knock. Silence. *Please.* Push. The door opened to Dirria's study, and there was no one there. She took deep breaths.

There were books on the shelves. There was an empty desk. And a stack of wooden boxes, four high.

Hridnaya placed the Doctor's tall stool before the door to give her a moment's warning of intruders, and lifted down the first box. It was heavy, and contained, as she'd hoped, bundles of twine-tied parchment. She untied one, and tried to understand it. The words **Monday, Tuesday,** and so on, had information written next to them. *These aren't letters. They're not what I want.*

It was risky, but so was everything, *everything.* She lifted down the second and third boxes, and opened the bottom one. The most out-of-the-way - the place perhaps to put what you didn't need, what you didn't want to think about.

Voices passed the window. She caught the word "unpalatable", but they didn't stop.

There weren't many documents in this one. She sat down with them under the window to be less obvious from a distance, looking through the first few words of each, searching for the word Bishop.

And she found it.

Sister Felicity of the Church of Holy Mourning – she was guessing some words in her hurry, but it must be **– to Deborah Bargadi, Bishop of the City and South Lake, with all reverence, greeting.** Reading this much was hard and slow, and she breathed in, looked down and saw the word **Gridor** – this was the one! Ittrad and the priest had both mentioned it, the letter that had sparked Dirria's interest, and started it all.

She put it beside her on the floor. This was what she'd come for. It wasn't much. Was there, might there be, anything else? She flicked through the pile, and came upon one that was unexpectedly short.

This is not an idle threat, Madrasun. You will do as you are told.

That seemed to be the whole letter, but someone else had written something more below and aslant – the letters were scrawled, and she peered closer –

The stool banged over. The door opened.

"It's you," said Ittrad.

Time passed, only a moment in fact. He shut the door, and his eyes flicked about the room. She watched him think.

"People are looking for you. There's a reward. They say you came to Sapientia to help a Jaryari spy."

No – no – no! She shook her head as firmly as she could.

"No? But anyway you are spying." He waved at the disordered boxes. "Why?"

She said, "Ii –or."

"Still Gridor? Why this? Don't move," he said, and stepped just enough across to bend over the open box.

She was almost as close to the door as he was, and he limped. But she was sitting down, and scrambling up would take time, and he would shout -

"These are old –they're left over from Doctor Madrasun."

His still round face and cold eyes pushed at her.

Ittrad took out the remaining papers, and shut the empty box. He pushed it back into place, somehow managing to keep his face turned to her the whole time. Then he drew out his knife. "Help me pile them up. If anyone comes in I'm questioning you before calling for help."

As far as she could tell, that indeed was probably what he was doing, but she helped lift the boxes back into their pile. "Sit against the desk." He poured two cups of wine, handed her one, and stood before her, a pillar of doom.

"Loyalty tells me to hand you over. I don't like Mobira. No one in the College does. But I've no love for the Jaryari either."

He said there's a reward.

"Give me that, if you please." He stretched out a hand, and she put the parchment into it. "This has nothing to do with Gridor. 'This is not an idle threat, Madrasun. You will do as you are told.' And – I think this is Doctor Madrasun's own hand." He stopped, and then his face went very still. He read, "'I am too old to delve into intrigues. I've done what I can. God help us.'"

He looked up and said, "Madrasun was Doctor of Law before Dirria. He fell downstairs in January and died. An accident. What d'you know about him?"

She made a "Nothing" gesture.

"God help us indeed. This is complicated." He blinked, looking downward; then he fished in the pouch at his belt. "Last night – after I left you – I went to The Morning Dream. This is what the landlady told me." He gave her another small piece of parchment, folded over. "Put it away." While she was doing this, he wandered over to the window, reached out to close the shutters, and stared at the wood. *Why?* "My wife's sister says you can tell whether to trust someone by looking in their eyes. I think she's probably wrong. But I don't know. I don't know about you."

There were footsteps outside. Ittrad jerked, and turned round. "I told Lord b'Nida this morning that you might come back here," he said, as the door burst open.

You told –! Hridnaya flung herself up and at him, hitting

and scratching at his fat kindless face. He pushed back at her with an "Ow!" As three College servants dragged her off, she snarled at him, like a furious dog.

Like an animal, as she was.

They put her on her face, on the floor, while a woman went to fetch Lord b'Nida. Ittrad stood by the window. He said nothing, except when someone asked him, "When's the Doctor due back?"

"About a half hour. There's a room at the top of the building that's unused."

So one of them went to confirm his words, and he must have been correct, for then Hridnaya was pulled up the stairs to a place under the eaves, with dusty benches around the walls. They put her in a corner, and opened a shutter to let in mid-morning light.

Lord b'Nida walked in with the messenger. There were three servants (in College black-and-white); Hridnaya, Ittrad and him. Someone set up and wiped a bench for him, and he sat down.

"See you hanged, as you deserve," he'd said.

At his gesture a man half-dragged her into the centre of the room. Then the Lord's face turned to Ittrad. "I thank you, sir," he said, a courteous dismissal.

But Ittrad didn't move. He said, "My lord, I came to you this morning because I thought you would want to find her before Mobira did." He paused. "And I thought she might prefer that also."

"*She* might?" Cold eyes on her. "Are you speaking on her behalf, sir?"

"No, my lord." Hridanaya saw he was holding parchment and pen. He bent forward – almost toppling over - to put them on the floor in front of her. "She can speak for herself, if you'll let her."

"D'you mean she can – worse and worse."

"Write," Ittrad hissed.

Hridanaya didn't look up. Almost she spat on his feet, but slowly she lifted the pen, and folded herself forward to scrawl her excuses.

It was a long terrible pause, while she wrote, and her back and stomach ached, and Balki maddened her about spelling. She'd finished – *no, she hadn't, she should be just to Kelji* – she wrote a last sentence.

She gave him her writing, and he handed it to Lord b'Nida.

I have not betrayed or spyed on you. I only lerned to rite after you put me out. Kelji of makayra tort me. I was in your studie to find out hoo my uncle who was killed came to the collej to see befor the b'shen killd him. I came to the collej to see doctor Dirria. Im not a spy for jaryar. I dont think Kelji is a spy aither.

He was short-sighted, and had to hold the parchment close to his nose. In her memory Hridnaya saw Lindet imitating him. She remembered him congratulating her on Brinnon's marriage, so many years ago.

She couldn't stop shivering.

The Lord read the message carefully, or seemed to. Then he took a knife and cut it across, tossing the pieces in her direction. They fluttered down, half-way across the space.

"My lord," said Ittrad, and she felt everyone's surprise at his intrusion, "she came back to Dirria's rooms this morning. She was looking for old correspondence. When I came in, she'd just found these, which I haven't seen before." He passed over the two letters, the one to the Bishop and the short note to the previous Doctor. As Lord b'Nida glanced down, he said, "My lord, you knew Madrasun. How did he die?"

"He was very old, and he fell downstairs," said the other curtly. "What are you – a man like you has no business meddling in such matters."

"I don't want any harm to come to Doctor Dirria, whom I wait on. Or to any other doctors here."

"You took these from her?"

"It was more that we looked together. I had to delay her. She could have overpowered or outrun me, and I knew your people would come."

"You!" Hridnaya looked up. "You claim that all this fuss was because of your uncle, and you were acting alone?"

She nodded hard, and put a hand on her heart.

"Did the visitor Kelji send you on an errand?"

What? No.

"Why did she bring you here, and help you?"

She shrugged ignorance. There was a terrible pause. Knowing his manner, she felt his worry. At last he said, "I certainly see no reason why any of the Families would be interested in this. You've caused more trouble than you can begin to dream of, and what am I to do with you, now that Mobira knows your name? You deserve death."

"That would be murder, my lord," murmured Ittrad.

"I've heard enough from you, sir. Thank you for your assistance. Please leave now, and say nothing to Dirria."

Ittrad hesitated.

"Get out."

One of the other servants grabbed his shoulder, and jerked him lurchingly backwards and through the door. It sounded as if he tumbled on the stairs. *Like this Doctor Madrasun.*

Lord b'Nida rose, and turned to face out of the small window. Distantly bells chimed the hour. Hridnaya watched the back of his thoughtful head. It occurred to her that no one can write without *hands,* and a bubble of scream began to build in her throat. Her fingers jerked on the floor.

He turned back. "You deserve death. However. Mercy is pleasing to God." More silence. "I don't want Mobira finding you, so you cannot go back to City Qayn. I own a farm along the road, where you can stay and work."

It was hard to grasp.

"You'll leave tonight. Do you have luggage stored anywhere?"

In the libraree stawr room, she wrote.

"Give her something to eat, and guard her here," he said to one of his servants, a thin pale woman, and held out his hand for another to give him his gloves. As he walked past her and out, he glanced down, and she dared to meet his eyes, surely for the last time. He didn't look as angry as she expected. She couldn't read how he looked.

A farm. She hadn't even known the b'Nida had one, up here.

She would never see a book again. Or Brinnon.

She wasn't sure which one hurt more.

*

A few hours later, the man and woman brought her satchel, and fresh clothes to wear that weren't hers, and walked her out to the Quadrangle. She guessed it was Vespers, and most people were attending chapel. The College, she understood, was strict about such things.

"Look happy," hissed the woman, a growling voice and a round gloomy face.

The three of them walked out of the College. Hridnaya thought there were significant looks with the porter at the College Gate, and assumed he'd received money not to tell. As they continued through the streets, she had time to wonder at the bright blue of the kirtle she'd been given – not servant colours. *I'm probably a whore being escorted off the premises.*

Watch me smile.

In an alley near the little tower, they found a stable, where a small cart and large horse awaited them. Assorted boxes and bales rolled around the bottom, and the man lifted Hridnaya in on top. "Lie back quietly. We're off to your new home." He covered her with sacking. Then he and the woman, whose name she'd gathered was Detti, climbed onto the front bench, and drove out. It wasn't yet dark. Perhaps they bribed more watchmen on the way out of the town.

"A farm along the road."

The cart bumped. Hridnaya pulled her cloak around her, and clutched the satchel, wondering how long the journey would take. After a bit she struggled out from under the sacking to sit up and look about, and they didn't forbid this. She thought of farmish words.

Ploughman. Milking. Threshing-floor.

Threshing-floors were in the Bible, but she didn't know what they were.

The man kept peeping back at her. "Stop that," Detti said to him. "Orders."

Why shouldn't he look at me?

"I know," he muttered. "But it – it's not like him."

"Ssh."

What's not like him?

I didn't know he had a farm near here, she told Balki. *But the Families do own small places away from their main estates.*

The waves sucked back and forth at the shore. Big brown animals (cows? deer?) munched grass in their pasture, as they'd been doing on the way in, two days ago.

"It's not like him." *What isn't? I don't understand.*

And then she did.

There's no farm.

"It's not like him," because Lord b'Nida was a kind and decent man. But he was desperate to keep her away from Mobira. Not so much because of what she knew – even the b'Nida secrets were half-respectable – but because of what Mobira could say she knew. The lies College enemies could torture her to endorse.

There was nowhere safe for her except death.

She sprawled between a large box and a sack of what felt like fruit, staring at the slowly darkening hugeness above. Cold terror was heavy in her bowels, and painful in her finger-ends. *It can't be, it can't be. It is.* The man and woman were taking her out to kill her, somewhere out of the city, where the body could be hidden.

She'd told herself it was only a matter of time, but – *not yet! Please, Lord, not yet! Oh please.*

How? Clenching her fists, she forced herself to think. No farm, so where would they hide her?

There was a new, additional, sound of water, this one running fast and merrily. "Now, you," said the man to the old horse, and slapped the reins, and the cart began to turn. Hridanaya pulled herself upright again, somehow keeping her face blankly interested, as would be natural. They didn't know she knew.

They'd lit a lantern, and were bumping along a track, just wide enough, away into the hills. On one side, a field of newly-stacked corn (a strong fresh smell that should have been pleasant) and on the other a stream bouncing down to join the Lake. She vaguely remembered seeing this on the way in, a road and river leading up the hill to a group of trees. "That way to the left's called the Haunted Pool." Mejorad was a liar, but maybe not always.

"If only we could send Mobira to the Haunted Pool" – that was what her lord had said once, grimacing. And then he'd looked up, plainly glad no one had heard except his wife – and a servant without a tongue.

The best way would be to slit her throat, bash her face to something unrecognisable, stuff a heavy stone in her bodice, and throw her into deep water, haunted or otherwise. Never to be found, or if found, never identified.

They didn't like it, neither of them did. But they would do it.

Please Lord.

They didn't like it, and they didn't know she knew. The world around became dimmer and dimmer. She thought frantically, words and pictures skittering inside her head.

*

Hridanaya sat up in a calm manner, flexed her stiff shoulders, and began to sing. Not Voiceless-mangled words, just sounds. "Ah *ee* yah – ah yee. Eyoo fa ay." She made up a tune. Her voice wasn't sweet, but that didn't matter.

Even to herself, the sound she made was a little eerie. *No one understands the Voiceless.* The man looked round. "Quiet, there."

She bowed her head, and was silent for a count of twelve. Then she began again, but very softly. The two in front would just be able to hear her.

The woman Detti shuddered.

Above, it was almost dark. The trees, she thought, were

nearer. The cart bumped up the track.

Her body was too tense to move, but she had to. She stopped singing. Balki didn't dare criticise. Quietly Hridnaya unhooked the satchel strap from round her neck, and unfastened her cloak. She stretched an arm to heaven, and laughed happily, crazily. And started to talk – nonsense sounds again, but clear and decisive.

"What are you -"

"What's she -"

I am a madwoman, I am strange. You are afraid of me.

And then she scrambled up, still talking, put a hand on the cart's side, and jumped, not knowing on what she'd land.

Grass.

Up, and run.

They were shouting, and jumping down.

Hridnaya pounded up towards the trees a little ahead. *Where's this bloody Pool?* She couldn't go quietly.

"Hurry up!" called Detti from the cart.

"Shit – shit!" panted her companion.

Under cloudy moonlight Hridnaya found the Pool. It was blessedly surrounded by trees, with a sharp drop to the water, a mansion's-height below. She dodged behind a tree. If she had a few moments she might just - *please* - she pulled out her jar of food, tore off her cloak, and curved it round the satchel. He was almost there. She laughed, loud and wild; then she screamed, all thirty years' fear in one scream, and flung the bundle away and out and down.

Splash.

She put a hand over her mouth, and breathed silently between her fingers.

"Oh – Oh God – Detti! Come! She's – oh."

Hridnaya could just see him through branches, staring

down. She heard Detti struggle up the slope with the lantern. "What -"

"Look. Maybe she slipped. Did you hear her scream?"

There was just enough light, it seemed, for them to find a shape bobbing, billowing out, in the water.

The two servants stared down, and Hridnaya pressed her back against ridges of bark. Heart banging; legs shaky.

"It could be a trick."

"How? She didn't even know."

"We could go down, and -"

We could scramble down the mud-slippery slope in the dark; grab the body, dead or alive. And if it's alive, or isn't a body? Find her, somehow, and then –

The woman made a growling noise that sounded like an ending. *Please.* They both turned away, but then the man looked back. "God rest her soul."

They didn't have to become murderers, after all.

The two half-tumbled back down between trees, cursing the dark. Hridnaya heard the man coax the horse around, and the cart at last lurch off.

She didn't dare to move, in case only one had gone. She waited, growing colder, tears dripping down her face for some reason, for a long long time, perhaps an hour.

She was alone in the dark, with nothing in the world but a jar of food and the new bright clothes she was wearing.

*

Mej didn't have to ride through the night. Wind's Son earned his name, and they arrived at the Friendship Gate just after it had officially closed. "I am Lady b'Shen's great-grandson. Thank you," and he was allowed through. He'd barely spoken to anyone all day, and his head felt empty and lost. *Where are friends when you need them?* Although he'd missed his little sisters more. *Not telling anyone that.*

He left his sweating horse at the b'Shen stables, but didn't go in at the front door. Eyanda would want him to tell Nadya first – tired and cross, he had a struggle finding the house. The shadows cast by the corner torches were confusing and hid dips in the road; and everyone was in bed or tavern.

Not everyone. Someone was shouting, no, more than one person, down a street off the Great Passage.

He got lost, and had to think. *Why can't she live with the rest of her Family, stupid Nadya? Stupid simpering Nadya; what does Eyanda like about her?*

But surely she's not a traitor.

At last, the house with what was probably a blue door – it was hard to tell in the torchlight. He knocked, hurting his knuckles, and conscious of Tor's absence. The sound was loud.

Eventually, "Greetings. I know it's late, but I have news for Nadya b'Astith."

He was disturbing the household at night, and the impudent woman managed to make it obvious that she wasn't quite tutting. "Please to come in, sir." She led him across the hall where Nadya transacted business on behalf of her horse-breeder brother and her cousin's monastery - empty but for a guard and a single candle at this hour - and into the private apartment to the left. An unfamiliar lanky youth was sitting by the fire, getting drunk. *Good plan. I'll do that later.*

The maid disappeared up a corner stair, and voices murmured. Nadya, a yellow bed-cloak wrapped around to cover her nightgown, brown hair poured over her shoulders, came down smiling. She lifted her skirts delicately so as not to stumble on the stairs.

"Be welcome, kinsman. Can I offer you wine? How was St Antonius'? You're back early?" She raised her eyebrows, gently teasing.

"I – I went with Kelji, to Sapientia," he said bluntly. "Some agent of King Aigith has arrested her. There was absurd talk of spying, and treason."

Nadya swayed. "I don't understand. Kelji?"

The boy by the fire jumped up. And he wasn't a boy – he was a lot older than Mej, only beardless. *Jaryari.* He was dressed all in green, brown-faced with mid-length untidy black hair, and one of his front teeth was missing.

"What d'you mean, 'spying'?" he said, and he wasn't so very drunk, after all. "Where is my wife?"

*

"Madam," said a servant to Doctor Dirria the next morning, "Lord b'Nida has an errand for your man Ittrad. I hope you don't object to losing his time."

"Of course I'm honoured to assist His Lordship," she replied, fluttering her fingers graciously; and neither of them was interested in whether Ittrad was also honoured, or that he might receive a black mark for missing Sunday Mass. He put on the meek face he was rather tired of, and limped with the silent messenger through various Quads, and upstairs to the Chancellor's office.

It was a very tidy room, daylight streaming in the windows but unlit candles ready for use in sconces on the walls. Blocks of books and round towers of parchment-rolls stood neatly arranged on shelves, and a desk held one pile of papers to the side, and one book open in the middle.

Ittrad approved, of the room.

It was the Chancellor's office, but Chancellor Irramatti wasn't there. Her husband was sitting behind the desk, stroking his long beard and staring at the single book. Lord b'Nida, not his wife. *This isn't official College business.* "Ah, thank you. You can go, Detti." She curtsied and left. "Please, sir," to Ittrad, "sit down."

Ittrad eased himself onto a chair, and rested his stick against the desk. "My lord."

Lord b'Nida looked straight across at him, eye to eye, beard to beard, gracious smile. "I'm grateful for your help yesterday," he said. "You were correct in keeping that woman away from Mobira, and bringing her to me. Your loyalty to the College, and to me, is appreciated."

"Thank you, my lord."

He brought his hand out of a bag with money, exactly five silver coins, which he laid on the desk one by one, and pushed in Ittrad's direction.

"I thank you," Ittrad repeated, but he didn't move to take the money. "My lord, your woman Detti spoke of an errand."

Eyebrows were raised delicately. "Yes. I'm leaving for City Qayn before noon, but I had something to mention before I go. Look at this." From between the pages of the book he lifted a small parchment, which Ittrad recognised.

"*This is not an idle threat, Madrasun,*" and the Doctor's scrawl underneath, "*I am too old for these intrigues.*"

"You told me this was found in Dirria's room? Doctor Madrasun died last November."

"Yes, my lord."

There was a short silence. Ittrad let his eyes drop politely. He heard the other man tapping the fingers of one hand on the desk.

"Errhm. A few weeks ago," said Lord b'Nida, "I was warned by someone that Madrasun had feared trouble at the time of this foreign visit. There was mention of his death, and of Mobira. You know of her?"

Ittrad nodded. Taking an intelligent interest, he said, "May I ask who gave this warning?"

Lord b'Nida paused again. "Someone outside Sapientia, but with access to high-level information. *Very* high-level."

A member of the Families, or of one of the Royal Councils? That must be over a hundred people.

"Had it ever occurred to you or your Doctor that there was anything wrong about Madrasun's death?"

Ittrad was conscious of a great longing for food. An apple pasty would be just the thing.

"My lord," he said, deliberately as usual, "Doctor Dirria told me she was visited by Mobira after the man Flower-in-Hood died. Mobira said his death, Gridor's, should teach Dirria not to interfere, and that other people should have taken such warnings in the past. I believe Dirria thought this was intended as a reference to Madrasun, but I don't know if she was right. She hadn't suspected anything before. It would be very easy to push an old man downstairs, and very difficult to prove."

"Yes." They were looking at each other again. "Did Dirria 'interfere'?"

"No. She heeded the warning." *And ran to Mobira with the Voiceless woman's letter.* In his head he saw his mistress' terrified tear-stained face.

"Understandably. But I have decided that enquiries should be made." Lord b'Nida didn't look terrified, but Ittrad was beginning to be. "I want someone loyal and discreet to look into that death. What would you do, if you were that someone?"

He disliked this question very much.

After taking time to think, as the other must surely be expecting, "It was nine months ago. I wouldn't be able to find out where people were at the time. I suppose it might be possible to talk to the physician who examined his body. And -" he reached out to touch the parchment – "this says 'not an idle threat.' So there must have been other threats, or warnings, and they might have been written down, or he might have mentioned them to his wife or his friends. I could search in his old papers that are now Dirria's to see if there were more, or to try to learn what Madrasun was doing that someone might not have liked."

There was no need to mention that he'd done some of these things already.

"Yes. Mobira has a room of her own. It's possible that she keeps secret documents there."

"Does she take precautions? She must know she's not loved."

"Remember, er, Ittrad, that officially Mobira is merely a general assistant to the doctors. We all know she's more, but she doesn't have her own guard. Yes, her room is locked, but there are rumours about the servant on that staircase. With the assistance of money, you should be able to get in." Now he was putting out more coins, this time a little column. "And this." It was a small key. "I'm told this will open many of the simpler locks on boxes and such."

Now we come to it. "If Mobira discovered a man using this key," Ittrad said slowly, "what should he say, my lord? On whose instructions should he claim to be acting?"

"Why would he be acting on anyone's instructions?" Then, "Do you have a family, sir?"

This isn't a good question. "My father lives in the north. I have siblings, but no one in Sapientia."

"No wife or children?"

"My wife died."

"Hum. I am sorry to hear it. All I can say is that the College would take good care of anyone hurt or – bereaved – in this enquiry. Generous care.

"You're thinking this is a hard task to be given. I have observed you, Ittrad, and you are a man of discretion and skill.

Your teachers speak well of you. You're hoping for a place as a physician, or a bonesetter, when you finish here, aren't you? There will be rewards. And I don't desire you to take excessive risks."

"I thank you, my lord. I will see what I can do."

So it was agreed. As Ittrad pulled himself out of his chair, Lord b'Nida added, "Be careful. You may know that some of the doctors – look more kindly on Mobira than the Chancellor and I do. Akraib, for instance. I will therefore leave it to your judgment how much to tell Dirria. She may have information."

"Yes, my lord. And might that woman Hridnaya know anything more? Can I see her?"

"She's not here. I've provided for her," and his tone was suddenly firm and sharp. "She's gone to a farm that I own. But she told us all she knew."

"My lord."

*

Nadya provided Mej with a long hot bath, several cups of wine, and a comfortable bed in the second guest chamber.

The first had already been allocated to Fejederic, the husband Kelji had never talked about, who'd arrived unexpectedly the day before. But he didn't use it, for he ran scowling out of the house as soon as the news was told. Nadya sat down flump, and put her face in her hands.

Now it was bright morning, streets washed by early rain and all fresh, and Mej felt a lot better. He dressed himself without servant assistance, and ran down to find food laid out in the living room. The woman who'd let him in and a manservant he'd seen before were standing about yawning.

Nadya entered just as he was sucking the honey spoon.

"Good morning to you, sir. I hope your sleep wasn't disturbed by the racket outside?"

"No – that is, I did hear something, but I wasn't yet in bed."

"Some rascals were running around breaking windows. Fortunately we have shutters on the ground floor." She was interrupted by a banging outside, and it was the way she jumped that made Mej wonder, and realise how strained her face looked.

Eyanda, his mother-aunt-tiresome-overlady, came running into the room, and took Nadya's hands in hers. "Nim – are you well? I saw the damage upstairs. What more trouble have you had?"

"One window is all. Should there have been more?"

"Some louts made a row last night at our house. They managed to smash several windows, and they waved torches about, and shouted abuse of b'Shen and b'Astith. The children were frightened. One of the Families must be raising feud – only a little, we hope, but we don't know why – and why you too? Have you enough guards?" She squeezed Nadya's hands, and lifted them to her mouth to kiss. Then, of course, "What are you doing here, Mejorad?"

And so it had to be explained again – and when he told them that a b'Nida messenger had passed him on the way, riding even harder than he was - "So that's it! Bloody b'Nida blaming us for the College's troubles!"

"Who would have thought the prim b'Nida would go rioting?" asked Nadya, trying to smile. "Do not fear, Eyanda, it will all pass."

"I'm staying here with you today, and tonight. I have servants to help protect the house. As well as this great boy who runs off to College and back again, and thinks we don't know." Her eyes were sharp, and Mej understood. *Tor took my money, and ran straight to Eyanda, the turd.*

"Poor Kelji!" said Nadya suddenly.

Mej realised that he was expected to stay around all morning, an extra guard – and the steward offered to find someone to clean and mend the damaged gown in the meantime. So while the two women went upstairs for a little while *(ugh - and on a holy Sunday morning, too!)* and then out to the hall to attend to Nadya's business, he sat in her living room strumming a lute, grumpily amused by how helpful and dutiful he was being for once.

Fejederic did not come back. But in the afternoon there was an unexpected visitor.

*

Ittrad was fond of food and quiet thought; less so of people. So he took his noontime bowl of pottage and cup of ale from the counter at the students' end of the Refectory, paid a half penny extra for the desired pastry, and sat down facing the wall, as isolated as possible.

Ittrad the spy. I'm to investigate whether Mobira makes a practice of murdering people for the Evening King. I'm to do this out of loyalty. Lord b'Nida or the Chancellor will pay me, and perhaps find me a position in future, when I'm finished my studies. If they and Dirria between them allow me enough time to finish.

If I'm blinded in his service, he'll see that I get fed, and if I'm killed, he'll look after my father. But he won't acknowledge that he sent me, and if I refuse, or use his name to justify myself, he won't be pleased. And he could have set any of his own people to this task.

Ittrad felt no great love for Lord b'Nida or his demands. *They expect us to do anything they want, for no reason, under no law. Some day I want to tell them so.* But he hadn't needed the morning's interview to dislike the idea of an old man being pushed down a tall flight of stairs. Anyone, and especially anyone with a bad leg, knows the terror of falling.

Slowly and methodically he considered what was wanted. As he pushed the last piece of comforting sweetness into his mouth he thought, *His manner changed at the end. When I asked about Hridnaya. He was not at ease.*

*

"I'm delighted to find you here, madam," said Mobira, curtseying. Eyanda waved a brusque hand to a seat, and they faced each other across their laps and six feet of floor. Mej stood at his mother's shoulder, hands fiddling behind his back. There was no one else present.

Nadya remained in the outer room, writing a letter.

"You asked to speak to me in my friend's house, without her. An odd request. How can I assist you?" Eyanda's voice was cold.

Mej realised she didn't know who Mobira was, and he did. This pleased him a little.

"Thank you, my lady. Yes. I am Mobira, daughter of Jentoretti, a humble servant of the Evening King. He's sent me to express his gratitude to you and your family. This little problem of the Jaryari spy will be much more easily solved, thanks to you."

Eyanda frowned, and gripped the chair-arms. "I am grateful for His Grace's good opinion, but Kelji of Makkera isn't a spy, and we've done nothing. Please explain."

"You sent your son to the College with her to watch for trouble. He said so, before witnesses, in Sapientia."

Oh. Shit.

A smile without amusement. "I sent him to St Antonius' Monastery. He ran off on a frolic of his own, but that –"

"I must interrupt you there, my lady."

Mej saw Eyanda's outrage. *You impudent commoner.*

"Your son was watching for signs of treason, doubtless on your instruction – *doubtless*. This demonstrates the wise precautions of the b'Shen Family, and the probable innocence of the b'Astith in this matter. Probable innocence."

Eyanda's mouth opened. She made a noise between a puff and a gasp, very angry. Mobira smiled.

"Nadya b'Astith welcomed a kinswoman from abroad. That's all she did. A godly act. Why should I ask my son to spy on the guest?"

Mej obeyed an urge to say, "I saw no spying. There was no -"

"The foreign woman sent secret messages and payments to the College doctors. Is that not spying? The King is eager to know how deep this runs, and he relies on me to investigate. Did Riodran b'Nida know what was going on, and did Nadya b'Astith?"

"Nothing was -"

"You see, my lady, how fortunate it is for your *friend* that you and your son can clear her name."

Messages and payments? Sent by a woman she'd only just met? The Voiceless had nothing to do with –

Silence. There was no fire in the grate, and the room was cold.

"You want me to tell you that Mejorad went to Sapientia on my orders," said Eyanda slowly.

Mobira smiled at her, and Mej felt crinkles down his back. "You and he will swear this, at the woman's trial. The King will be most grateful. He's asked me to say how he felt for your sorrow, in the matter of your elder son. You offered, I think, to do anything?"

Eyanda stared, and her mouth opened a little.

"It is within the King's gift to summon Rorash back from

Defardu, and restore him to the College."

Mej suddenly understood what kind of conversation this was, such a one as he'd heard of, but never witnessed. It was thrilling and disgusting at the same time. "The -" he began. His mother's head jerked a little, but she didn't look round at him. Mobira turned mockingly-polite eyes.

"The woman, the servant – what was she doing?" he said.

"Serving Kelji, and the Queen of Jaryar. For money, doubtless," said Mobira. "She's not been found yet – traitors at the College must be sheltering her. When we find her, as we will, we'll learn it all."

I don't think she was. "She can't talk."

"She can nod, and put her mark to a confession, saying whatever the judges need. By the time the Guards have finished with her, she will."

"Nadya is innocent," said Eyanda slowly.

"Of course she is. Your evidence will make that quite clear."

Eyanda stood up abruptly. "I understand." She breathed in and out. "I agree. We agree." As the other woman rose and curtsied, she added, "What will happen to her – to this Kelji?"

"How can I know what the King will decide? The penalty for espionage is death, but it's not always imposed. He will do whatever is to the benefit of Ricossa, and the discomfort of our enemies."

She walked out of the room and the two stood in silence.

At last Eyanda said, "Go away, Mejorad. Go and play, or something."

*

Hridnaya had come to the crossroads where the wagon had turned up towards the Pool.

Which way to go now?

It had been a strange night, huddled chilly between tree-roots in the rain, listening to the hoots and rustles and shrieks of Outdoors, thinking pleading prayers into her clasped fingers. Not much sleep, a few tears.

Balki couldn't make sense of any of it. "I don't understand. I don't understand" – until at last, *Shut mouth, Balki.*

I don't understand either, she thought now. *I'm confused. Why would they think Kelji's a spy? Is she? What's this about a Doctor Madrasun who was involved in intrigues, and was threatened?*

And I'm a little frightened. More than a little.

A little angry. Lord b'Nida. Ittrad. *But neither of them betrayed me. They owed me nothing. There's nobody in the world who owes loyalty to me, bannerless creature.*

But mostly some other feeling she couldn't make into sense. She heard again her own scream on the edge of the Pool; felt again her terror.

She looked out across the road, past strips of yellow and brown to the Great Lake. It was a gleaming band that trimmed the huge sky - and she laughed aloud.

It was triumph she felt. Last night They'd tried to kill her, and They had failed. She'd dodged that doom. God had saved her from her enemies, like in the Psalms. *"With the Lord on my side, I do not fear. What can people do to me? He reached from on high, He delivered me from my strong enemy, and from those who hated me."*

Thank You, Lord, Jesus! Thank You, thank You!

"But what does that mean? D'you think you're a holy warrior, or a prophet or something?"

Not a warrior. A prophet? Maybe. Maybe I have a task. And I'm here, still alive, and I will go on.

"Have you never heard of the sin of pride?" Balki was

seriously alarmed. "And none of that tells us which way to turn here. You can't stand at the crossing forever, like - like a signpost, or a gibbet."

This was true. She was hungry and thirsty. A stream chattered beside her, a foot or two below road level. She had to kneel on the grassy bank, steady herself cautiously, and stretch down to cup cold water – and almost all of it leaked away before it reached her mouth. *This is easier in tales.* But at last she'd drunk, and her blue skirt wasn't much more stained than it had been already. So she sat by the edge of the path with her mizzum pot. There was apple in this mix, she thought; and gravy, and turnip, but she couldn't taste much.

A herd of perhaps ten of the large brown animals she suspected were cattle plodded along the road before her; a skinny scowling lad drove them from behind. He glanced over, and she felt a moment's terror, but managed to smile a friendly greeting.

Please, Lord, he's just going from field to field, or farm to farm.

Please don't let anyone ask him if he's seen a runaway Voiceless.

Where am I going? Back to Sapientia, or on to the City?

What have I learned? Not much, truthfully, and that Ittrad may have been lying. Sapientia means books, but Mobira's looking for me. And the answer I'm looking for isn't in books. Who else can I ask? And I can't ask, so I need someone who wants to help, and is willing to take time and to guess. There is no one.

For a moment she remembered sitting in Singing Frogs tavern, watching Ittrad fill his cheeks with pie, and look up at her with a half-apologetic smile. But then, "I told Lord b'Nida."

It's a long way back to City Qayn. In the city there's Sister Felicity, and Aunt Miya, and the physician what's-his-name from the trial? She pursed her mouth. *Vreddo.*

One of them may know something more.

Abruptly she remembered *Ittrad gave me something.* She reached into the bodice of her smock for the folded piece of parchment no one had known to take from her.

"This is what the landlady told me," he'd said.

Bada of The Morning Dream says the death of Flower-in-Hood happened just as she said at the trial. He didn't seem to know (k-no?) the prisoner, or the woman Shina who quarrelled with the prisoner. He fell down and died very quickly, only gasping. The other b'Shen lad fell on top of him. It made Bada laugh, until she realised he wasn't moving. A few days later M came and talked to her about what had happened, and seemed amused, but Bada insists M didn't tell her to lie.

Who's M? Mejorad? No, surely Mobira. I don't think Ittrad knows Mejorad. I may be wrong.

If I'm meant to be learning, God will need to show me what to do.

Again she stared at the parchment, spelling it out in her head, and comparing it to the memorised evidence of the witnesses. *Yes, they all said much the same. He fell down, and that rich ragamuffin fell on top of him.* She pictured the ragamuffin Mejorad, just a little stockier than his cousin, she thought, with carelessly-worn expensive gown and cloak. He had a studded belt and an embroidered sheath for his knife – and a sword to make common people tremble.

Hridnaya went on sitting there, parchment in fingers, watching the events of two months ago. Until at last she noticed what she hadn't seen before.

The odd thing wasn't that a rich man had followed Uncle Gridor, and knocked him down.

The odd thing was that he had died.

*

"We agree. Go and play."

Mej decided to take the instructions literally. He wandered home and ran in, under the green banner above the front door, and up the stairs two at a time. "Orthon?" he accosted the Housefather. "Where are my sisters?"

Aladim and Firi were delighted to be taken out of lessons – ("by our mother's order") - and thrilled when Orthon said worriedly, "Do take a guard, honoured sir. You know there was trouble last night."

"The trouble was here, and at one of the b'Astith houses. We're going to the Water Wall." So the three scampered along, with the girls' tutor and a guard trailing behind, to the walkway on the sheltered southern edge of the City, where they could watch people boarding the Ferry to the unseeable north, and throw tidbits to the swans and geese. Which of course you shouldn't do, for it encourages rats and gulls.

"You mean you went to the College, the Sap-town, when you should've been praying at a monastery?" said Firi. "You're very naughty, Mej. Why don't you like praying? I do." She screwed up her eyes, and began to chant, "Our Father -"

"That is showing-off, not prayer," said her tutor repressively. Mej interrupted more effectively with a tickle under the arms, and then he had to swing them both round by turns, until all three were dizzy.

By the time he'd delivered them safely back, he felt clean and good. He'd done his duty by the b'Shen yesterday, and by his sisters today; and the fate of Kelji, daughter of Shanell, was nothing of his concern. She was a cross difficult woman, and no one was really going to hang her. Or, surely, her groom, what-was-his-name-beginning-with-V. And as for little Voiceless, who knew what sneaky dangerous game she was playing? She deserved – whatever.

He went for a reviving adult drink in The Dog and Boot, distracting himself with his friends' lives. Majilli moaned about her irritating uncle, and Narod dropped mysterious hints about his next military mission; and Mej found he didn't have to say much about Sapientia at all.

*

"Listen to me, young Defani. I haven't fed that bear for a week, and he's very hungry. So tonight you'll sleep in your cage, next to his, and in the morning you'll swear to sing for me forever, or the bear will have you."

Hridnaya walked on and on, filling her head with whatever she could. The Lord's Prayer. The Ten Commandments. The Mass. (Which she was missing today – *it is Sunday, isn't it?* – for the first time in years of her ordered life.)

Letter-shapes.

The evidence at Rorash b'Shen's trial.

The questions and answers in her invisible Box.

Looking around at the Lake and the farmland. Talking about it to Balki and God.

Now she was down to childhood tales.

Her feet were very sore, she was hot and thirsty, and she'd nearly run out of food. Soon she should find somewhere to curl up for the night.

Defani could see the bear's eyes shining in the dark, in the next cage.

*

But on Monday Mej woke bored and restless – so much

224

so that after breakfast he actually enquired of Uncle Yettrid if there were any errands to be done.

"You could have a wander round to the Great Square and see what announcements there are, or what signs of trouble. And your mother didn't come home last night, which is inconvenient. She'll be at that Nadya's. Orthon and the kitchen need to know her guest list for next Saturday's dinner."

"Indeed, uncle," and he grabbed up a cloak and went out. It was another sunny day, with just enough breeze to move everyone along briskly.

Will I ever be the one inviting people to dine and discuss politics with the Family on Saturdays?

He amused himself with concocting his ideal guest-list. He started, as most young men did, with Helen of Troy; and had added Samson, Gormad Kingsbrother the Lucky, St Ansha the Lesser, Odysseus and Rod Ribcrusher before he arrived at Nadya b'Astith's blue door.

"I believe Eyanda b'Shen has just left to return home, sir," said the dull middling-in-every-way steward. "Isn't that right, you – Imadal?"

The question was addressed to the foreign maidservant passing through the hall – Kelji's woman, he recognised. "Yes, sir," she said, after a surprised and miserable jerk. She rubbed her face, but not before Mej had seen tears.

"What ails her?" he asked.

The steward pursed his lips. "She's the maid of our foreign guest who was arrested with her groom, and taken to the Palace yesterday. And her master landed himself on our doorstep without warning two nights ago, and now has run off somewhere also. It is most distressing for everyone here, and especially for my mistress. Our hospitality has been so ill-used." Over his shoulder his eyes shot scorn at the poor woman, and Mej, contrary as ever, felt an impulse to say,

"It's not – er – Imadal's fault." And to her, "Surely matters will be put right soon."

"Sir," she said, turning at the door, "we've done nothing! It's all trouble caused by that beggar-thing -"

"Imadal!"

"Let her finish, sir."

"Who my mistress took pity on, and wanted to teach – I'm sorry, sir." She curtsied, and was gone.

"My apologies," said the steward, smoothing the last few minutes off his face and apparently out of his memory, "Your mother has left, as I said, but can I offer you some refreshment?"

"Thank you, no." *Not in your company, you cold-hearted stick. The poor maid, alone and in disgrace in a foreign land.*

Always feeling sorry for people, Mej. Like that beggar Tor wanted to punish the other day –

And then as he strode along the streets, thumbs in belt, a flurry of thoughts hit him.

The beggar the other day was the runaway Voiceless. I never did find out why Kelji took her to the College, and taught her to read. Surely she's not a spy, as that Mobira claims! What was she doing? She left a message behind.

In his pouch he thought he still had it. "You can beat me wen I come bak." Surely her disappearance had been a surprise to Kelji, and to the groom too.

"Servants have plans and ideas of their own, at times," his first mother, now the Queen, had once said.

Inside Mej's brain was a mess of different colours, each one a confusing thought.

Her own plan? – about what? Tor was right - she was spying on us in the Square! Perhaps even on me! Maybe she persuaded Kelji to take her to – she arrived in Sapientia, and at once ran away. Does she live in Sapientia?

No, but – but! I'd seen her before – I think – or someone who looked like her. Before that Sunday in the Square. It's connected to Sapientia. But how?

He leaned back against somebody's housewall, squinting against the sunshine, and thought, while the colours faded. A priest bustled past him. *The trial. She has something to do with Rorash's trial.* He rubbed his neck and squeezed his eyes together, and tried to remember. Flower-in-Hood had a family there – a widow – a nephew –

She looked like the nephew! That insolent fool who'd called Rorash a murderer. It's not chance. It's –

It was the whole family, with their poisonous slanders! So – so *either* –

Either they're all lunatics, like the uncle but worse, spreading wild lies about the b'Shen (there's a word for that. It's sedition); or someone's paying them to do this. One of the other Families. Or the Jaryari?

Surely not Kelji.

One of the other Families then. B'Iri, or b'Olim? Most likely the b'Nida, whom she'd worked for. *We're not at feud with b'Nida, are we? Or maybe we are, now their people've been throwing stones at our house -*

I need to find out about this. Someone does, anyway, and why not me? Clear Nadya! I'd like to prove Kelji innocent too if I could, if she is. Like an investigator in a story. Buddric the Wise or the prophet Daniel - or like Marod's Queen's Thirty! They investigate crimes and judge cases –

He fizzed with eagerness. *I need to find that woman –*

Hridnaya, they called her. Mobira's looking for her, but can I find her

first? I don't trust Mobira, no matter if Eyanda does.

Mejorad the Investigator pulled himself away from the wall, and set off again on his uncle's errands. ("Have a wander round to the Great Square.") There was a coldness in his head. Everything around him seemed doused in freshening water; made more real than usual.

"Traitors at the College must be sheltering her," Mobira had said. The thought of setting out immediately to ride all the way back along the shore to find her was not attractive. On the other hand, there was the brother, the one with all the mad theories – *Can't remember his name. Who could tell me? Who would know anything about them?*

He'd arrived at the Great Square, one side of which was the Hall of Justice. No one was being hanged today, and last week's corpses had been cleared off to the gibbet at the Crossing. Over to the right, City Guards had stripped some poor bastard of his shirt, and were tying his wrists above his head to the whipping-post. A small group of idle justice-spectators had gathered, laughing and tutting.

But he could tell Uncle Yettrid that no great announcements were being made.

Mej turned away, hearing the crack-thud-scream flogging sequence begin behind him.

I really definitely don't want to see Kelji hanging here. Very definitely.

So finding that woman or her brother was urgent – and as he entered the Great Passage, his eyes fell on a stall selling belts and harnesses.

Wait a minute. Flower-in-Hood worked for someone like that – was it the saddle shop on Gallows Walk Street? I think I've seen him around there. His employer might know his family.

So he wouldn't have to ride to Sapientia.

*

Lord b'Nida hadn't said his investigation was urgent, so Ittrad spent the rest of Sunday getting as far ahead as he could with his studies and his work for Dirria. But on Monday he made for the staircase in the Fourth Quad, where Mobira and other medium-level attendants had rooms. A smartly-dressed woman of perhaps forty called Emmia cleaned and laundered and ran errands for this staircase, and as the Lord had suspected, Ittrad had barely opened his pouch before she was offering assistance.

"You promise you'll leave the room exactly as you found it? I don't know when she's coming back – she's unpredictable."

"I promise." Ittrad handed her a five-silver piece, and received in exchange a large black key. He struggled up the stairs leaning against the wall, turned it in the lock, and entered.

Mobira's room, he thought, half-maintained the pretence that she was an attendant of no great standing. The furniture was simple: bed, chests and two chairs. The window was unglazed, and there was no fireplace. But she did have a private brazier, cold and grey in her absence, and the chairs were nicely carved, and a matching pair. There was a braided rug on the floor, rather pretty. His late wife would have liked it. (But he didn't want to think of her, and how unhappy they'd managed to make each other, so that when she died he grieved only for her loss, and not at all for his own.)

How does one search a room? He'd bargained for an hour. If Mobira walked in and caught him –

That was the choice he'd made.

Ittrad looked round very carefully, trying to remember where and how to put things back, and he began.

He took off the bedding to poke and examine the

mattress. He felt all round the inside of the chests and the bedframe. With some difficulty and pain, he crawled over the floor, tapping as he went. There were two books on a shelf, which he flicked through. The brazier and a pot of flowers by the bed contained nothing they should not. Picking up the spilt soil was fiddly. The ceiling looked undisturbed and undisturbable.

So it came down to the walls. All round the room on his knees. All round again standing up. All round again, dragging a chair to stand on –

And at last, above the bedhead, something moved. He wriggled a stone out, and found a space, and a box.

Why shouldn't she keep treasures in a hidden box? Most people do. I do.

It was wooden, about a foot long, with a metal panel inlaid on top, and a design of a man or boy etched onto the metal. The Girl-Box and the Boy-Box – he'd seen these things on stalls.

It was locked, of course, but Lord b'Nida's key, with a little fiddling, clicked it open.

Inside he found a few coins, a certificate of good character from a priest dated twelve years back, a posy of dried flowers and a lock of hair.

*

He thought carefully, and learned a speech. Then he locked everything up and jerked down the stairs to where Emmia was pretending to sweep the hall. She stretched out her hand for the key.

Ittrad looked at her: tall and only slightly stooped, wearing the College tabard above unbleached hose. But her shoes were smart, and a bright chain sparkled round her neck. A suspicious mistress would have noticed these things.

"Has she come back?" he asked.

"No, not that I've seen. Give it here. Did you find

anything?"

"I found a box. A wooden box with a picture of a boy on the lid."

Emmia allocated him a faintly-interested shrug.

"These boxes come in pairs," said Ittrad. "Where's the other one?"

"Didn't you find it?"

"No."

"Then who knows? Maybe she got rid of it, or only ever had -"

"Tell me where the other box is."

She lowered her voice. "How should I know that, you fool? I let you look round, which I shouldn't have done. That's all I can do."

"But it isn't all you do."

The sun shone into the doorway, slanting across a face just starting to be irritated. Ittrad began his speech. "Mobira has many enemies, we all know. These enemies come to you and bribe you, and you pretend to be shocked. But then you agree, take their money, and let them in. They search, and find nothing, because there's nothing to find, because her real secrets are somewhere else. And she's happy and you're happy, and she even lets you keep some of the money. So where," he said again, "is the other box?"

"Go to hell!"

"If you wish. On the way, I'll call on the College Chancellor, and tell her about all the people you've been cheating. No one will pay you again, and you may lose your place. Where is the box?"

She stared at him, chin trembling. "I don't know!"

"Guess then. You know she talks to people, questions them and frightens them. Perhaps they give her something, or she makes a memorandum? Where would she hide it? Somewhere near here but out of the way. Think hard if you want me to forget the money and time I've just wasted. Think. I'll come back in an hour."

He walked off, hearing his footsteps and stick tapping, hoping they sounded sinister.

*

It was hard to think of anything except how hungry she was, and how her feet hurt.

The famous outlaw, Hardi of the Woods, had many adventures, living among the mountains and sleeping under the stars, but in the end she was betrayed to the troops of Lord Arbeth, and dragged into his hall. There he sat warming his ringed hands before a huge fire, and drinking southern wine. 'Captured at last. And are you ready for death?' he said. 'In the morning I will be, my lord,' she answered. 'But for tonight I will thank you for a soft warm bed, and a tasty broth.' So he laughed, and ordered it done.

"And did he hang her in the morning?" Brin demanded.

"Here's a penny. Toss it up. Heads, she was hanged. Crosses, she escaped."

Most often, it came up Heads, which was a shame, as well as a shorter story. But now Hridnaya agreed with her. *A soft bed and a tasty broth, and then I could accept death.*

And a clean kirtle. It was slimed and torn, and she had no cloak to cover it. Anyone who looked closely would know her for a fugitive.

She stared at the ground – *I am an invisible nobody* – and a wagon rumbled past without seeming to pay any attention.

After a little, she walked out of the bright sun into a little grove of trees surrounding the road. She stopped to run a finger up and down a crease in the hard bark: so lasting and real. *What*

232

a strange thing is a tree. In the city tall pillars commemorate the dead, but a tree commemorates nothing: it just grows, and is. Above her spread layers of green ceiling, pitted with holes that flapped open and shut in the breeze. A small animal with a long furry tail ran straight up the trunk! She watched it in awe, and for a moment she allowed Balki to scamper also, bounding from branch to branch. Leaves and shadows danced in the sun, along with her friend. The glade felt safer than the road.

But she couldn't stay, and she walked out again, forcing her legs to move. One of the big brown animals stared at her from its pasture, making her nervous despite the waist-high wall. On the other side stretched rows of newly-harvested rigs, scattered with yellow house-shapes of stacked grain; and beyond, the Lake. She paused to watch the moving water for a little.

When she looked back, everything inside her jumped, for two riders were coming towards her. It was too late to hide, and she could only step to the side of the road. *Keep going, head down. I am an invisible nobody.*

The horses came closer and closer, quite fast, she thought. *They won't want to delay –*

But - "Greetings, madam – can I ask how far you have come?" She didn't like the voice. Her heart thumped as she looked up.

An ordinary woman her own age or younger had stilled her horse; a beardless man was turning back. His mount reared, sharing his surprise at the stop.

"Well – how far?"

Hridnaya made what she hoped was an ignorant innocent gesture. The woman wasn't deceived, and swung herself to the ground. "Would you hold Arrow for me, please?" she asked her companion, and then, "Aha, it *is* you," and knocked Hridnaya down.

She was on her back on the ground. Struggling to roll over, she felt a stick crack across her side and arm. And again. She cried out.

"What is -?" said the man.

"Her name's Jindi. She's a nasty little beggar-thief I've been searching for, for the King's justice. People feel sorry for her because she can't talk, and then she picks their pouches." The woman was kneeling on her legs, grabbing her wrists with one hand and winding rope round them with the other. A difficult thing surely, but she must have done it many times before. She smiled at Hridnaya, and the smile said *You can't deny it, after all.* Hridnaya wriggled hopelessly.

"Are you needing assistance, madam?" The voice was uncertain.

"Sir, I would be grateful if you would tie this rope to my saddle. I must take her back to the City for trial, and the easiest way will be to have her trot alongside."

Hridnaya stared up at the man, wildly shaking her head, but he didn't look at her eyes. He had foreign clothes, and a tooth missing in a large mouth.

She struggled and even screamed, but it was no use. Between them, the others dragged her upright and attached her wrists by a long rope to the woman's horse.

"Thank you, sir," said the woman. "I'm sorry to lose your company, but now I must turn back. My errand at the College will wait. God go with you."

"Fare well, er, Mobira," and he mounted and rode off. Wriggling in desperation, Hridnaya heard his hooves fade. There were two of them left, along with the big chestnut, snorting and shaking its shoulders.

Was there any way to escape? She was too tired -

"Behave yourself, rat, or I'll make you ride head

downwards. What a lot of trouble you've caused people. You'll regret that when we're back in the City. And before, I think. Now, Arrow, dear." She turned to mount.

No! Hridnaya pulled away as best she could, and slid or fell to the ground. Hooves near her head were a small terror. Everything was terror. "I'll have to teach you now, then," and the woman (Mobira!) lifted her stick. Hridnaya jerked up her bound hands, trying to ward off the blows –

She saw something move; the horse reared, and her enemy was falling, and someone was dragging her aside from the hooves. Then she was lying in the road. So was Mobira, still. Dead? High above, a man was grabbing the horse's bridle, leading it aside, and soothing it. "There, Arrow, isn't it? Fine fellow, fine, don't fear."

It was the same man – he turned with the reins in one hand to stare down at her. "Oh, shit, what happens now? Is your name Jindi?"

No, no, no!

"What is it then?" He narrowed his eyes. Slowly, "Tell me your name." She made a helpless gesture. "Ah. You *can't* talk."

His jacket and hose were both green and so was his floppy felt hat.. Something about his thin face seemed young for a murderer.

He looked rapidly up and down the road, and then down at Mobira, face wrinkled. "It would be good to have three hands now." Cautiously he stroked Arrow's nose, and then turned away to pull out a knife. "Stand still, Arrow, stand still, yes, beautiful," and as he crooned, he knelt to cut Hridnaya free. She opened her fingers painfully, and scrambled up under his eyes. "Hold the horse."

I can't – but he'd put reins in her hand, and she gripped them. "Tell me if anyone's coming." As she obediently looked, he bent over Mobira. There was a stone lying next to her – he must have hit her from behind. Her eyes were closed, but Hridnaya heard breathing. "Which is better, to be a robber, or a spy?" He took a deep breath. "Robber, I think." He crouched to cut the pouch off her belt, and tried to pull a green-stoned ring off her finger. Hridnaya felt a little ill. The ring stuck, and he shrugged.

(No one coming.)

With some trouble, he rolled the woman to the edge of the road, into grass, and turned. "She'll wake up soon, or someone'll find her. We can talk in the trees. I'm not going to hurt you," he added. He moved to take the reins; then "No, wait. I should just -" and she watched as he went back to tug shoes off his victim's feet, and then pushed them into Arrow's saddle-bag. "Right then." He took the reins, and they started walking back to the little grove that she'd come out of less than a half hour ago.

Who are you –why did you – am I safe?

"I don't think you'll ever be safe again," said Balki.

The man had left his own horse tethered among the trees, she supposed to creep up more quietly. He pulled out a water-skin, drank, and then handed it to her. "Fa – oo," she said, her voice loud.

"My name's Jedder. Fejederic. Jedder." He took back the skin, and they looked at each other. "I don't know your name, but I think you're the servant who ran away from my wife in Sapientia. She's in prison, and in a deal of trouble because of that. I'm going to get her out, and so I wanted to find you before your King's people did. Before they could force you to lie about her." He frowned, distorting his whole face. "Are you that woman?"

Hrindaya nodded.

"Good. So. I'm not certain what we do next."

She heard a cracked voice laugh. Her own.

"Are there people looking for you? In Sapientia, or City

Qayn? Which way is safer? D'you have friends? I'd prefer to take you to the City." She nodded again. "Are you hungry?"

Jedder rummaged in a bag, his eyes flicking up and down the little they could see of the road. If only he had parchment, or even one of those wax tablets the children used to learn on - but she could only see food and cloth. "Forgive me, but you're rather road-soiled. Better to change clothes." He politely looked away while she went behind a tree and pulled herself out of the filthy blue kirtle, and into shirt, hose and jacket, all too big for her. She tied her hair back, and he handed her a cloth and showed her how to tie it on over her hair. "Now you could almost be Jaryari. My servant, perhaps? Can you ride? If not, I suppose this lad might carry two. But it'd look strange." She prayed for strength, and put both hands boldly on Arrow's flank.

With some help from Jedder, she got up, *oh help,* much higher than the mule. Arrow's strong-scented warm body breathed and shifted below her, perhaps knowing her for an enemy. "Give me the reins, and I'll lead if you like. Go on," to the horse. They were riding along – bump frightening bump – out back along the road to City Qayn.

At any moment they'd be passing Mobira in the ditch.

They did, and she thought both looked very quickly down and away. Nothing had moved. Jedder crossed himself. Hridnaya was clutching saddle and kirtle-padding, and couldn't.

"She's not dead. Pray God she's not." He went on, "The horse isn't mine; I stole her yesterday from a farm. I don't know her name, but she's been obedient. So now you know my crimes. I've no love for your King Aigith and Queen Rommi, and I'll do anything to get Kelji free." His face was less hard than the words, and at once he said again, "But I don't plan to hurt you. I don't understand what's going on. I'm told she picked you up from the streets – she was teaching you – she took you to the Great

College, and you ran off. Who are you working for?"

"No one," she tried to say.

"Why did you – Tristar's bones!" he exclaimed. "This is going to be difficult. Difficult for you, too. Why did they – aah!" He screwed up his face. "Only yes-no questions. Nod your head or shake. Did you have a reason to run away?"

Hridnaya nodded. She supposed she owed him answers.

*

Afterwards she remembered the pain in her thighs: nothing at first, then discomfort, then worse. And she remembered realising that there was some benefit after all in covering her head from the sun. Now and again they shared some water, but sparingly, for there wasn't much.

Question after question, and to some she had no answers, or none that he could understand. But at last, "So, Kelji didn't send you anywhere. You wanted to go to Sapientia, and she brought you, and you ran away, on a private matter of vengeance, nothing to do with her. She was teaching you to read out of kindness. Or boredom, knowing my wife, or both. You ran away from the Guards. You're not sure where to go back in the City, and you've fallen out with your master. This is right?"

Nod.

"And of course you could be lying to me. You had every reason to, after I attacked your enemy. I don't know if I can trust anyone here, even my hostess." He scowled. "I mean you no harm, but my concern is for Kelji. I'll need you to swear all that you've told me, in some way. I suppose you have judges or courts or something in City Qayn? Who is this Mobira, why is your King doing this?"

The King? Hridnaya's astonishment showed.

"Oh, yes, it seems so." His face twisted with anger and worry, and he looked down at his saddle. Largely to himself, he muttered, "How did all this -? I come here after her, wondering what she'll say – Nadya b'Astith's very kind and says she's in Sapientia, will be back in a day or two – then some highborn lad drops in at night and says she's been arrested for spying! How dare they? And then -" He looked up at her, and she saw him decide not to care that he didn't know her, but to go on talking. No one in the Families, she thought, would have done so. "Yesterday this Mobira woman came – I didn't see her, I was out being laughed at and told *nothing* at the Palace, but our maid listened, and heard someone called Eyanda b'Shen and her son promise to tell lies, promise to help the King hang her if he chooses." He turned his face away for a few moments. "Imadal told me this when I returned, and that some servant who can't talk, you, was involved and was missing, so I ran out, and saw I was being followed. I got away and out of the city, and stole a horse, and came to look for you. She, Mobira, must be looking for you too. We fell in together on the road, she must've known who I was, but she didn't know I knew her. We made polite fellow-traveller talk. Then we saw you. So now –

"Now I've got to get back in, and do something – this is all completely mad. I'm telling all my heart to a stranger!" He breathed heavily a few times, and then smiled at her. "You're accustomed to smooth courtesy, I suppose, but I come from Marod, and we speak plain and ugly."

Where is Marod? Hridnaya thought.

They went on riding, and she tried to digest all that he'd said. Why had he followed Kelji here, apparently without her expectation? How had he got out of the city? *Did I truly get her into so much trouble?*

Once she glanced over, and saw tears running down his face.

A little later he said from nowhere, "Someone once

threatened to do that to me – 'cut your tongue out as the Ricossans do.' I'm sorry – that was a stupid thing to say."

Occasionally people passed them, going west. She put her head down, but she suspected they were staring. "A good day to you, in God's name," Jedder said, and normally received a just-courteous response.

What was going to happen to her when they reached City Qayn? Who could possibly help? *I can't go back to Stansha's – they'd tell Lord b'Nida I'm alive.* In her head she pictured Brin and Lulet – *dear Brin, I must keep him out of danger* – and then Sister Felicity. Which of them would she be least trouble for?

Perhaps she should toss a penny, like Uncle Gridor in his stories.

Still the sun burned down, through the clothes that were too good to be hers.

*

Ittrad returned a little early. He had time to practise his frown before Emmia flurried round the corner, scowling.

"I don't know where any box is, I've never seen one!"

"Guess."

In a whisper, "Only – sometimes – if she's met with someone Mobira comes here and puts on gloves and goes out again. Always gloves – she has a dozen pairs."

She does. I should've noticed that.

He repeated thoughtfully, "She goes out again wearing gloves? Even in summer?"

"Yes, very plain ones. As if she were about to get dirty. I thought maybe she – she might bury her secrets in the ground."

He made a scornful face, and she wailed, "That's all I can think of, it is! I swear it!"

She goes out every time she has something to hide, and digs a little hole, like a dog with a bone, hoping no one will ever notice. Absurd. But yes, she hides things somewhere dirty. Dirty for hands, but not for the rest of her – not like a cave or a loft. Dirty and private.

*

Hridnaya woke to find herself curled up on sand. She sat up, finding that someone, Jedder, had covered her with a cloak, and was sitting nearby, stretching hands to a small fire.

How strange still, to be out of doors at night! Before them, a small church-length away, the Lake whispered. Left and right, up and down, ran perhaps a mile of sand – grey-yellow it had been till the light started to fade. Beyond on their right the huge block-shape of City Qayn, slowly smudging into the dusk. But Hridnaya stared left, west, to a sky dark purple above, and below blue streaked with deep pink.

A sunset. "He makes the outgoings of the morning and the evening to shout for joy." The Psalmist, then, had lived in the country. There were tears on her cheeks.

"Yes, it's beautiful," said Jedder, handing her a refilled water-skin. He was chewing a piece of dried meat. It wouldn't have needed cooking, and surely a fire risked discovery by someone?

But "We need to make a fire and wait on the beach," he'd said when they turned off the road. Then he'd unloaded the horses and led them away, coming back without them, which also was a surprise. She'd dozed off, she supposed, while he was busy with tinder and flint. How long ago?

Now he said, "We're waiting for someone. There are people who – I hope – will get us back into the city. Then I'm not certain – I don't think I can take you to Nadya's. But we can't smuggle horses in, so that's why I let them loose. Anyway they're not ours."

"Smuggle" meant servants sneaking cakes to naughty

supperless children. What did it mean here?

Mobira, if she lived, would realise who had attacked her, and know he'd been out - would recognise him.

"Moh – ee – a." She repeated it a few times, and pointed back. When he understood, Jedder looked downcast. "Yes, you're right. I didn't give her my name, but I expect she guessed." He shrugged, like a child pretending not to care about the punishment coming, and picked up the stolen saddle-bag. "Let's see what she's left."

And he'd almost tipped it onto the darkening sand, where anything small would have been completely lost, before she stopped him. "You're right again," with a sigh.

So he dug his hand in, and laid the items they'd stolen out on his cloak, so both could peer at them.

There were her shoes, which would fit neither, and Jedder tossed away. There was a change of linen and a comb. A little phial, three-quarters full of some liquid. A small wooden box, containing a chunk of wax and a ring etched with a design - that must be for sealing documents. Her pouch of coins, and three apples.

No other food, as they might both have wished, but a second water-skin, not quite full.

"I don't like taking the money," said Jedder, crunching into an apple that had doubtless been intended for Arrow. "I don't mind anything else, but that's stealing, and I have some, enough, I think. But we're not throwing it away." He put everything back in, and handed the whole bag to Hridnaya. "Go on – you'll need things if you've no place." She shared his distaste, but took it.

So they were waiting for someone, and they sat, and Jedder pushed more sticks into the fire. Behind them the grass whispered. Jedder hugged his knees and gazed out at the water they could hear but not see.

Strange thoughts came to Hridnaya unbidden, as she sat there very tired, beside a man.

Four years ago, Sinavid b'Olim, visiting for two nights, had ordered her to bring fresh towels to his chamber. When she came, he put one hand on her breast, slid the other under her skirt, and said, "Your lord and lady want you to please their guests. They wouldn't be happy if I complained."

Afterwards he slapped her for getting blood on the sheets, gave her a piece of silver, and sent her away.

He was the first, but the following Christmas, getting drunk in a corner with Jantorad the cook, she'd thought she might as well. It'd been Jantorad who'd said afterwards, "It's not your fault you can't kiss properly."

And last winter she hadn't been the only one to lie awake thinking useless sinful thoughts about the handsome manservant visiting from the estate. She ought to be growing too old for such weakness, but she wasn't.

Now, all of a sudden, she'd been spending time with a host of strange men. Mejorad and Vaddras and Ittrad and now Jedder. What would it be like?

How would his skin be to touch or stroke; how might his hands move on her side? To lie in a bed or on the grass with him, or another of them – she came aware with a jerk. *What am I thinking? I don't even want to –truly, Lord! Jedder and Ittrad are married, even!*

She really didn't want to think such thoughts, and Balki tutted, but the pictures strayed into her brain, and she was too tired to chase them away. Her finger tingled as if it might reach out towards his sleeve.

She woke again, abruptly, to a new noise, out on the Lake, a regular splashing. It was almost completely dark, apart from the glow of what had been a fire. "I hope this is -" said Jedder, and then, "I'm sorry, I should've warned you, but I should just - I think you need to be blind-folded."

Why? She had no choice but to trust him, but it was more fear. He wound a cloth round her head – close up, he smelt of apple as well as sweat and horse. She waited in blackness, having missed her opportunity to perhaps see stars. *Please, Lord, how tired you must be of me, but -*

Splashes; then steps. A voice, not happy.

"Greetings – who's *she?*"

"There are two of us to go back," said Jedder.

"We could be hanged or burned for this!"

"Are two worse than one? We mean no harm, as I swore yesterday." She heard the clink of coins.

"Should cut your throats. Huh. Up you get, then." Someone pulled her to her feet. There was a pause. "Er, and you, sir, would you put out the fire? If it please you?"

"Just now you threatened to kill me, but you still say 'please.' The fabled Ricossan courtesy."

The man grunted. There seemed to be two people, and the second guided Hridnaya's steps over sand that slithered beneath her, before lifting first one leg and then the other into a boat. The floor was curved, and rocked, so she had to spread her hands wildly.

"Forward, forward, stop. Turn round. Sit down." It was a woman behind her, young.

This was worse than the horse. She clutched her bag with one hand and the bench with the other. Around her the other three began to push. The boat with Hridnaya in it went backwards slowly, then a little faster; and at last it was bobbing, and there was a confusion of people scrambling in, swaying past her, thumping down, and she supposed grabbing oars.

Long ago, a child with her parents and siblings, she'd watched little fishing boats come into harbour.

The breeze teased her shoulders.

"More to starboard – not too much. They're all in bed but one house-light. Straight in now. And you, sir, need to be blinded also."

"Very well."

Unexpectedly the man began to chant, rather fast.

"They cried to the Lord in their trouble, and He delivered them from their distress; He made the storm be still, and the waves of the sea were hushed. Then they were glad because they had quiet, and He brought them to their desired haven. Lord-save-us-and-protect-us-this-night. Amen."

"Amen," said Jedder; and Hridnaya inside her head.

"Must you do that every time? Amen," said the woman.

There was indeed quiet, and in a little the boat bumped against something, and stopped.

"You have to climb. There are rungs to put your feet on. Hold the rope – here."

Hridnaya had seen a rope ladder before, in a picture of a ballad-hero escaping from a tower. She'd never imagined climbing one, blind. She stood up, and then she sat suddenly down, on a seat that rocked.

At least she wasn't wearing a skirt. *Thank you, Jedder.*

The flimsy thing swung her aside as she climbed, away from the wall and into air. She almost screamed. It flapped back. Lifting each foot, moving each hand, became an effort of courage. Her knuckles scraped on stone. Inside her head she was sobbing.

And then someone above put hands on her arms, and she was dragged up and through a window. She was on the floor, and she reached for the blindfold.

"Please to keep it on." It was a new voice, female but

older. This person helped her to stand, and then sit on a chair. She heard someone else climbing.

"Hridnaya, are you -" Jedder.

"No names!"

When the room seemed full - "Welcome, whoever you are, to this house where you'll only stay till I've told you what you're doing next. You go out blindfold; you'll be taken to a lane. It's night, and quiet. When your guide leaves you, keep the blindfolds on till you've counted twenty-five - unless you hear anyone coming. Has he paid? Are you ready to go?"

"Yes," said the younger woman.

Hridnaya was guided by hand and whisper - "Ten steps down here, the stair turns to the right," out through what smelt like a backyard, and then they brushed a gatepost. Along a little way; a pause for the guide to listen. A rat or something similar scuttered. "Round this corner." Half a dozen more steps; then she was abruptly twisted around so that she became dizzy. "Start counting," and the woman was gone. It was dark and quiet, but she heard Jedder obediently murmuring numbers.

"Twenty-five." They pulled off their scarves, and they were in a little street. There was more than one lane off it - she didn't think she could have identified the house they'd come from - but they were back in the city. The sky was lightening. *Is it tomorrow?*

"I believe this is Abigail's Alley," Jedder whispered. "D'you know it?"

No.

"I got here off October Street. I can find my way back to the square with all the pillars, I think. And where then?" He reached out to touch her sleeve, quite gently. "I'm sorry, but I just - I need to know where you go. I need your evidence. If we had parchment, I could write it down."

He looked scared, she thought. He'd attacked and robbed Venomous Mobira. Could the Families allow a foreigner who did such things to live?

Brin, or Sister Felicity?

Or maybe there was someone else.

*

Long before she was born, before the War, some of the b'Asa family had lived here. They'd left behind an unkempt patch, and the name Burnedhouse Street. Gridor and Miya's home was three houses along. The outer door was unlocked, and they stepped into the very dark passageway. Its odd but perpetual smell of fried onions was strangely reassuring.

Please can I just sit down, and have a cup of ale? Hridnaya was thinking. *I don't know what comes after that. I need to know, but I'm too tired.* Yawning, she led the way up the tenement stair, hearing Jedder stumble and swear softly. There were four doors on the first landing.

I'm sorry to wake you, Aunt. She banged on the door and waited. Banged again.

"Who -? Wait a moment, please." There was movement within, and the door opened a little. Aunt Miya had thrown on a gown and lit a candle. She blinked at them.

"Who is it – oh! *You.*"

She was pulled inside, Jedder following.

"You! Where the hell have you – d'you know what you've done? *D'you know?*" Her aunt was spitting with rage; her hand holding the candle shook. Although low, her voice was spiked with venom. "Do you want to destroy us all – traipsing round with your -" she spared Jedder a glance – "How much more trouble can we endure?"

I don't understand, Hridnaya gestured.

"Oh, so innocent! You –aah!" Lost for words, she threw

her eyes up to the ceiling, and her candle onto the table, so that she could slap her niece's arm. "What have you done? Brinnon thought you were dead – what else could he think? It's your fault, what's happened to him! Your fault! Get out, and take this – whoever – with you! Get *out!*"

There was a flicker and a grunt from behind a bedcurtain. "Be quiet, Gita! She's just leaving. Get out!"

They were on the stairway again. The door was shut.

"Who's Brinnon?" Jedder whispered, but Hridnaya had to lean a hand against the wall, and gasp for breath.

What's happened to him? Oh, please Lord.

She ran down the stairs.

It wasn't far, but she couldn't run all the way, especially not in the streets at dawn. Cowards and children run – and thieves. She walked fast.

Is he dead?

In Jaydrich's Street, she paused for a horrible moment outside the door. Knock. Knock. Wait.

"Who -" Lulet's voice – distressed, exhausted. The door opened.

There was light inside, again a single candle. Brinnon was sitting, leaning forward with his elbows on the table.

Hridnaya heard herself scream.

*

"That's their house there, sir," said the passer-by Mej had accosted.

"Thank you." Surely so early in the morning the man Brinnon would be at home. Excitement crinkled up and down his back. *Now, sir, you will give me answers.* He gripped his sword, as he entered the passage and knocked.

Voices, and there was a little scream, and he pushed the door open.

It was a square poor-family's-room, with a lot of people in it. Someone was crying. Others were staring at him. Then –

"You!" The fury hit him first; then the words. Then someone struck him hard in the face. His head hit the door edge. His shoulders were thrust back and back, and the door went with them until it slammed shut. Skull ringing, Mej reached for his sword, but someone else's stronger fingers closed over his hand. That someone had an arm across his chest, and with his free hand held a knife close to Mej's chin.

The beardless Jaryari, Fejederic.

"You filthy fucking swine!" he said. "What did she do to you? What did she do? She – you – did you try to rape her on the road, and she kicked you in -"

The terrible word *rape* made everything black for a moment, and he could only squeak, "No!"

"Some kind of *revenge* -"

"Take your hands off – I don't know what -"

More slowly, "You are Mejorad b'Shen. You promised that Mobira woman to tell lies about Kelji, to help your King hang her. Kelji is my wife. If she dies, I will kill you. That's a promise. It's bloodfeud."

How did he know? "I didn't! I came here to help Kelji." That was true.

"To *help*." Over his shoulder his enemy said, "Madam, forgive my ill manners. I have a quarrel with this man." To Mej, "These people are already in distress. Where I come from, a stranger would put down his sword, and explain his presence."

He stepped back after one last jerk, and let Mej look past him, and see that he'd stepped into two stories, not one.

The shutter was still closed, so there was little light. A man sat leaning on the table, staring at his visitors. His back was covered with a sheet, and there were what looked like smudged lines of newly-dried blood coming through the cloth. He was breathing in slow gasps. A woman knelt on the floor at his knees, sobbing into her hands. Two children, one barely out of babyhood, sat clutching each other and staring on a box bed. A second woman, stocky and ordinary-looking, stood in the centre of the room. Her hands were clenched by her sides.

"Please, my lords," she said in a tiny voice.

Mej controlled his humiliation and fury. He drew his sword slowly, and laid it on the floor. "Madam, I mean no harm to you. I am here searching for someone. This man's wife has been wrongly suspected of spying, because she took a maid to Sapientia, and the maid ran away. She's called Hridnaya. I think you know her, and she needs to explain-"

The woman's eyes slid to the other, the crying one, and back again, but she said, "That's not possible, please, sir. My sister-in-law works for the b'Nida-"

"She did work for them, until they threw her out for some cause or other, and she ran off to Sapientia." He walked over, and yes, it was her on the floor, the little Voiceless. "You've caused a great deal of trouble," he began - but he couldn't but be distracted by the bloodied man. His face was twisted, and his eyes wide (Mej thought) with the constant effort of not crying out.

Now he noticed that the room was drenched in pain and terror.

"What happened to you?" he had to ask.

The other woman said behind him, "Four days ago, on Friday, Lord b'Nida's Housemother came here looking for my sister-in-law; saying she was missing. My husband thought – he thought she'd been murdered or – so he went to the Hall of Justice to enquire and complain." Her voice was dull but clear. "He only meant to ask, but then they made him angry. He shouted, and – they said it was some crime – disrupting the city's order and abusing the Families – so yesterday the Judge ordered-”

“How many?” Fejederic asked.

“Fifteen.”

Abruptly cold, Mej remembered the flogging he’d half-noticed the day before. He’d only heard the whip’s first two or three cuts, and the screams.

The sheet had slid a little off the man’s shoulder, so he could see where the flesh had torn and curled. And bruise-blackened, because whips are heavy as well as sharp.

Fifteen was the kind of sentence they called “firm”. The man would live. He’d be able to work again – just – by tomorrow, probably.

“And so his master said he’s brought disgrace on the business, and not to come back. There are plenty of others eager to take his place, just as skilled. So now -”

So now no work, no money, no food.

“Poor devil” and *“serves you right”* collided in Mej’s head. *But the wife and children – innocents always suffer.*

“I’m sorry,” said the man behind him. “As I was saying, my name’s Fejederic. Or Jedder – everyone calls me Jedder. I don’t wish to disturb you. Your sister’s helped me, given me some information that I need to write down, and then she needs a place where she’s safe. You, sir,” and Mej turned, “still need to explain your presence.”

I am Lady b’Shen’s great-grandson. I should be in command here. Boldly he said, “I don’t need to explain myself to you, *sir,* or to anyone. This woman -” He squatted down to look at her. She’d stopped crying, but her face was swollen and wet. Her eyes met his – reluctant and miserable. “You went to see someone at the College, didn’t you? It was a frolic of your own, nothing to do with Kelji. I think I know what. Both of you,” he nodded towards the man, “were at my cousin’s trial. And *you* were loitering round us the other Sunday, when Kelji met you. Seeking to cause trouble for the b'Shen. I don't know if any of our enemies was paying you, or if it was just because of the accident in the tavern, but look now what you've done."

The woman said, did, nothing; not even her face changed. But he heard the man Brinnon draw breath – and then the bloody Jaryari interfered again.

"What *she's* done? You're the one scheming against the innocent with this Mobira! How dare you say -"

"I'm not scheming, sir!"

Flatly, "You and your mother agreed with her on the precise lies you would tell, the day before yesterday, sitting in the living room at Nadya b'Astith's house."

Who told you -? "I didn't! There was a conversation, but nothing about telling lies!"

"My informant says differently."

"Nadya wasn't in the room! Who d'you think you are, sir?"

"Had you forgotten? I'm the man who's going to kill you if they hang my wife. Or if you hurt this woman or her family in any way."

"If you want to help prove Kelji's innocence," Mej began, but he was interrupted.

The sitting man whispered, "Not accident. In the tavern." Each word was a gasp.

"Brin -" his wife whispered, but he went on, "Not accident. B'Shen. Murderers."

"Fucking hell! Are you people not finished with that yet?" Mej thought of Rorash banished, and he was filled with rage. "You snivelling - muck-pokers! If I walk out now and fetch the Guards, do you know how much shit you'll all be in?"

Brinnon's wife wailed. The little girl – six years old? -

scrambled off the bed and ran to her mother, clutching her skirt and crying too.

"No more shit than we're in already," said Jedder. "Someone will come and arrest and hang me soon for what I've done. Everyone here is in more danger than I think you've ever known, you pampered rich bratling." He placed his foot on top of Mej's sword, just in time to stop Mej grabbing it up.

"Mother, mother," cried the little girl, unfairly reminding Mej of Firi, and making him feel bad.

And suddenly the mother cried, "I should be at work! Oh, God help us!"

Mej almost laughed. But she put the child aside abruptly, and whirled round to grab a cloak from a hook by the door. "I'll be so late!" She was wiping tears away with the back of her hand. "Minna, be good -"

She couldn't go. She was the only person here with any sense.

"Lulet," Brinnon gasped. "You haven't slept."

"If Fandis throws me off too, we'll have *nothing!* The children will starve!" She took a breath, and then another. She blew her nose. And before everyone's eyes, something strange happened.

"My lords," she said, and all were quiet, "I don't understand why you're here, but I beg of you not to – not to hurt each other or anyone else. I'm sure you're both good people." Mej could feel her hoping, praying, that this was true. "Please don't - my family has meant no ill to anyone. Please to take some ale, and sit down. Hridna -" she turned back to the other – "you know where things are – and you must be hungry. You might be able to manage the broth in the pot. Please." and the women looked at each other; words passing silently.

"In the name of God," she said to the two men.

"We do not kill children," said Jedder, after a pause.

Where have I heard that? "I didn't come here to hurt anyone," said Mej gruffly.

Then Lulet walked quickly over to kiss her baby son's head, and back to stroke her husband's hand.

"Love," he said, and a tear rolled down. She put a finger on his forehead, and then drew it down his face to the mouth. No one else moved as she walked rapidly across the room, and out.

"Sir," said Jedder after a moment, "you are most blessed in your wife."

"Yes."

The other woman crossed to a shelf. She took down a jug and cups; she began to pour. Suddenly Mej was visiting a poor person's home. There was ale, which she passed round. She poked the fire into life, and stirred the pot hanging over it.

Jedder sat down with his back to the door. "Let us be well-mannered, then, and talk, as our hostess asked."

Something extraordinary had happened to the room. Mej leant against a wall, and reminded himself that the self-confessed foreign outlaw had threatened to kill him, and the other oaf had called him a murderer. His anger rose again -

Then he remembered. *We do not kill children, we do not commit rape, we do not take pleasure in torment.* It was the rule of the Queen's Thirty of Marod.

And Marod is now part of Jaryar. So -

Fejederic Queensbrother? *Could it be? Have I walked into a story?*

"Where are we now?" said Jedder. He looked up at the ceiling, and then began to speak quickly. "You came here to arrest this woman, didn't you?"

"Not arrest! Can't you see, I'm on your side, Kelji's side, here!"

"You're on Mobira's side, and that's your King's, I suppose."

"No! Mobira – my mother has reasons for wanting to help her, but I don't. I swear."

"Do you?" The man looked at him warily. "These people said something about murder."

"They're lying; maybe they want money, or to make trouble-"

"Ssss!" Brinnon actually hissed. The woman Hridnaya turned round from the fire, and took two steps forward before kneeling, eyes still dull but fixed on Jedder. She traced something on the floor with the spoon she'd been using to stir the pot.

"L?" said Jedder. She jerked her head agreeingly, and traced again. "I. A. R." And she pointed the spoon accusingly at Mej.

"Liar?"

Inside his head boiled with fury, but somehow he managed to speak low. "Your uncle, whatever his name was, died by chance. You *know* this. You do. You've just seen what happens to slanderers, and I will make sure it happens to you if-"

"Don't threaten her, sir," said Jedder. He cast his eyes to the ceiling, and cried, "I can't believe this! What am I doing here, listening to this nonsense, while Kelji – do your people torture prisoners? And I can't spare – I must – no, very well then!" He jumped up, and strode over to the fire. The little girl was sitting there wide-eyed. "I don't know your name. Can you do something for me? Go and open the shutter, and peep out, and see if anyone who looks like a soldier is coming."

Why would they? Mej wondered.

"I'm Minna, sir."

"Can you do that, and I'll give you a coin?" Mej, Brinnon and the woman kneeling with a spoon all watched as the child scampered over and unhooked the shutter. A block of grey light fell on the floor.

"There's no one, sir."

"Keep looking, please. Warn me if they come. Now. What the hell is all this about a murder in a tavern? Do I have to find out what it means before we can talk sensibly to each other? This is what you were finding out about in Sapientia?" he asked Hridnaya, and she nodded.

"There's nothing to find out," said Mej. "Her kinsman got in my cousin's way, and was knocked down and most unfortunately for him, he died. That is *all*. These people were not there, and I was."

"How do you mean," asked Jedder, "knocked down?"

"My cousin was crossing the room, and -" he made a throwing-aside gesture – "and he banged his head against a wall."

Jedder looked at the other two, frowning. The woman said, in the ugly grunt of the Voiceless trying to talk, "Mo –ee – ya."

"Mobira wasn't there, and my cousin wouldn't take orders from her!"

"You think Mobira was involved? Tristar's Bones. Oh for Mistress Fillim. Sir, does your head hurt? Where you hit the door?" said the man suddenly.

"My head – yes, somewhat." Mej put up a hand, pressed, and winced.

"But you're not dead, are you? I am your cousin, you are this man. Push me."

"What?"

"Push me," and Jedder was striding towards him, and Mej pushed. The other man swayed.

"Harder than that, I think? Try again."

So he pushed, and Jedder stumbled backwards, and he

did indeed fall over on his arse.

"And he hit the wall with his head," Mej said crossly.

Sitting on the floor, Jedder said, "No one dies like that."

"But he did. I was there."

"Was a physician called? What did they say?"

"Not much," said the man Brinnon, staring.

"Was there blood?"

Mind your own business, Mej thought, but he said, "A little, not much, but however it was, he did die. I fell on him, and I saw him die."

"You fell?"

"It was getting ready to be a brawl, and someone tripped me up," he said sullenly.

"But was this man ill already? Did he use to get pains in his chest, anything like that?" Jedder asked the others.

"No. Sir," said Brinnon. The Voiceless woman's head moved, from speaker to speaker.

"Falling over doesn't kill anyone."

But it did!

Then everyone heard Hridnaya take a breath. She turned to the bed and lifted up the younger child, presumably some relative of hers. Three people watched.

She laid the child down on the floor, on his back. "Aunty, what -?" Aunty waggled a finger in a circle to make the boy smile. Then she reached for the knife at her belt.

She's mad – will she kill the child? Mej felt painful terror, but it was only a gesture. A stabbing motion near his midriff.

Then she looked up, tears still drying on her face, and pointed at Mej.

He stared.

"*After* he fell," said Brinnon slowly. "Stabbed -"

Now everyone was looking at him. "*What?* I should have

you arrested for – I didn't stab him!! Why should I – I didn't do anything!" Inspiration came to him. "There was no other wound on him. No knife wound!"

"The physician could have overlooked one," said Jedder. "Or been bribed to."

"But he wasn't! I didn't! He must have been ill before; he was swaying about – ill, or drunk."

"Or poisoned," said Jedder.

The world seemed to stop.

At last, "What do you mean?"

"No one would murder someone the way you describe, but unless your cousin was a Hercules the man wouldn't have died anyway. Some poisons take time to work. You saw him die?"

"I – yes – I fell onto him, and -" He shut his eyes, looking back. "He was just lying there – he tried to talk but there were no words. His eyes were -" he shuddered – "his eyes were all black, no colour, odd. Then his head jerked -"

"And some poisons do that to the eyes."

"He'd bought a drink. But -"

"D'you know where he'd been before the tavern? That's what you need to find out. It's not likely the landlady killed him, especially if he chose the place by chance." Jedder scrambled up, and looked over at the others.

It was at this moment that the little girl called, "People are coming, Guards."

"Shit." Jedder was at the window; then he turned back to the woman. "I need to get out of here, and if Mobira sent them, I think you do also. Is there a back way?"

"Back yard. Climb wall," said Brinnon.

Mej saw Jedder blink rapidly.

"Please God they don't yet know which house." His eyes swept the room, including Mej; then he said to the child, "Put away the cups." She stared, and it was Mej who grabbed them up and stuck them back on their shelf, his heart beating strangely fast.

An adventure. This really is an adventure.

Jedder bent over the table. "If they come, if they know we were here – say – say I forced my way in. I put a knife to your throat, or your daughter's throat. I've kidnapped your sister. Here." He reached into his pouch, and shoved a few coins into the man's fist. "I'm sorry for your trouble." Standing up, he looked at the woman. "Are you ready?" His eyes moved on, to Mej.

"Hridna," gasped Brinnon, stretching out a hand with pain.

She paused; then grasped it with a jerky movement.

"You're alive. Thank God. Go."

"Where are you going, Aunty?" Mej heard, as he pushed out into the passage with the other two. It was a building like a hundred others – four single-room homes on each floor, two each side of a smelly passage; stairs up; entrances front and back.

No noise from outside yet.

Mej opened the back door onto a hovel-sized yard: henhouse, privy, wall. Easily climbable wall.

"If they're wise, they'll have someone in the alley," said Jedder. Mej turned and looked the house up and down. Four storeys high.

"Upstairs," he said, and they ran back in. Up one flight, up two.

Why am I doing this? Is it treason? I don't care. I'm going to hell anyway.

The woman was panting. They reached the top landing. There were window-holes at each end - the pauper's exchange, light for warmth. Mej opened one shutter, looked out, and pointed.

Behind all the yards ran a messy alley between streets.

Yes, a woman in Guards' livery stood at one end, staring ahead of her. Plainly she didn't know exactly which part of wall to watch, but she was watching.

And now they heard a banging on a door below. The woman Hridnaya, Hridna, whatever her name was, moaned.

I can do this, but can they? Mej leaned out and peered. "Up?" he suggested to Jedder, and received an odd look and a shrug in return. He twisted out through the just-wide-enough gap, balanced on the sill, and stretched up –

Must be quiet.

If he were a holier man, he'd be praying the Guard didn't look up. And that the window was sturdy. One foot on the top of the frame, reach, grab, pull.

Pull.

He was up, swinging himself onto the roof at its highest point. It sloped to the front, diverting rain into the street's sewers rather than the yard's mud. He spread himself across the highest point, and looked down.

The Voiceless woman was squeezing out through the window behind him. He heard little gasps. Her face staring up was blank with terror, or other emptiness. Probably she'd never done much climbing. Jedder was helping her place her feet, as she clutched with one hand, and tentatively raised the other.

Mej had always climbed alone, and he hadn't often had to stare downward like this. Thirty feet to the ground –

poor creature. He stretched, and grasped her wrist. "Now the other one," he whispered. A moan or gasp, and she forced her fingers off the window frame, and reached up.

He braced his feet each side, and pulled.

Up, up. Don't you scream. Up. His arms were agony.

She was bent over the roof; her legs floundered in air; she'd made it.

Jedder had more trouble getting through the window, but less pulling himself onto the roof.

Now they only had to crawl along the slanting slate to the far end of the tenement – hoping windows and doors were unlocked in the end house. And making no noise.

A sudden breeze ruffled Mej's hair, reminding him that he'd often done this kind of thing before. For pleasure.

*

On Tuesday morning, Ittrad went to the back court, choosing a time when most people had finished getting ready for the day and were in lectures (he was missing Bones of the Upper Body). Between the kitchens and the stable was a little space too ugly to be overlooked by any windows. Only God and the heavens watched over the pigpen and muckpile, and the ramshackle privies for those like Ittrad who had nowhere better to go. It was a simple wooden building with a thatched roof, divided into stalls, the window unshuttered for light and rain to come in, and it smelt.

Not inside, he thought, *where anyone sitting bored or constipated might notice. But round the corner of the outer wall –*

And yes, snugly tucked beneath the eaves just above head height, was something – something wrapped in grey cloth, a little stained.

He edged it down, and took off the cloth, smiling with grim triumph. It was indeed the pair of the other box, the one with a girl's image on the top. Maybe Mobira had or had once had a twin. Babies often die. It was locked, but again Lord b'Nida's key fitted and turned. Ittrad felt his heart bump, and his face grin. He carried it into the privy, lit a rush-light, and sat down. If anyone came in, he could be reading old love-notes before tearing them up and then shitting on them. Someone had done that in some tale.

In the box was a bundle of documents, folded and bound together with ribbon. Quite a large bundle – was he to skim through, read them all, or take them awayl?

Thou shalt not steal. Ittrad remembered his Bible.

The bundle nearly filled the box, which seemed odd. He ran his finger over it – surely it was shallower than its mate. Which meant –

He gently pressed and fiddled, and the false bottom came out. There was one piece of parchment underneath, and he unfolded it.

The writing was unsigned, but the bottom right corner was marked with a seal. He'd seen that seal or something like it before, on very important documents.

12th November.

To the most faithful Mobira.

This follows our conversation. Fear not. What you do for a King is absolved, and I will protect you. He is a traitor and deserves it. Make sure it is an accident, as we spoke of. Within one week.

As you love me, dear one, destroy this letter.

The seal of the Evening King.

*

"Don't run," Jedder hissed.

The two men and one woman walked out of the end house and turned the corner. Hridnaya had wiped tears off her face with her sleeve, and painted on a jaunty smile. It looked as unreal as one of Aladim's dolls, but Mej admired the effort. He tried and failed to whistle.

But he felt alive.

It was mid-morning now, and there were people. They edged past a lad struggling with a bucket of water too heavy for him. Over there were two servants in red b'Iri tabards. Squeals and shouts from within a small church indicated that it was in weekday use as a childpen. A man and a little boy were arguing under the tree by the church door; the child was preparing to screech.

Jedder had lost his hat, but his jacket was foreign as well as dirty, and his hose were torn. Heroes are often untidy, and smell of sweat. If he took off his shirt, would they see the fabled brand on his shoulder, the mark of the Thirty?

"People are looking at us. Where can we talk?" he said. "Are you pretending to show us foreigners the city?"

There were indeed stares, which was bad. Mej waved hopefully towards a grubby tavern, not one he knew. Inside it was quiet and ill-lit, this early in the day. "Three cups of wine, if you please," he said to the landlord, and they sat down next to the wall. There was a still moment.

"What now?" said Jedder, his eyes unfriendly. Plainly none of them knew. "I don't understand your place in this, sir. What are they going to do with Kelji? Mobira -" he shut his eyes and opened them again -"doesn't care for innocence or guilt – she has her own purposes. I have to hope that there are others in your – courts or palaces, I suppose – who do care. That your trials are open, and your judges honest."

"They are!" cried Mej, remembering Rorash.

"Hridnaya is a witness that Kelji's not a spy. I need to get her evidence written down, I suppose, and she needs to be safe from the King's agents. She's not safe with me."

"Why not?"

"Should I trust you, or tell you?" He scowled. "I don't know your laws, but hindering the King's agent in her work, assaulting her with a weapon – these must be serious crimes?"

Mej nodded, longing to know more.

"So. She may even be dead, which would be murder. And I can't make myself invisible." He rubbed his telltale bare chin. "Soon someone will find me, any moment they may come, and I don't think either of you want to be with me when they do. I'd better go back to Nadya b'Astith's and try to look innocent. There's parchment there. But *you* – she needs a place. Do you have anywhere else to go?" he asked her, and his voice was gentle.

Slowly she shook her lowered head.

Arms were thrust over the table suddenly, and three cups placed before them. "Can I get you anything to eat, sirs, madam?"

The Voiceless need different food, mashed to mush, Mej remembered, but it would be unwise to draw attention to that. "Two bowls of porridge, if you please?" He wasn't hungry himself. When the man had gone, "I'll look after her." *How?* As soon as he'd said it, a bright idea came to him.

But *"Oh,"* she said, shaking her head, and giving him a very nasty look.

Ungrateful trout. "I helped you get out of the house," he reminded them both.

"Yes," said Jedder slowly, "but you may be reporting to someone –"

"I'm *not*, I swear." In the pause, he took a gulp of wine. It was terrible – worse than the College's. This was an ale-and-pie shop for the poor.

"What *do* you want with us?" Jedder's eyes flicked around nervously. "Be quick."

I want to go on being part of this. "I want Kelji not to be hanged." *You said you'd kill me if she is.* "My mother has reasons to want to please the King, and so yes, she promised to help –

but I don't want that. And – and – if Mobira or anyone poisoned that man Flower-in-Hood, I want to know, and prove it." He needed to decide if he believed that theory.

Another pause.

"I think you have to go somewhere," Jedder told the woman.

"Oh. I – ar." *Liar?* Her eyes glared with pointless time-wasting hate, and then she was looking down, blinking tears. Then, quickly and clumsily, she began to scrabble in her pouch. Jerking out a coin, she looked from one to the other, and tossed it. She fumbled the catch, and it fell on the table. "Heads," said Mej. She nodded angrily, took it back, and then - "Yeh," she said to Jedder. So that was the way servants made decisions.

The man said to Mej, "Don't hurt or betray her, or I'll kill you." The threat was weary but implacable. To her, "I'll write down what you said, and show – read it to you. And what then? I don't know what the – what your people, what anyone's going to do. If we separate, and we have to, we need a meeting place or a go-between, or a way to communicate -"

"I can come to Nadya's house."

"Yes - if they let me stay there. If not - Swear," he said, "both of you, swear that you'll stand up for Kelji, for the truth."

He thinks the King will kill him, when he's caught. Maybe today. And maybe he's right.

"I swear."

The woman nodded, and crossed herself.

The tavern's man came back with porridge. Jedder jiggled on his bench, and as soon as the server was gone, he leapt up. "Fare well." Again a pause, looking at Mej, chewing his lip. "Lord, let me have chosen right!" And then he was gone.

Mej realised with a shock that foreigners prayed, secret prayers of the soul, in public taverns, where others could hear.

He was left with a crazy woman whom he'd promised to protect. How, where, from whom?

"Who is he truly?" he whispered. "How did you meet him?"

She couldn't answer, of course.

And who are you? B'Nida castaway, criminal, trouble-maker, spy? At this moment she didn't look capable of being any of these things. Her face was blank and stupid, but tense, the marks of tears still on her cheeks; and he was reminded of her brother holding his mouth shut between words, determinedly not crying out.

Her hand shook as she lifted a spoon and began to feed herself. Mej tried to occupy himself with his own bowl. He hoped his bright idea would work.

There were two people in the world he trusted. One of them was in Defardu. But the other-

She took an age, but at last she was finished, and not too messy, although tears were again oozing, drawing attention to them both. *Civilised people weep in the confessional and in their bed. Nowhere else.* So he'd been told often enough after punishment. "Come on," he said, and took her arm, and she *shuddered,* but she stood up. "Smile," he hissed, and stopped to wipe her face with his sleeve. *Ugh.*

She seemed to have to make a huge effort to do it, but she put on the smile, lifted her chin, and said, "Ha."

"Yes, yes, ha ha. Come on."

He remembered to pay the charge, and they wove out into the street between people. The woman didn't look at him, so even with her eyes she asked no questions. That was as well, because he wasn't sure what he could have said.

*

They reached the Avenue of the Palace without meeting

anyone Mej knew. It was a wide street with trees either side, and no windows in the high walls. Long-dead King Mevander and Queen Jillida, larger than life in stone, stood either side of the Royal Gate. This stayed open all day, and people thronged the courtyard beyond, mostly doing nothing but throng. One or two were buying ale and spiced fish from an enterprising barrow seller. When he'd been six years old, it had been Mej's highest ambition to own a barrow like that, and sing of his wares.

On the far side of the courtyard, the Palace; and its great bronze doors were shut, and Guards stood before them. As Mej and Hridnaya sidled past the rich and middling idlers, he watched these doors grow bigger and bigger. They were one of the wonders of City Qayn (tutors said.) Yani herself had carved them with pictures of Solomon's Temple in the Bible.

However, the less fuss and explanation the better, so he turned aside. "This way." In the far left corner of the courtyard was a trio of brightly-leaved lime trees. They'd been planted long ago, to provide shade in summer. But also, as Mej's older sister had explained to him, to block most people's view of a set of steps built against the Palace wall, leading to a small entrance at the second level. This was the Quiet Door, that trivial people were discouraged from using. Mej knew it fairly well, mostly from genuine errands.

"Come on," he said again. The stair was narrow and handrail-less, but they'd both been clambering on a roof a half hour before, and she scrambled obediently beside him. The Guard at the bottom of the stairs passed them as harmless and only two, and the Guard at the top watched them come. There was a bell next to him to ring if he needed help.

And, *oh most excellent*, Mej recognised the man, both from a previous visit, and as one of his friend Majilli b'Trai's hangers-on. He was built large and strong, with a cheerful brown face and thick beard.

"Greetings." *Can't remember your name.*

"God's greetings, sir. May I enquire your errand?"

"I have a letter from my great-grandmother to deliver personally. She told me to be discreet. And to bring a Voiceless in case we need a private talk." He indicated Hridnaya. *A pretty good story,* he thought.

"For whom is the letter?"

Oops. Er –

"The Queen's Chamberlain," *oh, what's his name?* "Krothon."

"Will you -" Mej was ahead of him, and had unbuckled and handed over his sword and belt before the man could finish the question.

Down below, small figures clumped and strolled and murmured background noise. No one seemed to be looking up at them.

The Guard ushered them through out of sunlight, into the anteroom beyond. A comfortable square room, with a colourful tapestry, and no other people. "Thank you." The door closed. Mej blew out his relief.

So far, all well. But now he needed to find Queen Rommi, or some very confidential servant, and persuade them to allow him an audience. Which would be easier without this odd-looking woman who might already be on someone's Suspected of Crime list. So, "Stay here. I'll come back for you," he said. *But suppose –* He thought quickly. There were parchment and pen on a small table. He wrote **I am accompanying my lord of the b'Shen** in large letters, and gave it to her. "Show this if anyone asks what you're doing." An enquiring Palace servant might even assume "my lord" meant Uncle Yettrid. He grinned. "I'll come back. Don't weep, Hridnaya. All will be well," he finished, and walked out of the room, rid of her for the time.

He was standing on an empty landing, from which a staircase went up and down, and other doors opened. The stairs upwards were noticeably shabbier – downwards wasn't very grand, but there were at least pictures hanging on the walls, boring ones. Two servants with the white-striped-with-gold Palace tabard passed by down, arguing about their favourite types of soup.

He smiled pleasantly (on business but not in a hurry) and pattered down. *Now let's see. The Palace.*

When he was eight, he'd been selected to bring birthday greetings to Queen-before-Zinial Fayadi on behalf of the b'Shen. A little older, he'd attended two or three feasts or other ceremonies, the details too dull to recall. Two years ago, he'd been presented to the Evening King with twelve others, before leaving for military service in the south.

And then there was the time Majilli had dared him and Narod to sneak in at night to leave a box of horse-shit in the middle of the Council Chamber. Not a successful prank – they'd been caught brown-handed as it were, and the result had been the worst thrashing of his life.

But anyway he knew the Palace. *I need to go down to get to the better rooms. The Morning Queen's apartments and offices are on the Great Square side – which is that way, I think. But I want the grand place with the mosaic floor, where people come in.*

He reached street level, and went through a room whose sole purpose seemed to be to provide pegs for garments to hang on. And then he was indeed in the Mosaic Corridor, light and huge and buzzing with people, where the great and pretending-to-be-great gathered. Here supplicants who'd passed the first test by satisfying, or perhaps bribing, the Guards outside came to wait - and lowly dependants were summoned to make speeches of gratitude and entreaty, while peeping around in awe.

It was a high hall, the width of a small road, and he was standing at the far end. A long way ahead was the Great Stair, but the hall itself also led to many doors. More Guards stood around. Anyone unfamiliar with the place was staring at the floor - paved with thousands of tiny squares of coloured stone, placed together to form pictures inside white rectangles – pictures of fruit, or stars, or – Too many feet were in the way.

The people here were more purposeful than those outside. Some marched through the hall and vanished. Others talked in groups – but real quiet talk, not "look-I'm-here" stuff. The outer wall had windows high up but large, shutters pulled back. Light streamed down in squares on the wonderful floor.

Mej had time to look around, and know how out of place he was, grubby and moss-streaked.

Then, "Are we acquainted, sir?" asked a middling-old, middling-brown woman with gold-coloured threads looping through her black hair.

A polite way of asking what he wanted.

"Madam, I am Mejorad b'Shen. I am honoured to meet you." He bowed.

"Of course, Lady b'Shen's great-grandson, I think? What do you seek here? Can I be of assistance?"

He had enough sense not to ask for the Queen straight away. "I have a message to be delivered to Yikkeri, daughter of Janika. Is she to be found?"

"I will enquire, sir. Please to take a cup of wine." She moved away, and Mej wandered as indicated to a finely-carved table with jugs and cups and napkins.

He sipped slowly, heart banging, but pleased at his

success so far. But what would Rommi say to him – would she be willing to help her bad boy? Almost automatically he felt his face put on its defiant rogue expression. *("You can't make me respectable; don't waste time trying. Yes, we broke seven windows that night – if you say eight it was eight.")*

No. Smile calmly. Look like a courtier. Like that couple there –

"I've tasted better than this, you know," said the man.

"Ssh."

"As have you."

"Yes, yes. The foreign wines from Tell are better, we all agree. Don't be disloyal." The woman glared at her companion.

Or like him –

The fat man he'd spotted – grey beard but little hair of any colour – padded up to the table, took a cup and drank thirstily.

"How went it, Padrafor?" The loyal wine-drinking woman had a long nose, and red beads round her neck.

"Delayed *again*. But it's not just me. Everything in the courts is to make way for this most important new trial."

"Whose is that?"

"Oh, the foreign woman they arrested in Sapientia, the Jaryari spy. It starts on Thursday. Everything else is to wait. It's just within the hour been sent for crying round the streets, the Secretary told me." He'd raised his voice, so that his news would carry and impress, and several heads turned towards him, like pigeons on a roof.

Thursday. The day after tomorrow.

They were talking about Kelji. Yet somehow it was also the fool pauper he saw in his head, the sheet sticking to his bloodied back, and his wife saying, "The children will starve."

People shouldn't have to suffer like that. They shouldn't.

Kelji shouldn't be hanged. And Rorash –

He saw Rorash sitting on the floor in The Morning Dream, saying, "What have I done? What have I *done?*"

Taking the blame, according to Jedder's theory, for someone else's murder.

Mej's head fizzed with rage, but suddenly he heard sharp tapping steps, and he had to clear his expression and remember his errand. Two people were coming purposefully towards him, and one was Yikkeri.

Queens renounced their servants – most of them – as well as their sons, and Yikkeri had been one of only two that Rommi had been permitted to take after the Conclave.

She was pale-skinned but wrinkly-red-cheeked, and her hair was grey. She'd been the Queen's nurse, making her *old,* but spry and bright-eyed. She and the gold-threaded woman stopped opposite him, and she curtseyed.

"Sir."

"Yikkeri, good day to you, I hope you're flourishing here. I need your help."

"In what way, sir?"

"I must talk to the Queen. It's an urgent matter. And private." He tried to speak low, but a few conversations were already fading, as people turned heads.

Yikkeri frowned, and then held out her hand. "If you have a letter from Lady b'Shen, or your great-uncle, I will take it."

"No – it's me. I need to speak to her."

There was a little pause. "The Queen arranges appointments with people she wishes to see. Your name is not on her dayplan."

"She will see me," said Mej.

You are nothing to her any more. Yikkeri didn't say this, but she looked it. Mej said quietly, "It's urgent. I need to ask her to protect someone, a witness to crime. The trial is very soon. I must see her."

She leaned forward, and her face was not encouraging - but then heads were turning again, this time away.

A group of people were coming down the stairs, twenty paces off, slowly and formally. Guards were in front, priests and secretaries at the back, and in the middle, the Morning Queen.

Mej tasted sudden sick in his mouth. She was all wrong.

She was wearing a blue gown with silver sleeves, and a very wide skirt. His mother, who normally dressed as plain as a servant, and had more than once been mistaken for one. There were jewels round her neck, and her hair was piled up in a black heap, with a gleaming white star-shape fastened to the top. *She doesn't even have that much hair!*

In the middle of this finery was a woman, with b'Shen dark skin and a face without beauty. Her broad-shouldered frame made her look shorter and fatter than she was.

And she came slowly, so slowly - his mother, who talked slow but always walked brisk. All wrong.

She was still five or six steps above the hall. "No, Mejorad," said Yikkeri, but he strode forward past people, until he could kneel at the foot of the stairs. The end of the bannister was carved like a lion's head.

"Your Grace," he said loudly. Everything stopped.

"Who is this, ha?" asked a chubby man in a yellow gown. He'd stepped from the back to the Queen's right; a woman in priestly black had stepped to the left. They were like soldiers guarding her from him.

Mej looked straight up at the familiar still brown eyes. "I am Mejorad b'Shen, and I seek audience of the Queen."

The priest asked, "On what matter?"

"It's private."

Yikkeri said, "Your Grace, I apologise! I was even now telling him to go. The Queen's time is fully occupied, sir, and she doesn't see people from nowhere."

The priest smiled, an evil smile. The plump man scowled. Queen Rommi looked from one to the other. Someone put a hand on Mej's shoulder.

"Leave me!" he exclaimed. "It's important. Mother!"

The hall was full of twenty tutting people.

"The Queen for the Morning has no children," said the man, taking a step down, blocking his view. "This grows tiresome, sir."

"Who are *you?*" Mej shouted. "Mother!"

He dodged aside to look up at her. More hands were on him – this memory would give him nightmares for years – but he managed to stare into her eyes.

They didn't change – they never did. "I am sorry I cannot talk to you, sir," she said, her voice catching. She looked quietly again left and right. "Go back to your Family."

"I can't -"

She was coming on down, and he lunged forward, but the hands pulled him forcefully back. He struggled, hot and sick, watching her turn away and walk off, still slowly, down to the left.

"*Shame* on you, Mejorad," said Yikkeri. "She's rid of you now, and a good thing she is. Go and cry on Eyanda's shoulder."

"Is he a barbarian or just an idiot?" That was someone else, chuckling. The door was opened by a grinning Guard. The Queen and her little crowd moved even further away. Mej made one last struggle – "Sir, this is madness!" – and was put out.

He hated everything and everyone in the world.

Standing up as tall as he could, seeing a few curious faces in the courtyard turning to him, Mej felt he understood for the first time why some people killed themselves. Of course he wasn't going to. But oh to be *finished* – not to have to deal with moving on beyond this horrible place and time –

He stomped across the courtyard.

"She's rid of you now." His flesh cringed.

He'd trusted two people in the world.

He hadn't *loved* his mother, of course. He'd spent his childhood wishing to be someone else's son. Someone who might giggle with him, or tickle him, as some mothers (Eyanda) did. Rommi would never do that. She was always kind and calm and fair to him, but never playful.

Even before he knew what the terrible words meant, he knew why. Everyone knew why.

Mej had been about seven, probably, when he'd mustered his courage, licked his thumbs for luck before clenching them inside his fists, and walked into her study when she was sitting alone behind a desk as high as his head.

She'd frowned, although not crossly. "What is it, Mejorad?"

He knelt. "Please." His eyes pricked, and his throat suddenly hurt, so he had to stop.

"What is it?"

"Is – is it true what they say about my father?"

Her skirts swished around the desk corner, and rapidly towards him. She reached out a hand, and paused, and then placed it on his head.

"Yes, it's true. But Mejorad, you don't have to be like him."

That was all.

But he *was* like his father – everyone said so. Like him in his sharply pointed nose, in his bouncy dancing and carelessness with gowns and shirts, in his voice (after it broke) and in the way he lied to get out of trouble.

He was like his father, the monster. He hadn't yet raped anyone, but that was probably only because he hadn't yet met anyone he wanted to rape.

No mother would love such a son, and he couldn't please her, so he might as well be bad. He left goodness to Rorash the bastard, even after Rorash fathered a bastard of his own, and then shocked everyone by going off to study at the stupid College. (But Eyanda still adored him.)

No one would ever adore Mejorad.

My father was a rapist
My mother is a Queen.
I'm on the surest road to hell
That you have ever seen.

He'd made that up, in The Dog and Boot, the night she was crowned, and he lost her anyway. It was an updated I-don't-care version of what the other children, even Narod sometimes, used to sing at him, until Rorash stopped them –

Your father was a rapist -
Throw him in the Lake.
Your mother was unlucky,
And you're a big mistake.

Rommi had indeed been unlucky, but a good mother. Not like horror-story parents, who beat their children to death, or cut off their fingers so they'd make more lucrative beggars. He'd always known he could trust her. She would at least listen, and tell him the truth.

Until now. Now she couldn't and wouldn't, and hadn't – and he was going to run to a tavern and get as drunk as a fly in an ale-barrel -

Oh shit! The Voiceless woman's still in the Palace.

Where the hell can I take her? Nadya's? An inn? Will she be safe in an inn? Is she really in danger? He had to turn back, march across the courtyard, behind the trees, once again up to the Quiet Door; and it was still Familiar-but-Nameless on guard.

"You again, sir?" with an amused smile. "You forgot your sword, I think."

"Yes, and – I'm to pick up that servant I brought."

The door opened for him.

But the room was empty. Once again she had gone.

Once, *Uncle Gridor says,* there was a famous warrior. Once, and not so long ago. She was called Dark Defani, and she was the fiercest swordswoman, the most beautiful singer - and she could make the most amazing wiggly faces in all of Ricossa. There are many stories, but most tell of when she grew up. When she was a child she was still learning swordplay and face-making, but the fame of her singing had already spread up, down and around; and it came to the ears of the evil Wizard of Frow.

"Oh, yes!" cries Brinnon. But "Is that the story with the bones?" asks their mother. "Not that one – it's surely too scary." "Please, mother, please!" "Hmm," and she smiles. "If either of you screams with the nightmare and wakes up me or Baby, your uncle will never be allowed back here again." Brin puts his palms together and

prays "Don't-let-me-scream", and Hridnaya slaps her hands over her mouth as if to prevent any sound escaping, and Uncle Gridor twinkles at his sister Haidi, and goes on.

One day, little Defani was fetching water, and a very tall, very ugly man stepped up to her, and said, "Come over here; I have a secret message for your father." And she thought it wasn't his fault he was ugly, any more than it's yours, so she walked with him two steps, to the tree, and said, "What is it, sir?"

"Come further," he said, "I've something to show you." So she walked round the tree, out of sight of the village, but she was a sensible lass, and she said, "That's as far as is safe with a stranger. I'll not go another step."

But she didn't know that he was carrying his magic staff, and he waved it, and used the magic words, which were – what? Toss this coin, and if it's Heads, the magic word is

Hridnafidnapridna, and if it's Crosses, the magic word is *Brinniprinnigrinni.*

"It's Crosses."

So he shouted, "Brinniprinnigrinni! Be still!" and Defani found she couldn't move arm nor leg, head nor body nor even tooth. The Wizard bundled her into his bag, and took her off to his secret house, which was dark and smelly and filled with cages of animals. He tossed her into a cage, and said, "Brinniprinnigrinni! Be locked!" and then, "Brinniprinnigrinni! Release!" and now she could move and shout and bang the bars, but it was no use, for the cage was locked fast shut, and so was the door to the house.

"I've heard you're a good singer," he said. "Sing for me." So Defani sang, as well as she could, to please him. And he said, "That was most sweet. I will keep you here to sing for me night and morn, and I'll make a magic of your singing so that the whole world will do what I want."

"Then I won't sing for you any more!" said Defani.

"Oh, won't you? Well, then, I'll -" Toss the coin. If it's Heads, he said he'd throw her into the next cage, to be eaten by a fierce mountain bear. If it's Crosses, he'd toss her into a hive-full of angry bees, to be stung to death."

"Heads!"

"Bear, then. Listen to me, young Defani. I haven't fed that bear for a week, and he's very hungry. So tonight you'll sleep in your cage, next to his, and in the morning you'll swear to sing for me forever, or the bear will have you. Here's some bread for your supper. Good night."

So he went to bed, taking his magic staff with him, and Defani was alone, or not quite alone. She could see the bear's eyes shining in the dark, in the next cage, and she tried to throw it some bread so it wouldn't be so hungry, but either she missed, or bears don't like bread, and it snarled. She even sang it a lullaby, and it snarled a little more quietly, but it was still snarling.

In the morning, the Wizard came back, and said, "Swear that you'll sing for me forever."

Defani said, "I won't. But please don't kill me. Please, please, please!" She sang, "Please, please, please," so sweetly that —

"He changed his mind?"

Oh no, he didn't, not the Wizard of Frow. But he liked the singing, so he didn't wave his magic staff and make her be still. He unlocked the cage and dragged her out, still singing "please", but wriggling and writhing all she could. "Breakfast time for you," he said to the bear. But Defani wriggled and twisted, and reached up and grabbed the staff, his own staff. "Brinniprinnigrinni! Be still!" she said, his own magic words.

And the Wizard couldn't move arm nor leg, head nor body nor even tooth. Only his eyes, and they were scared. Defani stood up and waved the staff again and shouted, "Brinniprinnigrinni! Unlock!" She meant it for the door, so that she could escape. But —

"Ooh!" Brin bounces.

But suddenly the bear's cage was also unlocked and open, and it was leaping out, and it POUNCED! Defani darted quickly away, but the Wizard couldn't move. And maybe the hungry bear remembered who'd given it bread and who had not, for it tore and crunched and munched and chewed until the Wizard was quite dead and all eaten up, *except* – except two of his finger-bones, the littlest bones on each hand. And when the bear had finished, it pushed out through the unlocked door, and off it went to its mountains and woods. But Dark Defani picked up the two bones and went home. And she made the bones into a necklace to wear always, to remind everyone to be properly frightened of her, and remember the fate of the Wizard of Frow.

Part Four

Conspiracy In The Palace

Kelji had one of the bad dreams, where Larelna was still alive.

She was sitting near the fire at home. Jedder was kneeling before her making the child on her lap laugh with bizarre faces, and they were all three completely happy. But the dreamer-Kelji knew dread approaching, more and more terrible - and then she woke up. The pain ripped and banged her heart and was gone, leaving only the dreariness, and the daily decision whether to pull herself back under her blankets and stay there, or to do her duty and pretend the world was interesting enough to get up into.

Slowly this had been growing less of a pretence. Yes, after ten months she'd begun to abandon her baby to the past, as everyone told her to do - until last Friday night. Then those two scheming women –

Being imprisoned in City Qayn's Palace wasn't interesting. But she had to show strength, so she got up anyway, and sat at the desk to write.

Tuesday 21st August 641. The fourth morning of my captivity. I have not been tortured or starved; all are Ricossan, and therefore courteous. But still I have been told nothing more of why I am here, or who accuses me, or what I am to expect. Still no one will say what has been done to Vaddras and Imadal. I have only that woman's incomprehensible riddles.

Kelji laid down her pen, while she could write neatly - before rage took over and turned her report to scrawl. In theory it was intended for her Queen and Council, but the Ricossans would likely destroy it as soon as she was dead. It had to be plain and civilised, to prick what passed for their consciences.

One day on the road, and then two in this cage.

It wasn't a dungeon. The room was large, and considerably grander than her – their – bedchamber at home. There was a good-sized glazed window, from which she could stare down four storeys or so to an inner garden. Hateful people chatted there sometimes, gathered herbs from bushes, or drew water from a well. A Guard also stood there, to stop her tying sheets together and climbing down like a story-heroine. The window was hung with heavy curtains, woven with designs of snake-like plants, and so was the high bed. She'd been allocated a few books and other entertainments. She'd asked for needle and threads, and got them. Servants provided well-prepared food, and most of her belongings from Nadya's house had been brought up. But she'd not seen Nadya, or received any message from her.

If she chose, she could stare at the ceiling, which was scene-painted in dramatic colours.

Back in November, after so many hours (days?) of screaming and tears, she'd locked herself away for three weeks. But at last common sense and duty, those hateful things, had forced her out. So now how ironic a punishment was this! Just as life had begun to hold savour again –

I should never have talked to that devious little beggar, never let myself be tempted – Rage rose hot, and she jumped up to stride around and make the floorboards creak, but rage was less strong than shame.

"Be careful," Queen Nerranya had said, snatching a half

hour for her cousin before a more important and worrying meeting about landslides in Exor. "The invitation pleases me, but the last time we sent an envoy to City Qayn, he didn't come back. We know they spread lies about – about us. I believe I have my kinsman in exile to thank for that." She looked briefly away, her face harsh, and Kelji remembered stories of the Great Council of Vach-roysh. "Don't be over-friendly to Madrasun or Bekonin, for their own sakes. You've been told who to contact, and how, if you need to get out of the city secretly?"

"Yes, Your Grace. The Marshal's given me the names and passwords."

"And prices." The Queen gave a harried smile. "God go with you, cousin. Does Jedder not choose to accompany you? He may, if you both please."

He doesn't know I'm going. "He has an errand to Dendarry, Your Grace. He's wished me well."

Kelji felt guilt at her lies, but more at her failure. "Be careful," and she had not been. *I like to do things right! I'm clever, I'm forceful, but I let myself get swept away –*

Stupid, stupid, stupid! Her masters made her dumb, for their own reasons, and I decided to change that. It must be a crime. Everything's a crime here.

What the hell is going on? Is this her plot, that nameless one? she wondered for the hundredth time, swishing between bed and desk. *Or all Mobira, or both, or someone else? Nadya?* That hurt. She'd liked Nadya, kind and matter-of-fact, who'd never once reminded her that almost every family loses a child, one or more.

It was safe to miss Nadya; not safe to miss *him.*

Three days, and who knew how many more, to fill? She shook her head and arms about to remind her body how to move; and sat down by her window with her white cloth and threads.

Every day she removed the top sheet from the bed, and every night replaced it, with added embroidery. It was a little soothing to do what she was good at, and she'd covered nearly a quarter now with her design. First the Palace, then the Glory Cathedral – how much more of Makkera could she fit on? A picture of home. Her legacy in Ricossa.

She glanced through the window and downwards between stitches, for she could do nothing else except observe. It would be so satisfying to destroy the room – tear the books, smear blood on the curtains – tempting but not useful. *They must see me calm and innocent.*

An hour later, she'd stitched an outline of the River Angan, and the Guard down below had changed shift.

Up again to march, down again to sew, or read more battle stories from the provided Bible. She recited the old Song of the Peoples. *"Ricossa's fair shores saw the gospel alight..."*

At noon a servant, guarded, came in carrying excellent-smelling soup and cheese. "A good day to you, madam," he said nervously.

"And to you also. How long am I to be kept here? Where are my servants, and are they well?" She asked this every time. Poor timid Imadal, whom she'd abandoned for that other.

As ever, the servant made no reply. He laid out the food and wine, bowed, and retreated to the door. But just as she was about to forget him, he cleared his throat. Squeakily, as she glowered up, he said, "I am to inform you, madam, that the date for your trial has been decided. It will be on Thursday. The day after tomorrow."

He was gone.

"Ricossa's fair shores saw the gospel alight
On a land of great plenty, and zealous for right.
The people well-mannered, both handsome and tall –

If you sneeze out of place, you will hang from the wall."

The room Mejorad had left her in was square and white-plastered, with a glass window above person-height. There were wooden settles around the walls, high-backed with curved and carved arms; places to sit very straight and still.

Hridnaya walked slowly to a corner between furniture, and crouched down. Now at last there was peace and solitude. Now she could cry again, although crying would rectify nothing and atone for nothing.

"Your brother's blood cries from the ground." God said that to Cain.

"God has rescued me! I'm a prophetess, I have a divine mission!" So she'd thought, two days ago, walking the road. Weary in her feet, but lifted up, oh so high, in her arrogant heart.

She hadn't told Brin she was going away, because she hadn't wanted to endanger or worry him. But he'd worried anyway, because loving kindred do.

Like many children, the twins had been taken to the Great Square to watch justice – a warning or a punishment. *Mend your ways, or this is where you'll come.*

So she knew what they'd done to him, what she'd done.

Brin would forgive her. Had already forgiven her. "Hridna. You're alive."

Lulet never would.

The tears didn't come. She huddled in her corner, as in her mind the whip rose and fell. Over and over again.

A door was opening. Hridnaya jumped up to stand neatly, head bowed, feet together, as good servants do.

Are you coming to kill me? Please let me die.

As if that would help.

There were two men whose tabards were white with a

gold stripe.

"Who are you waiting for, madam? You have to leave," said one. "This room is needed."

She scrabbled for the parchment the b'Shen lad had given her. "I fear I don't care. *The room is needed.* Out." His friend opened the door wide, and jerked his head emphatically.

So she walked through, onto a landing with stairs.

She went up the stairs.

The whip rose and fell.

Oh God.

A servant scampered down past her, blowing his nose as he ran.

She came to a landing. Two youths were playing dice on the floor, betting for sweets. They ignored her.

She went up until there were no more stairs. There was only a passage with a light on the wall, and doors with holes in them for Narrim or her like to peer through. Servants' quarters.

Slowly Hridnaya walked through a door to find a row of beds, each with a box beside it, and each with a peg and a crucifix on the wall above.

At one end of the dormitory she found another corner, and she huddled down again. She put her arms round her shins, and her forehead on her knees.

Still the tears wouldn't come.

*

Mej trusted two people. But Jedder, against his better judgment, had trusted *him. I was given one thing to do, and I failed. Where's the little rat gone? Why didn't I tell the Guard -?*

"Oh, I'd forgotten, Yikkeri said she'd look after the woman," he'd said, picked up his sword and walked out and down the steps. What else could he do?

So now was Hridnaya wandering around by herself, or

had she been arrested? And if arrested, did that mean doom for Jedder and Kelji, or just for her? *I'm confused, and there's nothing I can do.*

So of course he made his usual way to The Dog and Boot. None of his friends were there, so he sat quietly, staring at his failure, and the way everyone had abandoned him.

"Can I get you anything else, sir?"

"Another of these, if you will. Have you seen Narod or Majilli lately?"

"No, sir. Um… Narod b'Lan is leaving the city shortly, sir. He's off to the north somewhere with his troop."

Ah, yes, he said he was expecting something like that. More soldiers to the border in case there's trouble? I wish I were going. Steel and terror, and everything clear and simple, teaching the bloody enemy a lesson.

But now the bloody enemy were Kelji and Jedder. They'd never been actual people before.

*

King Aigith wrote to her on 12th November last year. Madrasun died on the 15th.

The portress nodded to him, and Ittrad nodded back. *If you knew –*

Because he was almost Dirria's servant, he didn't knock. But as he was pushing the door, he heard a voice saying, "You see the importance of demonstrating -"

A voice, but not Dirria's.

He went in. The Doctor was sitting in one chair, and Mobira in the other.

Ittrad bowed, his back cold.

He'd never spoken to her, and he thought she didn't know him. She looked up casually, and then back.

Dirria, rather happy, said, "Oh, there you are, Ittrad.

Please put together what I need for a journey to the city. I shan't want bedlinen, but my clean gown. Urgent news has arrived, and I'm leaving - er, very soon."

She glanced at her visitor, who said, "Within the next hour or so will be sufficient."

"Yes, madam."

"I'm required for an important trial, as a witness," she said, looking, as she sometimes did, like an excited child. Mobira coughed and caught her eye, and she went on, "While I'm gone, Ittrad, I want you to thoroughly clean this room, and also my private chamber. Make sure the papers are in order. I'll be taking Mari." Mari was her personal maid, and he saw her glance again at Mobira, as if for permission. This was granted with a nod.

The rooms are already clean. The boxes are in order – I made sure of that after the other day. "How long will you be gone, madam?"

And it was Mobira who answered. "I can't be certain, but it's not likely you'll be needed beyond Friday."

"I can't travel on the Sabbath – you'd better not expect me before next Tuesday evening. I'll need you to take a letter of excuse to Doctor Dniren. So now, please -" and she gestured him to leave, with her tiresomely regal look.

You said you were taking Mari; why can't she pack? And I'd've expected you to take me along as well. You want me out of the way.

In her sleeping chamber next door, he dragged her satchel from its closet and laid it on the bed. Then with deliberation he took a cup, placed it against the adjoining wall, and pressed his ear to it to listen. His wife had spied on their neighbours this way.

"As I was saying," he heard Mobira say quietly, "this demonstrates your loyalty, and that of most of the other Doctors.

Your evidence will reveal how the Jaryari spy was plotting mischief and treason. You understand?"

"Yes – yes, of course. Her people dared to attack you? That's terrible. You will advise me precisely what to -"

"Of course. We'll have plenty of time on the journey. I suggest you tell First Doctor Dniren merely that the Morning Queen wishes to speak to you – the College is her province, after all."

He heard their footsteps moving towards the door. Ittrad turned back and started packing, very slowly, for it wasn't a long task, and he wanted to think. Whose trial? It must be that foreign woman's. *What has Dirria to do with that?*

It's about Hridnaya. What did Mobira say about her? "She sneaked out yesterday on an errand for her employer." *Except she didn't. I know that, and Dirria knows it, and Mobira knows it – but I'm not to be there. 'You can advise me precisely what to -'*

That means 'You can advise me precisely what to say at the trial.'

He already had news for Lord b'Nida. And now this was urgent.

"Thou shalt not bear false witness."

*

Hridnaya woke up stiff, knowing only that something terrible had happened. What was this quiet dim place? How long had she slept?

Thirsty. She reached into her satchel – but this wasn't hers. *Whose is it? What's happened? I was on the road – on a <u>roof</u> –*

I've destroyed Brin's life.

And I'm not supposed to be here. I came with that lad – where's he gone? Is he cursing me, looking for me, reporting me missing?

Am I missing?

She remembered back: she'd been at Brin and Lulet's - and that Mejorad and that Jedder had been there, as well as the children. There'd been a long talk, important things said, but she couldn't remember what.

Hridnaya was accustomed to remembering almost everything. It was a skill, one she'd practised. But this time the words were slipping away, as if she could see people but their voices were in Latin or Greek –

She was breathing very fast, and her chest hurt. Her head and shoulders were clammy and she was shaking. The world before her shimmered.

Is this death? Help me, please!

Breathe. This is a spasm, you've had them before. (In the early times, waking suddenly, finding her mouth unbearably still unbearably wrong.) Only a spasm of terror.

She breathed, and clutched the strange bag, and slowly she could see normally, and all the pain sank and congealed into a lump in her stomach.

She found a water skin, and managed to drink.

The saddle-bag belonged to Venomous Mobira, and she and Jedder had searched through it on the beach. Money, linen, a phial of something - and a box with wax and a seal-ring. Now she had enough light to see that the device was a crown entwined with what Kelji had taught her was the letter A.

A for Aigith.

This was very dangerous theft. Things crawled around the lump in her stomach.

And the little phial? She sniffed it, and it smelt of nothing in particular. It wasn't wine; it might be a seasoning.

But – Venomous Mobira.

"Or poisoned," Jedder had said. Memory was coming

back. "I need your evidence." Jedder, Kelji. Poison. *I am holding evil in my hand.*

The lump burst upwards, and again she was cold and gasping.

Breathe. Breathe.

"Think, you fool." Was that Balki's voice, or was it God's?

Think. I'm in the Palace, and I can't get out without the Guards finding me, and if anyone does find me – a thief, a criminal, a spy – unless it's that Mejorad – I'll be dead.

Why was he bringing me here? Does he have a friend, or was he going to hand me over -?

Perhaps I could die now. She fingered the little phial. *Dead, and trying to explain to God that I didn't mean -*

I wanted to find out about Uncle's death – and now I've discovered something, something possible, maybe, thanks to Jedder. But I've destroyed Brin! And – he said the King's planning to hang Kelji, because of what I did? Because I talked to Dirria and Ittrad?

She was kind to me, at first.

I'm hungry. I'm like a mouse, hiding between the tenement walls. A mouse needs food and a hole to sleep in. How long before the trap finds me – or the cat does? There must be other Voiceless here; there must be some food I can swallow.

I shouldn't be thinking about food.

Question 36. *What do I do with what I suspect?*

I've made such ill work of it. (The whip rose and fell, and she wanted to scream.)

Ill work of it, but – Kelji is in deadly trouble, because of me. I have to help her, if I can; unravel the consequences. If I can.

At her feet lay Mobira's possessions, and the parchment Mejorad had given her to hold. By accident, she saw, he'd swept up two sheets together. All around were the beds and belongings of ten or twelve Palace servants.

Hesitantly, she lifted a hand and crossed herself. After several days of unaccustomed walking and riding, every movement was small pain, reminding her to wonder what real pain, real torture would be like.

Jesus, Word of Truth, I don't know what hour it is, or when
people will come back to this room. I've done everything wrong. Please
give me enough time alone here to decide what to do.

She sat and thought, and shuddered, and thought more.

*

New Question 1: What should I do?

Answer: See how you can help Kelji and Jedder, and their servants. Stay alive as long as you can.

Question 2: How can I help them?

Answer: Write your evidence for Jedder. Find out things. Like where she and Vaddras are being kept: here or at the Hall of Justice. You might be able to see them. Find out when the trial is, and what the other evidence. It may be false. And who the Judge is to be. Jedder needs to know all that.

Question 3: How could I get any information to Jedder?

Answer. Leave that for now. *Please, Lord.*

Question 4: Where can I find this information? And how?

Answer: Use your brain, and your knowledge! You've listened to the b'Nida talk about the Palace for twelve years. The Morning Queen and her business to the east, the Evening King and his, which includes justice and trials, to the west, where the sun sets. There'll be rooms of archives and records and plans. Picture the words you're looking for.

(Terror rose with each answer.)

Question 5: How can I get into these rooms? There'll be

293

Guards everywhere.

Answer: Look like a Palace servant – and use the King's authority.

Question 6: What will they do to me when they catch me?

*

Hridnaya relieved herself and washed as best she could in the upstairs lavatories. She found a pot of mizzum in a private room that probably belonged to a Palace Voiceless, and ate (stole) a few mouthfuls, for her own was finished. She hid the (stolen) bag under blankets in a box. She dressed herself in a (stolen) grey kirtle and Palace tabard, and tucked a folded piece of parchment (forged) into her belt. She prayed again.

Look calm, but not too happy. Perhaps slightly bored – but also arrogant, for I am a trusted messenger on a serious errand.

And then she headed down the stairs – *I need to find a way to go left.*

It was easy to think this, but a little later how many turns had she made? Down two flights – *Yes, these rooms look business-like, and some have guards posted outside. Which one?*

High people in bright-sleeved gowns passed by, talking.

At the end of the white-plastered corridor, there was a window. The sky outside still shone pale, and beyond courtyard and roofs she could see the Cathedral spire.

This is the western side. I think, yes. And I'm loitering here for no reason. This will not do.

A woman marched up a corner stair, panting but brisk, carrying rolls of parchment. A woman in a secretary's gown! She went up to a door, spoke to the guard, and was allowed in. Hridnaya bent to adjust her sandal. A few moments later, the woman came out, without the parchment. *Ah.*

The man at the door was old and red-faced, with fierce eyebrows. *Please Lord, please Lord, please Lord,* as she walked towards him, scalp fizzing, sweat cold on her shoulders.

She pulled out her parchment and offered it.

Alow the bearer to colect what papers she needs. Sealed with the King's seal.

As she'd hardly dared to hope, he looked at the seal rather than the words. He grunted, and opened the door.

It was a long room, walls lined with shelves, shelves walled with books. There were high desks in the centre, three rows of four, about half of them occupied. No one looked up at Hridnaya, because they were all staring downward at their work, avoiding the attention of the two men in the centre of the room. She felt their fear.

A tired-looking woman in secretary's black was showing a book to a younger man, who also wore a plain gown, but red. Pushing the volume back, the man said, "So that's all arranged for Thursday. Thank you. I wish you a good day," and turned to go.

Hridnaya lowered her eyes as she stepped aside for him, receiving a sharp image of a large face scarred on one side, and white teeth in a black beard. He walked briskly out, and she felt the room breathe.

"Thursday! They're in a hurry for the execution," the woman murmured, and then she shook herself and turned her attention to the newcomer. "May I ask your business?"

She offered the parchment.

"I see. Can you tell what you're looking for?" She sighed, and began to recite, "Transcripts of trials over *there* – suspected person lists *there* – pre-trial procedure and arrests -"

Yes, nodding.

"This shelf here. Can you find what you need? Arrests are

in the blue book, of course. There's a ladder if you need a high shelf, or of course you may request assistance, madam." After a terrified moment, Hridnaya decided it wasn't mockery.

Such was the power of the Evening King's seal.

Arrests in the blue book. No one stopped her lifting it down, and carrying it to a desk.

She opened it to the difficult but fascinating words, part of her still wondering who they'd all been so scared of, the man in red. Not a person ever at the b'Nida house, an air of authority in the Archive –

Months ago, she'd seen someone else dressed in a long gown like that – the Morning Queen's Chamberlain, Krothon.

King Aigith also had a Chamberlain. He was called Brechad b'Iri, and yes, everyone was scared of him.

("Mobira's the prying rat in Sapientia, and Brechad's the snarling mastiff in City Qayn," Lord b'Nida had said once.)

The King's Chamberlain was talking about an execution.

Thursday? Kelji? Make haste.

With a deep breath, she plunged into the long words.

(19th August) Jaryari Kelji d of Shanell from Makkera, arrested in Sapientia on suspicion of spying by King's Agent Mobira. Kept pending trial in the Palace. Quarters 2. Good treatment.

(In another hand.) **Trial date 30th August.**

30th August! She'd lost track of the days – *but very soon!*

Vaddras, servant accompanying the above Kelji. Transferred to Hall of Justice, cells row 6. Decent treatment. To obtain confession.

Further doc'n W t V.

"Doc'n" means "documentation", it must. But "W t V?"

Bending forward, she learned it by heart. *Now what?* She replaced the book, shaking her head as one who hasn't found what she's looking for, and reached down another. "Suspected Persons." Was it possible?

Lists of names, each with a paragraph. *I'll only go back a few pages* – but suddenly –

Gridor, son of Arro. Also called Flower-in-Hood. Malcontent and whiner in re position of the Voiceless, of no great account.

In another hand, Comm - communicating with School of Law in Sap. Mobira to watch and obtain further information.

(4ᵗʰ June) Harmless.

(21ˢᵗ June) Died by violence 19ᵗʰ June. Note trial of Rorash Adam b'Shen (4ᵗʰ July 641) Trials Vol XIII.

"Harmless." But – Mobira?

"Further documentation W t V" – W t V must be a shortening of something or somewhere. "T" could mean "the", perhaps? "With the" something, or someone?

Suddenly she recalled a stuffy evening in the Gallery at home, pouring wine for a cross visitor. "Of course the documents in this matter are kept Within the Veil. That's what it's called, you know. A blasphemous name, if anyone asked me," and Lord b'Nida had soothed his old colleague with an agreeing head-shake.

Within the Veil's a Bible reference, to the holiest part of the Temple. But here it's where they keep the most secret papers. It must be a room, the room I need.

She half rose – *Wait. Is there anything else here? It*

wouldn't be wise to come back.

What did he say? Trial transcripts there – I know Uncle's, surely – process there – she didn't mention that red book. At home red means money. Finance, payments. Maybe –

Yes, there was a whole page for her.

Mobira, daughter of Jentoretti. Agent in the Great College. Trusted to the highest level, and reporting only to the King. Salary per year twenty-four gold pieces.

How much?

As if that wasn't enough, Mobira also claimed, or was allowed, money for expenses.

(19th Aug) up to seven gold in re trial of Kelji of Makkera.

Going back, **(6th April) three gold.**

And last year, **(12th November) ten gold.**

What was she doing last November?

Her head was thumping with fear and concentration. She yawned, and blinked, and yawned again. She was so sleepy, and people would notice.

But somehow I need to get Within the Veil.

*

I agreed to do one thing, and I failed. Of course.

Mej was sitting on a bench outside his second favourite tavern, Stars Above, staring at the sky between occasional raindrops, and laughing to himself. If anyone came within two arms' lengths, he'd say –

"*There* you are."

"Go to hell."

"Oh, of course. Get up, Mejorad! Get up!"

"Go to hell."

The maid Yikkeri bent down and slapped his face hard. "Leave me al -" he began, and had to tip over sideways to vomit, his palms hitting the paving just in time to save his nose.

"Get up. The Queen has a question for you."

"Whatjoosay?" He balanced himself with one hand, swallowing vileness.

Angry fingers squeezed his chin. "Listen, you drunken fool. What did you want to see Queen Rommi about? Tell me in one word. One."

"Nothing."

"One word. Now."

He dragged bits of his mind together. One word. "Kelji."

"What did you say?"

"*Kelji.*"

"Is that a name?"

"Of course it's a fucking name. It's Jaryari." (Only the lowest scoundrels are rude to servants, and he was hot with shame.)

"Then get up."

He moaned.

"I've thrashed you before, and I'll do it again. Get up."

So he scrambled to his feet, and wiped his mouth.

"Try to walk straight."

His head jangled with every step, but he could walk, as long as she didn't let go of his arm.

"Where -? The Queen -"

"Wants to see you, against my advice. Keep out of the puddles. Why did the angels choose to weep tonight?"

He'd trusted two people. As they walked, his own tears slid down his cheeks to blend with the rain.

But they crossed the Great Passage, and were among

large but quiet houses. They weren't going to the Palace. Yikkeri peered about her. Till today he hadn't realised how much she'd always disliked him – *no one cares for me but Rorash, no one* – perhaps this was all some nasty humiliating prank, and his mother hadn't – or even a trap, if he had enemies –

They went down an alley, and into a stable. "You lied!" he started to say. She glared. There was a torch in the wall, and a groom opening a door onto an inner stair. Mej put his hand on his swordhilt and stumped carefully up, into a plain room, with two people, and a bowl on the table.

"Be welcome -" said a man.

"One moment," Yikkeri answered from behind, and she took Mej by the back of the neck, and plunged hm face down into cold water. He gasped, and his head danced with familiar post-wine pain; he was pulled up from the bowl, pushed in and out again, and then handed a towel. "Dry yourself off. Are you sober now?"

Someone chuckled as Mej rubbed at his head, scattering water drops around. He pulled away to stare suspiciously at an elderly woman by another door, and a solid man with a mass of grey hair, wearing yellow. Both looked unsettlingly not-quite-familiar, especially the man, who finished chuckling, and then exclaimed, "Ha, this is the lad from this morning!"

Now Mej knew him. *You were scowling at me on the stairs at the Palace, you and a woman, a priest.*

"It is, sir. Shall we go in?" and Yikkeri poked Mej towards the woman, who opened her door for him. The man followed.

Inside, there were a lot of lights in beautifully-carved candle-sticks, and wood panelling on the walls. The main furniture was a large bed covered and hung with blue-and-white lace. But there was also a table with wine and fruit, and chairs; and in one of them sat the Queen.

Yikkeri pressed his shoulder, and he knelt. There was a long pause, while candles flickered, and Mej tried through the thumping in his head to remember what to call her. "Your Grace," he said at last, and looked up.

Thank God the jewels were gone, and the gown was plain single-colour brown – even shabby, in fact, and it didn't quite fit her. This was Rommi, and the world became slightly more right. He almost burst into tears.

"Mejorad b'Shen, welcome, sir," she said. "Please stand up – and sit down. This is my Chamberlain. You can speak freely before him."

The man stepped to her side, amused surprise on his loathsome face. "Your Grace, is this truly the one you wanted to meet? I – forgive my foolishness, but I hardly thought -"

"I know what you thought, Krothon, but this is the one." Her mouth twitched as if she also were amused. "Yikkeri, did he give you a word?"

Sourly, "The name Kelji."

"The spy who's to be tried on Thursday. Your Grace," and he smirked, "this is a little eccentric. What does that matter have to do with this youth – or he with you?" More gently, "You were once his mother, but if I may, you aren't any longer."

"And why should you believe a word he says anyway? This is *Mejorad.*" Yikkeri, of course.

"No, I'm not his mother. A citizen came to his Queen with a problem. He walked into the Palace without permission, recklessly, and he went on begging to see me until he was thrown out. That is not words, but action. Tell me, Mejorad, about Kelji."

Mej stared across the table, making himself look at nothing but her: her plain serious dark face; nose and right cheek lit, the other side in shadow. A drip from his wet hair trickled down his neck. *Clear and succinct as may be, and don't mention Jedder. Or that Mobira may be dead -*

He took a breath, and began.

But he'd only got two sentences out, when - "Teaching to *read?*" exclaimed the man Krothon in incredulity, and the Queen blinked.

"I know – but Kelji's foreign, she wouldn't have realised - and this woman wanted to talk to one of the Doctors, so Mobira said she was working for Kelji, spying. But she wasn't. She left this note behind." He handed over the scrap Vaddras said he'd found on the floor. **You have an errand. I have one to. You can hit me wen I come bak.**

Krothon sighed annoyingly as he read it. Mej trudged on. "She and her brother, I've talked to them, they've nothing to do with Jaryar, they're only interested in her uncle, Flower-in-Hood's death. They think he was murdered."

"You said you were here for Kelji," Krothon interrupted, "not for this Flower-in-Hood."

"Yes, I am -"

"My sister-in-law judged that trial, and his kin got as good justice from her as anyone would have given them, if not better." His face dared Mej to disagree.

In the midst of headache, resentment and worry, Mej realised where he'd seen the woman in the outer room before. Judge Adjefi b'Trai, who'd had Rorash beaten and banished.

"So, Kelji?" said Krothon, a tutor bringing him back to the point.

"Um - I think she's just being blamed for this stupid woman – maybe for teaching her. So anyway I promised to keep this Hridnaya safe so that she could give evidence on Kelji's behalf, and I brought her to the Palace, and left her in the little room by the Quiet Door – and when I went back she was gone.”

“Gone? I don’t understand.” Now Krothon showed some concern. “Young man, you’re saying that you’ve let a rebel loose in the Palace? Armed with a sword, or merely a knife?”

“She’s not a rebel!”

“Isn’t she? You tell us she’s a Voiceless who’s broken their every rule, and has some absurd grudge against the Families. You put her somewhere, and she immediately disobeyed you, and ran off. Ran off like a – like a criminal. Alarming, some would think. And why did she need your protection anyway? Who was going to harm her, merely an innocent witness?”

Mej wondered, cold, if he’d made the greatest fool of himself ever. And then he remembered what he hadn’t yet said. He kept looking past the man (whose fat face was less arrogant than his tone) straight at her.

“This woman Mobira says the King wants Kelji found guilty, whether she is or not. She came to us at Nadya b’Astith’s on Sunday, and told Eyanda and me to lie. To say I was sent to Sapientia to watch her, Kelji.”

“Whereas in fact?”

He shrugged, as if uncaring. “I – I just wanted to go. The Family were sending me to a monastery!” He felt that Rommi guessed the words as he said them.

Yikkeri said from behind, “Eyanda b’Shen agreeing to swear falsely? Not very likely.”

“Mobira said the King would bring Rorash home. And that she’d make Hridnaya say whatever was needed for the trial. Torture her. When, if, she finds her.”

There was silence. The Queen lifted a hand. “Krothon, what do you know of this matter?”

“Not much, Your Grace,” he said briskly, although he was frowning, and he cleared his throat for an explanation. “Kelji,

Nerranya's cousin, is a prisoner in the Palace. The trial is on Thursday; they say she was trying to bribe Doctors at the College into treason. Mobira has been about here somewhere in the last few days making the arrangements with the Hall of Justice. The woman Kelji has a husband who spent several hours battering at the doors and being turned away a few days ago. Some were surprised that he wasn't arrested also. I know of no intruders found in the Palace today.

"So, errhm, this young man may be - mistaken. But I suppose he may not be. I'm not told everything. Especially," and he paused, "about matters that aren't my concern. Or, some would say, yours."

Mej wondered what he meant. "I've told you the truth," he said crossly.

"In any case, this woman needs to be found. She could be intending to steal, or kill anybody, to poison us all."

"No, she's not!" Mej thought of throwing himself to the floor, and swearing he was telling the truth – but Yikkeri would laugh. Instead, "Why would I bring her to the Palace for that?"

"She may be deceiving you."

"It was my idea! She didn't want to come with me."

"We may return to this, but first, who is this Mobira?" asked the Queen. "I don't know the name."

The man flicked a smile and coughed. *This scares him.* He coughed again. "Umm. Your Grace," stroking his gown, "it is not wise to ask questions about that woman."

The Queen drew breath in and out. Her face didn't alter, yet somehow Mej was reminded of the night his stepfather died. Rommi wasn't always quiet. "You make me very curious," she said at last. "Curious" was an ominous word with her, and her voice grew in strength as she went on. "You have my thanks and my goodwill, honoured sir, for arranging this meeting for me. For me to meet my lover, as you thought. You will have my ill will if you mention it to anyone at all. But if you wish to do your duty as my Chamberlain, you will answer my question. Otherwise you may leave."

Krothon blinked several times. He lifted a hand and touched his forehead, then dropped it. "She's King Aigith's granddaughter."

"Indeed."

"Yes. Many years ago, when he was a b'Oto lad, he fathered a boy, now dead, Mobira's father. He employs her in Sapientia, at the College, like a – well, she *is* a spy, and more. She reports to him about the Doctors, and keeps them in proper order with fear. Some think she uses worse than fear, and they call her Venomous Mobira. In whispers." His voice had been growing faster; now he slowed. "But officially she is nothing, which is why you hadn't heard of her. That's all I know. The College isn't my concern."

"It's mine. She's not on the King's Council."

"Ha, certainly not. She's not acknowledged b'Oto, or of any rank. But he trusts her more than any of his Councillors, they say. To cross Mobira is to cross the King."

"She would have authority to arrest Queen Nerranya's envoy, then?"

"If she saw good reason, she'd have authority to arrest anyone. And the young man is doubtless right – that if she had suspicions, she'd not be very scrupulous about embellishing them. Between these walls -" Fingers of both hands were twisting in his gown. "Your Grace, you know and I know King Aigith's views of foreigners from the West. He believes them capable of all evil. He'd be very likely to think anyone Nerranya sent was a spy. As they might be. And of course he'll be eager to stamp out any treason. There are rumours that - he thinks war may be coming."

Mej thought of his grumpy companion, and then – "We were told to be ready for attack," he said, "when I was doing my military, down south."

"Border patrols must always be ready," said the Queen.

"The patrols are being strengthened, both north and south," said Krothon. "And I've noticed that the minstrels have lately been singing all the most patriotic songs, and reminding us of the Exile's stories about the Jaryari Queen and her people. This may not be chance."

"The Exile. That is the man in the mansion on St Stephen's Street, who supplies us with filth about his homeland in return for living in luxury at our expense. And we make the filth into songs, with little regard for whether they're true or not."

Krothon said nothing.

"Nerranya's Nineteenth Lover", "The Church-Burning at Mex", "Seven Thieves in Lefayr" – all fine songs with easy choruses to shout when drunk. They're a bad lot in the West, blasphemous and immoral, everyone knows that. I'd probably fit in well.

The Queen put fingers against her temples, and shut her eyes.

Krothon said, more calmly, "My sister-in-law always says, wait until the trial judge is named, and then you'll know if it'll be fair. Most of them, like Adjefi, are honest, but not all. Your Grace, it's growing late. *Is* all this your concern?"

"I don't know." To Mej, "This Voiceless woman. What does she look like?"

"Her name's Hridnaya. Just – just ordinary. Mid-brown, quite small." He shrugged.

"Of what age?" As he grimaced ignorance, "Is her hair grey?"

"No, no, black. Less than forty, but not young. Her

eyebrows are – feathery," he said suddenly, and a smile rippled for a moment across both listening faces. "She's not a rebel or dangerous, truly."

"Is she capable?" asked the Queen.

"Very capable at getting into trouble," he said, "and yet staying alive."

"Like you, perhaps? But she may already have been arrested by Mobira or her agents – I suppose she has agents."

"God have mercy on the creature if that's so," said Krothon unexpectedly.

"Yes. Well, Mejorad, I have listened to you. I understand that you wanted me to protect this woman, but I can't protect her if she's disappeared."

Krothon said, "Your Grace, she must be found, and surely she will be."

"By someone. Until then, what else are you asking of me?"

Mej realised, unpleasantly warm, that he didn't know. "Kelji isn't a spy. Can't you help her?"

"This isn't a matter for -" Krothon repeated, gently annoying.

Mej was beginning to sulk, but he heard her say, "I suppose not. And yet I don't like it. Mejorad, if you are to give evidence on Thursday, what will you say?"

"The truth," he answered.

There was a snort behind him, which was no surprise. Yikkeri said, "If anyone in City Qayn has to choose between believing Eyanda and believing you -"

"Yikkeri, you're speaking to my guest! Thank you for coming, Mejorad. I think you should go home now. Try to keep out of further conversation on this matter with anyone, especially Eyanda. If I need you, I hope I'll be able to find you either there or at – is The Dog and Boot still your favourite?"

That can't be all! Please! But Krothon's expression was saying a polite goodbye, and the Queen was looking at the ground. Mej was about to protest with a last futile wail, when she said, not looking at him, "Your one word was Kelji. Do you remember mine, from last Christmas? Chaos?"

He remembered. It was a small note of hope to leave on.

*

The Palace was a magnificent building where high folk lived and feasted in luxury, and therefore it was also a place where many lower folk wrote, cleaned, and cooked; and eventually slept. Hridnaya made some guesses about who would be doing what, where and when, and as a result of those guesses, she spent the evening curled up underneath the bed in a small chamber, rather like her own old place, the one where she'd found the mizzum. The Voiceless servant who slept here would almost certainly be waiting at a private meal downstairs –

It was dangerous, but everything was dangerous, and she couldn't keep her eyes open.

It was only when she woke in the dark, and heard someone breathing close by, that she realised how insane she'd been. She lay chilled and listening, not a person any more, not herself, only a woman-shaped criminal thing.

A few inches and a mattress above her came a grunting snore. *Lord, please.* She put out a hand on cold wood. Then another. She crept, slithered, out into the room.

Greyness came in through the hole to the passage. That door seemed the gateway to heaven, but not yet. First she had to open the chest in the corner – lift the lid so quietly – fold back the blanket inside – and retrieve the hidden saddle-bag. And then ease the lid down on to a finger, and edge the finger out without a sound.

There was another snore. Uncle Gridor had told a story about soothing a dragon to sleep with lullabies. Her body crawled with terrible what-ifs.

Edging so slowly – lifting the latch –

She was out in the passage, leaning against the wall, waiting. The what-ifs retreated just a little, and she became aware of cold and thirst, and her aching bones. Deep breaths. There was a candle in this corridor, wasn't there?

Once she'd got down the first flight of stairs, she lit it. Because she was a respectable servant – *King Aigith's errands can't wait for morning!* – and she should look like one.

Now to find the place Within the Veil. It was the most secret room, the one that would be guarded day and night. If guarded, she was gambling, it might not be locked. And she had the King's Seal.

She found the room, she found the writings, and the more she looked and wrote the more frightened she became.

Memorandum in re the evidence to be presented at the trial of Kelji of Makkera.

How many hours she spent in that place, reading, writing, pausing to breathe and frantically pray, writing again, she didn't know. The light of a summer morning grew. *People who know I shouldn't be here will be coming soon. Where am I going?*

Kelji's in Quarters 2, wherever that is. But she's a prisoner – will even this seal get me in? No, these writings (these terrifying writings) are for Jedder, but that means getting out of the Palace.

There would be kitchen doors, but they might only lead to kitchen yards, and in any case they'd be full of people at this time; people who again would recognise an intruder. There was the grand entrance – *what do they call it? The Mosaic Corridor?*

Or there was the little stair and door that Mejorad had

brought her in by.

*

Wednesday 22nd August. The fifth morning of my captivity.

Kelji was sewing again, bright and early, when abruptly the door opened to allow two women and a man to enter. The man, a guard, immediately went out again. One of the women had silver sleeves and jewels in her hair, and the other was presumably a maid.

They looked at Kelji, and she looked at them. She had time to think *Have you come to condemn me to death?* and to wonder if she wanted to die, before the one with sparkly hair said, "A good day to you, madam. May we sit down?"

"You are my guests," Kelji said sourly. However, there was only one chair beside her own, and she wasn't going to give it up for them unless she was made to. So the maid stood beside the bed, and the main visitor sat down opposite her, and smoothed her skirts.

She was a dark-skinned woman in late middle years, wide across the shoulders, and broad across the face. At the edge of her jawline, a small droplet of mushroom-shaped flesh cruelly and irresistibly drew the eye. She was possibly the plainest woman Kelji had seen in Ricossa.

She blinked as if nervous, but when she spoke it was slowly and with dignity.

"Kelji, daughter of Shanell. I understand you were brought here on Sunday. I hope you've been well treated?"

"I haven't been tortured, if that's what you mean. Have you been as kind to my servants?"

"Which servants?"

"My groom was arrested along with me, and I've no

310

doubt you've also brought in my maid."

"Do you mean the Voiceless woman?"

"That scheming creature ran away from me in Sapientia. I meant my Jaryari woman, Imadal. Is she well?"

Jedder would be so proud of her.

"Madam, please speak with more respect!" the maid exclaimed.

I'm not a child or a servant, to be shamed like that. "I've not yet been told who I'm speaking to."

"My name is Rommi," said the woman.

Kelji felt surprise twist her face. But she said brashly, "Is that Her Grace Rommi the Morning Queen, or some other? I'm a foreigner here. I don't doubt there are dozens of Rommis in City Qayn."

The maid's mouth hung open in outrage, so it probably was the Queen. Another mystery: how wearing. "Is this an official interrogation? I've been waiting four days for one."

The other woman looked worried, but smiled a slow unexpectedly pleasant smile. "It's not. You may know that the Morning Queen does not interfere with matters of justice. Those are for my colleague, King Aigith. Madam, I haven't heard of any arrests other than you and the man Vaddras. I haven't seen him, I'm afraid. But I've been told that you are to be tried for espionage shortly. Something to do with the Doctors at the College, to whom you gave a book."

The abrupt terror in her bowels told Kelji that she really didn't want to die. "At some point will I be allowed to deny such an absurd charge? The book was a requested gift! Is it a crime that it was damaged? No one has asked me how that happened. No one has said anything, except that Mobira alleging I sent the silent woman on an errand, and someone yesterday mentioning a trial. I thought this land boasted of its justice. I've seen little evidence of it so far."

The maid tutted. The woman – *Queen Rommi!* – frowned. "This is not official – but can you tell me about the silent woman? Yikkeri, please write this down." Yikkeri – *what kind of name is that?* - moved over to the desk.

Kelji almost ground her teeth with the effort to control her anger. "I don't know her name. But if there's any spying going on, she was spying on me. She tracked me down with something she wanted to have read to her. When I understood that she couldn't talk, I offered to teach her to read. It seemed to me unnecessarily cruel that no one had done this." The face before her tensed. Kelji didn't care. The maid was writing. "I let her come to Sapientia as my maid, leaving Imadal behind. I supposed she had some reason of love or family. But while we were on the way she snooped in my belongings, damaged the book I was bringing -" despite her resolutions she heard her voice grow furious – "and so in the College I shut her in a room, but she ran away. I gave her no instructions, and I haven't seen her since. I'd gladly pay for her whipping. Mobira knew almost at once that she'd gone, and arrested me, pretending that I'd sent her to spy, so I assume they were working together."

"And nobody has asked you about this since you've been in the Palace?"

"Nobody."

"You think that she was connected to Mobira, who brought you here, but you don't know that?"

"I don't know it, no. But what other excuse was there for my arrest?"

The woman sat still, looking at the hands in her lap. Then, "How did she damage the book?"

"She spilled something on one of the pages, smelt like wine. I found her looking at it, which she had no business doing, so I checked later, and I couldn't make it right again."

"Did she do anything else? Write on it, or tear it, or slip a message inside?"

"No."

"How can you be sure?"

"Because I checked carefully, of course! The stain was bad enough, but I didn't want my Queen to be blamed for anything – she could have defaced the pictures, or written blasphemy. She hadn't, so I delivered it anyway, a gift that your College requested, and so did the Prelate in Vachansha, and Queen Nerranya had the two copies manufactured, at her own cost. Before I left, she told me that you Ricossans didn't care for visitors." She really shouldn't have said that, *but it's been four bloody days, and Mobira was loathsome.*

The maid looked up from her writing to say, "You are insolent!"

"She is angry," said the Queen, before Kelji could prove her right. "I tell you frankly, madam, this is all very puzzling to me.

"You say you're not a spy, but you are the Jaryari Queen's cousin. Do you know why she chose you to send?"

Kelji supposed she had no reason not to be fairly honest. "I was - eager for travel, to see beyond the borders of my homeland, and when I heard of this embassy I asked my Uncle Haras to put my name forward." *To get away from home; to get away from him. And from everyone else telling me to forget Larelna, and grow up.*

"Indeed. As you say, visits between our capitals are rare. Forgive me, but when you returned, surely your cousin would expect you to add to her knowledge? She would ask you what you saw, and learned, in this strange country?"

She spoke quietly. Something about her, the gentle logic,

reminded Kelji of Jedder, the first time they'd met, at that absurd dance when she'd made a fool of herself.

"I was instructed, yes," she said, "to keep my eyes and ears open for the customs and views of those I met. But not to pry or offend. My Queen was clear about the distinction. She -" and then she was caught, and stopped.

"She?"

Well, she'd been rude already, and yes, why not?

"She said Jaryar hadn't often sent emissaries to City Qayn, and the last one died. A monk some years back. Brother Jude."

"He was robbed and killed in the street, as sometimes happens in all cities. Unfortunate, but years ago," said the Queen. "Who is the man Vaddras?"

Kelji shrugged. "He's just a servant. My husband employed him first, before we were married. Four years ago. I've no complaints about him. He looks after horses, and does what he's told."

"Has he any connections to Ricossa?"

"No one has any connections to Ricossa except me. Nadya b'Astith's uncle is married to my great-aunt, whatever kin that makes us. I've never been here before."

"Indeed. When you went to Sapientia, there was a young man with you, was there not?"

"Yes, Mejorad b'Shen was his name." It struck her suddenly. "Your son, Your Grace."

The voice was calm. "He is not my son now."

"In Jaryar," said Kelji loudly, "your child once born is your child for always." The pain in her chest and throat was so unbearable that she barely heard the maid's exclamation. She had to flick tears furiously off her cheeks.

"I am sorry for your grief," said the Queen, after a pause. Kelji hated her for having guessed. Queen Rommi waited; then she said, "My second husband was very dear to me. He died three years ago. I was angry, with him, and with the world. Even, Lord forgive me, with God. If someone had offered me a journey far away, to a foreign land, I think I would have been eager to go."

I don't want your soothing! But Kelji found her hate leaking alarmingly away.

"Yes, Mejorad travelled with me," she said tiredly. "He said he wanted to avoid some holy duty he was supposed to do, and I believed him. But apparently his Family or the b'Astith set him to watch me. Nadya's lover is a b'Shen, isn't she? I'm not familiar with the way you all work together here." *I did think Nadya was my friend. I was a fool.*

"Curious." The Queen thought. "What do you know of the Doctors here – I mean as individuals?"

"Almost nothing. Bekonin is the First Doctor of Divinity, who wanted the book, but someone called Madrasun had written the letters arranging the visit.. I was told the other night that he's dead. God rest his soul," she said with defiant charity. "I had no secret dealings with either of them, or with the woman Dirria, whom Mobira mentioned."

"You would take oath on all this?"

"Yes, I would. But if you don't believe my word, you won't believe my oath. And now are you going to hang me, or allow me to go home?"

"Neither is within my power," said the Queen. "I expect an official questioning will come. If you're not asked, there'ss no need to mention this visit."

"If it's unofficial and secret, Your Grace, why are you here?" *Four bloody days, and no fresh air.*

"That's a good question. Yikkeri, may I have a drink?" The maid poured wine from Kelji's jug into a cup for her. Kelji waved a refusal.

Her visitor leaned forward a little. "You come from Jaryar. May it please you to forgive my ignorance, but Marod is part of Jaryar, is it not?"

"My husband comes from Stonehill, and he would say, Not. We share a queen, that is all."

("What a good Jaryari you are," when she wanted to annoy him.)

"I see," though she probably didn't. "But have you heard of King Arrion of Marod, long ago?"

"Arrion the One-Armed. Yes."

"My father studied foreign history when he was young, and he told me a tale about Arrion." Kelji raised her eyebrows, and the maid stared. "He said that the King banished his dearest friend, tried and convicted and banished him for some monstrous crime, and then it became clear that he'd been innocent. And instead of sending him money and prayers, or even calling him home by royal decree, King Arrion changed the law of the land, so the man could be tried a second time. He said this is the reason why in Marod and Jaryar people can't be hanged without two trials, a first one and then an Appeal. Is that correct?"

"I believe so; something like that." Kelji knew little of law.

"We in Ricossa find this a very strange idea. Once a decision is made here, by judge or king or council, it is irreversible. If it's wrong, as it may be, God will set all right in heaven. My father said King Arrion must have been the stupidest man ever to wear a crown. But perhaps that was unfair.

"You ask why I'm here, madam. I was told you are to be tried the day after tomorrow. I want the verdict, being irrevocable, to be right."

*

"I'll be back in two weeks or so. I'll give your greetings to them all at Dendarry," Jedder had said for the severalth time, standing ready to mount.

When you come back, I'll be gone.

"Fare well," she said, still not looking him in the eye.

"Remember I love you," and he dared to touch her cheek. Then he and his servant rode off.

The charge was espionage. She'd probably not see him again this side of Judgment Day.

*

Hridnaya pushed the door open, and it was the right room. There was only one person in it, a grandly-robed plumpish man sitting covering a yawn with his hand. She might have seen him somewhere before -

She curtsied in passing, a humble servant on her way to the courtyard. The door to Outside was almost within reach, and hope was rising high, when she heard him stand up. "A good morning to you," he said. "Can you tell me what your errand is, so early?"

Please, Lord! yet again. She made the Voiceless gesture. His eyes flickered from her bag, not an indoor one, to her face, which he seemed to study. "You have leave to go out, that you can show me?"

Plese alow the bearer to come and go freely. Sealed.

Let him be satisfied.

The man didn't look satisfied. For a blink he looked amazed, and then he looked – what? She seemed to see anger – horror – fear – shock – all in his roundish face at once. And then it was blank, with the stare of rapid thought.

"I see," he said. He breathed. "Madam, may I speak with you?"

Madam?

His flowing yellow sleeves gestured, and she had to

precede him back out of the door. They passed from the square landing into an empty room, and across that to another. It was quite small, with a few chairs and stools, a high window, and nothing else. This was bad. She wondered what death she was going to die.

The man shut the door. Still politely, "I am Krothon b'Trai, the Queen's Chamberlain. Your name is Hridnaya, I believe, madam?"

Her trembling stillness was an admission.

"And -" he paused uneasily, "and you're in Mobira's service? Forgive me, I hadn't -"

The room spun around her.

She had a permission with the King's seal, Mobira's seal. He thought she was working for Mobira.

He was afraid of her.

Hridanaya started to laugh. She heard herself madly, wickedly, laughing, filling the room with monstrous mirth, and she couldn't stop. *Mobira!*

A part of her mind waited for him to slap her into sense, but he didn't.

It was loud, and someone put a head round the door. The man spoke to the head, and it went away, and Hridnaya, abruptly silent again, sat down on a stool, trembling and gulping, and clutching the saddle-bag that wasn't hers. She dared not look up. She heard him say, "You *are* Hridnaya, who worked for the b'Nida?" and she nodded.

The door opened, and a woman came in. She was plain, and very dark. She couldn't be the Queen. It wasn't possible. The man displayed the guilty parchment. "You guessed right, Your Grace." Hridnaya waited.

"'Please allow the bearer to come and go freely,'" the woman read aloud. "Someone wrote this, and sealed it. Someone who cannot spell. Was that you, or another?"

Could she claim -? But no, for everyone's sake she must stay clear of Mobira. She tapped her own chest. The man drew in breath. *Using King Aigith's seal for my own purposes,* she thought. *You will make me regret it with tortures, but I do not regret it yet.*

"You're mad!" Balki was fluttering her paws. There'd been no word from Balki for a long time.

"So you can write, as we've been told. Where did you get a royal seal? There are not many." She thrust the parchment back at Hridnaya, and the man gave her a pen. They stood towering before her.

Wearily she wrote **I stole it**. This was the end.

But she'd thought that before, and the End refused to come.

She sensed them looking at each other. There was a pause, and then the man's gown swirled towards her. He pulled a small box that hung from his belt up into his hand. "In here I have a bone of the holy martyr St Joro," he said sternly. He kissed the box, and grabbed Hridnaya's left hand. Lord b'Nida would have done this more impressively. "Write. And swear it on the holy relic. Tell us who you're working for."

Her heart thumped. One hand imprisoned on the reliquary, she wrote with the other **Justis**.

"What justice? Justice for whom?"

For Kelji of Maker. And for Flowerinhood.

Again a pause, and she heard the man breathing. (Krothon b'Trai. "That fat-souled smiler," Lord b'Nida called him with contempt.)

"We are not your enemies," said the woman, "and I think you're not ours. I have spoken to Mejorad b'Shen." She reached for the bag, and Hridnaya let her take it.

They opened it, and found the writing she'd copied, all those hours of work, and they sat together and began to look through it quietly.

("Memorandum in re the evidence to be presented at the trial of Kelji of Makkera.")

Hridnaya leant back against the wall, and longed for sleep.

"They're bribing her own servant to lie."

"Mm," said the Queen.

And then she heard gasps, and she knew what they'd come to.

("Item. As arranged and paid for, Doctor Akraib will testify that on looking through the gifted book after the presentation she found a hidden letter fastened between two pages, with money to the sum of ten gold pieces. The letter, which Akraib will produce, was addressed to Madrasun b'Olim, and said 'Your information has been useful. Payment is enclosed. Please supply further details when you can. N'.")

"This is -! This is not -"

"The Lake is deep," said the Queen, as people did, and her voice trembled.

The man grabbed her hand again, and his palm was damp. "I think you're lying. *Did* you copy or find these here in the Palace? Swear it on the holy things. Go to hell if you lie."

Almost, for a mad moment, she thought she hadn't. It was all too much. How much more likely, easier for the world to deal with, if *she* were the liar!

"I ware," she managed to say.

"This means -"

"Ssh, please, Krothon." Hridnaya saw the Queen shut her eyes. Without opening them, she said, "I spoke to Kelji not two hours ago, and she - Madam. Hridnaya. Did you see this book, that she gave to the College? Did you look at it closely?"

Rather nervously, she nodded.

"Was there anything hidden inside?"

Her hand was still on the box. She shook her head as emphatically as she could, and crossed herself.

"Indeed. Kelji would have had no reason not to lay blame on you, and she didn't. This allegation is certainly a lie. A planned lie. But that means her arrest had almost nothing to do with you, after all."

"Your Grace, please!" moaned the man Krothon. "We are in too far!"

Hridnaya saw the door open behind them.

All three gasped, but it was a pink little old woman whom the others seemed to know. "Your Grace, you're expected in the – whatever that room's called with the green fishy ceiling. To meet Brother Silas and his delegation. People noticed that you weren't at Mass. And just now I was given this." She curtsied, and handed over a parchment. The King's seal on this one was to fasten the letter shut.

"Who gave it to you, Yikkeri?" asked the man.

"His Chamberlain's servant, the short-sighted one who peers."

"Edda."

The Queen opened her letter and showed it to her servants. Hridnaya could see writing, and also a design of some sort, a plan of box-shapes.

Krothon read in a whisper, "On this fine morning Aigith the King for the Evening sends greetings to his beloved sister and colleague. To assist her in the onerous duties which are still so new to her, he encloses a plan of the *eastern* wing of the Palace." He paused; then, "Oh, dear God."

"The eastern wing," said the Queen slowly. "So he knows already where I went this morning, two hours ago - that I crossed to his side to talk to Kelji - and he doesn't like it. Am I the one being watched, or is she? She, I would think."

"Your Grace, you must step back. You must. This is a threat."

"It's a criticism, certainly."

"The Queen can walk where she likes! He can't harm her!" exclaimed the little woman.

Krothon said, "He can't harm *her*." His rather round face glistened with sweat. He was looking down at Hridnaya with horror. "This woman, and these papers, are very dangerous to us – to you."

The Queen shut her eyes tight again. They all waited, Krothon fiddling with his little box. *Which of us four is truly the most frightened?* At last she opened them. "He knows where I went, but he may not know about her, and she's got herself a Palace tabard. Yikkeri, you have access to keys. Find somewhere to lock her in, for her own protection. If anyone questions you on the way – can you think of a story?"

"Of course, Your Grace."

She looked directly at Hridnaya, and said, "I am asking you to trust me." Slowly, "Krothon, there was rioting in the street on Saturday night, because the b'Nida took offence about something that happened at the College. I think that I am very angry about this."

He looked baffled.

"We will discuss it further after seeing this priest as my dayplan requires. Yikkeri?"

Almost unbelievably, Yikkeri was grinning. "The woman's from the kitchens, and thought I had a kindly face. I found her in tears. I suspect she fears she's with child, but I haven't yet managed to learn the details."

"Brechad wouldn't believe that! It's your actions he may investigate, as well as hers!"

"Yes. Wait." The Queen frowned. Then she also smiled, looking for a moment like that Mejorad. "My actions are not Brechad b'Iri's affair, as you can tell him, but if he inquires and tries to insist, hint that you don't approve of them. There is no one so lost to propriety as a lonely woman besotted with a lovely face, and I've sworn you to secrecy, as I did last night."

"Besotted?" And then he understood.

My lovely face? Hridnaya had become a piece of contraband, a dangerous item to be smuggled around the Queen's own Palace, her existence covered with titillating lies. She wanted again to laugh, but perhaps she'd already laughed too much.

"Come, madam," Yikkeri said.

*

The wagon wheels bumped, and the plank seats swayed again. Ittrad gripped the sides and pressed his teeth together. Half of yesterday jiggling like this, and a night trying to sleep on the ground, wondering what the noises were. And it would still be most of today before they arrived in City Qayn. He couldn't even look forward to supper, for his stomach was in revolt.

Dirria and her maid weren't riding in the common wagon, of course, but were travelling on horseback with Mobira, an hour or so ahead. She didn't yet know how he had disobeyed her. He had to hope that Lord b'Nida would agree he'd done the right thing, and make good any difficulties.

The driver was a solid youngish woman chewing a straw, and there was one other passenger, a tall priest who was managing to read what looked like a psalter as they went. Ittrad's previous journey to the city to meet Gridor had taught him that reading would only make him sick, and he disliked talking to strangers, but he wasn't a man for savouring creation either. *God forgive me, I hate journeys.*

They paused at a little road by a river to the right, for the horses to drink. The driver spat and crossed herself.

"Where's that lead to? Is it the Haunted Pool?" the priest lifted his nose from his book to ask.

"Aye, where the great ones -" and she crossed herself again. *If you want to pray, pray,* Ittrad thought irritably, and then, *Where the great ones do what? Worship the devil? Torture babies? Commit adultery under the stars?*

Off they lurched again. He thought of what was waiting in the city ahead, beginning to grow nervous, and annoyed at himself for being so.

*

"This is most generous of you, er, my lord," said the woman Miya shyly. "I will be sure to pass the money on."

"Thank you." At least Brinnon's children wouldn't starve just yet.

Mej looked around her home, the second single-room commoner's place he'd been in recently. This one was higher-up its tenement than Brinnon and Lulet's. It was very tidy. There was a flower in a pot on the table, leaves drooping in the August heat. Wednesday laundry already hung from a line stretched from the window across to the other side of the alley.

Miya hadn't seemed to remember him from the trial, but had accepted, albeit with a surprised jerk, that a member of the b'Shen might still be concerned about Flower-in-Hood's kin. Now she twisted her hands together, and said, "Please assure your – that is, Lady b'Shen – we don't seek trouble. My niece, she's run mad." Her lips and lower face tensed disapprovingly, an expression Mej had often met in others, aimed at him. "But the rest of us only wish to be quiet and respectable. Brinnon has learned his lesson."

"Yes, of course." *Poor bastard.* "And are you well yourself, madam, and your own family?"

"Oh, yes, sir," and suddenly her face lit up with pleasure, even glee. "I earn, and the children are settled. I've had good reports of them both in the last week," she said proudly. "Thank you again – please to accept a cup of wine?"

He did so, out of courtesy, and it wasn't as bad stuff as he'd expected. As he said farewell and swung downstairs, he knew he'd done something *right.* And he *couldn't* report to Jedder, as he'd promised – a casual glance down St Patric's Street that morning had shown him the muscled brute, soldier without armour or tabard, idling in a doorway to watch Nadya's house. Mej had done duties like that himself down south, and knew the signs.

So he was genuinely unable (yet) to tell Jedder that he'd misplaced Kelji's main witness, and face his wrath. All he could do was hope – *the Queen and Hridnaya and that lick-glistening Chamberlain* – hope that they could sort things out.

As he crossed from poor areas of the City to wealthy, he came to the Great Square. No one was being whipped today. But among the usual bustle were extra workpeople, some sweeping around the empty platforms and laying straw; others hanging banners on poles. The great banner of Ricossa next to the High Gallows, and those of the Families around, all ten. They were preparing something big.

People were standing in clumps, pointing.

"Yes, tomorrow. I wish I could be there, but the childpen has to stay open, and my mistress needs me. We're expecting to be busy. Tell me about it, if you do decide to watch."

"The hanging, yes, but trials are dull. You can't hear what they're saying at the back. Last time I was stuck behind some bore explaining it all wrong to his in-laws, and then I couldn't get a place by the scaffold. Will it be more severe than hanging, d'you think?"

"Bloody Jaryari. I hope they make her squeal."

They were preparing for that.

Ears pricked for Eyanda's strident tones, he reached the house and ran in. His dash up towards his chamber was unfortunately intercepted. The Housefather said, "Ah, sir. There are messages," and handed him two pieces of parchment with a bow. "That one, sir, came from the *Palace*."

Mej's heart thudded, but he was contrary, and opened the other first.

Narod to Mejorad, in haste, greeting. Do not look for me at the D and B. We are told to expect to leave tomorrow across the Lake for some northern village. No one will tell us why, or what we're to do there, which aggravates. Say a prayer for me and buy me a drink when I return. May you flourish till then. N.

Soldiers being sent off at short notice; not good.

The other letter was sealed with an R entwined with a crown. His back tingled.

Krothon b'Trai, Chamberlain to Her Grace Rommi, Queen for the Morning, to Mejorad b'Shen, greeting.

The Queen has received reports of rioting and chaos in the streets of this city last Saturday night following a quarrel at her College between you and Lord b'Nida. She wishes to hear an explanation of this unseemly conduct from both parties. The Families should not be at odds, and the

College does not wish dissension between b'Nida and b'Shen. You are therefore requested and invited to attend at the Palace this evening at the sixth hour after midday, to dine, to discuss and it is hoped to make peace.

I remain in the Queen's service, Krothon.

Mej had read this letter several times, wondering, before he noticed the word she'd told him to look for. Last December, the b'Shen had been playing a game when everyone had to invent a password for others to discover. His own had been Queensbrother, not difficult to guess. And Rommi, to people's surprise – but it was Christmas after all, and a time for merry fooling – had said Chaos.

She had a plan. He had no idea why it involved b'Nida, that passionless stick, but there was some kind of plan.

*

Ittrad was waiting with a short brown hall-warden who evidently had nothing to do but stand silently making sure odd visitors didn't steal the b'Nida jewels, or set fire to the house. *At least my life's more entertaining than that.*

A pleasant-faced older woman swept into the hall. "You are Ittrad, son of Ambario?" He bowed. "You are to come up, if you please."

His bad leg ached from the capital's endless paved streets. Thankfully they only climbed one flight, and then passed into a small study, or library, where Lord b'Nida was sitting at a table. Ittrad glanced covetously at the books and documents covering two walls. It was a cosy place, only needing a mug of ale and a plate of toasted bread or stewed apples to make it perfect.

"You may sit down. This is Narrim, Housemother here." Lord b'Nida gestured.

"Madam."

"You said below you had a message for me."

"Yes, my lord, two." He cleared his throat. "Doctor Dirria has been summoned to attend the foreign woman's trial tomorrow. She didn't bring me, but I came of my own planning, first to give you this." He handed over the King's letter that he'd found.

"To the most faithful -" Lord b'Nida's long face quivered. "Where did you find it?"

Ittrad explained. "Mobira's been happy enough to have everyone searching her room, where she kept nothing that mattered."

The Lord nodded. The Housemother looked very serious. *Well, they're impressed,* he thought with sinful pride.

"'He is a traitor,'" Lord b'Nida quoted. "*That* Doctor Madrasun never was. And he died – when?"

"Three days after this letter. I also spoke to his widow. She said he was anxious, and told her the kingdom had a dilemma. She wouldn't tell me what, or he wouldn't tell her."

"Yes. He spoke to me, and perhaps to others." Lord b'Nida didn't elaborate. He tapped his right hand on the table, holding the letter. "So this is at last proof that Mobira is obedient enough to kill. I thank you. It's not clear what use we can make of it."

Ittrad said, "She's obedient enough to kill, but not enough to destroy the instruction, as he asked. He trusts her more than she trusts him."

"True; well thought. You spoke of a second message?"

He took a breath. "Doctor Dirria is here because Mobira brought her, brought her to lie. She is to say that her meeting with – with your former servant was part of a plot by this Kelji. As we both know, and I can testify, that isn't true. I overheard the

328

Doctor promise that she'd let Mobira tell her what to say, and Mobira told her this would establish her loyalty and that of the College. I'm almost certain that's the reason she came without me. Because she plans to give false testimony, and I would know it's false."

"Hridnaya was in Sapientia?" The Housemother was amazed.

"Yes. She can give evidence at the trial. Pardon me, my lord, you may already have brought her here."

The Lord had been looking solemn and concerned, but now he blinked sharply. "I – bring her here? What do – sir, what do you think is my concern?"

Ittrad paused. "To stop Mobira's crimes."

"I wish to protect the College from her conniving, if I can, yes. Kelji, on the other hand – it is hardly desirable to discredit Doctor Dirria as you suggest."

"But you could discredit Mobira, my lord," said Narrim.

"This Kelji isn't a spy," said Ittrad slowly.

"I dare say she is not. It might indeed benefit the College if she were declared innocent, but I doubt the King will permit that." He stared at Ittrad, who decided it would be wise not to stare back, and dropped his gaze to the table-top.

In a different tone, Lord b'Nida said, "Sir, does Dirria know you're here? Do you have a place to go?"

"No, and no, my lord, but I have enough money for a bed at an inn." Enough for one night, anyway.

"We can spare you some coin, then. At the sixth hour today I am summoned to dine at the Palace, with the Morning Queen. You will accompany me. Can you wait at table?"

He gaped, head suddenly cold. "Not – not very well, my lord."

"Do your best. Narrim will arrange for a bath and a meal,

and find you some better clothes. You should have a little time
from then to practise."

*But -! I'll be fed, at least. Me, to meet a Queen! Rich and
poor are the same before God, but – a Queen!*

Narrim was turning towards the door, beckoning him.
"My lord," he said as he rose, "this Hridnaya's evidence, if the
judge believed her, would make all clear, and expose Mobira, at
least to suspicion."

"She wouldn't be believed. She couldn't even talk." The
voice was forbidding.

"She can write."

"We cannot bring her. That is enough."

"Did you find her then, my lord?" asked Narrim, and the
simple curiosity in her face jolted Ittrad in a way he didn't like.

"That is enough, Narrim! We cannot bring her into the
matter. She is not available. Nor would she be useful."

Ittrad was used to thinking carefully, but not fast. But as
he looked across the table, he remembered his journey.

The Pool where the great ones - do what?

If you want to pray, pray, he'd thought. "Lord of Justice
and Mercy, let it not be true."

But surely it was.

*

*Am I going to have a future? Or am I in the pause in the
middle of a tale, before most of the characters are perhaps killed?
I need Uncle's story-telling penny to toss.*

After a very long time the door to the linen cupboard
opened. Hridnaya's fear stabbed her, but it was only Yikkeri,
carrying a largish cloth. "Put your things away, and cover them
with this. Now come." As Hridnaya scrambled up, "Look
ordinary." Almost as quick as this took to say, they were walking
out, down stairs and through rooms. There were people talking,

tidying or going about for Hridnaya to pass with stomach churning, but no one gave them a second look. Yikkeri trotted with confidence, and at last an anteroom opened into somewhere that had no other doors. There was a steaming bucket and jug, a dish of soap, and a pile of towels and garments. "Get yourself clean, and put these on."

They don't want me dead yet, then. She made her face as enquiring as was polite.

"Yes," said Yikkeri. "There is to be a dinner this evening, and the Queen wants you to listen to what is said."

May God put me where He wants me. I suppose.

*

"I'm dining out tonight. Tell the kitchens, if you please," said Mej. "And I'm going alone," he added, for Tor would just run to Eyanda with more tales.

"At the Palace, sir?" asked the Housefather in awe, as Uncle Yettrid walked into the room, and raised his eyebrows.

Mej made himself look sulky. "The Queen wants to force me and Lord b'Nida to kiss and make peace. I don't see how it was my fault, if his people break windows."

"B'Nida?" said Uncle Yettrid. "Hmm. Isn't his youngest daughter available still - Lindet? Clever and pretty, they say, and the b'Nidas don't object to priests. Be very courteous to him, Mejorad." He gave his great-nephew a sternly encouraging smile.

"Yes, sir." Mej gritted his teeth. A wife was something else he didn't want.

So once again as the bells chimed he entered the Palace courtyard, and this time he was dressed in his second-best clothes, and he walked straight and smarmy through the chattering idlers, and past the sausage-barrow, right up to Yani's great doors.

"May God bless you, honoured sir."

"And you. I am come to dine. Mejorad b'Shen, by

331

invitation of the Queen."

*

The room wasn't large, but there were tapestries and a painted ceiling. A square table of gleaming dark wood had been laid with four places, only four. A woman servant was arranging fruit and sweetmeats in attractive little piles at the base of a magnificent candelabra. To the left, the sideboard was already laden with covered dishes. Mej had rarely been privileged to attend one of these intimate suppers "where the true business of the realm is done", and he felt unreal.

Yikkeri, who'd led him here blank-faced, went back out.

Krothon the Chamberlain was standing by the sideboard, his hand on a jug of wine. He wore a long grey gown with golden trim at neck and shoulders, and his hair and beard were curled and – surely – scented. But his eyes went from Mej to the woman, and Mej followed his gaze, and gasped.

"It's you! Well met, Hridnaya!" His pleasure and relief surprised all three of them. She jumped a little, and he lowered his voice. "Where did you go to? I've been expecting to be murdered for losing you." He grinned, and she actually gave him a timid smile back.

"The Queen and I found her trying to leave the Palace with documents," said Krothon. "Now, sir. Can I pour you a drink?"

"Thank you."

"No, wait. Lord b'Nida will be here soon. Madam," and he turned to the woman. "You must be hidden before the regular servants arrive." He beckoned her to one of the tapestries, and lifted a flap. It didn't cover plain wall, but a narrow recess with a shuttered window beyond. "The Queen wishes you to listen, like a – listen carefully," Krothon told her, "but if I hear one sound from you, you'll regret it." She nodded. He hid her away, smoothing the tapestry with fussy jerks, and then he and Mej looked at each other for an odd moment, before Krothon rang a little bell. "You're alone, sir? Wine?" His voice croaked slightly.

Mej accepted a cup, and then removed his cloak, realising too late that it would have been more dignified to do these things the other way round.

Two women and a man in Palace clothes glided in. "Thank you. Deb, please inform the Queen when Lord b'Nida arrives. I believe he's bringing his own attendant, but Baidon, you'll be waiting on this gentleman." To Mej, "Please make yourself comfortable, sir. And do not be nervous. The b'Nida are a civilised house, and their Lord is not fearsome. Saturday night was surely an aberration." He attempted a kindly-uncle smile as he left with Deb. Mej, about to feel insulted, realised that after all it was for the benefit of the servants. One of them, a slender white-haired woman, began to tune her lute.

(But how do we talk secrets with these people standing at our backs?)

The door again, and voices. "The young gentleman is here already, my lord."

Mej bowed politely but not obsequiously to Riodran, Lord b'Nida.

*

He'd been kind to her for eighteen years. He'd ordered her death less than a week ago. Now he was standing a few feet away, separated from her by a tapestry and his ignorance.

Her instructions were to listen, but for a little time there was nothing to hear except an awkward silence. She looked around at the narrow space in which she stood – tapestry-thread-ends eight feet long and seven high on one side, and panelled walls or shutters on the other three. There was a candle on the floor, and cups of wine and water for her to mix. *Don't get drunk,* and she felt a horrified giggle grow within at the thought of herself interrupting the dinner with wild hidden singing. *Be sensible. Sit down – quietly! – and listen.*

The door opened again, and there were steps, and murmurs of "Your Grace."

The Queen is here.

Then she heard his voice, and sudden tears pricked. All he was saying was, "Your Grace. Please allow me to apologise most humbly on behalf of my Family for the disgraceful conduct on Saturday night. Your rebuke is deserved. We have no wish to be at enmity with the b'Shen, the b'Astith, or anyone."

"Thank you, my lord," said the Queen.

"And I apologise also for any – I never meant to imply wrongdoing, or cause trouble for the b'Nida." Mejorad was less smooth.

"Indeed, I was sure of it. You are both most gracious. Let us eat and drink to cordiality between the Families, and with the College – and after dinner we can share a few thoughts as to how to foster goodwill."

What happened on Saturday? Whatever it was, she made it an excuse to bring them both here.

There were noises of sitting down. Krothon gave thanks to God – his voice was still nervous – and the meal began. Hridnaya heard gentle music, the chinks of platter and spoon, and servant-murmuring. And she remembered "I believe he's bringing his own attendant," but didn't dare move the cloth to peep and see who this was. Narrim? Or had he already found a new Voiceless? That actually hurt. Whoever it was would need to be very trustworthy, for Lord b'Nida was clever, and he'd have guessed – something.

"Your family are all well, my lord?"

"Yes, I thank you. We're hoping for a new grandchild

down south in November, God willing. And my daughter Lindet is training a fresh colt for the hunting season – have you ever met her, sir?"

"Er, Lindet, yes. She's very charming."

"Thank you, and I'm glad to say she has more substantial qualities also."

Hridnaya briefly pictured Lindet at the altar marrying Mejorad b'Shen, and wondered if this would be a good idea for either of them.

She'd listened to so much dinner-table conversation over the years, and she felt the tension as they all avoided the topics they'd come for.

"So few cooks understand the need for the sauce to complement not merely the fish but also the accompanying wine. This is excellent."

"You are most kind; we are well served in the kitchens."

The Chamberlain even sank to the tediousness of "I hear the harvest is nearly all in. The farmers are thankful for the good weather." *He writes bad poetry,* Hridnaya remembered hearing from somewhere. *And he forgot to search me for the seal I stole.* It still sat, a lumpy irritation, inside her bodice.

Once there was a small crash, as if one of the servants had fumbled and dropped a plate. This was hard to believe, in the Palace itself. He or she went unrebuked.

But at last, "The evening wears on. Perhaps, Your Grace, we might manage the sweetmeats and wine for ourselves, and these worthy people can retire?" said Krothon.

That speech was prepared.

"Indeed."

"You can stay," said Lord b'Nida, presumably to his own man or woman, whom oddly he had not introduced.

There were noises of plates being gathered.

The Queen said, "Thank you, Yikkeri. May it please you to pour wine for everyone, and then stand outside and watch?"

The door shut. Music continued, but very softly – the lute-player must be Queen Rommi's Voiceless. Hridnaya guessed that there were five more people in the room. Four conspirators, and one presumably very trusted servant behind Lord b'Nida's chair. There was a silence, and she felt her heart thudding.

The Queen's voice seemed to shake a little. "My lord, thank you for coming. I wonder if now can be the time to speak more frankly. Your commitment to the Great College is of many years' standing. It's also under my care, and so of course I maintain spies in Sapientia. They have not found anything to concern me." She paused, and removed the shake. "And yet it seems plain that my brother the Evening King distrusts some or all of the Doctors, and what they do. This puzzles me. Can you shine any light on the darkness?"

A cautious beginning, but still someone – the Chamberlain? - shifted. *Yes, this is talk about the King, and he wouldn't like it.*

Lord b'Nida said, "You are asking for frankness, Your Grace. That can be dangerous. Before whom are you asking me to be frank?"

Hridnaya gasped almost admiringly at his daring. But the Queen was willing to answer.

"Mejorad b'Shen shares my concern, and consulted me for this very reason. Krothon b'Trai is my Chamberlain, as he was Queen Zinial's. Does that answer you?"

And then there's me, whom you didn't mention.

There was a surprisingly long pause. *Who is he staring at? Doesn't he trust Mejorad? Do I?*

But it was the Chamberlain's voice that said, "You know me, I think, my lord."

"Hmm. Yes. I have seen you for many years standing around the Palace, smiling. Does that mean I think you worthy of trust? Since we are being *frank*, no, I do not. This is a house of many spies."

Krothon said nothing.

But the Queen said, "Very well, my lord, *I* will answer. I agree that King Aigith has ruled so long that most people here have forgotten any deeper loyalty than to him. Lady b'Shen, who was my grandmother once, warned me of this when I was chosen. She said, and I've found, that I'm surrounded by people who smile and run my errands, and tell me that everyone other than them is reporting my secret thoughts to the King. As you say, spies - but I doubt they think of themselves that way. So I had two people in the Palace I trusted, those I brought with me. One is a guard at my chamber, and the other has served me since I was born, and is now standing outside that door. Then I had to decide if there could be a third person, and I chose Krothon."

"May I ask why?"

"That is not a fit question -" Krothon began.

"Indeed not," agreed the Queen. But she went on slowly, "Yesterday morning I was standing on the stairs between my Chaplain Sister Ansha, and my Chamberlain, two people who have lived and worked here and know everything. This impetuous young man begged to speak to me. It was most indecorous and unwise, and I thought it might mean trouble. One of the two looked pleased at the interruption, and the other looked angry. I thought anger was the more honest response. So I chose Krothon. I have seen no sign that I was mistaken." Nobody said "yet". Hridnaya, barely breathing, wished she could see their faces. "And then I chose Mejorad, and earlier today I chose you, my lord. Is that enough, or is this conversation over?"

A tinkling of background notes, but no other sound.

Then, "Very well," Lord b'Nida said. Someone must have gestured, for the music stopped at last, and they moved forward in quiet. "You asked about the College. Your Grace, some of us think that the Evening King may have been – misled, or induced, to see danger in the College where there is none.

"Some narrow fools of course believe all study leads to heresy or treason. We analyse and debate and invent, as we were set up by the New Governance to do, but we teach nothing contrary to God's law."

"Is this his only concern?"

"No. The Great College is the only place of its like on Ragaris, perhaps anywhere. It was intended to be the envy of the nations, and it is so. The nations, therefore, enquire about it, and this he appears to dislike. The Defardi ask about our lectures in theology, and the Jaryari ask about the idea in general. Over the last few years, Queen Nerranya has sent letters with questions. None of this is secret."

"No?" asked Krothon.

"*No*. We are loyal. We consulted the Morning Queen, your predecessor, and she saw all communication with Makkera, and approved all our replies. Your Chamberlain can confirm this. But then we noticed that the King, or someone in his name, had placed the woman Mobira at the College, without our agreement and not for our benefit. She enquires into what she chooses, and bribes students for reports on their tutors, and calls in soldiers at her whim, and sometimes gives orders that our frailer Doctors dare not disobey. All this without reference to you, or to Queen Zinial before you. We are loyal," he said with solid emphasis, "but we dislike this."

"Indeed, I see. And now there is this visitor, who's to be tried tomorrow."

"Yes." Hridnaya sensed effort behind Lord b'Nida's calm

as he said, "I've seen no reason to believe evil of her. I do not even know the charges."

"In brief," said the Queen, "the charge is that she was sending secret letters and payment for information to a traitor at the College called Madrasun b'Olim."

Hridnaya felt the ice. "Madrasun was never a traitor. And he's dead."

"That news might not have reached Queen Nerranya when she sent her cousin out."

"And what does the accused herself say to this?"

"The lady has not been formally questioned, or hadn't been this morning. This in itself I found very odd. And so I investigated. I have another spy, not in Sapientia, who found me the papers prepared for this trial, and copied them."

Me! thought Hridnaya.

"You have them here?" She could picture him raising eyebrows.

Perhaps the Queen gestured. Hridnaya heard footsteps and swish as Krothon walked over to fetch, presumably, her documents. He said, rather plainly trying to sound efficient and trustworthy, "Kelji was arrested and brought here by Mobira whom you've mentioned, and who made most of the preparations before leaving again on Sunday. A message came in from her yesterday morning, and the trial was then fixed for tomorrow. As I say, most of this is probably by her, but the final few notes were completed by someone else."

So Mobira's still alive, thought Hridnaya. *I hope Jedder is too.*

Krothon cleared his throat, and began to read, just loud enough for her to hear, a little faster than someone calm would have done. "Memorandum in re the trial of Kelji of Makkera. She should be referred to as often as may be as Kelji the Foreigner.

The charge is espionage, which is a heinous crime. The evidence to be produced is as follows:

"'Imprimis. A statement by her own servant that she came here with secret letters for Madrasun. This servant, whose name is Vaddras, was arrested with her'. Then someone else has written, '28th Aug. Now arranged. Vaddras denied this at first, but no torture was required, merely monetary persuasion. Six gold pieces and a good place in the capital.'"

"Her groom said that?" It was Mejorad's voice, expressing the same shock Hridnaya had felt last night. They'd both travelled with Vaddras.

"What filth," said Lord b'Nida, more calmly. "The Jaryari are careless in hiring servants."

"Yes. Then, 'Item. Eyanda b'Shen will testify that Kelji's excessive curiosity about matters of national security led Eyanda to send her son Mejorad to Sapientia to watch her. He will confirm this.'"

"This isn't true," said Mejorad. "I was there when Mobira bribed my – my mother."

"Mm. So thus far," said Lord b'Nida, "the evidence is fabricated. What, if anything, did Kelji truly do to alarm the King's agent?"

"'Item. We expect a statement from Doctor Dirria of the School of Law that a Voiceless woman called on her on 24th August and managed to convey her concern that something about Kelji was wrong. Mobira is to obtain this statement.'"

"I know that's not true either," said Mejorad flatly.

"And I," said Lord b'Nida. "This is a woman I was forced to dismiss. She and her whole family are crazed on the subject of her uncle's death. He was Flower-in-Hood, whom you may have heard of, and she wanted to talk to Dirria about him. My servant here was present at their very brief meeting."

Hridnaya heard surprised breaths, which covered the sound of her own. That man is here!

"Ittrad is a student-servitor at the College, waiting on Dirria. I employed him to look into Mobira's activities. He told me this afternoon that she's recruited Dirria, as you say she planned to do."

"Why is she, Dirria, lying?" asked the Queen.

Ittrad answered for himself, surprising Hridnaya and perhaps everyone.

"Because she's afraid. The man my lord mentioned died on his way to see her, and her predecessor, Doctor Madrasun, also died, and she doesn't wish to cross Mobira. She was warned not to."

"Many in the College fear Mobira," said Lord b'Nida.

"And *also*," said Mejorad, "that's not even what Mobira said when she arrested Kelji. She accused her of sending Hr – the woman to spy for *her*."

"She changes the story from hour to hour," Lord b'Nida agreed. Presumably to Krothon, he said, "Please proceed, sir. Is there more?"

"'If the Voiceless woman is found in time, a statement marked by her confirming the above can be obtained and used. If she's not, it may be suggested that she has disappeared, murdered by agents of Jaryar or in vengeance by the traitors at the College.'

"Finally, the meat of the matter. 'Item. As arranged *and paid for*, Doctor Akraib will testify that on looking through the gifted book immediately after it was presented she found a concealed letter –"

*

"'Your information has been useful. Payment is enclosed. Please supply further details when you can. N.'" I assume N stands for Nerranya," he finished.

"What?" cried Mej, almost leaping off his chair. "But that's nonsense!"

"Yes," said the Queen, but he barely heard her.

"I swear – I'll swear anywhere you like – there was nothing hidden in the book! I travelled with Kelji – she boasted of it and showed it to me, even!"

"The book was damaged, I think?" said the Queen irrelevantly, giving him an unexpected glance. "Wine spilt?"

"By accident," he admitted. "I -" and he made an explanatory gesture.

"And *I* was present when she gave it to us. Several people handled it, with care and reverence, and there was nothing strange about it. Sewing money inside and expecting no one to notice would be absurd."

"Yes, indeed. Please remind me, my lord. Who is Akraib?"

"Akraib is Bekonin's second in the School of Divinity. She has ambitions, which Bekonin is too unworldly to see." One hand was tapping lightly on the table.

"Indeed. Thank you, Krothon. My lord, when Mejorad first spoke to me, it seemed that the King's agent distrusted Jaryar so much that she took fright at nothing. Flower-in-Hood's niece spoke to Dirria, for her own reasons as you say, and Mobira responded by crying treason. But that's not what happened. The Voiceless woman only became involved by happenstance, or ill luck. This false letter, addressed to a man who is dead and cannot defend himself, must have been prepared, and Akraib bribed, in advance. And so Kelji wasn't arrested because she acted suspiciously; the arrest was planned all along. Queen Nerranya sent her kinswoman into a trap."

Trap? In Mej's mind there were pictures of trip-nooses for foxes on the lands of his childhood. Then he saw Kelji struggling and choking in one. He heard himself make a little noise. *I don't understand.*

Everyone was very still.

"A trap," said Lord b'Nida. "For her - and for the College?"

"So I thought I needed to speak to you, my lord. To ask you about the King's suspicions, and about Madrasun b'Olim."

Slowly Lord b'Nida said, "Madrasun was a wise and thoughtful man. To call him a traitor is a despicable lie." At last there was emotion in the man's voice. "He studied the laws and customs of other countries, and compared them with our own. Long ago I was his student, but of late I was privileged to consider myself his friend. It was his place to handle our correspondence with Jaryar, taking advice from Queen Zinial, as I said. He'd known her many years. Your Chamberlain can confirm this." Krothon nodded.

"In the last few days, I've been thinking back, and I remember dining privately with him last autumn. At the time I thought he looked worried, or ill, but after all he was over seventy. We were discussing his studies in law, and he asked what I thought was the greatest curse for any realm. I said, I think, 'Rebellion and internal strife,' and he answered, 'That, yes, we all agree on. But I've been reading the history of Israel and Judah. The greatest curse for any land is a king who does wickedly and cannot be stopped. Israel had prophets to challenge her rulers, but such brave and holy people are hard to come by.' I must have looked surprised, for then he told me to forget his words, they were just an old man's maunderings from the Scriptures." With a twisted smile, "If one is told to forget something, one remembers it."

"A king who does wickedly." Mej trembled. But Lord b'Nida went on, "Do you truly want me to speak freely, Your Grace? I have evidence that Madrasun was first threatened, and then murdered."

He acknowledged their stares with a tilt of the head, and then nodded to his man. While Ittrad was taking something out of his pouch, he said, "We've found a letter that Mobira had hidden away."

Krothon read it out.

"…What you do for a King is absolved, and I will protect you. He is a traitor and deserves it. Make sure it is an accident, as we spoke of…."

He showed the seal at the bottom. "It's the Evening King's."

"Madrasun died three days later." There was a silence. "He must have spoken unwisely. I know he spoke to Queen Zinial. Before she died in June she summoned me and warned me – you may remember, sir."

Krothon said, "Yes. We'd talked of Madrasun. After he died she was very uneasy. I admit I thought it merely a sick woman's fancy, but I suggested summoning you to calm her."

Lord b'Nida spared him a frown, and continued, "She told me to be careful, but gave few details. She said Madrasun had expected trouble on the occasion of this visit. She'd dismissed his concerns, and then he died, and I think on her own deathbed she felt guilty. Perhaps after he consulted her, word got out through others, to the King."

Did his eyes shift again to the man at his side? It occurred to Mej suddenly that he'd left his sword at the door. But surely he could knock down either of the oldish men if he had to, and the servant limped.

"Thank you," said the Queen. She laid her hands on the table, and stared at them. "So," she went on, "Madrasun suspected evil in high places, and connected it with the Jaryari visit. He spoke to people, and then he died. And now we have the evil. Either Queen Nerranya offered to send this book, or she was asked to do so, and someone in City Qayn made a plan. They recruited Akraib, and set out to accuse Nerranya's – what is she? First, second cousin? Mobira did much of the work, but her orders, it's clear from the letter your man found, come from my brother. Dangerous though it may be to say so, he planned this. He arranged false evidence, and an unjust trial. For what purpose? What does he want to happen?" Slowly, as if speaking her thoughts aloud, "It will humiliate the College, claiming you house traitors and Jaryari-lovers." Lord b'Nida nodded curtly. "What does it mean for Kelji? Some kind of - punishment."

"If she's found guilty," said Mej, but he remembered what he'd seen and heard in the Great Square.

"She will be. The judge has been named," said Krothon. "Simoren b'Asa."

"The most venal man in City Qayn." Lord b'Nida.

"So Adjefi says. I guess he'll be given this Memorandum, as an honest judge would not be. It describes espionage as 'a heinous crime,' which would normally mean death."

"Mobira told my mother it might not in this case," Mej remembered.

The Queen's face twitched slightly. "I suspect that was to soothe Eyanda's conscience. Our law says mercy is for God, but the courts are to do justice. And what else could we do to her, a severe sentence short of death? Banishment is just sending her home. And if we – put out her eyes or cut off her hands, that might be as bad as killing. I've heard the Jaryari are squeamish about such things.

"I was wondering last night, after Mejorad spoke to me. Twenty years ago, Lady b'Shen as she now is, his great-grandmother, went to observe the Great Council in Vach-roysh. If the Consuls of Haymon or the King of Marod had killed her, killed her publicly and on obviously false grounds, what would we have done? What will Queen Nerranya do if we hang her cousin? We don't know. We know so little of the West." She looked away, around the shadows of the room, as if the candle-light on her guests' faces was too intense.

"Raids on our borders, at the least."

"Yes. Raids, violence against anyone in Jaryar with Ricossan blood, hot words and hotter actions, and then we would surely retaliate."

"You mean war?" said Lord b'Nida. "You think he wants to provoke war?"

"I wondered, but why?"

Krothon had been fiddling with his napkin. Now he said, and his voice seemed to jerk, "Your Grace, what do we think will happen if the King learns of this meeting?"

"Is he going to?" asked Lord b'Nida.

Mej's heart began to race. "Trap", someone had said. The room had no windows.

Krothon stood up, fast and clumsily. He almost scurried over to the wall, and lifted a corner of tapestry to reveal again the shelves where documents were piled. When he returned to the table, he was carrying a scroll. The Queen watched him, and so they all did.

"Your Grace, and my lord," he said, "please look at this map."

Mej rather liked maps, and wondered if it was going to be something exciting. But no, what Krothon spread out and weighed down with cups was the familiar shape of the continent, Ricossa on one side, and the Evil-Lands-of-the-West on the other.

With a deep breath, "We have a rumour, a tradition," he said, "among those who've served here for many years. My mother was a high secretary before me, and she swore it was true. See here. Ricossa is the east of Ragaris, the whole east. Defardu and the mountains are the centre. In the west, Jaryar and its client states."

My youngest sister could tell you that. Is this a geography lesson?

Pointing, "We have a north-west border with Jaryar, *here*. On their side of it is Arbeth, part of what was once Marod, but is now ruled by Nerranya and her husband. Our border in the south-west is here, with her province of Lefayr.

"The tale is that King Aigith swore an oath long ago to win these two provinces for Ricossa. 'Arbeth and Lefayr,' he said, 'I will die happy with both, but one or the other I must have.' He cannot openly say that he wants war and conquest, not as a Christian king in a Christian country, but that is his aim. And the Families with lands on these borders - the b'Iri and the b'Asa in the north, and the b'Met in the south – don't discourage him, hoping that if Ricossa expands, so will they.

"It's always been his dream, and perhaps now he's growing old and his health is poorer, he may think his time is short. I should have told you before. I didn't think. I didn't think!"

There was a quietness in the room. Neither the Queen nor Lord b'Nida seemed surprised, but she looked sick, and he sad.

War. Mej thought of Hector and Achilles at the Siege of Troy, of David and Goliath, St-Ansha-of-the-Sword-and-Cross, Gormad Kingsbrother at the Battle of the Lither, and the book of Revelation; and part of his soul stirred. *But there are the Pillars in the Square! Soldiers are being sent out - I don't want Narod to die.*

Candle-flames flickered, and he suddenly thought, *Will this meeting be remembered in history? Are we talking of how to save our country? Am I?*

He knew he was showing his ignorance, but, "Can he do that? Start a war?"

Krothon and the Queen were silent. So it was b'Nida who answered, "The New Governance gives the Evening King authority in matters of warfare, but this isn't absolute. He cannot declare war without the consent of the King or Queen for the Morning – and also the Council of the Families. But he doesn't need anyone's consent to *wage* war, once someone else starts it." He paused; then, "Were Madrasun here, I think he would say that after the fighting begins, the declaration hardly matters. If we make the Jaryari angry, and they kill enough of our people, then war will happen."

"Yes," said the Queen.

The word "angry" reminded Mej of someone. "Kelji's husband is here – he won't sit still while we kill her."

Krothon said, "I dare say not. That's doubtless why he hasn't been arrested. Mobira is waiting for him to do something like – something public and rash, and as soon as he does, there'll be two dead Jaryari to taunt Nerranya and Barad with, not just one."

"But!" Mej cried. "The - the New Governance was to stop that! Its purpose is to prevent war! Peace at all costs, and the War that Must Never Happen Again! Isn't it?"

"No," said the all-knowing b'Nida. "The purpose of the New Governance is not to prevent all war, merely war between Ricossans. Foreigners, and even a few of our own soldiers, are expendable, if there's a reason."

"And does he think conquering Arbeth or Lefayr would be a good enough reason? He may do." The Queen shook her head, lifting her hands and dropping them again. "He's ruled for so long, and of late they say – he doesn't listen even to his own advisers – when I was a b'Shen people were saying -"

That King Aigith is mad. Even Mej had heard that whisper.

"My lord, you wish to protect the College. I wish to

protect our people. And not only ours. The foreigners in Arbeth and Lefayr also have souls. What then – speaking frankly – can we do?"

Mej dared to break in. "Surely we can prove it's all lies, and get her found not guilty! Show that Mobira's lying, and getting other people to lie. I can speak to that, and so can this man" (he'd forgotten the servant's name), "and probably Nadya and Jed – the husband - and Hridnaya." At the back of his senses, he thought someone shifted at that name. *Shouldn't I have mentioned her?*

"Young man," said Lord b'Nida, sounding a hundred years old, "what would all that achieve?"

"Proving Mobira's a criminal! Accusing her of murdering your Doctor friend!"

"Mobira is merely the agent who carried out the arrest.," said Krothon. "It's not likely she'll even be mentioned in court. And I suppose Madrasun's death has nothing to do with the Jaryari. So the Judge will say, and he decides whose evidence to hear."

"But he has to hear me! My name's on his list!"

"Yes. He'll hear you, and Kelji, and anyone else, ordering you to confine your words strictly to the issues at stake, and suggesting reasons why you might be mistaken or lying – perhaps this spy has bribed or seduced you, or - and then, as judges do, he'll sum up the evidence, and say who he's decided to believe. That's how trials work. This is Simoren, so he'll believe whoever the King pays him to."

The Queen added, "Poor Nadya isn't in a position to contradict Eyanda's evidence, even if she wishes, and maybe she wouldn't wish to. Fejederic – is that his name? – is our enemy, and no one will listen to him."

"But they'll listen to me – and you, my lord, about the

book."

"I cannot give evidence, and neither can Ittrad."

Mej stared.

His face sternly carved, Lord b'Nida said, "I would wish for Mobira's crimes to be exposed. I would wish very much for vengeance for Madrasun. But Simoren and the King won't allow that to happen. The trial will proceed, and she'll be condemned. I have to protect the College. We cannot be seen to be allied with traitors."

"And," said the Queen, "the more truth is told – the more obvious it becomes that the verdict is unjust and manufactured - the greater the insult to Nerranya when she's found guilty."

"Is there any way to get it stopped, or put off?" Krothon asked. "We have new evidence."

"It's tomorrow morning, sir. No one would listen. Your Grace, I agree with your conclusions and I share your concern. This matter is bigger than we'd thought. But I think, alas, that the King may get his little war." Lord b'Nida leaned forward deliberately. "'The greatest curse for any land is a king who does wickedly, and cannot be stopped.' I know of no way to stop him. *Unless*."

"Unless what?" asked Mej. No one answered him. The Queen and the Lord stared at each other across the table, and Mej thought perhaps she understood what was going on. He didn't. She looked haunted.

Lord b'Nida said, "Those who made the New Governance, our grandparents' generation, didn't intend for all power to rest with one person."

Haunted, but not surprised. "No," said the Queen, shifting a little. "For this reason we have two rulers, with their two councils, and also the Council of the Families, and the Church. No one of these is strong enough to defeat all the others together. If the others have a leader."

Krothon said timidly, "I think many of the Councillors would be very shocked, and might be willing -"

"But I can't be that leader."

"You have to be!" Mej exclaimed. "You're Queen, and you can stop him!"

Queen Rommi looked at him. "I can't move against the Evening King." They waited, and Lord b'Nida nodded sadly. "It's the basis of the New Governance; the Evening and the Morning don't meddle with each other! This is how we avoid civil war. Justice and war are his sphere of duty, just as commerce and learning are mine. I swore not to challenge him or interfere. I cannot step in."

"But you could disagree! Tell him he can't do this! Have Mobira arrested for Madrasun's murder!"

"*It's not my place.* The most holy oath, on my soul. 'Not to lift hand or power against, nor interfere with, the other.' I can do nothing." He felt her distress rising behind her quiet face. She turned to Lord b'Nida, and said, "Is there anyone else who can?"

He stared straight back. "I am here to protect the College. The b'Nida don't wish for war; we've always argued against war, but we cannot stand up alone and make accusations against the King. Our Family has enemies enough, and his ill will is vicious."

"If all the Families agreed?" asked the Queen. "Or members of his own Council?"

"Are you asking me to persuade the heads of nine other Families to oppose the King, before tomorrow morning? I would be in chains by midnight. Brechad and the b'Iri have long argued that Arbeth should be ours. The b'Met, the b'Astith, the others – who knows, but they don't all love b'Nida. Only you could speak to and for all of us."

"And I can't. I can't speak against the King."

"Not openly."

"Neither openly, nor behind the curtain; neither in person, nor through others. He would denounce me for treachery, and – he might be right. Even this meeting here may be a sin."

"Could the Church do anything? The Archbishop?" Krothon asked timidly.

"Before tomorrow morning?"

"Before war starts."

"The Archbishop got her place by staying out of trouble," said Lord b'Nida. "She will do nothing alone. With the Queen she might, but not without."

"And I cannot ask her. A Queen should protect her people; should make things better, prevent bloodshed - but I swore an oath!"

Mej remembered the night his stepfather died. He remembered her screaming. Screaming and screaming and screaming.

"I swore an oath," she said again, and her voice was a whisper.

Inside him, his heart tore.

"Your Grace," he said. He stood up and walked awkwardly round the table, feeling eyes on him. *Don't laugh,* he begged silently. The Queen turned slightly towards him, questioning, and he knelt, and put his arms around her. Someone gasped or clucked. But he held her more tightly as he felt her tremble; and dared to lay his cheek on her breast, and after a moment, her head dropped onto his, and she gripped his back, and there was absolute silence.

Then the Queen sat up straight. "Thank you, sir," she said, and her voice shook. "You are most kind." Her brown eyes glistened. Mej couldn't remember what colour his own were, and no one had ever mentioned his father's.

He stood up again, but he didn't return to his chair. Instead, he waited behind hers, like a servant. Or like one of the Marodi Thirty, whose duty and honour it was to protect their Queen. He stared straight across the table, over the head of b'Nida's man standing opposite and looking equally solemn.

We're here to find a solution, aren't we? But all the faces were grave and uninspired.

"I cannot oppose the King," Queen Rommi said again. "Even though he is authorising, commanding, murder - and endangering all the land." She looked up at the shadowy ceiling, and blinked, and he knew she was fighting tears. She said, "King David commanded the murder of his lover's husband. When the prophet Nathan rebuked him, he repented. Perhaps we need a prophet."

Mej rummaged wildly through history for a King David, and eventually found him in Holy Scripture.

"I think Madrasun saw himself as a prophet," said Lord b'Nida sadly. "And he's dead."

Krothon, staring at his clasped fingers, said, "If we – or someone – sent a message to Queen Nerranya?"

"What message, sir?" Lord b'Nida asked. "'Your Grace, we deeply regret having to inform you that our king has murdered your countrywoman. Please don't blame us.' Nothing would more certainly be called treason." Krothon flushed at that, Mej thought. "And she would ignore it anyway. She perhaps might think she could make use of division in Ricossa herself. Does she have her own plans for conquest? There are many bad stories about Nerranya. I doubt not that most are lies, but we know little of the lady. Even Lady b'Shen long ago met only her husband in Vach-roysh, not her."

Krothon was counting on his fingers. "He won't listen to persuasion. We have nothing to offer him in exchange. We can't

threaten. If no one here can oppose him, openly or in secret –
could the trial be postponed?" He took a deep breath. "If the
Judge were unwell?"

"Are you suggesting poison, sir?"

"Or if Kelji escaped?" said Mej.

"I think the Palace is well guarded," said Lord b'Nida.

The Queen said, "No. I can think of nothing but prayer.
And for any of us who can to use our influence for peace." She
looked at Lord b'Nida across the table, and he nodded with his
sad smile, which Mej was beginning to find annoying.

The Queen stood up, so they all did. It seemed that the
meeting was over. "Do – do you want me to tell the truth
tomorrow? Or will that make things worse?" Mej asked, for now
he was confused as to what the wisest course would be. If these
great people were in the dark, there was no shame in his being
so also.

"I'm not your conscience, sir." She thought, her head a
little on one side. "It is a risk for you, but I think Kelji would be
distressed if you did not."

Kelji, and Jedder too. "It's bloodfeud." "And Hridnaya?"
he added.

"That woman cannot give evidence," said Lord b'Nida, his
voice abrupt, almost a bark.

"No, she cannot, because she's dead."

It was the b'Nida servant (Ittrad?) who spoke, and
everyone was suddenly still.

Dead? She's hiding behind the wall, Mej just didn't say.
What stopped him was Lord b'Nida's face, as he jerked, and then
turned to stare.

"You had her killed, didn't you, my lord?" The voice was
quiet, but the man took a step backward.

"You – what nonsense is this?"

"If people are inconvenient, the powerful have them killed. That's what you've been discussing this evening. Madrasun was inconvenient; a man called Flower-in-Hood was inconvenient; and Hridnaya was inconvenient to you. I talked to her in Sapientia, and I had to decide whether to let her go, or to tell Mobira, or to tell you. God forgive me, I chose you."

Nothing else said that night had disturbed Lord b'Nida's calm, but this did. Mej couldn't read all the different passions twisting his face, as he stared. Then in one movement – "Lying dog!" He struck Ittrad's face, very hard, and the man fell over backwards with a grunt of pain. Krothon also jumped up.

"How do you dare -"

The man said from the floor, "I'm not under your banner, my lord. You mentioned prophets. Doesn't one of them say in Scripture – I can't remember it right," and somehow everyone waited for him. "'*Do justice, and love kindness, and walk humbly with your God?* Even you, my Lord."

"The prophet Micah," murmured the Queen.

"This is a lie!"

"Then where is she? She was your prisoner. Why can't you produce her for the trial? You told me you'd sent her to a farm. But your Housemother says you have no farms anywhere in the north. I believe you paid someone to take her to the Haunted Pool, and drown her there."

The three people who knew that Hridnaya was alive flicked glances at each other. Then they looked back at Lord b'Nida towering over the sprawled man. Towering but swaying.

"My lord, and you, sir, be still, in the Queen's name." It was Krothon, with a dignity he hadn't had before. Both turned to him, blinking as if they'd forgotten anyone else was in the room.

The Queen thanked her Chamberlain with a nod, took a breath, and said, "I do not think this debate assists us. But your evidence may do, sir, as to Mobira, I mean. Krothon, can you find a place for this man tonight? I do not wish any harm to come to him."

She didn't look at Lord b'Nida, but Mej tingled. *That's well done,* he thought, and almost laughed. More usefully, he picked up the man's stick, and helped him to his feet.

The servant bowed. He leaned on Mej and trembled. It was Lord b'Nida who was like a statue. At last he said, "Your Grace, have I your leave to depart? I share your desire for peace, but I fear I can be of no further assistance here." To the man, "You will be careful, sir, how you slander me and my Family."

"You may go, and God go with you. Please do not make threats in this place," she said, and raised her voice. "Yikkeri! Lord b'Nida is leaving us."

And so the great dinner which was to have solved everything ended. And nothing was solved.

Letter from Aigith, King for the Evening, to Captain Achandor of the Northern Army

Most secret. As soon as the Judge pronounces sentence of death on Kelji, daughter of Shanell, you will take ship with the second troop to the Lake's north shore, and then divide. Send the majority to defend our border with Arbeth at Jinner/Makaim. Take those you most trust to the village of Verndew. These people are traitors in league with Jaryar, but are under the protection of powerful nobility and cannot be openly accused. Let none in the village escape the hand of justice. Do not fail. You will be rewarded.

Part Five

The New Governance

Mobira walked out of Kelji's room, removing cruelty from her face, and replacing it with stern competence. As she'd ordered, the guard outside had been tripled, and the woman and two men met her eyes somewhat nervously.

"Still she will not confess," she said, to make them feel important enough to be informed. "Sirs, madam, you know that tomorrow's trial is a matter of great import. There are traitors in the city, perhaps even in the Palace. This prisoner doesn't leave the room until morning on any pretext whatever, unless the order is delivered to you *in person* by the Evening King, or his Chamberlain, or me. If the Palace burns down tonight, she burns with it. Do you understand?"

"Yes, madam," said the burly yellow-haired man in charge.

"No one enters unless you know who they are and their errand, and then only one at a time. Send someone in every hour, and if she's doing anything more suspicious than praying or sleeping, report to me. If she escapes, or is rescued," she ended firmly, "you will all die."

"Yes, madam." They eyed her with fear, and a little resentment.

"That is all." She turned away. Her head throbbed, and she wanted to sit down.

The Queen is taking an interest. I can't be certain the Voiceless is safely dead. And that Fejederic – he may, probably does, have my seal.

("He knocked you unconscious, and left you to die in a

ditch? I'll have him torn apart!" King Aigith had cried, trembling so much she had to help him to sit down.

"I cannot be certain it was him. We were riding together, both being vey civil, and I didn't think he'd connected me with his wife at all, and the next thing I remember is waking up by the road. If it wasn't him, why did he abandon me? But by the time his wife is in pieces, as you say, I think we'll have him."

"Yes, and when we do, my dear -" there were tears in the old man's eyes – "you may name what death you please for him. I promise you."

Mobira wasn't as vindictive as some people, but she liked the thought of that. King Aigith took her hands in his, and kissed her forehead.

But he is very old.)

Now she found her way back to the Archive of Justice. There she nodded civilly to the busy scribblers, ordered one of them to find her a cup of wine, and sank down on the corner stool that had become hers in the last few days. They were beginning to know, and fear – and dislike - her in City Qayn, as they did in Sapientia.

She hadn't told the King about the lost or stolen seal. She hadn't dared. What was Fejederic of Makkera capable of? He'd dodged his tail last Sunday by the simple trick of walking into a whorehouse and bribing the master to let him out at a window, while the Guards following him sniggered outside about the immoral Jaryari. He'd been missing for two days, and then abruptly reappeared at the b'Astith house, trying to look innocuous. She longed to have him tortured, but that wasn't politic – yet. An aggressive search hadn't revealed either the seal or the missing Voiceless. The troops Mobira'd sent all over town had also failed to find her.

She'd increased the guard detail at the Quiet Door and on

Kelji, and given Fejederic's description to those at the Great Gate. Simoren was ready. More she couldn't do.

Oh, how her head ached! It bothered her to have part of her life, even just a half hour, missing from her mind; but the physician in Sapientia had been fairly reassuring. "Your eyes look normal – that's a good sign – and your limbs move freely. Watch out for feelings of confusion or unnatural sleepiness." Mobira was always busy, but the last few days had meant a lot more riding than usual. Of course she was tired.

But she was on the brink of triumph, so exhaustion and even foolish fears were to be expected. She allowed herself to think of tomorrow with anticipatory pleasure. Defeat for the Jaryari – humiliation for the arrogant Doctors – exciting spectacle for the commons – success for her master, which meant rewards. And vengeance.

*

"No, she cannot, because she is dead," the man said, and Hridnaya gasped. Ittrad was speaking, whose face she'd scratched back in Doctor Dirria's room. "And drown her there." The horror of the memory turned her cold, and she found tears pouring down her cheeks. How had he guessed? Why were these great people discussing her?

Lord b'Nida couldn't deny it.

At last he was leaving. He was leaving. The door shut.

"Come over here, sir. There is something," she heard Mejorad say, and his voice held laughter. She was still wiping tears when the tapestry was pulled aside, and three men were peering in. Two of them seemed amused, but she stared at Ittrad leaning on his stick. She saw his utter astonishment – then his delight – then his embarrassment.

She also felt embarrassed, and looked away.

"So did the holy m'lord try to kill you?" Mejorad was

360

asking. "Did he truly?"

Even the lute-player, even the Queen, still standing by the table, were glancing at them with interest.

Did Lord b'Nida order you killed? She owed Ittrad the truth. *But I owe the b'Nida secrecy.* Attempted murder is a secret.

"Did he?"

Slowly she shook her head.

But her hesitation had already answered for her. "The dog!" said Mejorad, face shocked. Then, "How did you get away? Did Jedder save you? He said – I thought he said you met on the road."

Hridnaya turned her face away, wiping it again with her hands.

"Jedder? Who is that?" said the Chamberlain. Then, to Ittrad, "Was it necessary to anger him? Although he wasn't offering much help."

"No one can help," said the Queen. She looked round at them, and then upwards, as if seeing something invisible. Her lips moved.

Mejorad took two rapid steps towards her. "We must do something! Get Kelji out before tomorrow - a rescue! There must be a way! I can find people -"

The Chamberlain said sharply, "Rescue her? D'you realise what would happen to anyone caught doing that, or planning it?" Hridnaya saw him trembling.

"I don't care."

"The King was angry enough that you even talked to the woman, Your Grace! He'll have her guarded like – like his own life!"

"Hush, sir. Mejorad." The Queen took his hands. "You are kind and brave, but no. Krothon is right. It couldn't be done. You would not only have to get her out of the Palace, and there will be many layers of guards, you would have to get her – and her husband and her servants, or one at least – out of the city, and then out of Ricossa. Many days' journey, with pursuit - and torture for anyone you left behind. And in any case – as I said, I can't order or allow something like that. I can't order opposition to the Evening King publicly. Nor even privately. And I won't send you – or your friends – to a pointless death. No. Do you hear me? Truly, no." In the quiet, Krothon stepped back to her.

Ittrad lurched towards Hridnaya. "I," he said, and stopped. "Thank God you are alive. I ask your forgiveness for telling him how to find you. I try to do the right thing, and I thought I had, but I was wrong. I ought to remember that I make mistakes." He bowed a little, and then, "Wait. You were the spy who copied the papers? *You?*" His face burst into a grin.

"Of course it was her," Mejorad called over. Hridnaya blushed, not sure if she was happy or not. She'd lost something when Lord b'Nida walked out of the room. It was something she kept losing, again and again.

But then they all three looked back at the Queen and the Chamberlain, now talking in low voices.

The Queen gave a little shrug. She looked very sad, and utterly defeated.

It's easy to start a war. The War of the Throne was so long ago, it was legend. It meant the Pillars, and the empty space on Burnedhouse Street. Hridnaya's great-grandparents and some other cousins had been killed. Everyone had someone killed.

One more night, and then the trial. Tomorrow the corrupt Judge would condemn Kelji, and offend the mighty Queen of Jaryar; and *their* Queen could not, or would not, stop it.

"I try to do what's right," Ittrad had said.

Is there truly no way? Did God plan this meeting for us to find a way? Did He put us, me, here?

Is that arrogance?

The Queen stared over at them all. "I thank you," she said. "I shall pray. Krothon, I'd like these three to stay in the Palace tonight, and Mejorad, I rely on you to protect the other two. You'll need to send a message home. Say you're out with Narod, or something."

"Who do I send? Who am I guarding them from?"

"But where can we put them?" asked Krothon.

There was some more conversation.

Hridnaya's head buzzed. Somewhere in her memory –

"Breakfast time for you," he said to the bear. But Defani wriggled and twisted, and reached up and grabbed the staff, his own staff. "Brinniprinnigrinni! Be still!" she said, his own magic words.

"Come, then." Krothon waved them wearily together: Mejorad, Ittrad and Hridnaya. Ittrad was looking around like a man whose life will never be the same again.

She picked up her baggage, and then turned towards the Chamberlain, putting her hands together. Narrim would have understood this as a request, and so did he.

"What d'you want?"

She held her hands flat, and then pointed to a shelf. His mouth twisted.

"A book to read? You?"

"Why not?" said Mejorad.

The Chamberlain shrugged and walked over to lift one off at random. He handed it to her, trying to cover his fear with amusement, and she curtseyed her thanks.

The maid Yikkeri had appeared from somewhere, and gripped her arm to lead her out of the room.

Hridnaya should have been terrified: walking again through this grand place, an enemy and a threat to the King. But she had no time for terror. She clutched the book, mentally listing the words she needed to find in it. The words she had to spell right.

*

The woman Mobira had invaded Kelji's chamber with a secretary. She sat in the second chair, telling a ridiculous story about how Kelji had come to City Qayn to pass and receive secret messages and money to and from traitors at the College, and how her virtuous and shocked Ricossan maid had tried to report her to the authorities –

Kelji grew weary of saying, "That is not true," and stopped listening. She thought even Mobira seemed bored. In the back of her head an old chess match replayed itself – that one three years ago when she really should have beaten her sister-in-law –

"I said, Do you confess?"

"I didn't hear what you said I was to confess to, but No."

The secretary, writing at *her* desk, spluttered.

"That this Voiceless woman was murdered by your Ricossan associates."

"All this is lies."

"I don't think so. And it's no lie that the Morning Queen visited you this morning. What did you talk about?"

"She asked me about the latest fashions in Makkera. About hats."

Mobira rose, a block of spite in a red jacket. "Since you do not wish to assist us and yourself, I will see you at your trial, madam. While you were visiting your b'Astith kinswoman, and admiring the sights, I suppose someone took you to the Great Square?"

Kelji also stood, jutting her chin forward. "Yes, of course. It's magnificent. The centre of your beautiful city, and you fill it with devices for torture.”

“Say rather, devices for just punishment. I wish you a good night.” Mobira smiled coldly, and walked out. Kelji heard her talking to Guards outside the door, but couldn’t distinguish words.

She went to bed.

The woman hadn’t told her when to be ready in the morning, stripping her even of the power to plan what might be her last night here. Nor had she been told what was likely to happen afterwards.

How much time does this evil place allow between sentence and execution? she wondered, turning over and thumping the pillow in the dark. *A week, or a half-hour?* She couldn’t sleep and couldn’t sleep, crying with frustration, so she got up and paced the room in the dark, wrapping her arms across her chest and reciting the geography of Ragaris. At last she must have crawled back into bed, for she was woken by the opening of shutters, confusedly still trying to recall the capital of Falli.

*

At the Queen’s request, Mej spent the night sitting wrapped in a blanket against the inner door of her private chapel. Behind his back it led to her bedroom, a strange thought. He was there in case the dangerous commoner witnesses tried to escape, or hurt her as she slept - but also in case anyone tried to get in to do harm to *them*. Yikkeri, he understood, was lying on the other side of the door, and when they were all in, an extra unknowing guard was to be summoned to stand outside the bedroom.

They burned a candle all night. Only Ittrad seemed to sleep soundly. Once Mej woke from a drowse and saw Hridnaya crouching before the altar with book, parchment and pen. She didn’t see him watching.

Sometimes he thought he heard weeping on the other

side of the door.

Over and over he saw himself, sword in hand, ushering Kelji out of her cell, fighting Guards, putting her and Jedder on horses to ride north or west. "God go with you," he imagined himself saying with a brilliant heroic smile.

His back and his stomach crawled with terror and doubt.

She'd said *No*, and she'd seemed to mean No. But no one else was doing anything – *and I'm the bad boy anyway.*

If all this happens as they expect, we'll be going to war with Jaryar –well, the b'Iri Family will be pleased. The Queen and Lord b'Nida seemed to think it was terrible, and he supposed he agreed, but after all wars happen. But for Kelji and Jedder – maybe the timid maid also – for them to be hanged, or worse than hanged –

He felt sick. "Let her go, sirs, or -" Like a hero, like a Queensbrother. *Can Jedder do anything? In a land far from home, surrounded by enemies?*

Could I?

He sat, and dozed, and woke to the same question, and as the night grew on, it became clearer that he couldn't think how to, and wasn't going to; he was just going to sit here on guard as he'd been told to do. Obedience is adult and sensible. So, sometimes, is cowardice.

He woke with a jerk when Yikkeri banged the door in the morning. The other two were already awake; Ittrad standing staring out of the window, and Hridnaya smoothing her hair and looking understandably nervous. *How can a Voiceless be a witness anyway? Was it her evidence that she was writing – if I didn't dream it?* He'd slept in the same room with these strangers, and it felt awkward. They were beckoned through into the now empty bedchamber to tidy themselves, and ate and drank, sitting together on the unbelievably costly carpet – all save Ittrad, whose leg didn't bend, and whom Yikkeri allowed to use a chair. She frowned at droppers of crumbs, and told them the Chamberlain would be there soon.

Mej wasn't very hungry, and he wandered for no reason over to the great royal bed, where she had slept the night, a few feet from him, closer than he ever remembered them sleeping before. The embroidered cover was drawn wrinkle-less across. He touched it gently.

Will I be called by name, or need I volunteer? How can I make it clear? I'm not good with words.

"At what hour do trials start?" Ittrad asked the air.

They all jumped as Krothon came in with a guard, looking worried. "Now, good morning to you," he said. "Errhm. The trial is to start in less than one hour. I'll escort you to the Hall of Justice where you'll wait in the crowd until your name, sir, is called. When the listed witnesses have been heard, there is, or there should be, a call for anyone else with relevant knowledge. That's when you two -" gesturing to Hridnaya and Ittrad – "could step forward. You, sir, might be able to explain who they are, and that she can't speak, but could be asked to confirm, or she could write – which will look suspicious. Oh dear," he ended suddenly, "we don't know how it will be." He moved his hands around vaguely.

As he led their little line through the passages and out, Mej placed himself second last, just before the Guard, in case she couldn't be trusted. The air was still early-fresh, and the Palace courtyard almost empty. But as they approached the Great Square, there were already lines and clumps around the gallows -*have these commoners no work to go to?* People were laying out cloaks to sit on, and buying nuts and pies from equally early barrowfolk. Some were hanging around on the wide steps, obviously hoping to sit there if they could, to get a higher view.

Now and again, City Guards stepped down to chivvy them away.

Mej, Krothon, Hridnaya and Ittrad and their guard began to climb, and people shifted to make space for them. He was cold, and his head buzzed.

"Mejorad!" and he jumped.

Coming up towards them from the left were Nadya and servants, and Jedder. Mej and Krothon bowed. He saw Jedder's relief at the sight of Hridnaya - and Nadya had recognised her too. "Is this the woman you spoke of?" she asked Jedder, and then turned back. "I've heard strange things, Mejorad, about a woman called Mobira. Are they true?" Her voice trembled.

"Yes," said Mej - rather recklessly, but trusting Kelji's husband (the Queensbrother, after all!) was a decision he'd made long ago, the day before yesterday. He remembered courtesy and offered Nadya his arm. Together the little group climbed the wide steps, surrendered Mej's sword, and entered the Hall of Justice. He remembered walking through this anteroom three months back with Eyanda, peppered then with fewer excited people than today.

Jedder looked – not calm, but less agitated than Mej expected. But then he hadn't been at the dinner last night. *Ricossan judges are the fairest in the world. He may actually believe that.* ("This is Simoren, so he'll believe whoever the King pays him to. The trial will proceed, and she will be condemned.")

"Oh, Nim!" cried a voice. Eyanda-his-mother was sweeping towards them. She threw him the irritated glance he'd earned by not coming home last night, but her attention was on Nadya. He saw the way her hands itched for her lover's, but this was too public a place for gestures of affection.

Nadya, who was a tall woman, curtsied very low. "My lady," she said, and her voice was cold.

There were people all around them, passing through,

chatting. But in this little circle was stillness. Eyanda's face was blank.

Nadya rose, and with a polite gesture, said, "I don't think you've met my *guest,* Fejederic of Makkera? It's his wife, who was also my guest, who's on trial here, and I've come to give evidence on her behalf."

Uncertainly, "Nim?"

Nadya turned to Jedder. "I think we need to find a place near the front, sir, to be ready – you pardon, my lady." And Mej found himself and the others sweeping past, and Eyanda standing left behind.

"I've heard strange things about a woman called Mobira." Jedder would have told her what Eyanda had promised to do.

Ittrad impertinently touched his arm. "Where's she gone?"

"Who?" But as they approached the door, Mej's eyes swerved round, and Ittrad was right. The Voiceless woman had disappeared yet again!

He cursed internally. Would she never be done with her secret pranks? Had she run away, or been arrested under his nose? *Can I do nothing right?* The two men swivelled in the anteroom's centre, eyes trying to pierce through clothes and bodies, to assess everyone. And then Mej heard Ittrad sigh, and watched him jerk over to where she'd appeared at the courtroom entrance.

"What the hell are you up to?" Mej hissed as she joined them. Hridnaya gave him a quick look that, while timid, wasn't nearly as apologetic as it should have been, and the three pushed together behind Nadya into the doom-and-people-crammed room. It was time.

*

"Get up, madam," a man ordered Kelji, folding his arms and staring at her from beside the window.

Whatever she felt about Ricossa, up to now the servants

had been respectful; indeed more helpful than most would have dared be at home. This open rudeness was a bad sign. Also the sending in a *man* when she might have been naked. "I will rise and dress, when you leave me in peace to do so," she said, and he stalked out without bowing. And perhaps he wasn't a servant, for he wore a long gown – a cruel-faced man with a scar above the right cheek – some high official.

She'd always been called brave, as regards childhood whippings and bee-stings and the like – brave, until Larelna. Now she dressed in her best gown, the blue and purple with the pearled cap. Her hands shook, and she couldn't manage her hair tidily without Imadal. She'd look like what they wanted to see. The outlandish barbarian criminal, scapegoat for something or other that no one would ever explain.

The man came back in, and Mobira was with him, looking triumphant. *May you die an evil death.* She gestured for Kelji to walk out.

The passages and rooms were lined with people, faces dressed with silent sneers, intended to intimidate. *Go to hell, all of you. I will die without tears, and then I'll see my daughter again. Jedder will weep and rage for a little, but in time he'll marry someone else and be happy. Perhaps he'll even be relieved.*

Don't think of Jedder.

Behind her face was only the thump of her heart.

There was a door, and she went through onto a kind of low balcony, raised a few feet above the packed hall beyond. The balcony had two seats, and she was gestured to the one on the right.

Before her were more eyes, scores of pairs of eyes, looking around, noticing her. Then mouths opened in brown and black and pink faces, and there was a hissing. Prepared and planned by that bitch. Kelji put on a royal smile, took two steps forward to the rail, and curtsied. Two steps back, and she sank down.

There were words on the ceiling, one or two letters in each square. She read, and carefully translated from the Latin, "May the Lord guide us to justice." *Huh.*

Evil host of foreign faces, bared heads, bearded chins. Her eyes sped across them, and found one head that wasn't bare, one chin that was, round and brown and staring at her.

Jedder, preposterously here!

In as much danger as she, for he wouldn't let them kill her. "Remember I love you," he'd said before riding away, stroking her face. Her eyes blurred painfully. She was going to cry in public – complete humiliation, and his fault!

She didn't cry. She looked away, and saw Vaddras standing in a different row near the front, with some people she thought she recognised from the College.

Behind her, a door opened, and someone hissed, "Stand up." The Judge walked in, nodded to the spectators, sat down, and turned his face to Kelji.

He was quite a small man, beard long and curly, perhaps ten years older than herself. He didn't sneer; his face was quite expressionless as he laid a package of documents out before him on the balcony ledge, and unrolled them. A Guard poured him wine.

She imagined this insignificant creature saying, "Take her out and hang her," between sips. *St Mary-Christ's-mother, send me courage. Lord, help me.*

Her eyes leaped back to Jedder. He stared back, and no messages could pass, nothing. He was in a row of people, but at either end of it uniformed Guards stood with swords, not yet drawn. *Are you already under arrest? What are they making up about you?* Beside him she saw Nadya, face turned away to talk to that b'Shen lad. His family had sent him to spy on her, she remembered, so Nadya probably had betrayed her also. She supposed that hurt. And there, like a bizarre dream, was the Voiceless beggar! *Is this plot all yours, yours and Mobira's? Will I even find out before I die? I will tell the truth. I will shame them - how much longer? Will they let me say anything?*

The Judge was looking down pages of words, the stuff Mobira or her lord had concocted. A servant came through the door behind, coughed, and handed him another document – and also a small bag below the counter. Kelji saw an imposing seal. *Prejudice and lies aren't enough. They need bribery as well.*

He opened and read the new parchment, read it twice, and fingered the bag. Then he looked up and around, and Kelji followed his gaze to find Mobira standing at the very back beside a Guard, smirking in red. The Judge caught her eye and nodded, and Kelji thought the smirk grew broader.

Nadya looked miserable. Jedder seemed to be struggling to breathe. Mejorad b'Shen met her eyes, a young and apologetic look. The Voiceless woman stared intently at the Judge.

Someone called, "This court of justice is now in session, under Judge Simoren Ett Mai b'Asa. May God guide its deliberations. May God punish all liars."

The Judge stood up, and she was gestured to stand also. His voice was deep and rather beautiful. "Are you Kelji, daughter of Shanell, a visitor here?"

"I am." Her voice croaked infuriatingly.

"You are accused of bringing money and secret messages from your Queen in Makkera, to our College in Sapientia, attempting to corrupt Ricossans there to treachery. Are you guilty or not guilty?"

Firmly, "Not guilty." Another soft hiss in the room.

"Silence," said the Judge. He faced forward. "Listen

carefully, all present. As required by law, I have studied the documents presented against the accused. I am not satisfied with them. Even taken at their strongest, they do not amount to a sound legal case to answer. There is no reason to hold her, or to continue with this further. You can go, madam," he added to Kelji.

The whole Hall gaped at him.

"Did you not hear me? In the name of the Evening King, and of the God of Justice, I find her not guilty. Release her."

I – I – What? A hand supported her as she swayed. There was a little gateway and steps down from the balcony. Nadya and Imadal were there in front of her, beaming and crying –

"Oh, praise God, praise God, come on home, come now -" Then Nadya stepped back, for him.

Husband and wife stared at each other, perhaps equally baffled. "What are you doing here?" Kelji heard herself say.

He half-smiled, blinking rapidly. "Looking for you. Forgive me for coming." He looked away. "Is Vaddras free also?"

"Oh – we must see. I'll enquire," said Nadya, and gestured her man to do this.

"He was arrested with me, but kept somewhere else. He was standing over there just now." She was still dizzy.

That b'Shen lad touched her arm, saying, "I'm so glad. I don't know how this happened, but so glad."

Jedder to Nadya, "Forgive my doubts. You were right. Ricossan justice, even for foreigners, is indeed to be trusted." He spoke loudly, but a little less calmly than he probably intended.

They were a small bunch of people. Nadya and the returned manservant, Imadal, Kelji and Jedder, Mejorad; an island in staring hostility. Nadya smiled at them both, and turned towards the door. Her "Shall we go home?" was directed at the crowd as much as at her guests.

Jedder offered Kelji his arm, as he had on their wedding

day. Nadya led, and the two Jaryari followed, and people stepped back as they processed to the door, beyond all expectation vindicated and triumphant.

*

What? What?

Had their worries been unnecessary? Was there no plot after all?

"Shall we go home?" Nadya said. Mej stepped back to let them pass – there was no reason to involve the b'Shen further – and then remembered his irritating charges. Were they still in danger? He peered round and over people, and there was Hridnaya, but for a change, it was Ittrad he couldn't see! *(Is this some strange power of the common people, to appear and disappear at will? It might explain why there's never a servant around when you want one.)*

But the dour scoundrel Tor was peering from the back, looking for him.

All around was tumult. "What in the name of the Monarchs is going on?" "Bloody nonsense, this." "What's Simoren thinking of?" "Sh." "Mejorad! Hey, Mejorad, can you explain it? Was it the b'Astith who arranged this, or your people?"

He said vaguely, "I don't know, but I've no reason to doubt she's innocent."

The Judge Simoren b'Asa had disappeared. Guards were trying to clear the room, but the gossip wouldn't let them.

"Mejorad!" A hiss. He jerked round to see Yikkeri, looking cross as always, and beckoning an imperious finger from the side. Getting towards her out of the mess took longer than she'd plainly have liked. He bent over her, looking polite for any observers.

"Where are your – no matter. Have they left – the Jaryari?"

"Yes, just now. They're going back to Nadya's."

Almost too quietly to hear, "The Queen sent me to tell you: it's not over." Yikkeri glared.

"But the Judge – his decision's final, isn't it?"

She scowled him to silence. "The King wants them dead, or at least her. As soon as can be. Go after them."

"I –" Then he understood. There are more ways to die than hanging. *I don't believe – how far would Mobira go? That Madrasun fell down stairs –* Thoughts gibbering, he nodded to her, and turned away. He needed to get out fast, and there were fat talking shapes everywhere –

The anteroom was almost equally full of bustle. Mej found and joined the line to reclaim his weapon. Kelji and Jedder were foreigners, forbidden to bear arms. He'd never seen Nadya fight or wear a sword. She'd brought the Imadal woman, and one man, and they'd probably have Vaddras, who they shouldn't trust – would that be enough to protect them? His stomach grew a little colder.

"Here you are, sir."

"I thank you." Sword excitingly back on his belt, he was out in the sunshine, among *more* people. Voices around were grumbling. ("I lost good money to have a day off work!")

Which way is Nadya's house? Second Quarter, come on – Tor was at his heels. So many people, everywhere.

One face looked familiar – *surely that's Narod? Wasn't he supposed to be sailing north? No time for that now.*

He struggled to the edge of the Square, pushing gently and apologising, and the street beyond was still busy. There was a barrow, two barrows, in his way.

That house had a low porch. Why not? Over his shoulder he said to Tor, "Get to Nadya b'Astith's on St Patric's Street – there may be trouble," took a deep breath, put one foot on a window ledge, and reached upwards. Up, up, and onto the roof. *Look, crouch, run, measure, jump. Thank God for dry weather.*

Below, people laughed and pointed. Glorious mischievous energy surged through him, but he couldn't pause to savour it. With just enough care, he scurried along the empty roofs, hoping for a quick descent where the Great Passage was too wide –

A few minutes later, he was in and *above* the Second Quarter, a little confused by so many similar streets from an odd perspective. This one, no, *this* one was St Patric's Street. The roof sloped steadily but gently down. He scrambled to step onto a stable between houses, and perched panting, opposite the blue-painted door. The narrow road was quiet. He looked left. There they were: Nadya and the Jaryari and several servants, bunched up talking to a big man at the corner. Nadya and her man paused with this person - probably a beggar - and the others turned towards him, almost home. Relief washed him, but he felt a little foolish. *Why did I let Yikkeri frighten me?*

Then someone jumped out at Nadya from behind. Mej's foot almost slipped as he twisted to see. Two people were putting something over her head, it looked like – and her servant's - *Nadya?*

Kelji and Jedder, several steps further in, heard, and turned back. Then –

"Foreign filth!" A stone hurtled towards them, and with it a roar of hate, and people were running at them from several directions, one a Palace Guard, the others riff-raff. Mej saw a sword in someone's hand, and an evilly gleaming axe in another, knives - Kelji screamed. He watched Jedder reach for the swordless place at his belt, pushing his wife behind him – how many were there?

Not all armed, was Mej's last coherent thought, as he

stood, took two steps, and jumped down. The Guard below howled as he was knocked backwards. Mej jumped up, slashed at him, and twisted his sword away. He kicked the man's stomach – and ran for the others.

Kelji, Jedder, and the two servants hadn't reached the door. Four ruffians were coming at them, including the woman with the axe. Jedder had almost dodged her first blow - but blood was trickling as he grappled with her. Vaddras and another man wrestled, too close for either to use the knives they'd drawn. Kelji was screeching and whirling a satchel around her, but someone grabbed it –

Everyone was shouting, Mej too, wordlessly, as he rushed forward with a sword in each hand, knowing the man he'd kicked might follow his back. His arrival distracted the axe-woman: she turned, and Jedder hit her hard in the face. Mej knocked her aside – "Here," he said, holding out the second sword. As the Jaryari grasped it, Mej swung to the street, side by side with him.

Vaddras and his opponent were on the ground, Jedder was slashing at the man attacking his wife, Mej faced the others – the man he'd knocked down was running over. "Ricossa!" he found himself shouting, an excited soldier again –

But he knew it was over. They were five against five, and the maid was useless, but they had two swords and more training: those facing them were just street criminals, and hesitated to come on. He made a snarling contemptuous noise, and brandished his blade, dizzy with what was about to be triumph.

A voice boomed from the right. "Put the pins down, you fucking traitors." He looked. A bull of a man was pushing Nadya in front of him. Her head was covered in dark cloth; her arms were held down, and his other hand had a knife at her throat.

"Shall I kill her?" he asked, and everyone was still.

"You dare!" Mej cried. "She's Nadya b'Astith!"

"Fucking b'Astith shouldn't help our enemies. Put down the swords, heroes. Put them *down,* or -"

"I'm not your country's enemy!"

"Shut mouth, bitch. Tell your lovers to put them down." He jabbed and squeezed Nadya, and they watched her helpless struggle; heard her wail, horribly muffled. He was too strong.

The rest of the gang waited, smiling but a little nervous themselves.

"Now. I'm not asking again."

But a new voice, a woman's and surely familiar, interrupted.

"This is enough. Release her and go, all of you. In the King's name."

*

Ittrad had been gathering the strength he'd need to call Doctor Dirria a liar, only a day after denouncing Lord b'Nida for murder – and then abruptly he didn't have to. The Judge was setting Kelji free, and everyone was staring.

He watched the Jaryari woman he'd once seen climb into a cart - she certainly had courage – until she disappeared behind other faces, and then he turned to Hridnaya, and the expression on her face told him what he was beginning to guess. She was astonished, but in a different way from everyone else.

"You did this," he whispered, and her eyes flickered in answer. She almost giggled.

How?

But more urgently, *If you did this, They won't like it.*

He squinted at the back of the Hall. "Mobira's gone."

Gone for instructions, perhaps. *If I were the King, in such a case, what orders would I give? She has no conscience, neither has he.* "What you do for a King is absolved."

That letter gave me a thought. Can I really –

"If you pray, pray for me," he whispered, and left her, edging past and round. He was nobody; no one sought to stop him for gossip or opinion, and they courteously got out of the way of the man with the stick.

Mobira wasn't in the anteroom. Ittrad was out in the air, looking down steps to people complaining about the bad news. He watched Kelji and her husband stalk out, look around, and be joined by another man. "Give way, there!" called the Guards. Their party, a very small party, descended between suddenly silent watchers. Someone somewhere was hissing, but they ignored the noise. *Their dignity's impressive,* Ittrad thought, as he scanned the stew of people below him, cloaks and wagging heads and shrugging shoulders. He wondered how many entrances the Hall of Judgment had.

There she is! Over to his right, Mobira was already talking to two people, a huge scowling man and a thin woman. Talking intently, as if they might mean mischief, and even as he stepped hesitantly down, the others broke away from her. They set off, towards the Square's edge, going fast.

He could never catch them up. Who could? Mobira turned away, *praise God more slowly,* and Ittrad jerked himself at speed down the steps towards her, grunting and every moment expecting a disastrous stumble. At last he was on the flat, and he pressed his eyes to her non-descript red-jacketed back. He thumped his stick to push himself along, and ran over what he'd thought of saying. What he'd sat in that bumpy wagon crossly thinking that *someone* should say to her.

Just at the top of Lower Justice Street, away at last from crowds, he was close enough to gasp, "Madam – I have a message."

She turned her ordinary sharp-chinned face, disdainful

but not doubting. "What message? From whom?"

Ittrad panted, a little dizzy. *Say it firmly.* "He will not live forever." *Wait. Let her wonder.*

"What – who will not, fool?"

"He won't live forever. You've made many enemies. And when he dies, no one will protect you from them."

"Who are you?" Her hand twitched, as if wanting to slap him.

"Many enemies. I'm here to warn you." He made himself implacable. "If those Jaryari die, there'll be a war, a war no one wants but him. When their children start dying, the Families will look for someone to blame, and they'll tear you apart. How many hate you already? The b'Astith, the b'Nida, the b'Shen. Perhaps the Queen. The College is hers, after all. Who am I? I am nobody."

Protecting herself had been in her mind. The letter's preservation had told him that. He forced himself to hold her eyes, and lifted his left hand. "It's time to repent, Mobira. Time to be the Good Twin."

He turned his back with as much dignity as a fat lame man could, and behind him he heard her gasp. "Who sent you?"

He walked away, legs shaking so that he almost fell down. She didn't come after him. Then he thought he heard her steps, rapidly in the opposite direction.

How strange, if all his guesses had been right.

*

"Release her, and go. In the King's name."

Mobira was walking round the corner. A plain, drab woman, as she'd always been, but radiating command. Mej, everyone, watched her. She reached up to slap the big man's face. "Release her!" And he did.

"But your orders," one of them said.

"Orders have changed. Go!"

We should arrest them, Mej thought, but he didn't move. Mobira was helping Nadya pull the bag off. The man ran past, and the others moved with him, even the plainly baffled Guard, off to the far end of the street, dragging one of their number whom Jedder – or Mej? – had cut and made groan.

"Your servant is injured," Mobira said to the staring Nadya. It was Mej who found the man sitting bloody head in hands by the wall, and helped him over to the group by the b'Astith door. Jedder, Kelji, and a sobbing maid; Vaddras sitting up and rubbing his arms; Nadya, gasping; the house guard at last poking his nose out at them; and Mobira.

Jedder leaned against the doorpost, blood coming through his shirt. He held up the sword Mej had given him, and asked, "Who are you?" *(As if he didn't know,* Mej thought.)

"Please put that down, sir. I mean you no ill. There's been a misunderstanding." To the guard, "Your guest is hurt."

"You're King Aigith's rat," said Kelji.

Mobira hesitated, something Mej didn't think he'd seen her do before. "Do not insult the King. I serve my country. I'm glad to have been in time." She bowed to the Jaryari, and then to Mej – "Honoured sir" – lastly to Nadya. "Honoured madam, I am sorry for this confusion."

"Confusion!" said Nadya, high and wild. "We were attacked! He threatened – you let them go! You *commanded* them!"

"I commanded your release. Please, lady, listen to me. I need you, for the benefit of all of us, to let me see the Queen."

They stared.

"See the Queen – who are you?"

"Her name is Mobira," said Jedder, gasping.

"Mobira. *You* bribed Eyanda b'Shen." Nadya's voice was

hard. "Get out of this place. Run away and be hanged."

"Please, lady. Please. I have information – and help – for the Morning Queen. Please, in the name of Our Lord."

Kelji had been released, and then attacked, and this woman had stopped the attack. Nothing made sense to Mej, but he looked at Mobira, and thought her pleading was real. It was a problem, what to do. When it came to problems, he trusted two people.

Perfectly in time, Tor marched round the corner, and stared. One more fighting man. "Madam," said Mej, and he tried to make his voice deep and authoritative, "kneel and give me your sword, and we will consider your request."

Her eyes snapped murder, but she obeyed, offering the blade hilt first. Mej handed it to Nadya. "Very well," he said. "Tor, go to the Palace, find Yikkeri, daughter of Janika, and tell her that we have a woman in custody whom I think the Queen may want to question herself. And we need guards – trustworthy guards – to protect our guests here."

His heart pounded, and he wondered if he'd forgotten anything.

But then Jedder slid down the door to the step, and Imadal screamed at the blood pouring over his chest.

*

"Where's the cripple gone?" Yikkeri snapped. "Huh? Where?"

Hridnaya, poked, made I-don't-know gestures.

"Huh. Come then. Quickly."

The Hall of Judgment was still untidy with jabbering rich people, but Yikkeri knew her way. Once through to the anteroom, they nudged along its wall - not to the outdoors, but round into the back corridor that Hridnaya had herself discovered a few frightening minutes ago. And on. It became very grand –

382

the backyard of the Hall of Justice connected to the Palace, she realised, useful for transferring prisoners.

"Lower your eyes," Yikkeri hissed, as they turned a corner, and Hridnaya hastily made herself back into just another servant. There was no panic or surprise around her: these people hadn't yet heard, or didn't care.

She allowed herself to be pulled.

"Let her go," the Judge had ordered, the dishonest Simoren.

"You did this."

Did I truly? Pride before a fall, but – I did! I used their own magic: a corrupt king's magics are money and unthinking obedience. Once again, as on the Lake road, glee and terror fought in her head and soul, and she could barely see or hear. *Where's Ittrad? And Mejorad? Are they all safe?*

There'll be consequences.

These rooms were familiar. A Guard nodded to Yikkeri, and let them into the dining-room from (only) last night. The Voiceless maid was playing the lute in the corner again.

The Queen stood with her back to the far wall, and her palms against it.

"The Jaryari have left, Your Grace. I sent Mejorad after them – I hope he understands. But I couldn't see that whatishisname student anywhere."

"Thank you." The Queen seemed to realise that her stance was that of a cornered criminal, and she lifted her hands deliberately away from the wall and took a step towards her chair and the lute-player. Of course she wasn't going to discuss any thoughts she had with any of them.

They waited, and their breathing calmed. There was music.

But a knock, and the Chamberlain Krothon almost ran

into the room. He shut the door, and leaned against it, and his eyes darted around, to fall on Hridnaya. "You! Oh, dear Lord – you match the description! We have to hide her!"

"Have you news?"

"Your Grace, yes – can we hide this woman? I mean 'yes.'" He took a breath. "The King is - Simoren swears he obeyed a command – an instruction to release her after all, giving him more money for his trouble, he admits, and sealed with the royal seal." Hridnaya heard the Queen swallow. Her own heart beat wildly. "He swears this – he's produced the message – it was given him by his man Daragor. And Daragor doesn't deny it, says it was given *him* by a female servant he didn't know. So they're shutting the doors. No servant to be allowed out of the Palace, and all are to be questioned – and when they come to this one, they'll see she also is small and brown, and they'll start enquiring and all we've done will be discovered -"

"All we've done?" said the Queen. "I didn't do anything. Did you?"

"Of course not, but - it's chaos, like a - like fury! There are only three copies of the King's seal, and one of them must have been stolen or misused. Brechad is calling that no one's to follow any orders that aren't given in person. They say the King's talking of hanging Simoren and Daragor, as well as the traitors when they're found -"

Krothon put his hands over his face. He was shaking.

Everyone was still; then the Queen said abruptly, "Sir, is there any water in this room? My mother used to tell me, when you're distressed, it helps to wash your face. Make yourself fresh and calm."

She didn't look quite calm. Krothon had no water, but he wiped his face with a sleeve. He took several deep breaths, and a step towards her. "Your Grace," he said more solemnly, "if

Mejorad b'Shen did, arranged, this – you cannot protect him."

She nodded slowly, but looked past him for a moment at Hridnaya. *She knows; he doesn't, but she does.* "What was the description?"

Krothon recited, "A woman in a plain kirtle, small and brown, nothing to remark. She didn't even speak to Daragor, she was in such a hurry, panting and breathless."

Hridnaya had thought panting was a good excuse for not talking. But *am I going to have to confess, to save these others? Word of Truth, oh Lord.*

"You need to hide," Krothon said again, and beckoned her desperately towards last night's curtained recess, which any searchers would find immediately.

"Your Grace," Yikkeri was saying, "it may not have been Mejorad."

"No. And -" Queen Rommi drew herself up – "what you're saying, sir, is that *somebody* did what we hoped, and that the Jaryari woman has been released. I wanted this to happen; I prayed for it, and it seems my prayers were answered. However it happened, there would be anger, and so there is. That is all." Her voice trembled.

Yikkeri daringly reached up to lay pale triangular palms against the Queen's cheeks. "Your Grace, you told me before the Crowning, you believed God would equip you."

Quietly, "He needs to."

Hridnaya was wondering what the King would do before killing her, when he found out.

The Queen said slowly, "They're locking the doors, and checking the servants they *know,* from their lists. They know you, Yikkeri, but you're not brown. It may take a little while to reach the ones they *don't* know." Her eyes moved from one servant to the other. "Do you have anything with you, or did you leave anything in my chapel, that might – resemble – a royal seal?"

Krothon gasped. Hridnaya was able to shake her head, honestly. *Thank God I found a privy to drop it in.*

"Then, yes, get behind the curtain. Jeril, keep playing, please. I need to think how shocked to be by this very surprising news, although of course it has little to do with me. Krothon, plainly your next task is to check the whereabouts and security of all *my* seals. And in the meantime, I will pray for the safety of everyone at Nadya b'Astith's house."

If Hridnaya'd been a kinder person, she thought, she'd have stopped worrying about herself to pity the Chamberlain as he left the quiet room. Who knew what was happening in the corridors outside? What had it been like for him, to live in this frightening building for so many years?

But when he came back a little later, he had a message with the b'Astith seal; a message from Mejorad b'Shen.

*

The last time Kelji had been in Nadya's hall, it had been for courteous goodbyes, with quite a few people present. Some customer and his servant had been waiting scowlingly for Nadya to have time for him. Imadal had been receiving last instructions, happy to be left behind. (Or not. Kelji didn't know, and hadn't cared.) There had been bustle.

Since then, much had happened, and she'd had four days of solitary anger and wondering.

Now all again was noise and people. Someone arrived from the b'Astith mansion with guards; Mejorad came back from the Palace with more; physicians had already carried Jedder and Nadya's bloody-headed servant into the business-room on the right, where either of them might even now be dying.

She stood to one side while Nadya told the story (with gestures, showing the bruises on her neck) to her tall grand and shocked-looking elderly kinsman, and Imadal questioned Vaddras.

Mejorad with drawn sword watched Mobira standing by a wall. Her fingers twitched, but her face was thoughtful. As Kelji watched, she pulled down her hair from its plaited coil and began to comb it free. She was refusing to talk to them, and somehow they were letting her.

Everyone else waited for instructions, and Kelji was still. She wondered why. Perhaps it was only the effort of not jumping forward screaming to scratch that woman's face with her nails.

And a monstrous part of her thought, *I'm the one who's been locked up expecting to die, but now all the danger and the worry are for Nadya – and for him –*

St Mary-Christ's-mother, pray for us, please. She could formulate no better prayer.

All around her strangers jabbered.

Then - "Kelji. Cousin." Nadya swept up and took her hands. "I'm sorry for all this confusion. Has no one even brought you a drink?" She swallowed, and smiled shakily. "We've thought – I will go to the Palace with Mejorad and that woman, and three guards, but we'll leave plenty here. Whoever those murderers were, it's plainly you they wanted to hurt, so you can't go out yet. This is my kinsman Ettuar, Lord b'Astith, and we're hanging the Family banner above the door. No one will dare attack that."

Ettuar bowed, a small superior bow. *An assault on Nadya the Family takes seriously – and an assault on him would probably be insurrection.*

I should go to the Palace with them. I need to find out, and scream at them all – but she's right. And Jedder's here.

"Cousin." Nadya embraced her closely, her voice trembling. *Yes, cousin and friend, after all.* Kelji felt tears prickle as she squeezed her hands in the back of the other's gown. "We will find out what this is. And deal with it. God bless you."

Almost as quick as that, most of them were gone – Nadya, Mobira, Mejorad, several guards. Others were left in the hall. Some had Palace tabards. Kelji wanted to kill them, remembering humiliation. The place was almost quiet.

Imadal brought her a cup of wine. She stood for a moment staring at the door on the right, through which she could hear nothing; and then she turned the other way, into Nadya's living room where she'd sewed and dined and given reading lessons. She walked over to the corner stairs, and sat down on the second from bottom step. The house-cat strolled over to be stroked.

And still somehow she could do no more than "St Mary, pray for him. Please."

*

Mej had battled in the streets before, but never with a sword or for such a righteous cause. His skin tingled with life as he led the way (led Nadya b'Astith!) across the Palace courtyard to the doors. *"We are summoned by the Queen," that's what to say, not too casual but not worried – will the Guards know Mobira?* She plainly didn't want them to. In a borrowed cloak covering her drab clothes, hair combed over her shoulders and threaded with ribbon, she looked like quite a high person, even a Family member. She hadn't explained anything – *is she a murderer or isn't she?* And somehow not even Nadya had insisted. Because the Lake is deep, as people say, and all of them were floundering.

The Guards looked worried, but more concerned to question anyone trying to leave. They were allowed in to where the Chamberlain Krothon met them, smiling solemnly while his hands twitched, and they left two of their three guards in the Mosaic Corridor. Krothon led them to last night's room.

Queen Rommi sat listening to her musician and studying

a list. Yikkeri stood in front of the curtain. Hridnaya and Ittrad weren't visible, probably hiding behind it.

Mej bowed. *Now, can we have some explanations?* "Er, Your Grace, this woman is Mobira, who – she begged an audience, but -"

"Your Grace!" Mobira interrupted. She stepped firmly forward, raised her arms, and fell to her knees. "Please, Your Grace! I've come to throw myself on your mercy. My name is Mobira. You may have heard evil things of me, and yes, they're all true. I've been foolish and misled, and I've sinned. I've committed terrible crimes. I was ordered to deceive and kill, and I did so. But God is merciful – today I was called to repent and make recompense, and to serve and help you. I beg you to hear me."

She waited with bent head. Mej blinked. Everyone stared.

"Please explain, madam," said Krothon, passing her to stand beside the Queen.

Mobira lifted her chin, but kept her eyes downcast. She spoke more slowly. "Three years ago, the greatest man in this land sent me to Sapientia, to be his spy and agent there. Whatever orders he gave, I obeyed. I – I stained my hands with innocent blood." She lifted those hands and stared at them. "When our guest from Makkera was coming to the b'Astith's and to the College, he told me to prepare a false case against her, and I did. I bribed and threatened, and fabricated evidence. This man -" she waved behind her, vaguely in Mej's direction – "knows it's true. Today when Simoren b'Asa did what was *right,* my master was angry. He ordered the foreigners' deaths, a half hour ago, and I sent dogs I knew to do it. May God forgive me. And then I was changed." She lifted her face to the beams criss-crossing the ceiling, and Mej wondered if he saw tears. "Someone met me in the Square, angel or prophet, I know not – and in his words I saw what I was, clearly for the first time. He told me to repent, to be the Good Twin." Her voice altered a little on the last words. "And so without delay I went to the b'Astith house, and praise God, arrived in time. Now I am come in sorrow and repentance to offer myself to you. I wish only to make amends, and serve my country. I can be useful. If you fear what the King is doing, may still do, in the north and south-west. I crave your forgiveness, and God's."

"You sent those brutes to kill Kelji and Jedder?" Nadya cried.

"And to blindfold you, my lady, so that you couldn't interfere, or identify anyone. I meant no hurt to you, only to the foreigners. Such were my orders. I've now disobeyed them, and he will kill me when he finds out. And, Your Grace, he may try again. Even now -"

"And, ahem, then you met an angel?" Krothon asked.

"Mortal or angel, he appeared as a limping man. God sent him to me, and perhaps to Simoren also, I know not, to turn me from my wickedness."

A limping man. For a worrying moment, Mej struggled desperately not to laugh. He kept his eyes away from Krothon's and the Queen's.

"And you bribed Eyanda b'Shen." Nadya's voice was ice.

Still on her knees, Mobira twisted towards her. "She wrote to my master after her son was banished, offering to do anything if the Council would bring him back. So she wasn't hard to persuade. But yes, I was her temptress."

"You entangled her in your plot against my guests. Your dogs attacked us - Jedder may yet die, more killers may be at the house again *now,* and you evil creature, you came here for *pardon?*"

Mobira dropped her eyes meekly. "We are told that God

390

forgives any who truly repent.”

"Enough!” The Queen jumped from her chair. Mej’s heart bounced. She took a furious step forward, and Mobira quailed. “Have you never heard the Third Commandment, madam? ‘Thou shalt not take the name of the Lord in vain.’ For some reason you’ve decided to betray your master, whose banner you’ve served with murder and evil for many years, and you seek to creep under mine. You are not repentant, and every word you speak is an insult to God.” She glared down. “But you claim you can be useful to me. And I have to decide whether that’s true – or whether I simply send you in chains to King Aigith with a message that his jackal has turned traitor.”

Mobira paled. “Your Grace, please. I am sorry, truly I am –”

"Save that for the confessional. What knowledge have you that I want? I already know that King Aigith planned to slaughter our innocent guests by law, which through God’s grace Simoren prevented. Then you say you were told to slaughter them by street-murder, and, as my friend says, one may indeed be dead. You have questions to answer, madam,” and she looked over at Krothon. “Ask them.”

He shifted a little to draw Mobira’s attention. “You say your hands are stained. This means murder. Who have you killed?”

Mobira spoke clearly, but less readily than before. “There was a Doctor Madrasun. He was asking treasonous questions, making trouble. I was ordered to dispose of him without the mess of a trial.”

"And how did you –?”

"I confused him with a draught of menatol, and then pushed him downstairs. He was old, and it killed him.”

Mej felt sick, and Krothon looked as if he did also.

"Menatol, yes. Who else did you poison? Or stab, or push, or pay others to kill? If you seek mercy, you need to be frank. Names."

Mobira licked her lips. "There was a servant at the College who threatened me – us. Her name was Mari, or Marit. And – a priest, Brother Thomas, who kept praying at Mass for the welfare of our enemies. And." She peeped up, and down again. "The riots last year, when some of the students wanted permission to travel west of the mountains to Makkera and Vachansha and Vach-roysh, I arranged for the attacks on them."

"In which as I remember some people died."

"Three," said the Queen.

"Yes, Your Grace. The deaths weren't intended."

"But you caused them. What else have you done?"

"I watched and reported, and if my master asked me to scare and threaten people, at the College, I did."

"What did you threaten them with?"

Mobira shrugged. "Whatever they seemed most likely to fear. Death, rape, for themselves or their families. Or if I knew of anything shameful in their lives, I threatened to expose it. I was under orders. My master told me it's absolvable, if it's for the country. He's determined to crush the College, and now I think he wants to use the Jaryaris' deaths to make war. He hasn't told me all the details." Her voice had risen steadily, and now she looked at Mej. "I have wronged you, sir, by involving you."

She was turning away, when Mej suddenly remembered, and said, "Rorash. And Flower-in-Hood."

She jerked. "That man I didn't kill. I wasn't even in Sapientia that day. Your – cousin, was it? - struck an unlucky blow. But I confess that I made use of his death to scare the Doctor, Dirria. The School of Law tends to be the most troublesome, and needs to be kept in harness."

"Like Madrasun," said Krothon.

A little arrogance had been returning to Mobira's face. Now she removed it. "I deeply repent of that. I will do penance. I seek to serve you, Your Grace, because you are good. You are what a Queen should be."

"I dislike this flattery, liar," said the Queen. "Do not make me say it again. So much for the past. What else has the King planned? He's been thwarted twice today. You will tell me what you meant just now by 'may still happen.'"

Mobira remained on her knees, four people looking down at her with curiosity and contempt. Almost in a whisper, she said, "Please understand, Your Grace, I don't know all the King's thoughts. I live in Sapientia. But he was hoping that hanging Kelji and her husband would lead to trouble with Jaryar, even war."

"So I've guessed. Go on."

"And since they're not hanged, and the b'Astith are protecting their guests, as they should, he will try something else. He may send more people to kill them, perhaps later, on their way home. He'll want vengeance on Simoren, he'll think of it as treason. He'll be wondering where I am, now. And – I think he had some other plan as well, in the next day or so. It wasn't just the execution, there was to be more."

"What other plan?"

"I don't know, I swear, Your Grace. He shares thoughts with very few. He thinks people only serve a King for their own advantage, and he trusts no one. He has no friends, only subordinates. But there was something else he hadn't shared even with his Council or me, and all I know is the word Verndew."

"Is that all? You're lying," said Nadya.

"Verndew?" said the Queen. "What is that? A place somewhere? Or a thing, a poison?"

"I don't know! I swear it! He told me the Sunday before

last, before I went to arrest Kelji, no one else was there, not even Brechad his Chamberlain – he said, 'Pray it all goes well. The trials and the executions, and I'm sending a few people for a little scheme at Verndew ,or he may have said 'with Verndew', and these together should be enough.' I think he meant enough for war."

"It's a place," said Nadya shyly. "Somewhere in a ballad, but I don't remember precisely."

The Queen frowned. "If his original plan had worked, he would have expected trouble, and would have reinforced the border." She looked up. "Mejorad?"

"My friend Narod was about to be sent off with his company – but he hasn't gone yet. I saw him in the Square when I was on my way to Nadya's."

"Sent where?"

"Somewhere in the north - he didn't know; he was annoyed."

Krothon said, glancing at the door, "If they don't die, Queen Nerranya has no reason to attack. Narod's company must have been waiting for the execution. Does he have any other plans?"

"I know of none," said Mobira, "but he will not stop. He won't stop unless someone stops him."

"And I can't," said the Queen again. She looked at Nadya, and said, "They're your Family's guests."

"Yes, but – I don't understand! We'll defend them, but the b'Astith can't accuse the King!"

No more than the b'Nida, thought Mej. *And yet -*

"And this is all," the Queen was saying scornfully to Mobira, when Mej found her brown eyes suddenly turning back to him. "You always loved ballads of war, did you not? Is Verndew a name you know?"

"Yes, Your Grace. As Nadya says. It's the 'Tale of the Enemies' Cairn.'"

"Tell me. Sing it if you wish."

Krothon was looking anxiously at the door.

"Umm." Mej shut his eyes to think. He felt strangely shy. "It's – it says there was a quarrel between the master of Verndew and Alida Queensister of the Marodi Thirty, long ago. Her brother had run away into Ricossa with his sister, or something, and taken a pile of treasure, so the tale says she gathered her Eastern Six and other soldiers, and rode across the border after him. They rode for half a day to Verndew, but the master – his name was Miko – was waiting and ambushed them, so they all battled for half a day, and then Alida fought Miko for half a day, single combat, but *then* they decided they admired each other's honour and spirit, and made friends. They feasted together -"

"For half a day?" murmured Krothon irritably.

"Yes, and the young lovers begged forgiveness, and returned the treasure, and they all built a cairn for the dead of both sides. That's all. Long ago."

"I don't think this helps us." Krothon dared to scowl. "What are any of us to do, Your Grace?"

They were back to last night's problem. Who can say "No" to a King?

The Queen's head was bent, and he saw tears on her cheeks. "I wish to consult with my Chamberlain. All of you, wait outside."

*

"Listen," the Queen had told Hridnaya when hiding her again behind the curtain. Hridnaya was aware of the huge compliment, one the b'Nida had rarely paid her; and so she scrubbed her tired eyes with her fists, and knelt with her palms on the floor and listened.

(So that's what Ittrad rushed off to do!)

She was sickened by Mobira's calm list of crimes, and got a little lost when Mejorad started reciting an ancient story of battle.

But then, "Wait outside." She heard people leaving, and now she supposed no one was left beyond the curtain but the Queen and Krothon – and perhaps the silent musician.

Krothon spoke first. "Your Grace." He sounded nervous. "Before you tell more secrets. Lord b'Nida has always disliked me. But last night you told him you trusted me because I looked angry when that lad came to the Palace."

"You did. As if your comfortable safe life, and mine, were being disturbed."

"Yes," he said. So low Hridnaya could hardly hear, "Comfortable. That's a good word. This house is a hard place to be comfortable in, but I've tried to be – and to stay out of trouble. I don't, didn't, want to be – hurt, or – my life has secrets that the King's people know, which I don't want told. So I'm not sure your choice was wise."

Hridnaya hardly dared to breathe. But after a pause the Queen said, "I think that if you'd gone running to the King or his Chamberlain after last night, we wouldn't be here. Most of the people who dined with me, and the ones out there, would be under arrest."

"I didn't run to him. Please don't ask me if I was tempted." He went on, "But God help me, I'm saying that I do wish at least to deserve what you said – to be like – like a good soldier. Your true servant."

Was he kneeling? Hridnaya wondered. Nothing happened for a moment.

"I thank you, sir. And now -"

"But now you should consider that all this may be a trap."

"Why would that be?"

"The King sent you that message yesterday. And Mobira is conscienceless, and works for him."

"Let me think." After a pause, "You're right, it may be. But there's no doubt that he wanted them dead, and Mobira helped to prevent that. And why would Nadya b'Astith and Mejorad lie? No, I think this change of allegiance is real. So I wish to discuss with you what I do now."

"You do nothing, Your Grace."

"Nothing?"

"Your prayers were answered, and the Jaryari are alive. Their protection is now the b'Astith's responsibility. We can be thankful. If we can keep out of Simoren's disgrace, and protect the Voiceless through there, weather the storm, that will be well. It's all you can do. Trust me in this. War has been prevented."

"For now. He will try again. They have a long way to go home."

Hridnaya shivered. Krothon said nothing, but she thought his silence sounded frustrated.

"Verndew," said the Queen thoughtfully. "What, and why? Something so secret that even Mobira doesn't know – but someone must."

There's one person who may know – one person who can't and won't tell.

"I see I am a troublesome mistress to you, Krothon. The King is angry, and I wish to protect you, and myself, and others, from the consequences of this morning. I've done almost nothing; perhaps I stirred the water, but nothing more.

"He is still – dangerous - now, and in the future. But it's not my place to stop him. Oh God," she said slowly, "You appointed me, and to do what? My uncle said after the Conclave they chose me because I thought. I swore not to interfere."

"You did," said Krothon, in the tone of a parent cautiously leading a child back from tantrum to the path of reason.

"What did Doctor Madrasun say? 'The greatest curse for any land is a king who does evil but cannot be stopped.'" Hridnaya heard pacing steps. "He has so much power, but only because the Families and the New Governance allow him."

"Legally, there are some things he cannot do. There are restrictions," Krothon admitted. "But you cannot criticise him, and without a leader no one else dares."

What restrictions? Hridnaya had sat in nurseries while b'Nida children learned the New Governance by heart. She ran through it yet again, and - *Oh!* Her gasp was loud.

"What's that noise?" Krothon flung back the curtain in alarm turning to relief. "You."

Hridnaya'd used her last parchment on Simoren. Heart beating, she stepped towards the Queen's staring face. She lifted a hand, and with one finger on the palm traced letters.

T. A.*(How's it spelt?)* K. S.

"What are you -"

F. O. R. W. A. R.

She saw the moment the Queen understood her. "Indeed. 'He shall not without the consent of the Council levy tax.' So does it all come down to money?"

"Your Grace, your oath – I will be your servant, but I must advise -"

"I know!" She whirled away from them. "B'Astith, possibly b'Olim, b'Shen, probably b'Nida – I don't think it's enough. And we don't even have all the information. Verndew. Why Verndew?" Krothon and Hridnaya had to step back out of her way as she marched across past the dining table, turned, and marched back; turned again. *("Quiet and dull as moss on a wall",* *Jeruma described her as.)* "Da *da* da *da*...but. But."

She stopped, and looked at Krothon. "They rode for half a day."

"Yes…?"

"They crossed into Ricossa, and rode for half a day."

Hridnaya didn't understand, but she saw that Krothon did. "Verndew isn't a border town."

"No," she said, "and – but -"

Hridnaya watched rapid thought. "Please wait." And then, "No. This is too much blood. I cannot endure it, oath or no.

"But I *think* it may also be a mistake. Perhaps it is now the King who is in too deep."

Krothon's frowning face was scared.

*

Mej and the others waited a long time. B'Astith and b'Shen and a Voiceless musician stood together in the anteroom with a self-confessed murderer and two guards, none of them venturing to sit down, although there were chairs in the room. Nadya stalked to a window, and stared out. Mobira stood with her hands clasped and her eyes lowered, like a saint in a picture. Yikkeri watched her with fierce eyes.

Mej wandered in little circles, hating the silence. Once he dared to break it. "You swear you weren't in Sapientia that night, when Flower-in-Hood died?"

Mobira gave a little shrug. "It was 19th June, was it not? I was attending a dance here at the Palace. Spying on one of the b'Olim, as ordered. My master had no reason to order Gridor disposed of. He was an annoyance, but a trivial one."

Could that be true? Am I trusting Jedder too far? Or - did she recall the date too readily?

Is Jedder still alive?

Time dragged on, and he began to feel very thirsty. Surely a day of such excitement and significance oughtn't to have dull bits. They don't in tales. *What hour is it?* But at last the door opened for Krothon. His eyes passed by all the others, to rest on Mej. "The Queen asks if you know, sir, the name of your friend Narod's captain."

What about that brute he doesn't like? "Umm. Oh… umm. I think Achandor."

Krothon nodded soberly, and beckoned to the Palace Guard. They spoke quietly, and the man left. Krothon went back into the room.

More silence, and more thirst. A Guard, a different one, came in looking curiously about her.

The door opened again. "Return, please."

Hridnaya was waiting by the wall, which surprised Nadya, but all attention was on the Queen.

She stood on the far side of the table, squat and suddenly (he thought) unbudgeable. She looked like herself.

"Mobira, daughter of Jentoretti," said Krothon, at her side, and Mobira knelt, not before time. "You are a disgusting creature, and the blood you've spilled cries out for vengeance. But you're right that some matters are more urgent still. The Queen makes no promises, but she demands that you serve her today and tonight, and if you are faithful she will *consider* your future."

"I thank you, Your Grace," Mobira whispered, eyes flicking around.

Krothon turned his head towards his mistress, just enough that they all followed.

"Yes, you will serve me," she said. "And Yikkeri and Jeril, you always do, and Krothon is my trusted Chamberlain. For today, I claim the service of Hridnaya here also. But you two –" she looked from Mej to Nadya – "you I cannot command, but I would be grateful for your help."

"Whatever you need," Mej said, the words catching in his

throat, and he knelt.

"Your Grace, I don't understand," said Nadya. "I – I have obligations to my Family, and I came here to report an attack on my guests. I'm eager to protect them, and – if it's true that war's being planned, we would all wish to prevent that -"

"Very well. I will risk a little explanation." Mej thought Krothon looked nervous.

"Today one of your guests was cleared of all suspicion, irrevocably cleared in Ricossan law – and then criminally attacked, but the attack failed. Also today I've received a report that one of the King's seals has been misused, and he is rightly concerned about this." She paused. "So far as I know, nothing else, *officially*, has happened. I think my duties and my oath require and allow me to take an interest in the safety of a visitor to the College.

"Unofficially – we know that a company of soldiers led by Captain Achandor was waiting, perhaps is still waiting, for instructions to sail north. Achandor's reputation is cruel and without scruple – like you, madam, he's killed people before now for the King. I have a theory as to what they were going to do."

Mej felt the ripple run through the room. *Are these words treason?*

"So I am going to act. We, I, have one advantage. Everything the King is doing is covert. And that's why I'm saying that very little has happened today. One trial concluded early, a little violence in the streets, and a lost seal. Apparently there is some agitation about these matters in the Palace, but I am the Queen, and they do not concern me."

"But you said they do," Nadya began timidly.

"No. The King's servants may be worried and angry, but the Queen's are calm. Officially my thoughts are turning to tomorrow's feast day of St Aidan, for which my preparations are incomplete. So, Yikkeri."

"Your Grace?"

"Krothon has a list of names for you. They are servants or officials here on the surface work for both of us equally, but in practice report to the King; people I would like distracted from whatever he is worrying them with. They have no reason to disobey my polite but urgent command, so you will think of orders for them. I require new clothes, of the humble plain kind that St Aidan would approve, for me and my people; I want a dinner consisting entirely of fish and bitter herbs – think of some details, please. Find people to give orders to."

"Your Grace." Yikkeri grinned, looking the happiest person there, and she and the Chamberlain stepped aside together.

"More urgently, I have people to summon, and to summon today. So I need to dictate, if any of you can offer a good writing hand?"

*

Mej was still writing – *no blots, sir!* – and wondering, when Yikkeri slipped back in, about a half hour later. "I've got them scurrying round for sackcloth and fish. But there's still a search on for someone looking like *her*. Soon or late, they'll be here."

Hridnaya was sitting un-useful in a corner, and she looked up with wide eyes. But it was Mobira, next to Krothon, who spoke urgently. "Your Grace, they mustn't find me either. The King will be wondering why I haven't reported to him."

"Indeed. And now my dayplan tells me I have a meeting with churchwardens about Sabbath curfews and Monday markets, and since I have no reason to fear or worry I should not send an excuse. Where can we hide you two?"

"There is a place," said Mobira. "On the first floor, near the wardrobes. Almost no one knows of it." In response to several expressions, "I don't want him to find me!"

"And we don't want to trust you," said Nadya.

"I – I'm not lying, I swear it! I swear on – on my brother's grave." Krothon raised an eyebrow, and the Queen held Mobira's eyes. "He died when we were five years old."

"Come then," and as quick as that the little group gathered to leave the dining-room, a place that Mej felt almost seemed safe. Outside its door was the rest of the Palace, and it belonged to Aigith.

Hridnaya sidled up to him, and he tried to give her an encouraging smile. She seemed to need it, for her face was sand-coloured and she was trembling, but into his hand she slipped a scrap of parchment.

The kings voysless knos evrithing.

Hmm. He passed it to Krothon, whose eyebrows rose.

They were at the door. As they took deep breaths and walked through, the Queen said clearly, "Young sir, I am shocked by this ignorance. You've truly never heard of St Aidan of Northumbria? And you to be a priest, I hear?"

He scrabbled for a sensible reply, and then realised that it didn't have to be sensible. "North Umbria: is that a Marodi name?"

They put Hridnaya and Mobira in the middle of the group, Nadya's and the Queen's Guards at front and back - a band of cheerful unworried people walking along passageways that most of them knew well, teaching him about long-ago ascetic monks. "Which, then, is more pleasing to God, Your Grace – a day without food, or a night without sleep? I've often sat up till dawn, but not in prayer."

Nadya managed to laugh.

They climbed together, carrying their possibly treasonous letters, passing other people on the way. There were servants lighting wall-candles on the stairway, looking worried.

Mobira led them to an empty room. She strode to the far wood-panelled wall, and twisted something, so that one of the panels opened like a door. Inside was a hole, an empty cupboard, with just enough space for two people to sit or crouch. They all stared.

"Both of you, get in. And, Mobira, you will not harm this woman. Indeed, you will protect her with your life if necessary."

"I will, Your Grace."

Mej watched as Krothon pressed the panel back into place; hiding and imprisoning.

Outside, the Queen and Yikkeri went one way; Mej, Nadya and Krothon another. To the Mosaic Corridor, smiling calmly.

Guards bowed to them and opened the doors. As the Queen had said, officially little was wrong, so no one had reason to stop them, great people, all of them known. They were out in the Court, and it was still afternoon.

They were silent as they headed down Upper Justice Street to the Great Passage. This was speckled with taverns, benches outside many of them in the summer warmth. *I could be in The Dog and Boot now – or The Second Queen, over there, is endurable. But even though I'm terrified, I'm glad I'm here.*

Outside The Second Queen, he saw a face he seemed to recognise, and jerked. It wasn't someone he knew from taverns, but recently, from these extraordinary few days – not Jedder, but–

"Another, if you please." The man's voice to the server was thick.

Mej felt his companions' annoyance as he turned aside. But he couldn't help grinning. "You, sir! What are you doing here?" Whatwashisname – Ittrad – looked scared as he struggled to stand and bow. "My lord."

"Mejorad, leave your friend. We cannot delay."

"This is Mobira's limping man." He watched Nadya's face as she understood. "D'you have nowhere to go?" He hadn't thought of the man as a drunk.

Ittrad blinked at him. "I have accused the Chancellor's husband – offended and disobeyed – your pardon, my lord. In my foolishness I could think of nothing better to do than eat and drink and be merry, before I – before I'm arrested." He was not (yet, quite) as drunk as Mej had thought.

"Lord b'Nida won't want you back," he considered aloud. *And we don't want Mobira to see him.* "I – maybe you could come back with me."

"With me," said Nadya. "I can bring guests to my own home without explanation. But hurry."

Her servant hauled him upright.

"Your way is down there, is it not? Good fortune, Mejorad, and you, honoured sir," and Nadya wrinkled a nervous smile.

"Greet your other guests from me," he forgot to say.

"Come," said Krothon impatiently, and they walked on through the late afternnon, with one Guard only, the man who'd watched b'Shen doors until the Conclave moved him to the Palace with the Queen. They came to the Water Walk. To their left, the night-fishing fleet of little boats were making ready to leave, but on the right the wharves were almost deserted, for no one took ferries at this time.

Almost deserted. One boat rocked on the darkening water, and soldiers stood above it, with the cross waiting look Mej remembered so well. *Are we leaving or not?* The nearest two looked up.

"Mej!" exclaimed Narod. "What're you doing here? Your pardon, honoured sir -"

And Krothon said clearly, "I require to speak to your

captain. We've come from the Palace. I am the Chamberlain, and there is a difficulty with the King's seal."

*

So Hridnaya sat in some sort of upright coffin, squashed next to Venomous Mobira. It wasn't like a bedroom, where one could think peaceful thoughts. It wasn't even like the linen cupboard Yikkeri had put her in. It was darkness, and her enemy pressed against her.

She heard them both breathing. The other woman's arm brushed past her face, and she *felt* the moment they both realised that the panel didn't, couldn't, open from the inside.

Mobira's breaths grew ragged. *She hates this worse than I do. Is she my enemy? If so, my duty to God is* – After a little, Hridnaya squeezed her own hand up to touch the other woman's arm gently. Mobira jerked it away.

What is the Queen doing? What's happening? That's for her now, I can do no more.

My enemy. Did you kill Uncle Gridor? I still can't ask you. I still don't know.

"Justice," she'd said she wanted. Yet again, partly for something other than King Aigith to think about, she ran through the evidence at Rorash b'Shen's trial – if Jedder was right about poison, the actual events in the tavern weren't as important as the before and after – *who was spying on him? How many people? Four (one of them was Ittrad.) Why?*

A poisoner should be stopped. And I want to know. So does Brin.

He went to Sapientia, to see Doctor Dirria – and he died.

There was something else I wondered – the night Jedder and I came back to the city, why did –?

Oh no. Oh <u>no</u>.

In the dark place, next to a murderer, she shuddered with

406

her new thought. It made sense. Horrible sense.

Time is strange, when you can't even share looks. How long had passed, she couldn't know–

Abrupt noise, and brightness. She blinked.

"One, and *two*," said a Guard. "Well-a-day, it's the lady Mobira! What an interesting place to find you. So the King's Chamberlain was right. Both of you, out."

*

The ninth hour of evening approached. Brechad b'Iri, the Evening King's Chamberlain, sat at supper with his master in a small six-sided room high up. Windows whose panes were blind with night looked down over the courtyard, and the reflection of candle-flame shimmered off the glass.

One wall was almost covered with an embroidered map of Ragaris, its cities and holy sites marked out with gems, and the kingdoms' borders in gold thread. The King glanced at it often.

On the table were plates of spiced vegetables and fried fish for the Chamberlain, and a humbler bowl of honeyed porridge served with white bread for the King. He rarely ate much in the evening. Brechad had drunk one and a half goblets of wine; the King only water.

By the door a very young, very tall Guardswoman stood to smart attention; a much greyer man, King Aigith's Voiceless, waited on the diners, and poked at the brazier when its flames forgot to dance.

A piece of parchment lay on the table. *"For the urgent notice of Simoren b'Asa. She is to be set free without stain. Matters have changed, and additional payment reflects this. Fail not."*

"I'll banish Simoren to the furthest coast, the idiot!" the King muttered, for the fifth time.

The Chamberlain shared his anger. The temptation to

wring Simoren's scrawny neck had been severe. But that punishment could wait. He tapped a smaller map on the table between them, to draw his master's mind back to the current point of discussion. "Of the two they might use, the northern route through Arbeth seems more probable. We can manage either, although an ambush would be easier in the mountains -"

"Before they cross into Defardu. Nerranya must have no doubt who she's dealing with."

Brechad barked a laugh. "Very true, Your Grace. As soon as their courtesy-guards have gone home, which I guess will be early. The Jaryari have been troublesome guests. Lord b'Astith will thank heaven when they've gone, and provide as little protection for as short a time as he can. But we needn't forget the foreign groom. He may be willing to buy our favour by killing -"

"Too sanguine, Brechad!" The King angrily squashed a corner-crust of bread on the table. "That whole Family may have been corrupted – they must be either gullible or treacherous. Think what was done today! Someone knew of all the trial plans; someone knew of Simoren; they stopped Mobira's attack, and she's missing; and *they had access to my seal!*" He paused to cough. "Foreigners, with assistance in the Palace! We cannot underestimate Nerranya. Who knows what she's promised Nadya and her cousins?"

Brechad dared to murmur, "As to Mobira -"

The King's face was bleak. "If he, they, have killed her, their punishment will frighten children for years to come. I will bring back the nine-day death."

Brechad prided himself on being without softness, but still he shuddered at that.

The King had always been a big man, both up and across, although at seventy-five he was somewhat stooped. The hair coating his shoulders – a wig, now – was pure white, and his square-cut beard faintly yellowed. Vertical wrinkles gouged his parchment-pale face, and his eyes gleamed from deep hollows. They gleamed brightly, but his fingers juddered on the tablecloth.

Brechad was young for his post, not yet forty. His hair and pointed beard were thick, black and curly, but his face was hard and plain, a thin white scar running from eye's-edge to right ear. Now he paused, wondering whether to say anything about the nine-day death - or about Mobira, whom the King trusted too much. But there were noises outside, and abruptly the door was flung open.

"Her Grace Queen Rommi, to wait upon the Evening King!"

And she didn't come alone.

She was preceded by two servants carrying trays. Three steps behind them, the Queen herself, in a silver-sleeved red gown, and white jewels in her hair. Behind her, several – half a dozen? – highborn and mostly familiar people – one very old, leaning on a stick and a companion. At the back the inevitable Guard, who took up his stance next to the King's own Guard by the door.

What is this intrusion? Brechad had to rise and bow, furiously folding his map away. The Queen nodded in response, but addressed the King. "Brother, God be with you. I am sorry to disturb you so late, but I've brought some delicacies to excuse the interruption." Her ancient maid and the Voiceless woman she'd inherited from Zinial laid out platters with pyramids of yellow plums, surrounded and surmounted by raspberries and red cherries. There were also jugs from which fragrant steam curled. *Very tempting, but what the hell are you all here for?*

King Aigith was a great man. "My dear little sister," he said, seeming unruffled, "this is an unlooked-for pleasure. Please present me – Jeriet, is that you? Come and sit down."

The aged woman in grey and blue shuffled forward in response. There were only three chairs in the room, so Brechad had to give up his seat for her, while the Queen claimed the third place with a hand on its curved back. She said, "Indeed. Jeriet, Lady b'Shen, with her great-grandson Mejorad. Your Grace knows Lord b'Nida, Lady b'Olim, Lord b'Astith – and of course my Chamberlain Krothon."

The most craven peace-mongers on the Council. How has she dared – and they -?

The shiny newly-minted Queen sat down, almost looking dignified. She smoothed her skirts and gestured to the servants to pour. They handed cups round, and a few of the intruders sipped, for something to do. Brechad felt their nervousness and his own anger saturating the room. Everyone waited for the King – everyone perhaps except the two Guards, who had not been introduced, and whose business it was to ignore undercurrents and obey orders.

"So what is burdening you tonight, little one?" He was still smiling.

"Errhm. Are you aware, brother, that two high-born visitors to this land and the Great College have been vilified and attacked by people purporting to act on your instructions? I wish us to agree together that this abuse of our guests must now stop. The Jaryari will be treated with courtesy, allowed to leave in peace, and not hindered or hurt on their journey home. This is my urgent desire."

Brechad, the King's guard-dog, glanced for permission to engage. He removed a cherry stone from his mouth, and flicked it onto the carpet. Clearly and contemptuously, "Your Grace? How do these alleged matters concern you?"

"Kelji was invited by my College -"

"*Your* College? Is that your excuse for this interference?"

"I protest," the fool Krothon whined. "Please do not address the Morning Queen in -"

He leant forward, placing his knuckles on the table. Face close to hers, voice raised, "The Morning Queen -"

The King interrupted, calmly. "The Morning Queen should mind her own affairs. Was it but a half hour ago that she was plain Rommi b'Shen? I fear she has much to learn. If -" he paused to cough and then drink, and they all waited – "if she intrudes on my evening with this nonsense, like an impertinent little girl, I fear she should expect to be rebuked."

"Sir, it's not nonsense. The Jaryari are God's children, as we are," said the Queen. "Kelji is not a spy. You and your people will not hurt them or their servants. You will not hurt Simoren, either."

"Simoren! You did that?" Brechad demanded.

"I praised God for the act. But I didn't command or authorise it," said the Queen, blinking again. Her voice trembled. "What your agent had prepared was a murder, not a trial."

"My agent? Wait." Before the King's face the room grew colder. "I have a loyal servant called Mobira. This Kelji's husband or lover tried to murder her, but she escaped. What have you done to her?"

"I haven't hurt her. I swear it."

"So you say. *I shall find out.*" The King slumped backwards. "Very well, then, child," he said. "I would shed no tears for these scheming Jaryari. But send them home, if you love them so much." *It's no matter. We can dispose of them on the journey,* Brechad thought. "And then go back to your markets and musicians. That is your province. I shall not forgive those who have tempted you out of it." He caught Brechad's eye meaningly, and their joint gaze made Krothon flinch. Brechad showed his teeth. "Now you may leave."

But it seemed the b'Shen bred tougher than that.

"My actions are my own. We are a kingdom of law, and vengeance on servants is beneath you. Yes, we will send the Jaryari home with guards, but I fear we are not finished. There was a purpose behind all this, and I have warned the Ten Families that that purpose was needless war. War with Jaryar, to conquer their north-eastern province. This is wrong."

You "have warned?" How dare you?

The King's eyes gleamed. "I do not discuss strategy with children. Nor with the hem-lickers cowering behind them."

Krothon, who seemed suddenly to have grown a backbone, fluttered a hand. "Tonight you must, Your Grace. The Morning Queen and the Ten Families will not permit you, today or tomorrow, to start a war for Arbeth and Lefayr. Here are b'Shen, b'Nida, b'Olim and b'Astith represented, and I speak for b'Trai -"

"*Will not permit?*" Brechad's step forward forced Krothon back. He let his anger blaze through the room. "What is this treason? Five Families conspiring against the King, conspiring and boasting of it! Have you forgotten what Ricossa does to traitors? And to their kin? Siblings and children and *grandchildren?*" He heard the softer visitors gasp; saw them squirm. Good. This night would teach them a lesson.

The King came in smoothly.

"Thank you, Brechad. I repeat that I will not discuss strategy. Jaryar is our ancient enemy, and they remember that if we forget it. Nerranya is dangerous to us, and withholds what is ours. It is for me to defend Ricossa." As Rommi opened her mouth, the King, still calm-voiced, lifted a hand. "It shames me, little sister, to have to remind you, remind all of you, of the very basis of the New Governance. Our wise ancestors who signed its terms to end the most terrible war in history, would be shocked to hear what you have done tonight. Matters of crime and diplomacy are not for you, *madam*. This is our most fundamental law -" he rested his eyes on the Queen -"and your most sacred oath.

"Now, it is late and I have heard enough. You will all leave, and I will be gracious enough to forget this evening."

Someone's feet shuffled. The Queen looked scared. But to Brechad's amazement, "My sacred oath and yours," she said quietly. "I am not leaving. Your woman murdered Doctor Madrasun in Sapientia. The interference was yours."

"Sapientia? You mean that nest of fools, and worse than fools, who weaken and damage this realm?"

"No. Elder brother," she meekened her tone, "please. Why is this what you want? Queen Nerranya need not trouble us. For twenty years she's been a peaceable neighbour."

"Peaceable? The Jaryari?" cried Brechad.

"She is dangerous," said the King. He took a deep breath. "All of them, all - vermin - adulterous, filthy, lying -"

He's getting tired.

"Those are the Exile's spiteful lies."

Krothon said, "It's not treason but honesty to advise the King. And to remind him of what the New Governance says he can and cannot do. The Evening King cannot declare war *or levy tax* without the consent of the Queen, and the Council of the Families. Wars are expensive. Here are four Families, and they will not pay, nor ask their people to pay, for such a war. We think the soldiers will not fight without coin and food."

So that's your little trick, is it?

"You want the Council of the Families to listen to b'Nida and b'Astith? About money? I think not," said Brechad scornfully. "If the soldiers disobey orders they'll be hanged. The Evening King will protect Ricossa."

"Yes, I agree," said the Queen. "And Ricossa includes Verndew."

"Verndew?"

The door banged open again.

*

Mej was standing by his great-grandmother's chair. They were just outside the circle of candle-light shining on two faces: the Queen's and the King's; one dark, one pale. Her hands were squeezed together in her lap; his clenched around chair-arms. Their Chamberlains stood beside them. Brechad looked as if he could knock Krothon down with a single blow of his clenched fist – and as if he wanted to. These four people stared at each other, and everyone else watched. Past Mej's shoulder poured the silent gaze of those behind and beyond him: the three servants (Yikkeri and two Voiceless); b'Nida and the other high folk; the two Guards by the entrance. He was cold.

Everyone jerked as the door was pushed open. More Guards stamping in, and dragging between them –

Oh God, please no!

Hridnaya and Mobira were pushed to their knees by the table.

"You were right, sir, about the closet," a thin pale woman said to the King's Chamberlain. She drew her knife, and with her free hand dragged Hridnaya's head back, so that blade touched throat. Her colleague did the same to Mobira.

"*There* you are, madam," said Brechad, with a grim smile. Then he glanced sideways. "Small and brown and ordinary – this is the rat who bribed Simoren!"

Hridnaya gave a tiny terrified moan. Wild thoughts ran through Mej's brain, but he didn't even have a sword.

The King wasn't listening. His eyes were fixed on the other woman on the ground, his granddaughter, Mej remembered.

414

"What did they do to you?" he whispered.

"Mobira came to us freely," said Krothon.

The Queen managed to make her voice irritated. "You two, put your blades away. Your prisoners cannot escape, and you make us all nervous."

The Guards didn't obey at once, Mej noted crossly, but glanced for permission first to the King, who ignored them; and then to Brechad, who nodded curtly, and said, "Wait outside." They stepped back, behind the great folk, and left the room (he heard the door shut) leaving the two people still kneeling and stared at.

"Forgive me, Your Grace," said Mobira into the silence.

Queen Rommi gestured, and Krothon held out a folded parchment. When nobody moved to take it, he placed it on the table. The King flicked it across to Brechad. "Well?" he said.

Brechad read out with contempt, "This is the true confession, made to ease my soul, of Mobira, daughter of Jentoretti, the King's agent in -"

The King uttered a wordless sound, reached and grabbed. With the other hand, he pulled forward a candle. Everyone watched him bend forward to peer at the writing. While he read, Brechad scowled at Krothon. Mobira stared at the floor, trembling. The Queen watched her royal brother, and Mej thought her face looked sad. He himself could think of nothing except how scared he felt. *Treason, he said. Do they burn traitors alive? Or worse? "And their kin"* – *not Aladim and Firi!*

Moments passed. The King's face creased. He made another inarticulate sound, and snatched at the parchment with tearing and trembling hands. They watched it crumple, and he tossed it onto the floor. Nobody moved. With an effort, he said, "What did they do to you?"

Mobira hesitated.

"I think you have to choose now, madam," said the Queen quietly, "which of us two you least wish to offend."

At last, looking sideways, "They did nothing. What I wrote is true. It was me – I wasn't forced. I wish to be clean."

"Clean!" exclaimed Brechad.

"I am betrayed," the King whispered. Mej thought his eyes glistened. There was breathing in the room.

The Queen turned to Brechad, and her voice faltered only slightly. "You see that there is indeed proof of what we say. Mobira arranged the false accusations and attacks on Kelji - but she also mentions a secret plan regarding the town of Verndew. Your Grace, this is what we were about to discuss."

"Verndew?" said the King's Chamberlain again. Mej heard faint noises of puzzlement from behind and the side. His heart beat very fast. *Everyone's wondering* - suddenly he remembered Hridnaya's message.

The kings voysless.

He took a small step back, not quite bumping into someone, and his eyes found the little old man standing by the wall with the map, gazing with wide and rheumy eyes at this extraordinary evening.

"Your Grace, where is Verndew?" One of the people they'd brought; Mej hadn't concentration to spare for her name.

"Verndew is a small village in our north-western mountains, some two dozen miles from the border. You sent Captain Achandor there, to take Nerranya's vengeance for her," said Krothon. He began to read. *"Take those you most trust to the village of Vermdew. These people are traitors in league with Jaryar, but are under the protection of powerful nobility and cannot be openly accused. Let none in the village escape the hand of justice.'* Sealed with the King's seal."

"The King's seal was stolen!" There was something in the Chamberlain's voice. "This is nonsense!"

"He didn't tell you?" asked Krothon; and sudden as toothache, he spun to his left. "That *was* what the King intended, was it not? You know this."

The Chamberlain spluttered, but no one watched him. They all, the whole room, stared at the insignificant Voiceless man who'd spent a lifetime listening to King Aigith's secrets. He stared back at them all, and his face crumpled.

"Did you hear plans for these murders?"

He looked about; he hesitated – and nodded.

"Kill him," said the King.

His tall Guard ran four steps from the door along the wall, and grabbed the old man from behind. There was a glint of metal, and a gurgling cry, and bright red spurted forward below his chin.

Someone squealed.

The man was thrown down on the floor. He gasped once, making blood burst out again; and he died.

"What – what have you done?" cried the Queen.

"And kill *them.*" The King gestured to the kneeling women.

Squeaks and flurries, and the Guard was marching forward, past the shocked women in their chairs -

"No," said Krothon.

"No!" cried Mej, and stepped in front of Mobira.

The Guard met him by the table. He grabbed her knife-arm by the wrist, and pushed upwards and back, with all his might. She tumbled awkwardly backwards – somebody cried out – Krothon stepped with hands wide and raised.

Mej grabbed the woman and held her still.

"Enough!" shouted the Queen. "Enough bloodshed, brother! We came to talk."

"To lie," the King gasped. He was leaning forward, one hand pressed to the front of his gown, and the other gripping the table.

"Give me that letter," said Brechad.

He'll destroy the evidence! But the Queen nodded Krothon to do so, and the other Chamberlain looked at it, lifting a hand to request, or demand, time. Then, "Let none in the village escape justice," Brechad repeated. "Protected by powerful nobility."

"Brechad," said the King.

"Your *Grace,*" responded the other. "A village in our north-western mountains. Verndew, east of Jinner. You ordered this!"

Mej was confused – and then suddenly, blazingly, he understood. The b'Iri mountains.

Brechad b'Iri.

A harsh man, a man whose anger terrified, and that anger was now staring at the King. "How many years has my Family followed you, and agreed with you? *Arbeth should be ours. The Jaryari are dangerous. We kill our enemies.* How many years, for *this?* So are b'Iri farmers your enemies, then?"

"Treachery –"

"No. She is right. You are mad. To kill our own people, to provoke – The Council will not allow this. The b'Iri will not pay for such a crime, such a war, and where b'Iri leads, the b'Met, the Council, will follow. You have made us take sides with them."

The Queen's voice was almost calm. "This afternoon your Cousins have already come near to provoking bloodfeud with the b'Astith. You cannot now make war without splitting the Families, and upsetting the Governance." More gently, "There are enough names on the Pillars."

"The Pillars! The Governance! You're all traitors, all!" The

King looked from Brechad to Mobira. With plainly a huge effort, he pushed himself upright. "No! Get out! Foolish – senseless - children! Arbeth - is ours! King Osgar promised – we need Arbeth! To be safe – I've waited too long." He bent forward, gasping. From his mouth came a thin noise, and a little wet stuff. "Ah – ah." His face twisted, and kept on twisting, and he was clutching his chest.

Perhaps the Voiceless man would have known what to do.

"Help him, one of you!" The Queen flung her fingers at the two Chamberlains. Krothon took one arm, and the young Guard the other, and they got him back in his seat. He leaned back staring at the ceiling, breathing in gasps and moaning a little, tears running down his face. His Chamberlain grimly lifted a cup to his lips.

Oh God, what do we do now? Is he dying? Have we killed him?

Mej saw the Queen's lips move, and she crossed herself.

It was Krothon who asked, "Has this happened before?"

Mobira whispered, "Twice at least that I know of – perhaps more often. The first time was last spring."

And then Brechad said with great bitterness, "He knew his time was short."

"Fetch a physician."

The King rolled his head in agonised rejection. "Not to this room now," said Brechad, and everyone glanced again at the dead man on the floor. "Be quick, madam, Your Grace. What do you want?"

"Oath-breakers," the old man muttered through his pain, staring at the ceiling.

"God has shown me that some things are even more important than oaths. I want peace, peace for all of us, and peace abroad if we can. We have stopped Achandor, and the King will not, must not, try anything like this again." She looked at the old man as he gasped. "Execution without trial is murder. Pay blood-money to your servant's family. The Jaryari will go home unmolested and with honour. And you will abandon this claim to Arbeth.

"In return – all the Families and the Archbishop knew I was coming here tonight, but I won't broadcast this evening's events to the whole Council. Or your schemes against our people in Verndew.

"But on your orders Mobira murdered Madrasun b'Olim, Doctor of the College, who deserved a better fate." She turned. "Lord b'Nida, Lady b'Olim, are you willing to give up vengeance and justice for him, in the name of our country's peace?"

They murmured consent.

"You will not hurt Simoren or his servant. You will make no more enquiries as to the events of this morning. Replace your seal." She stopped. A dead man still lay on the floor. Two women knelt by the table.

"This will be our agreement." A long time seemed to pass.

The King made a little grunt and moved his face. As quickly as that, it seemed, it was done. Mej and perhaps everyone in the room remade their pattern of how things were.

"We will write this, two copies, and all sign," said Krothon, with a would-be competent air. "And then we will leave you in peace."

It was the two Chamberlains who did the writing, which took a long time. Mej thought Brechad b'Iri, blank-faced, wrote a surprisingly beautiful hand. The King's breathing slowly calmed. His face was very old, waiting. As they held a parchment for him to scrawl a signature, he opened his mouth. "B'Olim wants vengeance for the old Doctor. Take it. Kill *her*."

Mobira gasped.

"She deserves death. But I won't kill her for what she did to please you. I'll make sure that you never have to look at her again – or at this other woman, who's under my protection.

"One more thing. Do not think this can be undone. Enough people know about it. Do not seek vengeance, for I value my people. And now, good night."

"Tell – me." His words were very slow. "Wise child who knows everything – you have ruled for a day. For twenty-nine years I guarded Ricossa. In 612, when I was anointed and crowned, Ragaris had seven kingdoms. Tell me, how many has she now? How many?" His words came quietly and with difficulty, but she did not answer or interrupt. "Jaryar has swallowed up Marod, and Falli has swallowed Baronda. Haymon and Falli claim to be free, but they do what she tells them. Three nations only are left. Three. Holy Defardu, and Jaryar, and us. Jaryar grows and strengthens, and this is not accident. Soon or late, she will cross the mountains." A tear crept out of each eye, and wandered down the pale cheeks.

"When she does, our soldiers will be ready," said Brechad. "And now I will have the floor cleared, and call your physician."

*

Question 38: How are great decisions made? Answer: by a few
people, in secret, in small rooms.

Hridnaya thought everyone was trembling as they walked back through the Palace, Guards either side of the Queen, and Krothon just behind her. She herself felt buffeted inside. *The King, that was the King!* She could still feel the Guard's knife against her throat.

It was getting late, and there were few people about. They took their pace from the Queen, and at first she walked slowly, but then faster and still faster, until she was almost running, and behind her the group began to straggle. They came at last back into the now-familiar little dining-room, and Queen Rommi grabbed up a large bowl. Yikkeri held it for her while she was sick.

There were people crowded waiting for them, attendants for the great ones of b'Nida and b'Shen, b'Olim and b'Astith who'd dared to respond to the extraordinary summons. Among them, Attar and Narrim from Scholars' Street spotted Hridnaya, making Narrim gasp.

One of the b'Astith servants said, "Is all well, my lord?" and received a curt nod. Then they were quiet. Lady b'Shen, frail and slow, came in last, leaning on Mejorad.

The Queen wiped her mouth, and sat down. She gestured, and Lord b'Nida and Lady b'Shen sat also. There was one seat left, but none of the others presumed. The stench of vomit hung in the room.

"I thank you all," she said, and her eyes met the lords and ladies one by one.

"Until tonight," said somebody, "I'd believed the Jaryari were the enemy."

"Indeed. But some in Ricossa think we need enemies abroad," said the Queen. "We sing filthy songs about Queen Nerranya so that b'Shen don't sing them about b'Astith or b'Met, and knife each other in the street."

"What remains now?" asked another of the high people.

"My lord, I think we all go home, and sleep. But with guards on the doors. After tonight, some will hate us all." It was Lord b'Nida.

As he stood up and held out his hand for his gloves, his eyes fell on Hridnaya. She didn't know what to do. She'd begun a curtsey before she realised that he wouldn't want the other

Families to know of any connection between them; and she stopped, hoping no one had noticed.

But the door opened before he reached it, and after a surprised moment, he made way for Brechad b'Iri and a Guard. The King's Chamberlain stared at him for several moments before turning to bow to the Queen. "Common cause with b'Nida," he said bitterly. "Strange allies."

Perhaps they're all thinking that.

"Indeed. I thank you, sir."

"Don't. My children may curse me for this softness in years to come. He's mad, but he's right in this. None of you know that the Queen of Jaryar and Marod hasn't got ambitions in the east. And if she hasn't, some day her grandchildren will. Do not thank me. What I came to say, Your Grace, was: he's sick, and I think this is finished, but I'm sending home for a guard for myself. Do you and yours need any?"

"Lord b'Nida had the same thought. I thank you, but I hope there is no need to fear - a moment. Lady b'Shen? Will you lend me your great-grandson to guard my room tonight?"

"Of course, Your Grace," and Mejorad bowed.

"But it's true that - Krothon here, for example. Some might think to use my Chamberlain to send a message. He has not deserved to be a sacrificial pawn."

"Ardan?" Brechad turned to the man he'd brought. "Protect him with your life."

The Queen nodded, and "Th-thank you, Your Grace," said Krothon.

"Very well." Brechad, the man who'd shared all the King's plots but one, looked round at them all. Then he walked out.

Lord b'Nida followed him, Narrim peeping back just once, and Hridnaya lost the last eighteen years, *again.*

People were turning towards the door. *Where am I going?*

Please not back to that cupboard?

Krothon handed a piece of parchment to the man who was apparently Lord b'Astith. "Show this to Nadya's guests. They need to know not to trust the man Vaddras. If he chooses to knife them in the night, we could still have war."

I should have thought of that! Hridnaya shivered.

"And what of me, Your Grace?" Only Mobira would have dared. She swept a curtsey that was perhaps less graceful than she intended. "I have served you tonight, as you commanded."

"Indeed." Everyone left in the room was still. "Well. I have promised him that he need not see you again, so you will never return to the Palace. Lord b'Nida and Lady b'Olim have released you from bloodfeud, but you will not return to Sapientia either, on pain of death. I will find something useful for you to do far away, but in the meanwhile…" She shut her eyes, a tired heavily-dressed plain woman sitting at a grand table. "I will write you a letter, and send someone to escort you to a monastery, where you will stay for a month. Try to find the repentance you pretend. Your grandfather loved you, and you abandoned him when you realised he was dying. You told us this afternoon that he trusted no one, and thought people only serve a King for their own advantage. In your case he was right."

*

So for a second strange night Mej slept just outside the Queen's bedchamber, but this time it was at the outer door, and he lay in blankets across it. Cheery guards took shifts standing with their boots next to his head. When morning came, they heard Yikkeri opening shutters, and then she came out to fetch food. There had been no violence in the dark.

On her way back with her tray smelling tormentingly of bacon, she stopped beside him. "Perhaps you could wash your face and comb your hair, sir? The Queen wishes you to join her for breakfast."

Once again the bed was already made up smooth and perfect. He was beckoned to a place beside her, sitting in the window. As well as the bacon and ale, there was white bread, and the nut paste that she unaccountably liked - and his own favourite, eggs cooked in mushroom sauce. She'd remembered.

The Queen took a jug from her maid and smiled at her. "Can you wait outside for a little, Yikkeri?"

So the two of them sat together. Mej found he was very hungry. Also shy. He peeped at her between mouthfuls, wondering, and thought she looked tired. Then she yawned, and he jumped.

"Your pardon, sir. I didn't sleep well. There was much to consider and pray over. I couldn't sleep, so at last I distracted myself with other matters."

Is this what she's called me in for? "What matters?" he asked, forgetting her title.

She slowly lifted a crumbed finger to pat it clean with her tongue. "I thought of Gridor, son of Arro. Mejorad, truly, how did he die?"

"I don't know. I mean, Jed — Fejederic said he might have been poisoned before we met him."

"He claimed he was followed that night."

Oh, mother. Why do you always know? "He must have spotted us. Rorash and I – we were only bored. Rorash recognised him, and we wondered what he was doing there, far from his stall, and – we sneaked along behind for a few streets. It was a joke. I remember him looking over his shoulder, and swaying. We thought he was drunk. We meant him no harm." He saw again the black frightened dying eyes. He shuddered.

"Indeed. The trial is over, and nothing more can be done about his death. But his life interests me. I read the letter his priest wrote for him to Bishop Deborah. He was fortunate in Sister Felicity. She wrote it well." She smiled to herself. "Mejorad, in your history lessons, did you ever hear of King Arrion of Marod?"

"I don't think so."

"Arrion the One-Armed – Kelji had at least heard of him. He changed his country's law something like seventy years ago, so murderers in the west have two trials, or some such. A foolish idea. But there's one thing I've always admired about King Arrion."

"Your Grace?" *Is it permitted to admire foreign kings?*

"He made a change to the way things were. He seemed to think that kings shouldn't just sit in Palaces and give gifts, and make war or peace. The purpose of a ruler is to improve the world. To make life better, if possible, for everyone – or anyone, if needs be. Gridor wanted to do that, but Gridor wasn't a king."

"You – we can't change the New Governance," said Mej, feeling his way. *What is this – history, philosophy? For me?*

"No. And yet perhaps we broke it last night. And we barely succeeded. If Aigith hadn't taken that extra step, hadn't decided to betray his own friends – would b'Nida and b'Olim, would four Families have been enough? Perhaps. Perhaps not. But that extra evil was too much for Brechad, and we won." She shook her head, staring out and down at the inner garden, where two priests and a servant were talking. One of them waved her arms about, and laughed.

"Sometimes things need to change. I think I shall ask this Sister Felicity to arrange a memorial Mass," she said. "We could all pray for the soul of Gridor Flower-in-Hood.

"And now I must let you go home. Please say to Eyanda and to your Great-Uncle Yettrid that her son has served me well. Thank you, Mejorad."

"Your Grace." He was about to stand, when she coughed, a shy please-wait cough, unlike her.

"I," she said. He looked at her dark round face. "I was a disappointing mother to you, Mej."

They were forbidden words. His body tingled. "No," he began, and then, "I disappointed you." Because he never had, and wouldn't have the chance again, he said, "I know every time you looked at me, you remembered -" He couldn't go on.

Her hands were tensely-flat on the chair-arms. She shook her head a little. "At first I did. I couldn't feel for you the way I felt for Annamet – for any of your sisters. I couldn't love you happily, with play and kisses, like Eyanda does Rorash. I hoped it would be enough to love you with duty. I tried to be kind."

"You were kind." He jumped up, and found himself walking about, his feet making a small circle. "You gave me a good stepfather."

"Yes." They both thought of Skandar, a gentle man who had died too soon. "I meant to do my best for you, but sometimes I've thought – you might have done better, been happier, if I'd given you up to be fostered as a baby."

Fostered by whom? Would he still have been a b'Shen? She would have chosen a kind family. It was too much to wonder.

"But what I also thought last night was, if I had done that," she swallowed and looked down, "we might now be on the brink of war."

"I didn't stop the war! You did that!"

"You marched into the Palace, and made me look. You showed me Kelji, and brought me Hridnaya, and knew about Verndew, and made me trust Krothon. That was you. Thank you."

Mej couldn't speak, so he bowed. She stood up.

"Are you soon to be a priest? Do you hate the thought?"

The sudden change of subject was again unlike her, but

perhaps she was thinking, as he was, that they would never be alone again.

"I likely am. I don't hate it so much as I did." Priests help people, and some of them even wield swords. And no one pokes into why a priest chooses to be celibate. Trying to smile, he said, "I'll preach the words of St Micah that Whatwashisname threw at us – about kindness and justice."

Her face lifted in a smile, reminding him of Rorash. "The Prophet Micah, I think you mean. Old Testament."

"Oh. Yes, Your Grace."

*

Hridnaya woke in confused darkness, thinking herself a child again, listening to the breathing of her brothers and little sister. But why was she so scared? Then she remembered that she was lying on a pallet in the servants' dormitory at Nadya b'Astith's, with four other women in their beds above her head. No one was hurting her. For the rest of the night nothing bad happened except waves of sickening terror (*"Kill them"*, *a blade on her neck*) and almost equally sickening guilt. *The man on the floor. I pointed to him, no one would have involved him if I hadn't –*

She longed for the dawn.

In the morning she was provided with water and mizzum, and then the steward thought hard before directing her to the spindle, a never-ending task in any house. She learned that Nadya's injured servant was recovering well, but that Jedder had lost a lot of blood, and was being nursed and worried over by his wife and her maid in the room downstairs, the one on the other side of the hall. Also, surprisingly, that Ittrad was here. Ittrad, "mortal or angel" - or even Prophet. Nathan to Mobira's David.

Two days passed. She sat spinning in the corner of the room where Kelji had given her her first reading lesson. It was a place Nadya and others passed through or chatted in, generally ignoring her. There were curious and faintly hostile looks from servants and guards, and especially from Nadya's own Voiceless, an old man called Moyder. Already eerie to the others, Hridnaya was an alien, somebody else's secret-keeper, and one who'd disobeyed the rules.

She wouldn't have dared to send a message to Jedder, Kelji, or Ittrad, even if she'd been able to, and she wasn't. She had no permission to enter the sick-room, and Ittrad had apparently been put to work checking and sorting old accounts somewhere upstairs. Servants, and especially visiting servants, stay where they're put. Occasionally he manoeuvred himself downstairs for some task with quiet grunts, and they smiled uncertainly at each other. The first morning she saw Vaddras the foreign groom carrying a box – and then she didn't see him again.

What the Queen had done had never been done before. She tried to understand that this had happened, and that she'd been part of it., the Battle of the King's Supper.

Am I to blame for that man's death? She'd never know his name. It would have been so good to have a friend to talk to about that. And about Uncle Gridor, and his sad – now horrifying – death.

But it seemed she herself wasn't after all – after *all* – about to die. She must be very grateful for this.

She sat for a long time conscientiously thanking God while she worked, and then found she was cold, and crying.

Why? What's wrong with me?

As the second afternoon wore on, she imagined herself back in her own old room in Scholars' Street. (She missed that private place, spoilt as she had been, where no one would see her tears.)

Inside her head, she sat in front of her piece of carpet, and opened the Box.

Questions 35 and 36: What do I know about Uncle's death? What can I do?

Answer: He was murdered, I'm almost certain. I can do nothing.

Question 37: How do you stop a bad king?

Answer: It can sometimes be done, if people work together. But the New Governance shouldn't have made it so hard.

And now, Question 38, or is it 39: What is going to happen to me?

Answer: That must depend on Lord and Lady b'Nida. "I shall have you hanged, as you deserve," he said. But he did seem to believe my explanation. Can they forgive me? They won't want me to work for any of their rivals, but they might let me come back home. I can't forget how to read, so I can't be a proper Voiceless, but I could do other work. I think – I do think – that if he tried to send me to a farm again Krothon b'Trai and Mejorad would make sure it was a real farm. She swallowed.

Or perhaps one of them might find a little place for me in the Palace kitchens, or something like that. Or just let me go and look after Brin's children. (But he's lost his place, and can't even keep his own

family!) Or Gardyish's. Please Lord help Brin and Lulet.

Maybe I can get my baggage and money back from Stansha's, now I'm not supposed to be dead. That would pay for my keep for a while.

I think the Families will find somewhere to put me, a place to be. I'll have a bed and food. My life will have a pattern again, which is

good.

So, you fool, why are you whining? What have you lost?

If I don't go home, I lose Narrim and everyone there.

Though I might still see them at church.

I'll lose books. The memory of the morning at the inn on the road blew through her, unbearably sweet. *I was mad, I planned to read every book there is, think every thought – and I never will.*

And it's not just books. Tucked into her bodice was her last scrap of parchment. When that was gone, she'd be back to grunts that people who knew her understood as long as she wasn't saying anything unexpected.   Parchment and pens are expensive, and in any case Brin and Lulet couldn't read.

It doesn't leave me worse off than I was before.

I'll lose the sunset on the beach, but I can always remember it.

As evening came on, and people around her were laying tables for supper, she remembered the b'Oto Voiceless, the one who'd been taken on a delightful journey as a reward, and killed himself when he came back. *I think I know why. He was content before – had made himself content – but going away had shown him all the other ways there are to live. Travel and choices and sky – marriage and children and conversation. All the things we can never have. He'd discovered the world outside the b'Oto house, and then he'd seen the darkness closing back in. And he could share it with no one.*

Oh, Lord, she thought, gulping down the sobs that no one must see, *help me to be grateful for my life.*

*

There were still two guards outside Nadya's house, hands on swords. One wore the blue b'Astith tabard; the other the white and gold of the Palace. Sending a message, Mej supposed.

Inside, Nadya smiled up at him from her desk. "I have an invitation, madam, for you and your guests, including the servants – and also a letter for you."

She led him into a room to the right, where he'd never been before. Kelji was sitting at a table, writing something, and Jedder rested on a settle by the wall, sharpening a pen for her. His jacket hung open to allow for the bandages bulking his shirt. He looked pale and tired and wary, Mej thought, but cheerful.

"Imadal, fetch our two other guests. Be welcome, Mejorad," said Nadya, following him in. "Wine?" She looked at the letter he'd given her, recognised the hand, and moved towards the brazier.

"Please, madam, read it." Eyanda's fury and misery were making a nettle-patch of his home.

She scowled, but cut round the seal to unfold the message, as he asked, "How are you, sir?"

"I can move everything, so I'm getting well. We – I haven't yet thanked you for helping us the other day. I'd like to learn the trick of leaping into a fight from a roof."

Mej smiled humbly. He was still wondering about Jedder.

Nadya looked up from her letter. "Your mother claims she doesn't understand why she's no longer welcome in this house." They stared at her back, as she threw it into the flames. "She begs my forgiveness for choosing her son's interest and safety over that of my guests. She forgets that her son is merely living in Defardu for two years. My guests would have been dead."

They all waited with pity until Eyanda's pleas were ash. She turned round and shrugged. "How is the city today?"

"I think much as usual." Yesterday the extra guards at certain houses had caused many tense whisperings. They were still there this morning, but the peaceful continuance of markets and church bells reassured.

"Who is it we're waiting for, please?" asked Kelji, always impatient.

Nadya had to explain who Ittrad was, and what he'd done – making Jedder laugh, although it looked as if laughing hurt. "That's a tale – the limping angel of City Qayn!" he was saying, as the two servants entered. They looked humbly at the floor; but by now Mej knew enough to distrust humility in either of them. Ittrad's round face was blank as unshaped dough, but Hridnaya looked nervous. Jedder smiled at her; Kelji did not.

Instead, "Sir?" she asked Mej, with her sweet voice and taunting look. He'd forgotten how uncomfortable she made him.

He recited, "Krothon b'Trai, the Queen's Chamberlain, has sent me to invite Nadya b'Astith, Kelji, daughter of Shanell, her husband and all their party, to a small dinner in their honour at the Palace, in two days' time, Monday 3rd September."

"Oh, my," said Nadya, blinking pleasedly.

But Kelji said, "Will we be coming back again? And after that, be permitted to leave City Qayn? Do we need to take guards, or will the Queen send an armed escort?" She really was abominably rude. But he remembered her scrambling into the cart in Sapientia, sucked at by enemy eyes; remembered also the scaffold in the Square, and he didn't know what to say.

"It's an invitation, cousin, nothing more," said Nadya gently.

Jedder wavered a smile, and said, "The Queen honours us."

"And, madam," turning to Nadya but gesturing at the servants, "the Chamberlain says that 'all the party' includes these two." He'd been looking forward to surprising them with this, and he had.

But not Nadya. "I suspected they'd not be staying here forever. You lost your place at the b'Nida's, did you not, madam? Do you have other home, or any money?"

"She has the money she and my husband stole from from

433

Mobira," said Kelji. "A dozen gold pieces, was it?"

"Ssh," said her husband. "Something of that."

"Um," said Ittrad, who had no business interrupting. "Wasn't it eleven? Wasn't that the amount you sent the Judge?"

And that did surprise everyone, rather more than Mej had.

"*You* bribed Simoren?" Nadya stared.

Ittrad looked at Mej. "You remember, sir, just before the trial began, we couldn't find her."

"But I – we thought it was the Queen," said Jedder.

Mej said, "The Queen told us she could do nothing."

"*You?*" said Kelji slowly. "Then I – I perhaps owe my life to you?"

Hridnaya was staring, not at the floor, but at people's skirts and legs. She gave a polite little shrug.

Queen Rommi had realised, Mej was sure. *"I praised God for the act," she said.*

"I offer you my thanks," Kelji said slowly, graciously. With a grim smile she added, "I suppose that more than compensates for the damage to Paul's book."

"What damage?"

"Er, that was me, in fact," Mej decided to say. Ittrad looked politely interested, Nadya and Jedder puzzled. Hridnaya looked sharply up at him. Kelji froze. "You?"

"I didn't mean to – only -" and as before he made a knocking-over gesture, wondering why the room seemed cold. It was just a book.

She said slowly, "You stood there – you stood there and let me -" He saw that she was blushing. She jumped up and swished firmly forward four steps, until her face tilted down just above Hridnaya's. For an extraordinary moment Mej thought she was about to curtsey, but she didn't. "I see that I was unjust, misjudged you and wronged you," she said. "I ask your forgiveness. How can I make amends?" Hridnaya, obviously embarrassed, tried to smile. Kelji took a breath. "What do you need? Can you tell me? Give me some parchment," she added, turning; but the other woman was already pulling out a small piece. They all watched her walk to the table, take the pen Jedder offered, and write. Mej saw that her hand shook. He was shaking himself. He couldn't ever remember wanting so badly to get to confession, and kneel at the cross.

Kelji read out, **My brother Brinnon lost his plays and his family needs help.**

*

"She was here all yesterday, and I didn't know," Kelji said as soon as they were alone. She dropped herself onto a chair, and shoved away the report she'd been writing for the Queen and the Marshal back in Makkera. "Hating me, I suppose." *How I loathe being in the wrong.* "She saved my *life*."

Jedder gave her a maddeningly timid look from the settle that had become his. "Is it any comfort that I probably saved hers on the road? I don't know what Mobira would have done with her."

"Yes, it's some." Her heart lifted, and she found this annoying. "I hated Mobira the moment I saw her. One who makes her living by evil. You should've killed her. And Vaddras."

"That might not have been a good idea."

The timid look again, and she felt childish crossness. "I hate this country," she said. "I hate it so much."

"Why did you come?" Pertinent.

"The Queen sent me. Why did you?"

"Well - I got home from the Dendarry christening and the house was empty. They told me where you'd gone, and I thought," he made himself smile, "in twenty years' time I don't want us to be sitting by the fire together knowing that you've seen City Qayn and I haven't."

"You've seen Dendarry."

"It's a majestic house on a hill, but it doesn't compare. Oh, and Lida sends all the greetings that are proper, and reminds you to keep me out of trouble."

Kelji was silent.

His feet were planted on the floor, and he leaned forward, looking away and then back at her. "The house was empty," he said, and his voice had changed. "The Queen sent you because you asked her to."

Two days ago the b'Astith bone-setter had pushed a block of wood into his mouth to stop him screaming while the gash across his chest was burned shut with a white-tipped poker - and Kelji had gripped his hand and smiled at him while it was done. The hardest task she'd ever given herself.

Since then they'd exchanged stories simply, and argued about whether to give Vaddras any money before throwing him out. And his wounds were healing, thank God.

They'd said nothing about why she'd lied to him and abandoned him, running off on an errand that had nearly got them both killed.

Now, uncultured northerner that he was, he'd plainly had enough of empty politeness. Inside Kelji was still a heavy ball of pain, but on the outside every part of her skin tingled.

"So do you want to go home?" he said.

"D'you think I could stay here, where I hate everyone but Nadya?"

"Are we – are you -" He stopped, staring at the floor. The fire in the brazier snapped, loud in the quiet room. She didn't know if her silence helped or hindered him. At last, "But you went away. Are we going back to the same house? The same bed?"

Still silence.

"We – we can try not to have more children. Not until you wish – maybe not ever. We can try. I know where the herbs grow," and he managed to smile, up and across at her.

The bloody man was going to make her cry. Kelji hated crying.

"Are you asking me to come home?" *Asking* her. "You want me back?" Six months of shouting, slamming doors. And then hiding away from him and everyone. Breaking things.

"Yes. Of course I do. You screamed a lot, but I wanted somebody to scream. I couldn't. I want – I don't want you to be unhappy. But if you're going to be unhappy, be unhappy with me. I mean – I don't know –I don't know why you felt – what it was about me, about us, you couldn't endure – apart from Larelna…" It was Jedder who was crying. One, two tears crept down his cheeks. She could almost feel them tickle. He wiped them away with the fingers of his unbandaged arm. If he opened his mouth, she'd see the gap in his teeth that Larelna loved to poke her finger in.

It was hard to say it, but she had to. "I'm not unhappy with you. That's why – I ran away because you make me happy. I can't bear to be happy, going *on* and leaving her behind. Forgetting." *My darling, my baby.* Even the pain was so old and tired.

"But," he said, and stopped. Then, tentatively, "Kelji, d'you remember when she was born, and you said we could name her Meribet, after my sister? Even though it's not a Jaryari name."

Jedder had been eight years old when his baby sister, and his father and his mother, had died of fever in three days.

"Mm."

"That was so lovely of you, so generous. But I said I didn't need that. Meribet was herself, and Lari was, *is,* herself. Always. And I don't know, Abbot Paul found me crying once, and talked to me, even if we did, forget I mean, she's still real. More real than we are. She's not left behind anywhere. I hope she doesn't forget *us*. Where she is."

"Holy talk," said Kelji, just as he'd sometimes complained to her.

"Holy talk." He wiped his face again, and smiled a little.

Kelji thought about it, and he waited, not entirely patiently, fiddling with the cords on his jacket.

"We're going home," said Kelji. "I have to keep an eye on you, and make sure you don't sleep with the maids."

She could hardly bear the relief on his face, as he said, not for the first time in their marriage, "I do not sleep with the maids."

"Imadal wishes you would."

"Imadal was very helpful, eavesdropping for me." Jedder was a fair-minded man. "But what about this lad Mejorad you've been running round the country with?"

"You're jealous."

"Of course I'm bloody jealous! If he even touched your cloak with one of his fingers, I want to cut it off him."

"You idiot. He's barely weaned, and I scare him."

"You scare everyone."

Except you, she thought. *The timid looks are a game between us. I think.*

But she was bubbling inside, and at last she could do it.

"Can you move over a little, husband?"

The three steps over to his settle seemed the most important she'd ever taken. She felt herself blushing as if she were naked, and he was looking at her as if she were. He managed to make space, and she sat down and kissed the fingers of his good hand. He stroked her face, and then her breast.

"I want you to be strong and healthy again very soon," she said.

*

Mejorad had said "small dinner", but it was a large room, and the table was set for – rapid calculation – twenty-three people. Some had already arrived – Lady b'Shen with her son Yettrid and great-grandson Mejorad; Lady and Lord b'Met. More streamed through the wide doors behind the b'Astith-Jaryari group. Hridnaya heard a voice she knew, and for a moment her skin went cold. "Madam Kelji, we meet in happier circumstances," Lord b'Nida was saying.

Ten heads of ten Families, accompanied by nine spouses or other relatives, sat down around the great oval table. A servant stood behind each chair to wait on them – none of them Voiceless, for this dinner was official. Guards and the additional servants, including Hridnaya and Ittrad, lined up neatly against the back wall. When all was ready, the Queen walked in, accompanied by the two Chamberlains, Krothon and Brechad, and a priest, who was there to give thanks. The King was too ill to attend. The feast began.

Hridnaya had seen almost all these great people before, though never all at once. Only Lord b'Iri was new to her, for b'Iri and b'Nida did not mingle. He was a surprisingly unimportant-looking man compared to his nephew Brechad, with square-cut grey beard and narrow eyes.

Ittrad perhaps knew only Lord b'Nida, and he was less used to such events. She felt his shock when he realised they would be standing statue-still for at least an hour, watching more fortunate people eat.

They ate, and they conversed, as great people who aren't

open enemies do at banquets. The Queen's many skills didn't include putting ill-assorted guests at instant ease, as Lindet could do, or indeed Aunt Miya. Everyone avoided the questions they really wanted, she thought, to ask. Like: *Are*

you really spies? Are the songs about Queen Nerranya and King Barad true? What happened with the King four nights ago? Who attacked you in the street, and am I suspected of involvement?

Jedder smiled awkwardly and said little. But for the first time Hridnaya understood why Kelji had been chosen for this errand. She ignored any undercurrents; she smiled and even laughed; and she calmly answered all the dull questions about Makkera's green Glory Cathedral, her journey through Defardu, and her exact relationship to the

Jaryari Queen and the b'Astiths. Hridnaya was more interested when she described the life of Paul of Lintoll, from his less than happy start in the service of a murderer, to his reorganisation of Lintoll Abbey, and his first notable book, a Commentary on Psalm 104. Then he'd become absorbed in the "Blessed are the poor" paradox. Lord b'Nida stepped in to explain this word, and went on, "All of us at the College are delighted by the Queen's gift. I think my colleague Bekonin is planning a lecture series."

Several people looked bored, and Krothon moved the conversation by asking, "And this was the Paul of Lintoll who was one of your Queen's delegates at the Great Council, madam?"

"Yes, he was one of four, with King Barad and – others."

"Ah, yes, I remember." It was the ancient Lady b'Shen, who'd been following the conversation with the aid of a large shell-trumpet and her great-grandson's whispers. "King Aigith sent me to the Council, to watch and carry words." Many people looked as if they'd heard this story before. "I do recall the Marodi Abbot. A fat man who tripped over his own feet. He had little to say, but what there was worth listening to."

"My husband was there also," said Kelji, and heads turned back. Hridnaya saw Lord b'Iri scowl.

"I was a child in Mistress Fillim's service, getting in everyone's way and contributing nothing useful." But the way Jedder's eyes met his wife's told Hridnaya for certain what till now she'd only hoped, and she was glad.

But, disagreeably, "You're speaking of the Council in Haymon twenty years ago where Jaryar stole all of the north?" said Lord b'Iri, and there was a tenseness suddenly at the table.

"That is not, sir, my lord -" Kelji began with an indignant breath, but she was interrupted.

"Young man." Lady b'Shen stretched a thin arm to tap Lord b'Iri on the shoulder. Courtesy to the aged forced him to turn and listen. "Nobody stole the north in Vach-roysh in 619. I was there. There was a full debate, and a free vote, and each side offered incentives. I carried the bargain our Evening King had struck with King Osgar and Duke Haras, to divide Marod, giving us Arbeth, and Jaryar the rest. So the Duke, with our help, was able to offer the Jaryari nobility war and conquest. But they chose Nerranya, they chose peace."

"That's why the King said Arbeth should be ours," said Mejorad indiscreetly, echoing Hridnaya's thought and solving the puzzle.

"Yes, Aigith's arrangement came to nothing. And as far as I understood at the time, Arbeth was not King Osgar's nor the Duke's to give."

"Nevertheless, my lady," said Brechad, showing teeth. "You tell us they chose peace, but still the result was Jaryari expansion."

The food was eaten, and Ittrad's stomach growled, but the polite words drifted on. Until at last Lord b'Astith rose and said, "Alas, time is passing, and I am old. Before I ask leave to seek my bed, may I offer a toast?" He lifted a cup, and the wine-attendant scurried to fill the others round the table. "In the name of the Families, I drink to our guests, Kelji and Fejederic. May God smile on them and their kin."

"Amen." All stood; all drank, even the Queen, even Lord b'Iri. Plainly this had been pre-arranged.

"You are most kind," said Kelji. "I would repeat the good wishes I've already brought to many of you from my Queen and my King. Their desire is always to remain in friendship."

She managed to sound sincere.

And the Queen, also without obvious sarcasm, said, "May your journey home be peaceable and happy. I know you have your own guards, but each of the Ten Families here has offered a trusted man or woman to escort you home to Makkera. On the oath of blood-protection."

Kelji bowed.

There was a chorus of thanks, and a confusion of gathering people and sticks and cloaks, and the guests departed, group by little group. Kelji and Jedder stood by the door for last formal farewells.

Ittrad was casting agonised looks at the table, but Hridnaya kept her eyes on Nadya for instructions. None came. The room that had been so full of wide skirts, elaborate gowns and decided voices grew almost empty. The b'Nida and b'Astith servants left, with Imadal and Narrim. But no one spoke or gestured to Hridnaya.

There remained Lord and Lady b'Nida, Kelji and Jedder, Nadya b'Astith. The Queen and her Chamberlain. A Guard at the door; and two hungry servants.

"Your Grace," said Kelji, as the door closed behind Imadal, "I am ignorant. What is the oath of blood-protection?"

The Queen was the only person still sitting at the table.

"You will have ten guards on your journey. They've been chosen already, and have sworn to protect you until you release them, in Makkera. If you or any of your people die before you're home, from any cause whatever, their lives are forfeit. It is a holy trust, and an honour."

"From *any* cause?" said Jedder.

"Do your Queen's Thirty not swear a similar oath, and for life?"

"Not quite the same. We are honoured." He bowed – and Krothon noticed how tired he looked, and waved him to a seat. This was the first day Jedder had been out of the house.

The Chamberlain went on, "This night is not over. The Queen wishes to thank all of you here for your help in the last few days. And in some cases, for your forbearance." He bowed to Kelji. "It has been a strange time, but we pray it's almost finished."

There were wise noddings. Nadya, Lady b'Nida and Krothon crossed themselves.

"What remains, however," said the Queen, "is you two."

And everyone's eyes turned to them, the servants left by the wall.

In the silence, the Queen poured wine into two cups. She moved briskly for someone of rank. "Please drink with me," she said. "Hridnaya, daughter of Haidi and Ittrad, son of Ambario. Your country owes both of you a debt. This cannot be said in the streets, so I am saying it here. I thank you."

Hridnaya was frozen with amazement, grasping her cup. *The Queen. If I had children to tell this to* – Ittrad spluttered, warning her to sip cautiously. The wine was undiluted, the way the rich drank it.

Queen Rommi smiled and stepped back, looking around. "How can we reward you? Where are you to go?" To Ittrad, "You are a student, I think? Do you wish to continue there?"

Ittrad slid his eyes to Lord b'Nida's blank face. "I am content at the College, my lady – Your Grace. I need nothing."

"But you have to work for your fees and your keep – you serve Doctor Dirria, don't you? I will arrange for all to be paid."

"You are very kind, Your Grace," he said slowly, "but I can work. I don't wish to surprise my fellows by being set above them."

"You want nothing?"

"You've removed Mobira from the College. That's enough for me."

"If you change your mind, sir, speak. Then we have you." Hridnaya felt the eyes in her turn. "I would offer you a place here, but I fear you wouldn't be safe. Some day someone might connect you with Simoren." Their eyes met, and Hridnaya saw kindness.

She didn't know what to do, or if she was meant to do anything. But she'd served the b'Nida for eighteen years, and she looked to the right, up towards her master and mistress.

"Come here," he said, and she walked over. Her back tensed and her fingers trembled. He glanced at his wife, who nodded.

"We now understand, and we accept," he said slowly, "that you intended no disloyalty to our banner when you crept into my privatestudy to look at my private papers. You had your own reasons, which were nothing to do with us. But still it was a betrayal. And you have disqualified yourself for your post."

"She served you for how long? Fifteen years, or was it more?" said Krothon.

Hridnaya, very familiar with his face, saw the faintest flicker of annoyance. He didn't like being pushed.

"You worked very competently for the most part. My wife

and I -" Lady b'Nida nodded again – "will take you back under our banner. You cannot attend the most secret meetings; we will find a new Voiceless; but there will be work for you."

Hridnaya heard a little noise from behind her, somebody's sigh.

Please let me be grateful. Please.

"Um," said Ittrad. "May I ask a question?"

Everyone turned, and Hridnaya, supposing herself dealt with, stepped quickly aside to her place next to her master. *Let me be grateful.*

"What question?"

Ittrad looked down at both hands wrapped around the head of his stick. "In my studies I haven't fully covered the New Governance. What does it say about the College?"

Krothon opened his mouth, but it was Lady b'Nida, the Chancellor, who spoke louder. "The first Morning King or Queen shall establish and provide a College of learning, to be erected on the grounds of the former Shore Palace, and here men and women of good parts shall be encouraged to learn and develop all lawful kinds of knowledge and skill to the benefit of the land and the glory of God." And paused.

"Thank you, my lady," said Ittrad, and then, "Your Grace. My lord. You spoke of *rewards*. Think how Hridnaya learned to read in two weeks, what she did and found in the archives. Was the College not founded for people like her?"

Hridnaya actually rocked with amazement, her own and everyone else's.

"Like her?" exclaimed Lord b'Nida. "She can't -"

"What can't she do?" It was Kelji. "She can do any number of things. If you don't value her skills in City Qayn, I'm sure my Queen would."

"Madam!" said Krothon, horrified; but suddenly he almost

laughed. "We've just spent a great deal of trouble proving that you and your husband are *not* spies. We cannot permit a Voiceless to leave Ricossa. But, Your Grace, I see no reason why she couldn't study in Sapientia. 'Men and women of good parts,' as the Chancellor says."

When am I going to wake up?

Lord b'Nida, slowly. "It cannot be done."

"Why not?" His wife looked at him, her eyes passionless as ever, but with a hard smile on her face. Lord and Lady b'Nida were allies, but not friends. "She was never stupid. I think it an excellent idea." And she looked at Hridnaya almost with kindness.

"You think we should send a Voiceless freely into the world, with all she knows of us, and able to tell anyone?"

"But she won't tell," said the Queen, and her eyes flicked to Hridnaya and back to the Lord. "Last Wednesday night, we tested her loyalty by accident, and she was faithful to you. Perhaps more faithful than you deserved." She met his gaze, and Hridnaya watched him understand her meaning. She saw also his anger, and the way it changed to shame; and she was embarrassed for him.

"Studying costs money," he said, a sulky grumble.

"Indeed," the Queen answered. "The College is mine. Hridnaya, it's growing late, and I think you are hungry. In recognition of your service to me and to Ricossa, the Palace will pay for you to live and study for two years - or seven, whichever seems appropriate. After that, if you have been successful, and you have betrayed no secrets, you may come to my Chamberlain to ask for work. If this is your wish?"

Hridnaya's eyes were full of tears, and she could see none of the people in the room. She could only see books.

*

It was St Ansha's Day, a great festival in City Qayn, and

446

the Church of Holy Mourning was full. Many, several dozen, Mej thought, who might normally have made unholy holiday on such a day, or merely stayed in bed, had been tempted out to attend Mass, and even to attend it in this obscure church. For the Queen herself was there, sitting at the left in front of all, in a grand chair probably borrowed for the occasion.

Mej stood with Eyanda and her maid and Tor. Eyanda had peered about very obviously until she found Nadya, over in a corner with the Jaryari; and Mej, rocking on his toes, was looking for Hridnaya and her brother. He couldn't see them, although he just recognised Rorash's old sweetheart Yadiana, looking dutiful-holy, and for once without their child. And then he saw a little solemn group set aside on the right and sitting on a bench. Hridnaya, the sensible sister-in-law and her children, two youngsters (one in nunnish garb) and an older woman twisting her hands together. Abruptly he remembered Flower-in-Hood's wife and family.

The first prayers were over. An acolyte walked forward carrying a tall candle, to stand next to the pale-faced old priest, Sister Felicity, at the lectern. Mej was leaving for Defardu in two weeks, and was beginning to pay some attention to orders of worship. *Scripture reading next.*

But no. "Today we praise God for St Ansha-of-the-Sword-and-Cross, but we are also remembering Gridor, son of Arro, who died last June before his time, deeply mourned by his kin." She gestured, and heads turned to the little family, their faces blank with awkwardness. "He was an ordinary man, whose life changed eighteen years ago. Before I read from the prophet Micah, I present to you a letter that he asked me to write in his name, because he had no learning himself." The priest, hair bright red, face bright pink, lifted a parchment. Mej felt the surprise, almost disapproval, of the silent congregation. She began.

"2nd May 640 AL. Gridor, son of Arro, to Her Reverence Deborah Bargadi, Bishop of the City and South Lake, greeting. Honoured madam, your name is renowned in the city for holiness and charity. May your most excellent labours for the gospel and kingdom of God prosper on earth and be rewarded in heaven. I am most grateful to Felicity Mikana, priest of the Church of Holy Mourning, for writing my clumsy but sincere plea, as also for her prayers and counsel. Although I am one of the least account in your flock, I have been emboldened by prayer and long sorrow to lay a matter before you."

There were a few giggles. Mej clenched his teeth, suddenly imagining the two of them, ignorant pauper and nervous priest, putting this letter together last year - as polite and humble a beginning as they could possibly make it, before they began to be so terribly impertinent.

"It is on behalf of people like my niece. Her tongue was cut out in the year 623 when she was twelve years old, because she would be more useful to one of the Ten Families without it. This is permitted by law and custom, and by the New Governance, but I ask simply: is this harshness necessary?

"If I give my wife a secret, she keeps it out of love. If my master gives me a secret, I keep it out of loyalty.

"My niece, my sister's daughter, is a sinner like the rest of us, but she was a well-disposed and loving child – not over-talkative, but merry and clever. From when she was six years old, she could invent riddles, and recite old ballads to cheer our family firesides and make us laugh. She can never do that again. However long she lives, she will never be able to tease her twin brother, or tell a lad she likes him, or give her name.

"I believe the Family are kind to her, and they did not trick her. I have no complaints against them, and she has most certainly made none. But I will grieve for her voice till I die."

Mej didn't hear much more of the letter. When it ended, there was a single titter, and then silence. Sister Felicity rolled up her parchment. Then a sigh of surprise went round, as the Queen stood up. She marched to the centre of the church and bowed towards the altar. From the other side a woman in a Palace tabard carried forward a small table on which were – what? A clay bucket and a bag? *Mother, I mean Your Grace, what are you doing?*

The servant, whom he'd seen before but wasn't Yikkeri, looked very scared. The Queen's voice began low and nervous, but she steadied it. "Sister Felicity's letter was written fifteen months ago, and it recently fell into my hands by chance. I read it, and I thought about it, and I enquired about this Gridor. He died on 19th June last. Rorash b'Shen struck the blow, and has paid the price, but clearly without intent to kill. We will never know if there is more hidden behind this curtain. Be that as it may, I read what you have just heard, and I made enquiries about his life.

"This man wanted to change the world, something we do not approve of in Ricossa. This is strange, I think, because we are the people who founded the Great College, desiring to seek greater knowledge and wisdom than we now have. Yet for some reason we are afraid of proposals to alter the way things are.

"But in any case we certainly do not approve of such ambitions in men like Gridor, ignorant and poor as he was. Many of us have seen him going about over the last eighteen years, and laughed at the flower on his back. Few people asked him why he wore it, and let him explain. And of course many of us here have Voiceless servants, as I do. This is Jeril, daughter of Doumi." She gestured to the woman by the table, standing with bowed head.

"Like Gridor's niece, Jeril will never again be able to give her own name, or ask a man to dance. She came to Mass today, but she cannot recite the responses, or even the Creed.

"Is this harshness necessary? We say we need the Voiceless. What we mean is that our petty secrets are more important than other people's lives.

"The New Governance permits this, but it does not command. I lay in my bed a few weeks ago, and I thought of all the words I speak, all the uses I have for a voice, for a tongue. Perhaps you may wish to do the same." She paused. "And in the morning I made a vow to God. I will never instruct anyone to be made Voiceless, or to allow it done in any house of which I am mistress." She nodded to Jeril, and the servant scooped soil into the bucket on the table. Sister Felicity walked over with a flowering plant of some kind, pink petals dripping, and the Queen put it into the bucket and patted it down. "I won't wear this flower on my back, because I'm less brave than Gridor Flower-in-Hood. But I will keep it as a reminder. That is my offering to God this holy day. And now, Sister," with a gracious nod to the priest, "I have trespassed too long. Please continue with the Mass."

*

Had anyone understood? Had anyone cared? Mej looked around as they all wandered out into mid-September chill, and he saw a few sober faces, but perhaps no more than usual. Gusts of cold slapped cheeks and lifted the edges of cloaks. In the slow post-church scattering, he edged away from Eyanda and Tor, searching with his eyes. *There* was Hridnaya, with her sister-in-law and the two children, but he still couldn't see Brinnon. "Fetch Nadya b'Astith," he told Tor, and began to push up to them as politely as he could. The little girl recognised him, and responded shyly to his smile.

"Greetings." To Hridnaya, "Was your brother not well enough?"

The woman (Lulet?) answered timidly, "He is recovered,

450

thank you, sir, but he's working today."

"He's employed again? I'm glad." (The tailor Hanno had already been visited by Kelji and Nadya before Mej got there, and all this must have had its due effect.) "I have something for you," he said to Hridnaya. "Can you come?" She followed him, and Lulet uncertainly followed her, and they met Nadya, Kelji and Jedder by the wall of the church.

Mej manoeuvred the parchment out of his satchel. "Take good care of it." He watched her unroll it, and with great pleasure saw her eyes shine as she understood its meaning. "It was Kelji's idea." An order, formally made out and sealed, instructing any and all City Qayn and Sapientia merchants to supply parchment and writing equipment to Hridnaya, daughter of Haidi, for the rest of her life, at the expense of the Families b'Shen and b'Astith.

She curtsied again, and made grunting "Thank you," sounds. Everyone smiled.

Then after a slightly awkward pause, "We wish you well for the future," Kelji said, and Mej realised that this was goodbye for several people.

"May I wish both of you a good journey to Makkera? You leave on Monday, I think?" There were still enough people about for misdirection to be useful. They were really leaving the next morning, with their ten-strong escort. Just in case.

"Yes, thank you. And soon you will also be going west? I wish you well also, Brother Mejorad," said Kelji. "Have you chosen a priestly name – you do that in Ricossa, I think, as we do?"

"Yes, I mean yes we do, and no, I haven't." He'd never really liked the name Mejorad.

"I complained to you once of the constant bell-ringing in Vachansha. But it's only for two years."

Only. "Mm. Fare well." He bowed. He'd been waiting

nervously to do this for some time. "It has been a privilege, honoured madam. And Master Fejederic Queensbrother."

Two surprised and amused faces told him that he'd been wrong after all. His face burned. "Are you not a Queensbrother, then? You come from Marod, and you know the Queen, and you fight."

"Yes, and I squired for a Queensister long ago, but now I live in Jaryar. When Queen Nerranya came south, she left our strange customs behind. The Queen's Thirty guard Prince Gonnach in Stonehill."

"Oh." He would never understand how Marod could be ruled by the Jaryari Queen without being part of Jaryar.

"But I'm truly flattered by your mistake, sir. Mistress Fillim and Abbot Paul would have found it very surprising."

"I don't. Not at all," said Kelji. Her husband leaned across to kiss her lightly by the edge of her hat. "This is a public place, you barbarian!" But she was laughing.

Mej ("Ugh") looked away.

Nadya followed his eyes, and they both spotted the same person approaching. So, "Forgive me, but my cousin is waiting for us to eat," she said, and with very few more words the Jaryari were hustled away, Jedder looking back for a last grin. Eyanda stopped and stared after them, and Mej wondered a little sadly whether her love would outlast Nadya's indignation.

But then Hridnaya touched his sleeve. She made the Voiceless "request" gesture that he knew from home, and turned to the other woman with a gathering motion of hand and eye. Lulet looked first puzzled and then scared, but said, "Sir? I beg your forgiveness, but I think my sister-in-law is inviting you -" vigorous nods - "to our home for a cup of ale, or - something."

She must be staying with her kin while her place at the College was arranged.

He'd been planning to go to today's pageant. It was a ritual, standing in the raucous crowd, swilling ale, and cheering St Ansha's great victory over the pagan hordes. But it wouldn't be the same without Rorash, and he didn't mind being kind to Hridnaya, to Flower-in-Hood's niece. Her cloak had an elaborate design of flowers on the back, and he suddenly realised why.

So he got rid of Tor (at least in Defardu he wouldn't be accompanied everywhere) and the little party set off together – an odd group who received curious looks from the crowds heading for the entertainment in the Great Square. Hridnaya carried the wriggling younger child. She stared downwards, rather solemn, as if she thought she might be making a mistake. The older one looked up at Mej-the-rich-person with round eyes. "Good afternoon to you, my lady," he said, and she giggled.

"I think you came to our house before."

"Yes, once."

"I think you had a fight with that foreign man who gave us money, from the west."

The child's mother looked even more nervous.

"Yes, I did, but we're friends now."

The family's room was smaller than he'd remembered.

Brinnon was sitting bent forward over a table strewn with cut out pieces of cloth, but he pulled himself up with a face of welcome - turning to scared surprise. "Please come in, be seated, please." He was moving still with discomfort, Mej thought, and raising worried eyebrows at his wife.

"Hridnaya has a guest. Please sit down, sir."

Mej was gestured to the only chair. Brinnon poured ale for everyone, and then he and Lulet sat squashed together on a small bench. Hridnaya was standing stroking her niece's hair.

It was time to be courteous adult b'Shen. "I was very glad to attend the Mass for your uncle, sir. I hope you and yours – and his family also – are better?”

“My husband is almost well, I thank you. And we learn that Hridnaya is to do great things, and live in Sapientia.”

“And your late uncle’s family? Do they have enough?”

Brinnon answered this time. “Miya – my aunt – is working hard, and planning to marry again. His name is Treveth – he and his sister run the tavern where she works. It’s a good match for her. Her daughter Gita is taking vows at the All Ways Monastery.” (“She’s going to be Sister Phoebe,” interrupted the girl. “Ssh.”) “And her brother’s not in any trouble, at least. And, sir, I believe I have you and your friends to thank. I – I seem to be the most sought-after tailor in the city.” *So busy*, Mej thought, *that he’d been unable to come to his uncle’s memorial Mass*. “I – we – are very grateful.” Speaking fast, “I ask your pardon for my unforgivable words against you and your cousin.”

“I understand why you were suspicious and angry,” said Mej hastily. He wondered why Hridnaya had brought him. One never knows what the Voiceless are thinking.

But she’d found another piece of parchment, and now she folded over a sleeve on the table to give herself some space.

“What are you doing, auntie?”

“These are words? But you can’t do that,” said Lulet.

She passed her writing to Mejorad.

I beg your indulgense but I wish to tawk to my brother and hoped you coud read for me.

After all this time, her impudence could still surprise. *You brought me here for that?* She seemed to read his thought, and made the request gesture again, pleadingly. Her relatives looked puzzledly from one to the other, perhaps speculating if he - if he’d seduced her, or something –

He recited her message.

"What – what d'you want to talk about?"

Uncles death.

Her hand was shaking.

"Oh, Hridna, no! Not still!" exclaimed Lulet. But Brinnon stood up slowly, clenching his fists, and his face was dark.

Is this a trap? Mej almost reached for his sword. She was writing again.

Rorash b'Shen ment no harm but I have thorts. I may be rong.

"He *was* murdered?" asked her brother.

I think so but we can do nothing about it.

"I don't care. I want to know. Whoever it was – the Families, or the Cousins, or whoever – I won't do anything rash, I promise."

Lulet laid a restraining hand on her husband's arm. He touched his head to her shoulder, scowling. Then he looked up at Hridnaya, and Mej, who was tingling. *I thought we were finished with all that.* "Go on then, Hridna. We're ready."

She wrote for a long time.

Jedder from Makkera sujested poison. I found a book about poison. There is one cawled menatol. It confuses a person and makes them seem drunk and in a little time it kills you if you have enuf but not at once. He coud have been given it hours before. Being pushed down would make it work faster.

Mej read this out. "I suppose he did look drunk, when he came in."

"Who gave it to him? Someone at the College – or even on the way there? All those people spying on him!" Suddenly

Brinnon said, "I don't want you going to that place!"

Hridnaya gave him a quick smile, and then back to her scrawl. **I dont think anyone at the College ment him harm. But why woud anyone? Why woud the families?**

"He caused trouble."

Not much truble. Why kill him?

Brinnon shrugged, tears in his eyes. "I don't know! People were watching him! They were!"

Yes. At the trial you said you and uncle saw a man with a stic one night following. And you said he told you he or his house were wached by a man a different one and also a woman.

"Yes."

And Aunt Miya said he told her of a woman with a pale face. And that she and he together saw a woman one night perhaps that same woman.

"Yes."

A woman called Mobira who worked for high people (Mej thought she was wise to be vague) **told me she wached the house. She is a bad person and she has killed more than once. She uses poison.**

There were gasps as Mej read this. Lulet put her hands to her mouth. Brinnon stared at them, waiting for more.

But she is brown faced not pale. So that is four people two men two women spying on one man. It seems too many.

"Even one is too many!" said Brinnon.

The man with the stic you saw is called Ittrad. Doctor Dirria sent him to invite uncle to go to the College. He only came once and ment no harm. That leaves three.

"And one of those three was paid to kill him?" said Lulet, stroking her husband's hand.

No.

"No? But you said – mena-something."

I think Ittrad visited him and Mobira wached him. No one els.

"But Uncle told me there was another man – and both of them saw the pale woman! Uncle and Aunt Miya!"

They saw a woman. I think it was Mobira. No other woman. I think Miya lied.

"Why would she?" asked Lulet. Brinnon was staring. Mej heard Hridnaya breathing slowly and heavily, asshe wrote, **When I came back from Sapientia with Jedder we came here but we went first to Miyas. She was angry with me. There was someone els hidden behind a curtain. Miya cawled her Gita but I didnt see who it was.**

"But Gita's at the monastery."

Yes. Miya lied. Her face waited miserably. When everyone continued to stare, she began to write again. **What uncle saw was a straynge man at his house when he wasnt there.**

Oh! That's what you mean. He saw the moment Lulet

understood and said, "You mean you think she had a lover."

Brinnon made a little noise. "He's not been dead half a year, and she's getting married in two weeks! The banns are up!"

There was something remorseless but miserable in Hridnaya's face. She went on writing, while Lulet said, "When she – she told the Judge they'd never a cross word and all, you said at the time that wasn't true. They argued so much. She didn't like his flower and the way he lost work."

The people Mobira worked for wouldnot have needed to kill him but they would be happy for him to be dead if someone els did it. Maybe. He went to the College which is a long way and he woud have taken some food or drink for the jerney. From their house.

"No!" Brinnon cried, jumping up. "No, no, no!"

Mej tried to remember the widow, how she'd looked that morning. Her twitching hands. He felt his eyes pricking. "You think your uncle was murdered by his wife?"

Slowly, **I dont know. I think maybe.** She pushed away the parchment, and stood hugging her arms across her chest.

Distressed by something in the room, the little boy ran to his mother, who hugged him close. The girl crept away to sit by the fire alone.

"Who is this Mobira?"

"A bad person," Mej echoed. He sat still, staring at the torrent of words, wondering. Gridor's life destroyed, Rorash's blighted – it was nothing, almost nothing, to do with the Families at all!

Brinnon jumped up and thumped the wall with his fist. "By his *wife!* He was poisoned by his wife and her lover, like in some bloody fucking ballad!"

Maybe. Hridnaya had to nudge Mej to read the word.

"And if it's true, you said we can do *nothing!*"

The trial is over. If we coud prouv it it would excuse bloodfyoud if we killed her. I dont want bloodfyoud for Gita and Vren.

Brother and sister stared at each other across the room. His face crumpled, and Lulet went swiftly over to him. He buried his face in her shoulder and wept.

Mej thought, *I can find Rorash in Defardu, and tell him. It won't bring him home any sooner, but he'll be relieved to know. And maybe someone could make enquiries.*

He looked at Hridnaya, and saw tears trickling down her face. "The Queen promised this morning never to make anyone Voiceless. I think she hopes in time other people will agree. That's what your uncle wanted, wasn't it?"

She nodded, not looking at him. She scrabbled in a pouch, and took out a coin. It came up Heads.

*

The College provided mizzum for its own Voiceless, but it was embarrassing to be the only student needing it. Hridnaya walked to a dim corner and sat down on the edge of a bench, in the hugely long Refectory. There was a fire in one wall, but not big enough to warm the space. She looked along tables at the other students, almost all younger and much better-dressed than she, who were clattering and munching - and lowering voices to complain about one of the Doctors. Just like b'Nida servants grumbling about Jeruma's temper.

She'd woken that morning in a cell allocated to her alone, with bed, candle, stool and box; slightly smaller than the one on Scholars' Street. Her new home. Later, she'd sat on a floor (a cold

459

floor; *bring a cushion next time*) trying to understand what
Doctor Akraib said about St John's gospel. Some of the students
whispered or stared out of the window, but others copied bits
down. Hridnaya thought her best plan would be to listen hard at
the time, write the most important points later, and recite what
she could recall when alone, as she'd done with the trial evidence.

She hadn't yet been to the Library, but her body tingled
at the thought.

The first morning of a new pattern. She looked up and
down, trying to swallow, and wondered whether to send Balki
floating about to explore the ceiling. But perhaps she'd grown
beyond Balki at last. It depended on how lonely she was going to
be. Brin and Lulet and Narrim were a long way away.

She heard footsteps, and looked up politely. Ittrad was
carrying a bowl and a mug, cradled awkwardly to his side to
allow the other hand to hold his stick. He tilted his head in a
"May I sit here?" gesture, and she nodded "Yes."

His bowl was full, and there was a hunk of bread on top.
He lifted over a candle from an empty table, and took a piece of
carrot out of his pocket. After a munch, and a long swallow of ale,
he also brought out a folded parchment and a pen. It was friendly
of him, she thought, although she had her own. But as she
reached towards it, he began to write.

This one is for me. A good day to you, madam.

He picked up his spoon.

Hmm.

She wrote, **A very g d to y also.**

He wrote, **When did you arrive?**

Yesterday.

And how do you like the College? (*That is how you*

spell it!) **The place, and the people?**

The place is. She paused. **Like heven. Thank you. Thank y. It was your idea.**

It seemed the right place for y. And I need someone to talk to who can think.

The peepl - *No!* **people stare.**

Y are new and different. But someone with a memory like yours will be popular I think. Everyone will seek your help preparing for exams.

That was a strange thought. Another was that she seemed already to have a friend here. An actual friend.

She wrote, **Y dont need help. Your in your fifth year?**

Yes, and I'm stubborn. I don't take help from anyone. He was smiling.

Is that why y wouldnt let t Q give y money?

Probably. I don't like rich people's scraps. Tell me I'm stupid.

I dont want to be discerteus. But maybe y are.

Ittrad's eyes met hers over his bowl. **We can have a long argument about this, but is there anything y need to know today about t College?**

She shrugged, and then suddenly there was, a very small thing. **Why do all t Library books say tim dom init?** She couldn't remember the last bit.

It's Latin. It means t fear of t Lord is t beginning of

wisdom. They say it's from t Bible, but I haven't found it yet.
I don't know t Latin.

She couldn't resist. **I thort y new everything.**

Almost, in fear, she reached to scratch the words out. But Ittrad gave her an evil look. **I know how to spell <u>thought</u>,** and Hridnaya laughed.

He went on eating, and politely looked away while she spluttered down a last mouthful. There were perhaps a dozen other students, none of them paying her any attention, and she felt very happy.

He looked at her enquiringly. She wrote **I was thinking how pleased my uncle would have been that I was here.**

Yes, he answered. **I'm sorry I couldn't go to his Mass. Tell m about it.**

So she did.

Epilogue
Two Years Later

December cold nipped at ears, noses and necks, so the two young men were glad to push into the Grandfather's Folly tavern. Fat candles round dark-grey walls and on tables beckoned them into the unfresh warmth of people and fire. In one corner a man played a lute, while a handsome woman, no longer young, sang a sad but seasonal ballad about twin children who went sliding on thin ice. She sang well, and a few patrons were sniffling. There were at least two dozen people in the room. Grandfather's Folly was a popular place.

The newcomers ordered wine and water-to-mix from a brightly-scrubbed lad, and found themselves a bench with just enough space. Brother Jacob rubbed the shaven chin that he wasn't yet used to. His hair was trimmed to ear-length, and his gown was plain black, but some things do not change, so his fingers tapped on his thighs, or fidgeted with the swordhilt that most priests don't wear. *("We may need it.")*

Rorash was still neat and smart, in a blue gown with red sleeves, but his hair and beard were also shorter than they had been. He was silent as he looked around, and they both remembered the last time they'd sat together in a tavern.

Brother Jacob pulled the parchments out of his satchel, and flicked their corners. One signed statement by Mobira; one, unwillingly given, from Herion who sold physic and less savoury items down Bottle Lane; one written admission of what the physician Vreddo had failed to look for.

But what he said was, "How do they fare then, Yadiana and Jixi?"

Rorash smiled carefully. "All seems well. I met her new husband, and they've taught the girl to recognise my name. She didn't know me, but she will."

"Has the visit helped you decide about going back to the College? Unless of course they make you Evening King tomorrow."

"Don't say that, even in jest." King Aigith had died in his sleep three weeks before. The One Hundred and Two were gathering for the Conclave, and Rorash had been astonished to be named to the b'Shen delegation. "My future depends on what mother and Uncle Yettrid say. I hope to be around for Jixi. But some day, if God wills," he said more cheerfully, "I shall travel again."

"Back to Defardu?" *It's so cold, and everywhere is uphill. And the bells!*

"It was good for me, but there are other lands. Ragaris is a large place." And then he tensed. "Maybe we shouldn't have -"

The tavern singer had followed "The Ice Under the Moon" with "The Ballad of Faithless Raidar", but now she was resting her voice, and moving from table to table. "Welcome, my lords. We are honoured." She curtsied. "Is the wine to your liking? Do you have a favourite song I could sing for you?"

Rorash shrank back, almost cowering, his eyes large as he stared at her. Perhaps indeed they shouldn't have come. But Jacob said, "You don't remember us, madam? My cousin and I once met your husband in a tavern in Sapientia."

"I don't think so – Sapieintia?" Her puzzled frown was half a smile.

"Your first husband. It is Miya, daughter of Eve, is it not?"

"Oh." She remembered, and identified Rorash. "Oh, sirs, that is forgotten and forgiven."

Perhaps he would have said nothing after all, but the

464

word "forgiven" roused fury in Jacob. "A favourite song, you said? Do you know one called 'The Poisoned Husband'?"

She stepped backwards, hand half-raised. "How dare -"

"Mobira sent you to Herion, Herion sold you menatol, and Flower-in-Hood died." He spoke low, again flicking the documents Nadya and Eyanda had prepared for him. "Can that be forgotten and forgiven?"

"Let's go," said Rorash abruptly, standing up. To Miya, he said, "The law cannot touch you, because there was a trial, and I went to Defardu for your crime. But make sure no one else dies the same way. None of your kin, or friends – or enemies." He was already striding to the door. Jacob-Mejorad paused to make the first priestly pronouncement of his career.

"Go to confession – repent – and be made clean. Some time before you die."

They left her standing there, and went out into the cold. They walked back to the b'Shen mansion, where Jacob had to explain why there was a geranium painted on the wall by the front door.

Extracts from Hridnaya's Box of Secret Questions

Question 1 (aged 12): Will it ever stop hurting?
Answer (eventually): Yes.

Question 2: How can I love Brin, when I never see him?
Answer: I will see him sometimes, and can always pray for him. But my life is here now, serving the b'Nida.

Question 7 (aged 15): Bakker and Sister Judith and the priests are always talking about our duty to please God by obedience to the rich and highborn. Could it be that the highborn people of long ago *invented* God and the Bible and the Church, in order to make us obey? (Merciful God, please don't send me to hell for this thought. Please.)
Answer (aged 16): I have listened for the last year, and there are many verses of Scripture that speak on behalf of the poor. And our Lord became a servant. So that must mean that the poor and servants are important to God, even though the rich try to hide this and explain those verses away, and so He can't be just their lie.

Question 12 (aged 21): Will I ever have a friend or a lover, apart from Balki?
Answer: It is possible, but not likely.

Question 15: Which is the most powerful Family?
Answer: I've noticed that the b'Iri are the ones everyone fears most, because they shout at Council meetings about war, and they're close to the King's Cousins, who thrash people. They have power to hurt, but maybe there are other kinds of power. Lord

b'Nida says the College has power to make discoveries. When Narrim is kind and makes the kitchen a happy place, that is power too.

Question 24: Do rich people want different things from the poor?
Answer: Surely everyone wants to be as comfortable and loved as they can be, and also wants the people they love to be safe. But rich people want more – or perhaps merely expect more - than this.

Question 28: Does God want me to care only about my duty in this house, or does He have any other purpose for me?
Answer: I don't know. I hope so.

Question 34 (aged 30): Does a poor person receive the same justice as a rich one?
Answer (after the trial): Sometimes. It depends on the judge.

Question 37: How do you stop a bad king?

THE END

The Origins of "The Servant's Voice"

*On 27th September 2018, I posted on my blog
(www.penelopewallace.com/blog) a few thoughts about the third
Tale*

from Ragaris, then being revised for publication:

Where is it coming from, and where/when is it set?

The country of Jaryar first appeared in the unpublished volume
called "People of Makkera". Jaryar was always on the brink of war
with another country called Ricossa, which at that time was more
warlike and more formal in manners, and ruled, oddly, by two
monarchs. (This isn't unknown in history.)

Remembering Ricossa when I was writing "We Do Not Kill
Children", it occurred to me to wonder why Marod, even at a time
of internal turmoil, managed to have such a peaceful eastern
border. I casually solved this problem by providing Ricossa with a
civil war (The War of the Throne, 568-575). This is referred to
again in "The Tenth Province of Jaryar". The Jaryari decided to
have an election rather than risk civil war ("looking to and fearing
the example of the seven-year War of the Throne in Ricossa, in
which it is said ten thousand died", TPOJ chapter 1).

. . . .

So then I started speculating about the aftermath of this war, and
its conclusion; and a possible peace settlement aimed above all at
keeping powerful families at peace with each other.

By 641 AL (twenty-two years after the Great Council at Vach-

"

roysh) the Ricossans have become accustomed to the terms of the New Governance, and their two monarchs, who do not inherit but are chosen. ("Nobody knew, Lida remembered, how the Ricossans chose their kings and queens. Nobody in the world knew", TPOJ chapter 8).

This was one of the inspirations for "The Servant's Voice." Another was a minor character in George RR Martin's "Song of Ice and Fire"…… Cutting out someone's tongue is such an easy way for an author or film-maker to show that a fictional society or tyrant is Totally Evil (Martin's Joffrey does it, and there's an example in the film "Solo") – but what would it actually be like?

I found I wanted to tell the story of someone intelligent and law-abiding, who's been removed from normal social life in this way. Ricossa seemed the kind of place where this might happen. ("The Ricossans have some vile customs," TPOJ chapter 5). And so Hridnaya daughter of Haidi, Voiceless servant to the b'Nida Family, was born.

Following the pattern I've invented in the two previous Tales, I also needed political intrigue and a murder to solve. And this time I wanted the murder victim to be a man. (In fiction, unlike in life, murder victims are disproportionately female.)
Fourthly, looking back at Dorac and Makkam, Talinti and Meriden and Arrion (and Darilsa in "People of Makkera", twenty years ago) – I thought it was about time to see if I could ring the changes, and write a character who is fairly sympathetic (or is he?) but dishonest.

So The New Governance + voiceless woman + murder of man +

amiable liar = the foundations of "The Servant's Voice."

If you have enjoyed this book, and would like to know more about Ragaris, or the concept of Swords Without Misogyny, or just want to receive advance notice of future Tales in the series, your best source is the website www.penelopewallace.com, where you can explore maps, history and other details - and the blog, which comes out weekly, and deals with a wide variety of topics, not merely literary.

There is also a Facebook page, www.facebook.com/SwordsWithoutMisogyny.

The fourth Tale from Ragaris is expected to be set in the north-western land of Falli.

Have you read the first two Tales?

"We Do Not Kill Children", the first Tale from Ragaris

"We do not kill children, we do not commit rape, we do not take pleasure in torment."

Are the King's Thirty of Marod always as noble and heroic as legends claim? Or did Dorac Kingsbrother really walk into a small room and cut Lord Gahran's three children to pieces?

Sentenced by King Arrion to lifelong exile and disgrace, Dorac heads for the Old Stones, where Death will come to those who seek it.

A troublesome ten-year-old and an obstinate Kingsister believe he's innocent, and act accordingly. What happens next shakes the whole kingdom.

"The Tenth Province of Jaryar", the second Tale from Ragaris

"To the hall with six flames
Call the great of the nine
For an heir to the King.
They will seek for a sign."

Why do the nobility of Jaryar choose the foreign Nerranya for their Queen at the Great Council in Haymon? Behind the neatly-choreographed debate and election attended by Jeriet b'Shen lies a complex mix of bribe, threat and blackmail – and murder.

Some secrets will never be revealed.

Both are published by Mightier Than The Sword UK Publications
(http://mightierthantheswarduk.com)

Acknowledgements

"The Servant's Voice", unlike its predecessors, had an actual focus group supplying comments as the revisions went along. I am very grateful for the feedback and encouragement of Katie Attwood, Judith Leader, Esther Pawley, Clint Redwood and Mark Wallace.

All of these have also continued to encourage, and to assist with advertising on social media and elsewhere, as have many others. A huge thank you to all of you who have read, commented on, reviewed (Amazon, Goodreads, or wherever) or given away the Tales from Ragaris. I can't resist naming the sterling work of Vicky Cox, Sally Hodges, Gill Kirkwood, Judith Renton, Stephen Sheridan and Ian Storer.

My family are always supportive and helpful.

Judith Renton won the competition to name a character (Simoren b'Asa). Jane Hing and Stephen Sheridan also supplied names that I used for characters or places.

Jon Batchelor continues to be my medic-on-call for questions. Regarding the effects on speech and otherwise of losing a tongue, I am most grateful for discussions with speech therapist Margaret Metcalfe. She also pointed me towards helpful chapters of John Diamond's moving book "C: Because cowards get cancer too" (1999).

All mistakes and improbabilities are my own, of course.

Ittrad's text is from Micah chapter 6 verse 8. In her triumph on the road, Hridnaya mixes verses from Psalms 18 and 118. The smuggler in the boat quotes from Psalm 107.

Once again Ian Storer (http://scipio6.wixsite.com/scipio-designs) produced the pictures for the cover and Stephen Hall the map.

CS Woolley and the Mightier Than The Sword UK Publications team did a great job as usual.

Ser Ilyn Payne is a minor character in George RR Martin's fantasy epic "Song of Ice and Fire". When I first read it, I was filled with enormous indignation on this man's behalf. (Kelji's comment on page 412 is relevant here.) I wondered about the point of view of the deliberately unvoiced, and in due course Hridnaya was created.

Finally, thank you Mark. None of this would have happened without you.